T0036312

my darling DREADFUL thing

A Novel

JOHANNA VAN VEEN

For Hilke, who has read it all before, for Lieke, who has part of it still to go, and for Corinna, who has it all yet to come.

Copyright © 2024 by Johanna van Veen
Cover and internal design © 2024 by Sourcebooks
Cover design by Katie Klimowicz
Cover photo by Thais Ramos Varela/Stocksy
Internal design by Laura Boren/Sourcebooks

Sourcebooks, Poisoned Pen Press, and the colophon
are registered trademarks of Sourcebooks.

All rights reserved. No part of this book may be reproduced in any form or by any electronic or mechanical means including information storage and retrieval systems—except in the case of brief quotations embodied in critical articles or reviews—without permission in writing from its publisher, Sourcebooks.

The characters and events portrayed in this book are fictitious or are used fictitiously. Any similarity to real persons, living or dead, is purely coincidental and not intended by the author.

Published by Poisoned Pen Press, an imprint of Sourcebooks
P.O. Box 4410, Naperville, Illinois 60567-4410
(630) 961-3900
sourcebooks.com

Cataloging-in-Publication Data is on file with the Library of Congress.

Printed and bound in the United States of America.
WOZ 10 9 8 7 6 5 4 3 2 1

PRAISE FOR *MY DARLING DREADFUL THING*

"Dark and decadent, with the haunting allure of a true Gothic tale, *My Darling Dreadful Thing* is a sensation that horrifies as acutely as it delights. Johanna van Veen is a force to be reckoned with and will stain your thoughts a brilliant shade of crimson. I adored every page."

—Rachel Gillig, *New York Times* bestselling author of *One Dark Window*

"A sapphic séance of preternatural proportions, *My Darling Dreadful Thing* summons a stunning new literary voice to be reckoned with. Johanna van Veen reaches beyond the veil to conjure up a Gothic shocker like no other."

—Clay McLeod Chapman, author of *What Kind of Mother* and *Ghost Eaters*

"*My Darling Dreadful Thing* is a disquieting delight—an exciting and original Gothic tale, told with tremendous flair."

—Cherie Priest, author of *The Drowning House*

"*My Darling Dreadful Thing* is an unabashed Gothic treat, with a plot that propels you with restless, creeping logic towards its brutal conclusion. Van Veen's imagery is lushly cinematic, evoking the very best work of Guillermo del Toro. This is a delicious novel."

—William Friend, author of *Let Him In*

"This book got under my skin, all the way down to the marrow. It's as dark as a grave and throbbing with queer desire. I won't forget it."

—Kirsty Logan, author of *Now She Is Witch*

AUTHOR'S NOTE

This book is a work of fiction. Above all, it is a work of *Gothic* fiction, that most slippery of genres. To be *Gothic* means to refuse to be easily defined. That being said, Gothic novels generally have, at their heart, at least one secret so gruesome it has been dropped down a well, locked away in the attic, or buried somewhere in the garden. Left alone in the dark, this secret festers, until everything around it is infected with its rot and it has become impossible to ignore, forcing us to witness the most depraved sides of humanity.

I won't exactly spoil the dark secrets you'll encounter between the pages of *My Darling Dreadful Thing*; those are for you to discover, if you dare. I will, however, warn you in broad terms, so that you may prepare accordingly, that this book contains discussions and instances of trauma, the stigmatization of those considered mentally ill, child abuse, sexual violence, racism, misogyny, and homophobia.

These are dark themes indeed. I hope they will not deter you from reading this novel for two simple reasons:

1. I have done my best to handle these issues with the sensitivity they deserve. I have, for example, done a lot of research, and I have made grateful use of sensitivity readers. For more information, please see the Q&A at the back of this book.

2. If you strip down *My Darling Dreadful Thing* until nothing remains but its essence, you will not find a horrific secret at its very heart. You will find, instead, a love story.

Thank you for embarking on this journey. Darkness lies ahead, yes, but so do joy, solace, and, above all, love.

Part I

"No, no—there are depths, depths! The more I go over it, the more I see in it, and the more I see in it, the more I fear. I don't know what I don't see— what I don't fear!"

—Henry James, *The Turn of the Screw*

Prologue

EVERY SÉANCE I CONDUCTED WITH Mama followed a pattern.

In the small room at the front of the house, we—the clients, Mama, and I—would sit with linked hands around a table covered in dark velvet. The only light would come from the cheap candles she had lit before. They were crumbly, and the wicks often spluttered, throwing fantastic shadows on the wallpaper. As the candles burned, the wax tended to run dreadfully, staining the sideboards as it congealed. It was for this reason that she kept buying them. She said it created the right sort of ambience.

Poor Mama truly went to a great deal of trouble to spin her illusions. Not only did she invest in that black velvet tablecloth and the candles that would gutter out unexpectedly, she had also bought a crystal ball and large age-speckled mirrors that she would drape with gauze, giving the impression of a house in mourning. The way I addressed her, too, was part of the elaborate fantasy she spun. I called her *Mama* because she demanded it be so; it made us sound genteel, which gave her an air of respectability and made it seem as if she organized these séances not from a need for money but to help the bereaved.

"These communications are a terrible strain on my darling daughter," she'd tell new clients, though she preferred to call them our *guests* because, although she desired money, she thought it vulgar to speak of it. "Frankly, there are times when her little talent seems more like a curse than a blessing. The war left so many dead, didn't it? And in such gruesome ways, too. Starvation and bombs and gas chambers... But she's so eager to help, the dear girl. 'I must help these poor souls, Mama, and it doesn't matter how much it hurts.' She's such a selfless thing, you see."

Then she'd take a handkerchief hemmed with frothy lace from her pocket and dab at her dry eyes, her silver bangles clinking around her wrists. The shivering sound they produced when they clanked together could hide a multitude of sins. She wore black dresses of thick stiff materials that rustled as she moved. Her hair, she piled on top of her head in complicated heaps.

I, on the other hand, wore my hair loose. Mama brushed it before every session so it looked neat and shiny. I wore white summer dresses that were invariably too thin for the weather. Those dresses hung around my frame, making me look small and thin, a proper waif dressed in a child's nightgown. This, too, was intentional: she wanted me to look like a little girl, innocent and defenseless. When I got into one of my trances and thrashed and moved about, the dress would slip down my shoulders and reveal the satin slip I wore underneath, and some of our male guests would suppress a moan.

Mama presented me as a child, yes, but one ripe and ready.

"Nothing," she told me, "appeals more to a man than a young

girl who's not been had yet, apart from a girl who's not been had yet and gives the impression she'll be had by him." She made me think of myself as a piece of fruit and the act of sex like plucking a plum with a rough hand, bruising the flesh.

Once we were all seated and holding hands, we called on the spirits to join us. It was all pretense, of course. The only spirit ever present was Ruth, my protector and only friend. After Mama gave me my cue, I'd invite Ruth into me to tether herself to my flesh and the white meat of my spine, and once she went down my throat, I'd be possessed. After Ruth had introduced herself to our guests, we would pretend to let other spirits inside me. We would speak in voices, would move around the table with a sailor's swagger or an old woman's shuffling gait. We'd chew my hair like a shy girl or laugh raucously and wink and snap my fingers. We'd bedevil and confound, beguile and seduce.

Mama had strict rules about touch. She always told our guests they were not allowed to break the circle of linked hands—this so they would not take hold of me. It proved a difficult rule. Who does not wish to embrace a departed loved one made flesh for a few brief minutes? And so Ruth and I would have to do the touching. We'd sit on men's knees and stroke their bearded faces as we pretended to be a deceased daughter, or we'd manfully embrace a bereft widow and fold her against me.

Of course, there were always clients who did not care for Mama's rules. They had come not to speak to someone they had lost, but to be entertained or to expose me. They liked to pinch me or suddenly grab me around the waist and kiss me to see if we would lose composure and show ourselves to be a fraud. We had been fondled more times than I cared to remember—spanked, even. Once, a man had smuggled in a birch rod and struck at us with the glee of the truly sadistic. He managed to get a few good strokes in before the other guests came to my defense, leaving me bruised and bleeding and afraid, with Ruth hissing from the rafters. Still, as Mama liked to say, that happened only once, and it could have been much worse; at least he had not damaged my face.

When Ruth and I had conjured up enough dead husbands, aunts, and sons, Mama would banish the spirits who had come to live inside me, and we'd sink in my chair like a wilting flower with a bruised stem, breathing in shallow little pants and moaning softly, my fingers atremble. Ruth would slip out of me then, leaving me cold and bereft. When I'd come to, I'd do my best to look sleepy and shy, asking softly, "Did I fall asleep? I'm ever so sorry. I don't know what came over me, but I felt so very tired all of a sudden. Shall we begin?"

And I'd try and get to my feet, only to stumble and falter, proving to everyone how much the séance had taken out of me. Sometimes, if Mama felt it would result in a handsome tip, I'd bite the inside of my cheek and in that way cough blood into a handkerchief of virginal white.

This was how things had been for a long time, although not for as long as I could remember, and how things might have gone on for a while longer, had Agnes not decided to attend one of our séances.

I sometimes think it would have been better if she never had, for her and me both.

FIRST CASE EPISODE

PATIENT R–, A CASE STORY: INHABITED BY ANOTHER

(D = DOCTOR, P = PATIENT R–)

FIRST EPISODE, CONDUCTED ON 1 OCTOBER 1954:

Notes to self: First impressions of the patient: different from what I expected. Thought she'd be large, coarse, sullen. Didn't expect her to be so wan and thin. Must talk to her physician, see if she eats properly.

During the talk: She seemed nervous. Kept tilting her head. Hard time keeping eye contact (possible sign of madness?). Speaks with a slight stammer, but generally responds quickly to my questions. Large vocabulary speaks to a high level of intelligence; must keep careful watch for inconsistencies (Police officer S– thought her an excellent liar).

D: "Do you know why I have come?"

P: "To examine me. To see if I'm crazy, or whether I'm just pretending."

D: "And are you pretending?"

P: "Of course not."

D: "Then are you, to use your word, crazy?"

P: "Perhaps. Some things are so horrible that the only sane response is a bit of madness. A– [Mrs. K–] often told me that she had to laugh or else go mad."

D: "The police have asked me to talk to you because they have a hard time believing what you told them is true. Why do you think that is?"

P: "Because the truth scares people. They're always afraid of what they can't explain, and my Ruth can't be so easily explained."

D: "Why not? Because Ruth is a ghost?"

P: "I hate that word, always have." [*grows animated*] "It reminds me of children dressed in white sheets trying to scare each other, or of those fake apparitions made of cheesecloth and cardboard that Victorian frauds conjured up when they said they talked to the dead. Ruth is nothing like that."

D: "Then what is Ruth like?"

P: "It depends. Sometimes she is barely visible, no more than a quicksilver haze. It's like the shapes you see when your eye waters and you rub at it a little too hard. At other times, I can touch her, and she feels much the same as you and I do, only quite cold, as if she's been outside in winter without a coat."

D: "And when you can touch her, does she look like you and I do?"

P: [*laughs*] "Of course not. You look like you, and I look like me, and Ruth looks like Ruth."

D: "Let me rephrase that. Does Ruth look human?"

P: "A little. It depends."

D: "In what way?"

P: "Sometimes, she looks almost alive, and at other times, she's unmistakably dead. There's something off about her features. I can't explain. I think she's been dead for so long that she doesn't quite understand anymore what a human being should look like, although the longer she was with me, the better she got at it. Before that, I think she rested under the floorboards for a long time." [*nervously drums fingers on the tabletop*]

D: "You said Ruth doesn't really look human. Did that not scare you when you were little?"

P: "At first, but children accept so much as normal, don't they? And for a long time, she was my only friend and companion. Then, when Mama realized she wasn't an imaginary friend, she made me the medium of her séances. Ruth was my spirit control then."

D: "Your spirit control?"

P: "Yes. A spirit control is a powerful spirit who draws other spirits, like moths are drawn to a candle. They're supposed to soothe and help those spirits so the medium can talk to them. The Victorians invented them. Their spirits weren't real, you see, just people dressed up and pretending. By using the concept of a spirit control, mediums could conjure up the same spirit time and time again without their guests becoming suspicious. Mama read about it and thought that perhaps Ruth could be a proper spirit control. We'd become famous and very rich then, because our possessions would be utterly real."

D: "But?"

P: "But Ruth was never any good at being a spirit control.

Other spirits never came when she was with me. I've started to think that perhaps most of us don't become a spirit when we die, and there was never anything for her to lure. Or perhaps other spirits do exist, but Ruth scared them away. She was fiercely protective of me. In fact, I don't think she'd like me to talk to you. She might think you mean me harm." [*becomes agitated and incoherent*]

D: "Let us go back a little bit. When is the first time you saw Ruth?"

Chapter 1

I WAS NEVER A HAPPY child. I think that, if I had been, things would have gone very differently with me. For one, I don't think Ruth would have become my constant companion. Spirits like her are not drawn to the happy and carefree; they want salt, be it blood or be it tears.

The question everyone wants answered is this: Was I or was I not actually possessed? But it is not so simple as that.

The policemen who questioned me all believed I wasn't. In this, they agreed with one another, if not in much else. You see, some believed I was a little fraud feigning a disorder of the mind so I could plead insanity and escape being sent to jail. One even clapped his hands and called me a marvelous actress halfway through hearing my story.

They weren't all so cruel, though; some pitied me because they argued that I was, in fact, insane. Because they couldn't agree whether I was mad, they brought in a doctor to see if I was fit to stand trial. His name was Doctor Montague. He was young, eager to help, eager to prove himself. I found him easy to talk to, which

I suppose is why he was of such value to the police. He made the words tumble out of my mouth one after the other, all these things I felt and thought and remembered, like how I felt about Mama or what my earliest memory was.

The latter is thus: I am crouching underneath the floorboards of the sitting room in which Mama conducts her séances. It's a small space with strings bound to hooks protruding from the earthen walls. These strings all do something different when I pull them. One makes a lamp levitate; another causes a shelf to tilt, making books tumble down. I must know what each one does and when to pull it. For this, I listen to Mama as she pretends to be visited by spirits; certain phrases are my cues.

I am perhaps five years old, and I am scared senseless. The space is cold and damp and smells of mold and earth. Though my eyes get used to the dark, I can't help but be terrified. Sometimes I weep from fright. Mama explains away these sounds as the spirit of a little child who is lost, and though her clients believe her, she still thrashes me after such a session.

"Do you want our guests to think the afterlife is a horrible place?" she hisses at me.

"But Ruth is down there, Mama, and she wants to bite me and drink my blood!" I howl as I clutch Mama's skirts, trying to stay out of reach of the birch rod she holds in her hands. I have not yet learned to take what is coming to me without a fight.

"There's nothing down there, you horrible little lunatic! You're letting your imagination get the better of you. Now stand still!"

But despite everything Mama says, Ruth is in that little room

underneath the floorboards with me. In the dark, her eyes sometimes flash green like that of a cat or fox. At other times, she doesn't
have eyes at all, just skin growing over the place where her empty
sockets should be. Her skin changes all the time, too. Sometimes
it's the warm brown of an acorn; occasionally, it's black—not in the
way that some people are, but black like certain types of wood, with
a grayish tint to it. The one time I manage to smuggle a flashlight
down with me and shine it in her face, I see that her jaw is horribly
dislocated. It hangs open and crooked. No wonder she can't speak,
only moan!

I know what she wants: to curl herself around me like a comma
and press her gaping mouth to my throat so she can drink my
blood. I fear she'll drain me. To stop myself from crying out, I bite
the soft flesh between my index finger and thumb. I worry at it with
my teeth until I taste blood, rich and salty and sickening. So often
do I chew at that little bit of skin that the cuts I make won't heal.
Mama has to bandage my hand to stave off infection.

Mama has tried to feed me mixtures of pills and alcohol to
take away my fear, but those just make me sick and sleepy. I've got
a doll with me, a rag doll I've named Trudy. My father brought her
home with him from America. She is stiff and stained with the
blood from my bitten hand. One day, Mama will throw her away.
"She was a filthy little thing," she'll say, "and you're much too old
to play with dolls." I'll weep for my Trudy for days.

But that is later. I am in the hole now, chewing on my hand,
trying to listen to Mama pretend she can talk to the dead. I ignore
Ruth as well as I'm able. There's not a lot of room under the

floorboards, so a part of me is always touching a part of her. She's cold as stone. Sometimes she groans softly at me, but most of the time, she's a quiet creature. She smells like autumn—that is to say, like wet earth and leaves sweet with the first touch of rot.

Aboveground, Mama booms, "Spirits, give us a sign!"

I unfasten a piece of twine from its hook and pull at it, making an empty biscuit tin fall down on the piano. It crashes on the keys. The piano releases a shuddering twang. I knot the cord back around its hook, my eyes watering against the pain of the fibers rubbing against my torn skin. Many of the strings have brown streaks of my clotted blood on them. When I'm done, I shake my hand to get rid of the pain. Drops of blood fly from the wound. Some hit the earthen walls, but one or two splash against Ruth's face.

She shudders. She wipes them away, then licks her fingers with hoarse little moans.

"Ruth, hush," I hiss.

She pushes a palm against her jaw. With a horrifying jolt, it slips back into its socket. She opens and closes her mouth, and though each movement is accompanied by a soft grinding sound, her jaw doesn't fall back down. She sucks her fingers for remnants of my blood. She doesn't look so bad anymore.

And now something extraordinary happens. For the first time—and though this is my earliest memory, I know this has never happened before—Ruth speaks. Her voice is like the wind among the branches, high and keening and strangely beautiful.

"Roos," she whispers. Her breath smells like pennies. "You need never be alone again now, Roos. You have named me and let me drink from you. We are wedded to each other now, you and I. You're my helpmeet and yokemate, and I am yours. I shall keep you safe."

Later, when it all went to hell and I was smeared from cheek to chest with blood so dark and thick, it seemed like sealing wax, I thought about that moment a lot. If I had not so carelessly spilled my blood, would Ruth have found another little girl to love and hold and feed from?

Chapter 2

THE DAY I MET AGNES, I had gotten my monthlies for the first time in almost half a year. Mama looked at the blood staining my knickers. It was so dark, it looked black. "How relieved you must be," she said coldly. "Now go wash yourself."

In the bathroom, Ruth put a cool hand against my feverish forehead. "All shall be well now," she said. I leaned against her. She put her cool dark arms around me and held me tight, the smell of peat rising from the folds of her dress.

I washed myself carefully, the water in the bowl turning pink. Ruth flitted around the bowl. When I was finished, she lapped from it, pleased as a cat with a saucer of cream.

Sometime in the future, Agnes would read a part of the *Odyssey* to me, the bit in which Odysseus wants to enter the underworld and has to sacrifice a black ram and a black sheep over a mixture of flour, honey, milk, sweet wine, and water. The spirits flock to his sacrifice, wishing to drink from it so they may regain the ability to speak. "They were on to something, those Greeks," she said as she took a drag from her cigarette. "All spirits have a thirst for blood."

But all that happened later, and I must not rush and leave parts of my tale untold.

When I came downstairs for breakfast, there was nothing on my plate. "Mama, please, I'm very hungry," I said, hoping against hope.

"You've eaten enough lately. You wouldn't be bleeding if you hadn't," she snapped. She buttered my slices of bread for herself and covered them with cheese. The smell made me sick with longing. From the quick pecking movements with which she ate her own breakfast, I could see something important had happened, something that excited and agitated her. I did not have to wait long.

"You must be at your best today," she said. "We've got an important guest coming: Agnes Knoop."

The name meant nothing to me. Miserable and faint, I removed the wad of cotton wool from a glass bottle of aspirin and shook out two tablets in the palm of my hand. They lay against the scar caused by that client with the birch rod; he had struck so hard, he had exposed the bone. That night, Ruth had unspooled the bandages and nibbled at the dried crust of blood, nearly purring with the pleasure of it.

"Is Mrs. Knoop an acquaintance of yours?" I asked as I poured myself a cup of tea.

Mama stared at me, then gave a humiliating little chuckle. "My dear child, don't tell me you don't know who Agnes Knoop is. It was in all the papers."

"I haven't read the papers in a while." When I finished the housework, I was often too drained to do anything but watch Ruth grind up a piece of glass with a nail file. She kept the grit in a little bottle. I liked to hold it up to the light and see all the powdered glass inside glitter like snow.

Mama leaned close to me, her face flushed with excitement. "You've heard of Lockhart stockings, haven't you?"

I nodded. Who hadn't? Those stockings were of the highest quality, soft and lovely and durable. I had seen advertisements for them in magazines but had never held a pair, much less owned one; they were far too expensive. Mama did allow me to wear stockings, but the ones we bought were cheap and scratchy, liable to get ladders and never fitting quite right. They had a seam at the toe that often drove me to distraction. When I removed them at the end of the day, they left a red, raw-looking line on my toes.

"Well, the company is owned by some Americans nowadays, but it was founded by this Scotsman named Boswell who made his fortune with it. Nouveau riche and all that. Well, to get to the point, he kept a mistress in London. She was Asian, God knows from which country; they all look the same, don't they, whether they're from China or the Dutch Indies?"

"It's called Indonesia now, Mama. Remember? It's no longer a Dutch colony."

She made a quick impatient movement with her hand, as if batting at a fly. "Remember? Of course I do. What I don't understand is why you care so much what it's called. Ungrateful bunch, the lot of them. Before we came, they were no better than a bunch of godless children, playing with sticks in the mud. I say, if they don't want our help, let them rot in their jungles. And don't interrupt me and don't try to act like you're so much more clever than me. It's very unbecoming."

I took a sip of tea to keep from responding. Even if I had been able to muster the energy to argue with her, it would have been of no use. She never changed her mind about anything if she could help it, even if her opinions were poorly supported and small-minded. The only people she knew who had lived in Indonesia were white Dutch people who had moved back to the Netherlands after surviving the Japanese prison camps during the war, only to lose their homes and wealth when Indonesia had become independent. They were usually bitter, scarred, and homesick. All her other information she had gleaned from a nationalistic newspaper she favored, and two nineteenth-century library books, one written by a phrenologist who was convinced of the white race's superiority, the other by a missionary. In Mama's mind, anyone who was a published writer was an authority, never to be questioned or doubted.

"I'm sorry," I murmured.

"Now you've done it. You've made me lose the thread of my story. Where was I?" Mama complained.

"You told me that the founder of Lockhart stockings kept a mistress in London."

"Right. Well, his mistress bore him a daughter, whom they named Agnes. It seems they were happy for a few years, until they weren't, and Boswell broke with his mistress. That's when she decided to kill herself." Mama put some bread in her mouth and chewed it noisily. She had the infuriating habit of telling a story and then taking a bite of something halfway through, forcing her listener to wait till she had chewed and swallowed.

"It was all very dramatic," she went on. "She sent Agnes to his London office wearing a threadbare coat with a suicide note pinned to it, and while the girl was away, she drank half a bottle of lye. By the time they found her, she was dead." She shivered in delight. Ghoulish stories gave her a sense of satisfaction because they reminded her there was always someone who had it worse than she did, someone she could look down upon and think herself superior to.

I pictured a small girl with cold-chapped hands and very large eyes, the note written on cheap paper and carefully pinned to her lapel. The poor little thing must've been dreadfully lonely, without a Ruth to guard and guide her.

"Mr. Boswell rallied to the challenge most admirably. He couldn't have Agnes around to shame his wife and true children, so he sent her away to some Catholic boarding school and later a finishing school in France. Seems she had a talent for the piano: there was a lot of talk at the time of her becoming a famous pianist, only she suffered some sort of breakdown, and nothing ever came of it. She met Thomas Knoop not long after and married him."

She took another bite of her breakfast and scowled at my lack of recognition at the name. "Thomas Knoop," she said with great emphasis, "was the heir to his family's estate, the Rozentuin. It has been in his family for generations. He lived there with his younger sister, Willemijn, a great beauty. She would've made a tremendous match of her own, no doubt, had she not gotten sick. I heard she became a bit of a recluse these past few years. Truly, dear, do these names mean nothing to you?"

"I don't know," I murmured. If only my stomach didn't pulse with hunger pain, I might've been able to remember, but as it was, I felt so sick and weak, it was hard enough to make sense of Mama's words, let alone dredge up past conversations to go looking for the names of people who didn't interest me.

"It was the talk of the town at the time: the esteemed Mr. Thomas Knoop marrying a foreign bastard! Of course, she's said to be very beautiful, and there were rumors at the time that the Knoops had some money trouble that Agnes's dowry would fix, but it was a curious match all the same. Many said it wouldn't last. Well, they were wrong; their marriage was a tremendous success."

She finished her sandwich. My stomach contracted painfully. "Was?" I asked.

Mama nodded. She smiled, revealing her large white teeth. "That's why she's coming to see us today, my girl. You see, for the past nine months, Mrs. Agnes Knoop has been a widow."

Mama went to the library and brought copies of magazines and newspaper clippings home for me to study. "Just imagine," Mama said as she put a collection of pictures down in front of me, "what will happen if Agnes Knoop gives us her patronage! God knows we need it. Better prepare as well as you can, girl. God, but I wish we'd known she'd come sooner."

Mama kept folders on all our guests with personal information we could use to seduce them into believing us. After every séance, she'd add to them, leaving little notes in her large handwriting. I flicked through them once in a while to refresh my memory and keep myself from making mistakes. I could imagine her writing out Agnes's name on the cover of a clean new folder, scoring the paper with the pen's nib in her eagerness. I tasted something foul. I swallowed thickly to clear my mouth, then began to read the articles she had gathered for me, feeling slightly sick, like a child reading a forbidden book.

Agnes Knoop, I discovered, had been married to Thomas Knoop in 1938, almost fifteen years ago. She had been twenty-one, just as I was now. They honeymooned in France, traveling along the coast. When they had come back, they had moved to the Rozentuin, the family estate. Mama had copied an article on the house and grounds.

It had many pictures: one of a white summer house somewhere on the estate, of the family chapel with its stained glass windows, and of the house itself, with its mullioned windows and almost unbearable symmetry. Then there were pictures of Mr. and Mrs. Knoop: in the library, him standing near the window with a cigarette between his long fingers, her sitting on the window seat with a thin greyhound pawing at her skirt; Mr. Knoop on horseback in the woods, his hair so pale, it seemed white; Mrs. Knoop in evening dress, handing her husband a drink, a hand resting on his shoulder, a large stone flashing on her finger. In every photo, she looked a little sleepy, her eyes half-shut. Perhaps the flash had taken her by surprise, and she had shut them to keep the light from burning her eyes. That, or the photographer had managed to click the shutter every time she had made her way only partly through a blink.

Curiously, there were no pictures of her at the piano. There was a single picture of Thomas's sister, Willemijn, too, an open book on her lap. She was as pale as her brother, with watery hair and eyes and a strange mouth that spoke of discontent despite its plumpness.

I studied the photographs carefully, then closed my eyes and conjured sights and sounds and scents so Ruth and I could act the part of Thomas Knoop convincingly during the séance. I imagined myself walking down the drive, the cobblestones hard beneath my shoes.

The drive takes me through the woods, past firs with their feathery needles, always green, past proud oaks and birches with their queer white stems and bark peeling like strips of sunburned skin. They'll be naked now, those oaks and birches, their branches in harsh relief against a gray sky, but within two months, the first leaves will unfurl, soft and damp and tender. The harsh smell of frost and pine will make way for the good, clean scents of green things growing.

I walk down the drive, my shoes not the poor, cheap things Mama buys for me but made of good leather, with thick soles that do not allow the cold to travel up and nestle itself in my bones. In summer, the canopy will be so luscious that no sunlight can penetrate, and the woods will be strange and still. I put my hand against the trunk of a fir, feeling the rough bark. When I pull it back, sticky sap clings to my fingers. I pull out a handkerchief monogrammed with initials not my own to wipe it away.

Down, down, down the drive, past the hydrangeas blooming a powdery pink and blue. The road winds close to the wall of rhododendrons that marks the edge of the property and then away again, deeper into the grounds. The line of trees thins gradually, respectfully making way for the lawn.

I take a cigarette out of the golden case in my pocket and light it as I survey the house, feeling that strange constricting of the throat and chest that denotes pride, that breathless sort of happiness that this is mine, mine. The door opens and out she comes, running to meet me, my wife, my little love…

A hand on my shoulder jerked me out of my daydream.

"Time to get ready, my girl," Mama said, gathering the clippings and tucking them into a folder she had marked *A. Knoop.*

"Yes, Mama," I said and fled upstairs. I had the bizarre urge to cry, as if something precious and lovely had been crudely ripped out of my hands, and not even Ruth could comfort me.

SECOND CASE EPISODE

PATIENT R—, A CASE STORY: INHABITED BY ANOTHER

(D = DOCTOR, P = PATIENT R—)

SECOND EPISODE, CONDUCTED ON 5 OCTOBER 1954:

D: "In our last session, we discussed Ruth. You didn't like me calling her a ghost, but if she isn't a ghost, then what exactly is she?"

P: "I've always called her a spirit because that's what Mama called the departed when they came back to visit. Ruth was alive once, and then she wasn't, so I suppose it made sense."

D: "Where did Ruth come from?"

P: "I don't know. She doesn't remember. I think she died a long time ago. Sometimes I dream Ruth dreams, but they are almost always the same: just darkness, and pressure all around, and the smell of peat and the taste of earth and water in my mouth. Sometimes there's a little flash of something else: my face being striped with something wet, paint, I think; a horrible pain in my throat; a little child sobbing. I think those are her memories, but there are very few of them, and they're oddly muted."

D: "Do you know why she didn't go to the light?"

P: [*laughs*] "You mean why she didn't just disappear after she died, why she lingered? I'm not sure. Some spiritualists say that a person who dies a violent death is shackled to the earth. I don't know about that. Europe would be teeming with the undead then, wouldn't it? Yet the ones I've seen, I can count on one hand. I think it does play a part; all the spirits I've met did die violent deaths. Yet something else also matters. Ruth always says that where you're buried has something to do with it."

D: "You mean whether someone has been buried in consecrated ground?"

P: "Maybe that plays a part, but she means places where bodies don't decay as they should, like mounds and bogs. Mounds are dry and cool, so any body placed inside mummifies. In bogs bodies don't really decompose, they just tan and dye like leather."

D: "Why do you think the rate of decomposition has anything to do with whether a person becomes a spirit?"

P: "Well, Ruth died in a bog; she remembers that much, and she has shown me through her dreams. She said she slept for a long time before she found me. I think that her death was a shock to her, and it took her a long time to recover. When she woke, her body was still there, tethering her to the earth, keeping some parts of her whole. But when you are buried in a different kind of soil, your body seeps into the water and earth and air. You disintegrate. There's nothing keeping you bound to this world then, nothing keeping you together. I think you just drift away then." [*rubs* *the scar on hand*] "I'm sorry. I'm doing a poor job of explaining. It's very clear in my mind, but it doesn't sound very clear when I put it into words."

D: "I think I understand. Why do you think Ruth chose to be with you?"

P: "I woke her up."

D: "How?"

P: "I was lonely and sad and vulnerable, and that disturbed Ruth's slumber. Mama wasn't a very nurturing person."

D: "In our previous session, you said that Ruth was your spirit control during séances, but that she kept other spirits at bay. Yet multiple of your former clients have testified that, during séances, you were possessed by, or at least seemed to be possessed by, the spirits of their deceased relations. Can you explain that?"

P: "It was pretense. Not all of it; Ruth inhabited my body during those séances so I could dazzle all of them. But I never let another spirit in."

D: "You needed Ruth to be able to perform?"

P: "In a way. She made it easier."

D: "Easier how?"

P: "When she possesses me, I'm not really responsible for what happens. I'm not hampered by shame then, and that makes it easier to pretend to be someone I'm not."

D: "You said you never let another spirit in. Why make an exception for Ruth?"

P: "Because she was mine and I was hers."

Chapter 3

AGNES KNOOP ARRIVED WITH THE other guests. I was in the drawing room already, sitting with folded hands at the table. Ruth had turned insubstantial and fluttered around the room, making the gauze wrapped around the paintings rustle. There were three of them: a bowl of fruit on the cusp of rot, a winter landscape, and a vanitas painting with a brown skull clenching a flower between its remaining teeth. Mama had painted them in her youth, before her fingers had become swollen and painful, when life had not yet turned her bitter and casually cruel.

I heard our guests come into the house, heard them chatter as they unbuttoned their coats and hung away their hats, folded their umbrellas. It was pouring outside, the rain drumming steadily against the windowpanes. It was not even four in the afternoon yet, but it was already dark.

My palms were damp. I wiped them on the tablecloth. My body felt swollen and tender. There was that heavy, pulling pain low in my belly and hips, the soft flow of blood like a dark rope trickling out of me. Mama had made me brush my teeth so my breath smelled fresh. The minty scent mingled with my hunger and left a bitter taste on my tongue.

"Shall we go in?" I heard Mama suggest, her bracelets clanking together as she grasped the doorknob, and in they came, hushed now by my presence, wringing their hands in eager, slightly frightened expectation. There were five of them: three women, two men.

Agnes was the last to enter. From the moment I laid eyes on her, I could not stop looking. Of course, I'd known she was beautiful. I'd seen her pictures, hadn't I? But to see it up close and in motion was different from seeing it on a well-thumbed bit of paper.

She had that kind of radiant beauty that seems effortless, with hair that stood out from her face like a black halo and eyes large and liquid. She wore a black blouse, exquisitely cut, and a skirt to match. Curiously, no wedding ring. No jewelry, only a wristwatch.

Agnes did not sit down straightaway but looked around the room first. At the piano she paused. She reached out to touch the keys, then pulled away as if she had burned her fingers.

I remembered then that Mama had said she was to become a famous pianist, only something had happened to prevent it. Did she not play anymore? She sat down in a chair opposite me and looked at her watch, moving it over her wrist with her fingertips. Her skin was very smooth, the color a light brown, somewhat similar to the tan Mama labored to acquire in summer but without the orange undertone.

When everyone was seated, Mama began the séance by explaining the rules, then bade us to join hands. I lay my hands on the table, the sides touching the hands of my neighbors, Mr.

Bakker and Mrs. de Jong, both of them familiar and devout; after the birch rod incident, Mama would only let long-term guests sit next to me. Mr. Bakker had lost his wife during the bombing of Rotterdam and had come to visit us soon after. Mrs. de Jong wished to commune with her little girl, who had died of measles nearly three years ago.

"Spirits, I call on you. You are welcome here. We ask that you join us." Mama looked around the circle. "Let us sing a hymn to make the spirits feel welcome." She sang the first line of "Be Thou My Vision" and was swiftly joined by the others, her strong voice leading the atonal mumblings of Mrs. de Jong and the enthusiastic belting of Mr. de Vries on her right. As I sang, I worked my foot slowly out of its slipper. Just a little longer, and then I'd crack my toes against the floor. Such spirit rappings helped prepare our clients for the strange spectacle of possession.

I looked through my lashes. Agnes was not singing. Her eyes were on me. They were dark as jet and curiously wet, like licked-at liquorice.

Her gaze was very strong. I felt the blood beat in my throat, forcing the color up to my cheeks. I could not rap against the floor with my foot then, not with those piercing eyes on me. The words "O ruler of all" died on my lips. We were silent for a moment then, our clients frowning and looking at one another; normally they would have been assured of the presence of the dearly departed during the first hymn.

Ruth brushed against me, prickly and eager. When she was insubstantial like this, it was like walking into fog: just cool, damp fronds of cloud caressing my skin. Mama looked at me from the tail of her eye. I stared at the tablecloth.

"Mrs. Knoop, is something wrong? Why do you not sing?" Mama asked in that creeping, fawning way she employed when currying favor, her brow furrowed with concern.

"I did not know we all had to sing," Agnes said. Her accent was perfect; only her intonation betrayed that Dutch was not her first language.

"Oh, but you must. We must all make the spirits feel welcome, or they shan't come. Would you like to choose the next hymn?"

Agnes paused for a moment, then began to sing, "O come, O come, Emmanuel." Her voice made the hairs on the nape of my neck rise; it was peculiar, high, with a slight tremble. We joined her a little hesitantly; it was not a hymn we typically sang. I kept my eyes closed so fiercely, it seemed my lids would bruise. Still, I felt her gaze on me. I focused on the pain in my belly, at the pulling of it so low at the hips. A little blood trickled out of me.

Once we reached the second "rejoice," I cracked my toes against the floor. The space underneath the floorboards was hollow, so the sound reverberated around the room. Mr. Bakker startled, his hand twitching against mine.

"Keep singing," Mama encouraged them. Whenever we reached the refrain, I cracked my toes on the "rejoice." By the end of the hymn, my foot felt sore. We sang out the last words, then fell silent. The quiet was charged with want.

"Spirits, we thank you for coming. We wish to speak to you," Mama said. "Now, is Ruth there? Ruth," she explained to Agnes, "is my daughter's spirit control. She soothes and guides the spirits. Ruth, please make yourself known."

I rapped my toes again.

"Good." She looked at me. "Go on, invite her in."

As if I need your permission. "Of course, Mama."

I let her wait, spinning the silence, and stretching the expectation till it was almost unbearable. Then I let my head droop slowly, as if I were overtaken by sleep. I made my breath punch out of me quickly, in hoarse little pants, and rocked myself from side to side. The repetitiveness of the motions and Mama's continued "spirit, come to us" helped to put me in a light trance. I opened my mouth and invited Ruth in.

Greedily, she slipped between my lips and crawled down my throat. She tasted of brine. Years of possession had taught me not to gag and spit her up again; that only led to a fierce scrabbling inside my throat and mouth, tearing the pink flesh till my mouth was full of blood. Once inside, she anchored herself to my marrow, then stretched and stretched and stretched. It was like a flooding of the brain, dark and wet, hot like blood. I was no longer my drab little self then.

"Ruth, are you there?"

She opened my eyes. "Yes," she said.

Mama grinned in satisfaction. "There. Now let us talk to our dearly departed."

THIRD CASE EPISODE

PATIENT R—, A CASE STORY: INHABITED BY ANOTHER

(D = DOCTOR, P = PATIENT R—)

THIRD EPISODE, CONDUCTED ON 6 OCTOBER 1954:

Notes to self: Maybe a good idea to use these coming sessions to explore possible motives. I've read the reports from the police and the coroner. I've seen the pictures, too (won't be able to forget them anytime soon, either). What, I wonder, could have moved my patient to an act so vicious and brutal? Avenues to explore: sex, hate, jealousy, fear.

> **D:** "Describe to me what it feels like to be possessed by Ruth."
>
> **P:** "It's like swallowing something sharp and slightly salty. I need to submit to her, because if I don't, she won't go down easily. She'll bruise and scratch me, though not on purpose. Once I've swallowed her, she grows bigger and bigger inside me. It's like a fever of the brain then, no longer cold but warm and rich as blood. Ruth moves me, speaks for me, and I know it is happening, and it's still my body, but it isn't me doing it."
>
> **D:** "Could you stop it if you wanted it? Exorcise Ruth, I mean? Or are you completely at her mercy as long as she's inside you?"
>
> **P:** [*laughs uncomfortably*] "I just ask her to go and cough her up."

D: "But what happens when you want Ruth to go but Ruth doesn't want to go? Could you fight her then?"

P: "It's never like that. Ruth is my friend. She would never stay when I ask her to leave. She protects and loves me."

D: "Does it bring you pleasure to be possessed by Ruth?"

P: "I don't know."

D: "Does it arouse you?"

P: [*starts to rub scarred hand*] "You make it sound sexual."

D: "That's because you've described it with sexual imagery. Possession as penetration. The salty taste as you swallow her down, the need to submit or else bleed and be in pain..." [*laughs*] "Well, you see what I mean, don't you? Any psychoanalyst would conclude that Ruth is your love object and you wish to have intercourse with her, to put it bluntly."

P: [*through gritted teeth*] "It's nothing like that, and you've a filthy mind for thinking it could be. Ruth was my protector and companion, but not my lover. Would you have intercourse with your mother, Doctor? Or with your sibling? Because that's what Ruth was to me, and more besides."

D: "I can see I've touched a very sore spot. Let's talk about someone else. Mrs. K—, for example."

P: "What about her?"

D: "How did you fare during that first séance with Mrs. K—?"

Chapter 4

WHEN RUTH POSSESSED ME, SHE could slip into the people I had carefully stitched together from tales and photographs and things imagined. All we needed to do was to imagine a chain of sensations that linked us to these personas: scents and feelings and tastes.

The cool smooth surface of porcelain against my plump little hand; the chalky taste of milk in my mouth, and then the sweetness of sugar-dusted strawberries; the scent of cold cream.

Ruth gave a little cry, high like that of a bird, clawing my fingers into the tablecloth. She came to my feet, my eyes closed, swaying a little.

"Wake, spirit," Mama said.

She made my eyes large and my voice high as she slipped into the role of Mrs. de Jong's little girl. "Mammie," she said, and she ducked under Mrs. de Jong's arm and sat down on her lap. She threw my arms around her neck and rested my cheek against her bosom. Mrs. de Jong was warm and smelled of laundry detergent and a whiff of cold cream.

"Oh, Elsje," she moaned.

"Mammie, have you missed me?" Ruth lisped.

"You know I have, little mouse." Mrs. de Jong was not allowed to embrace us, but she pressed against us and kissed my head with little wet kisses. When Ruth looked into her face, it was swollen and streaked with tears, her nose running. She put my hands against her cheeks and wiped away the snot with my thumb. *You fool*, I thought desperately, *you stupid little fool. Do you not see that we're only pretending?*

"Oh, Mammie, don't be sad. You mustn't be sad," Ruth said, giving her a stern look. "You know I'm happy where I am, Mammie."

"Yes, little mouse, of course. You're with the angels, and you ride your little pony every day and play with the other dead little children."

"And I eat strawberries with sugar, my favorite, remember, Mammie?"

"I remember." Mrs. de Jong sobbed and kissed me again. Ruth put my cheek against Mrs. de Jong's chest. Her heart was beating very fast, and her skin was slightly clammy from excitement. "My poor little darling, my dearest little mouse," she murmured, rubbing her chin on the crown of my head.

"We shall be together again in the next world, Mammie," Ruth said. She yawned, my eyelids fluttering. "I must go now," she murmured with the slightly slurred speech of a sleepy child.

"No, Elsje, don't go! Don't go, my little mouse, not just yet!" She moved to put her arms about us and cling to us, but Mama, seated on her right, grabbed hold of her hand and clutched it tightly.

"You know the rules, Mrs. de Jong," she said.

"Please, just a little while longer!" Mrs. de Jong begged.

"Elsje's spirit is on its way back already. There's nothing to be done."

"Please, please, please," she whispered, choked by emotion.

Sometimes, when Ruth and I were alone, she mimicked our guests to make me laugh. I always felt sick and wicked afterward, but I simply had to laugh or else go mad.

"I love you, Mammie. Try and be happy for me," Ruth whispered, and she kissed Mrs. de Jong's wet cheek. Then she stumbled back to my chair and let me crumple with a sigh. She lay there breathing softly, looking at our clients through my lashes. Mrs. de Jong sat with her head hung, her shoulders shaking as she sobbed. The others were doing their best not to look at her, ashamed by this display of emotion. Only Agnes did. She reached into her pocket and held out a handkerchief to Mrs. de Jong over the table.

"Mrs. Knoop, put that away at once. You mustn't break the circle," Mr. Bakker said with the pomposity of someone who figures himself an expert. "You'll disturb the spirits. You'll…"

"Do shut up," Agnes snapped.

Mr. Bakker gaped at her. "Excuse me?"

Mama screwed on her professional smile and said in a mock whisper, "There, there. Emotions tend to run high during séances. That is why there are rules. They guide us when our feelings get the better of us. Your fellow feeling does you credit, Mrs. Knoop, but please link hands again and keep your voice low. We mustn't disturb my darling daughter, or else the spirits will take offense, and then they won't come."

Agnes didn't say anything. With a blank face, she tossed her handkerchief into Mrs. de Jong's lap, then put her hands back on the tabletop.

"Thank you," Mama said. "Now let us see if there are any other spirits, shall we? I am sure we all wish to contact our dearly departed tonight, especially you, Mrs. Knoop."

This was a sign for Ruth. She made my fingers twitch against the table to let Mama know she understood.

"Spirits, are you there? Spirits, come to us!" she called out.

Ruth began to rock again. It made my chair creak. My hands and feet had gone numb with cold, and my belly hurt. I turned into myself, so I did not feel it, soothed by Mama's voice, by the rhythm of my rocking, by the feeling of Ruth flicking inside me. She let my head fall back, opened my mouth, and gasped.

The soft, silky feel of a flower in my hand as I ripped it apart with my fingers to perfume the air; a thrush singing from deep in the woods; a woman running to me, her dark hair dancing around her face.

"Wake, spirit."

Ruth came to my feet. She felt strong and sure of herself. When she locked eyes with Agnes, she smiled crookedly. She put the palm of my hand against my scalp and smoothed back my hair, then she thrust my hands into the pockets of my dress and sauntered over to where Agnes sat. Agnes did not move, but her eyes followed me.

Ruth halted right behind Agnes and placed my hand on her shoulder. Agnes tensed, and though she sat so very still that we could hardly make out the rise and fall of her chest as she breathed, there was a humming sort of energy to her, coiled and taut. No amount of powder could hide the dark bruises of insomnia under her eyes, no amount of rouge liven the ashen hue of her cheek.

Slowly, Ruth took a lock of Agnes's hair between my fingers and pulled it back, revealing a small round ear. When she brought my mouth close to Agnes's ear, Agnes shivered and closed her eyes. Ruth was close enough that I could see the gooseflesh ripple over Agnes's throat.

"Agnes," Ruth breathed. "Oh, Agnes." She bent over her. Agnes leaned her cheek against my arm. We could smell her, Ruth and I, her expensive perfume and scented soap, and underneath that the sweet, intimate smell of her body. My belly clenched, and I felt that constriction of the throat again, which I first felt when surveying the Rozentuin, that tightening caused by pride and desire.

"My darling, my love," Ruth murmured.

Agnes looked up at me. In the dark pool of her irises, I read, curiously, fear, and dread—and pain. But as well as the horror, I saw a strange yearning, potent and raw. She pressed her lips firmly together. Her eyes, bruised by sleeplessness, said, *I am hurt.* The harsh twist to her mouth said, *I am proud.* And the tremble in her fingers that she strove in vain to hide from me by balling her hands into fists, what did that say?

That a part of her wished to seize me and not let go?

Mine, I thought.

Mine, Ruth echoed. She put my hands around Agnes's throat and kissed her tight lips. "Agnes, my darling," she murmured. "Have you missed me?"

Agnes parted her lips and began to speak.

Ruth and I stared at her proud mouth, feeling horror twist in my stomach.

We had no idea what she was saying. The sounds would not translate into any words we knew.

Agnes looked at us expectantly, then when she got no answer, she repeated herself.

English, I thought, now recognizing a word here and there. *God damn me, did she and her husband speak English to each other?*

When the war had just ended, Mama had paid a nervy-looking woman named Mrs. Smith to come and teach me English once a week to attract young girls who wished to contact their dead Allied soldier lovers, those brave Brits and Americans and Canadians who had come to liberate us from the Nazis, but none of those clients had stuck around for long after their Johns and Henrys had told them how loved they were; besides, the whole thing smacked of vulgarity, since hardly any of those girls were married, so Mama had decided swiftly to ban them from the house, and with them my English teacher.

I felt sick and faint as I grasped after what Mrs. Smith had taught me. With just a handful of words, Agnes Knoop had exorcised her husband and left only drab, shy little me, weak with hunger and pain, Ruth flailing about inside me like a cornered cat, her grip slight.

I flickered into possession of myself. I screwed on a smile as gossamer-thin frown lines etched themselves between Agnes's brows. "*My darling, I love you,*" I said in my best English. To shut her up, I bent down and kissed her again, touching her hair like I had seen Mr. Knoop do in a photograph. My hand was steady, and at that I marveled. I felt the rich texture of her hair against my fingers, the throb of my heartbeat in the scar on my palm, the blood running down my thighs, but no emotion.

It'll come to me soon, I thought, *when she denounces me and exposes me for a fraud. Then I'll panic and hate myself.* In the meantime, I kept kissing her haughty mouth, murmuring English sentences of love that I had learned by rote, feeling as I suppose the dead do, which is to say, nothing at all. I wished she'd push me away already and tell everyone that I was not her husband instead of letting me kiss her so dispassionately.

It was not right, to kiss a woman so beautiful and feel so little.

When Agnes finally threw her chair back and got to her feet, it was a relief. *Thank God,* I thought as the other guests gasped and one of them tried to pull Agnes back. She seized me around the waist and pulled me hard against her, her arms locked tightly around me. She was very tall; I had to crane my head back to peer into her face. Her eyes flashed with something fierce.

She'll hurt us, I thought and almost welcomed the blow.

But she did not beat us. She whispered something to us, harsh and urgent, and then her mouth was on mine. It was not tight and hard now, but wet and warm. Our tongues touched, and it seemed to me that with her soft sucking, she drew the blood up into my cheeks.

It did not take long before she let go—mere seconds, a quarter of a minute, maybe. I shuddered first, and then she. Agnes sat down, placing her hands on the table, looking straight ahead of her as if nothing had happened. I, on the other hand, could not pretend this was normal. The feeling that had so far eluded me now flooded me, clutching at my throat and making it hard to breathe.

The room tended to get stuffy after half an hour or so into a séance because Mama would not open a window. She said it helped the ambience; the lack of fresh air made people more susceptible to our tricks. She had read in some vulgar little book that there were people who opened windows to let spirits out, and with this she justified our closed windows to our guests.

I tried to inhale deeply, slowly, but my chest hitched and jumped, and I couldn't.

Did she kiss her husband thus? I thought wildly. *Did she just kiss me as a lover?*

If only Ruth would tighten her grip on me and help me as she had done so often before! She could mumble that I had to go back and then walk to my chair and let me drop into it like a puppet with cut strings; we might still convince everyone we had things in hand.

But I couldn't even breathe.

I staggered to the window. If I could open it and inhale the cool night air, if I could let the rain splash on my hands and face, I would be better. The water would cleanse and anoint me. I fumbled with the sash, but my arms were weak, and I couldn't open the window.

"Ruth," I murmured. "Ruth, please help me."

I saw my face reflected in the pane, queer and pale, and then behind that was another's face, beautiful but cruel, with a grin like that of a fairy-tale wolf ready to gobble me up, like Mr. Mesman.

I screamed.

Ruth jumped up my throat to defend me, spouting from my nose and mouth.

I was on the floor then. Someone was dabbing a wet flannel against my forehead. I tried to push the hand away, but I felt very weak, very sick. I had a throbbing pain in my head that made me groan.

"My darling!" someone said, and I recognized the voice. It was Mama. She was kneeling over me, her bangles clashing together when she moved to wipe my face with her cheap handkerchief drenched in eau de cologne. My mouth was bloody from where Ruth had scratched me.

"And this, Mrs. Knoop," a man said, "is why we have to obey the rules!"

Agnes stood a little behind the others and did not look at me but at the windowpane where I had seen that wolfish face. It was gone now, but the fear still held me in its grip, like those first few minutes after waking from a nightmare when the body is still ready to flee or defend itself, the heart pounding and the muscles taut.

Mrs. de Jong squatted next to me with a cup of tea on a saucer. I drank a little, scalding sips. After a minute or so, I felt a little stronger and less afraid, and I sat up. My head still hurt. I touched it and winced.

Agnes came to me then. I raised my arms to fend off the blow I still imagined she wished to dole out, but all she did was kneel next to me and peer into my face. "You and Ruth were very impressive," she said. "Quite a marvel. Thank you."

She looked at Mama. "I shall send for a doctor. Do you have a phone?"

Mama wrung her hands. "I'm afraid not, Mrs. Knoop. Our lodgings are very humble as you can see. The money..."

I hated her then, hated her with a passion so fierce, it scared me. It made tears spring into my eyes, sharp, bitter tears that pricked and burned. Even the fact we weren't really related couldn't soothe me.

"You need not worry about the money. I shall pay for a doctor and write you out a check for your daughter's performance."

"Oh, Mrs. Knoop, that is most kind of you," Mama fawned. "Doctors are so expensive these days, and medicine, too."

I passed a hand over my face, wincing when my fingers brushed a bruise. "Please," I whispered. "I just want to sleep."

Mr. Bakker was the one who lifted me and carried me to bed. I lay in the dark listening to our clients paying and leaving, mingled with Mama's high silly chatter. The pain in my belly was fierce, and I lay nursing it under the thin sheets, so I need not think.

After a while Ruth crawled into bed with me. She took me into her long cold arms. She was still trembling.

"Where have you been?" I asked her.

"Chasing that man. I hunted him over the rooftops and through the alleys and down the warrens of moles and rabbits, but I couldn't catch him. I know one thing, though: he's like me."

"You mean the face I saw in the glass was a spirit?"

"Yes."

"Perhaps my blood attracted him."

"I don't know. I think he might have come with Agnes. I really don't know."

Ruth shivered still. I kissed her cool mouth so she could taste the blood there and be comforted. Something in her throat clicked as she swallowed. When she spoke, her voice was high and reedy. "There's something else," she whispered. "She could see me. I swear that Knoop woman could see me, darling Roosje mine."

Chapter 5

I WAS ASLEEP WHEN MAMA switched on a light and sat on the edge of the bed. I moaned and tried to shield my eyes, but she ordered me to lower my hands and twist my face this way and that so she could see the damage done.

"Nothing a little powder won't hide, though that nick in your lip is unfortunate," she said and lit a cigarette. "It's your own fault, of course, fainting away like that. You were overdoing it. What were you thinking, pawing at her like that? We're a decent establishment, not a brothel."

"Please, Mama, may I have something to eat now?"

She sucked on her cigarette. "Luckily for you, Agnes," she said, and the familiarity of Mama using her Christian name made me taste something vile at the back of my throat, "seemed very impressed with you. A shame you had to faint."

"Is she still here?" I asked.

"Bless you, child, what a funny thought to have. Of course not. Time's money and all that." She patted my head. "There'll be a doctor here soon; I couldn't persuade her not to send one. Best behavior, sweetheart."

When she was gone, I ran my tongue over my lips, feeling how swollen and raw they were. The cut was on my lower lip; Agnes must have nicked me with her teeth. I relished the sharp sweet sting, touching it over and over until my mouth was filled with the salty taste of blood.

The doctor examined me carefully. He bade me to stick out my tongue, pressed his warm fingers against the lymph nodes in my throat, took my temperature. He pulled up my eyelids to check their color, listened to my heartbeat and lungs. He weighed me, too, frowning at the scales.

"You're awfully thin for a woman your age," he said. "Do you eat enough?"

"Oh, Doctor." Mama tittered. "She's like I was at that age. Always eating, eating, eating, and not gaining an ounce!"

"I see. Would you be so kind as to get me a glass of water?" he asked. As soon as she was gone, he smiled at me. "Do you truly eat enough?"

For one desperate moment, I thought of telling him the truth, but what use would that be? What could this man possibly do to help me? "Mama says I'll eat her out of house and home. I'm just naturally skinny. My father was like that, too."

He kept smiling. "I see. And your menses, are those regular?"

"My menses?"

"Your cycle, your monthlies?"

I could not look at him. I began to pluck at a thread in the sheets, winding it around and around my finger.

"There's no need to be ashamed. I know it's a funny topic

to talk about, but I'm a doctor." He had a kind voice, sweet and warm.

I pulled the thread taut and watched the top of my finger turn red. "Yes," I said. "They're quite regular. One came just this morning."

And I was glad to see that dark splash of blood because… But there are some things one doesn't talk about, so I did not tell him.

"Do you often faint?"

"No."

"When you get up too quickly, do things go black for a little bit?"

"Sometimes."

When Mama brought him his water, he drank it quickly, then bent over his notepad and wrote out a prescription. "Just a temporary faintness caused by your cycle. Best to rest for the coming days and eat plenty of hearty food. I'll also give you a prescription for iron tablets—I suspect you might be a little anemic."

Mama showed him out, then came back and sat down on the edge of the bed again, looking at me. "You didn't tell him anything you shouldn't have, now did you?" she asked.

"No, Mama."

"Are you sure? You didn't tell him about Mr. Mesman, for instance?"

The name made my heart race and my insides turn to water. I wiped my hands on the sheets; they were wet. "I'll never tell anyone about that," I whispered.

She smiled at me and began to remove her bangles one by

one. "Good, because it would be very unwise, you know. He didn't press charges, and for that we should be grateful." She tightened her hand around the bangles, making them grind together. "Well, it's all over and in the past now. Best to focus on the future. If we secure Agnes's patronage, Mr. Mesman will be naught but a bad dream, half forgotten already."

She looked at the prescription the doctor had left on the nightstand, then ripped it into little bits. "Iron tablets discolor your teeth. It's hardly attractive. Now help me with my stays, will you? I'm dead tired. I've had such a long, hard day."

Chapter 6

EVERY SATURDAY, MAMA TOOK OUT her accounting book and the tin box with the lock on it, in which she stored the money we earned, and she set to counting. While she stacked coins and fingered bills, she sent me out to do our groceries and change out our library books. I had no need of money—we had accounts at every store, and Mama settled the bills once a month—but she gave me a little pocket money to spend as I saw fit. I usually bought things to please Ruth.

She took a childish delight in the bright, the shiny, and the sweet. In an empty cigar box, she kept the treasures we had collected over the years: a pack of colorful cards with gilded edges bearing the images of Catholic saints, which she liked to hold up to the light and move this way and that to see the gold glitter; three pieces of sea glass worn smooth by the salt water; an empty tube of lipstick; a striped candy wrapper shot through with silver; and feathers from parrots and parakeets.

Mama did not want me to buy food with the money she gave me, though she did allow me to buy some sweets. She needed some way to incentivize me to go out, for I hated doing our groceries almost as much as I hated performing during our séances, though in a different way. The séances were shameful because we abused the suffering of others for our own gain, but at least our clients respected me. Grocery shopping was shameful because the godly shopkeepers thought us no better than sly little frauds full of pride, deceit, and greed. Naturally, they despised us.

It didn't help that they thought I was slightly insane. Some of them talked to me slowly, in a loud voice and with easy words, as if I were stupid. They'd look at me with pity and share looks with other customers that made me want to lash out and hurt them, or cry, or wish I were as invisible to them as Ruth was. Others refused to have me inside. I had to stand on the threshold and call out my order, then put down my money because they didn't want to touch my hand accidentally as they took it. They did the same with a woman who had been a German officer's mistress during the war.

It was a good thing Ruth came along with me. It gave me strength, her dead hand with the curled fingers holding mine. She talked to me all the time to distract me, saying spiteful things about the shopkeepers to try and make me laugh through the tears or babbling about the sweets she wanted us to get this time. She had a hunger for them: saltwater toffees, sheets of liquorice, bonbons wrapped in gold foil. The ones she liked best were a kind of cheap red lollipop that splintered and sharpened the more you sucked on it, cutting the gums and tongue. I suppose that was why she liked them so much: she relished the taste of the cheap sugar mixed with the tang of blood.

"Next time, I won't let you possess me anymore. You can eat those lollipops with your own body," I'd complain after she'd sucked one down to its wooden stick. With each word I'd feel the cuts on my lacerated tongue open and close like little mouths.

She'd laugh and kiss my stained lips. "They wouldn't taste half so good, darling Roosje mine!"

The Saturday after that disastrous séance, I came home with the groceries as always, the taste of sugar and blood lingering in my mouth. A sharp little remnant of lollipop had lodged itself behind the molars of my right lower jaw, where I could not reach it well with my tongue. Every so often, a drop of blood welled up around the shard, only to be swallowed. It made me nauseous.

"You could have plucked it out," I told Ruth as I struggled to open the door with all the bags. Their strings cut into my flesh, striping my hands and wrists.

"I didn't notice," she said.

"Just because you can unhinge your jaw doesn't mean I can."

I shoved the door open with my shoulder and took the groceries into the kitchen so I could put them away. First, I had to take care of my mouth, though; it throbbed and stung. I placed the bags on the kitchen table, then went to the little mirror fixed to one of its walls. I opened my mouth as far as I could, but I couldn't see the embedded bit of lollipop. With my fingers I felt for it, gagging a little. Soon my eyes began to water, and my fingers were coated with saliva, pink from blood and lollipop both. Finally, I managed to dislodge the shard. I spat it out in my palm, then swallowed the saliva and the fresh blood that trickled up from the cut.

When I smiled, the lines between my teeth were pink, too.

"There," Ruth said, "that wasn't so very bad, now was it? You didn't even need my help." She rubbed her face against mine like a cat. She could be a needy thing, my Ruth.

"Not now," I said. "There's all this stuff to put away." I washed my hands, then put things in their proper places. When I was done, I called out, "Mama? We're back."

"I'm in the drawing room, darling. We have a guest," she called back, her voice artificial and bright.

My heartbeat sped up so that the blood buzzed in my ears. I went into the drawing room.

There she sat, facing Mama: Mrs. Agnes Knoop. I had thought of her every day, of her soft lips on mine, her husky voice, her scent. So much had I thought of her that I wondered if I had somehow drawn her to me. She hadn't changed since the last time I'd seen her, although she wore different clothes now: a black jumper and a long skirt with matching stripes, exquisitely cut and very lovely.

"Mrs. Knoop," I said stupidly. "What are you doing here?"

"I've come to take you away. Your Mama and I were negotiating the terms," she said simply. She gave me a little smile, very sweet and pleasant.

"We were doing no such thing! I would never just let you take Roos from me. I love her, and if she's to go, how would I make a living? I'm an old woman in poor health. Surely you would not deprive me of the only one who would tend to me in my final years? We don't have a lot of money, Mrs. Knoop," Mama said. She spoke in that fake, overwrought manner she always adopted

when appealing to people's sense of pity and charity. I felt suddenly
revolted by her, so much so that it made my mouth twist.

If Agnes felt the same way, she did not show it. "We had
already discussed the fact that I would reimburse you—and Roos,
too; I wouldn't dream of not paying anyone in my employ. And,
of course, Roos could come visit as often as she'd like. If I may…?"
She wrote down a number on a slip of paper. Her little diamond
watch caught the light and threw it back on the table in fragments. She slid the paper to Mama, who snatched it up and read
it greedily. Yet when she looked up, she had composed her face
into a look of sadness.

"It won't do, Mrs. Knoop. A mother's love for her daughter
can't be expressed in a sum of money, but all the same, my Roos is
worth more than what you offer."

"I see." Agnes wrote a different number on the paper before
giving it back. "And this sum? Shall that suffice?"

I daren't move or speak for fear Mama would refuse. I daren't
even think; I was gripped by a superstition that to put my yearning
for a different life into thought would put it out of reach forever.
But I could not help the sudden image of Agnes running to me,
her halo of hair dancing around her face, holding out her hands
for mine. Neither could I help the flash of desire that accompanied that image, so strong that it made gooseflesh ripple from my
soles to my crown. Part of that desire belonged to the Mr. Knoop
Ruth and I had stitched together for our séances, but part of it was
undeniably mine.

Sensing my anxiety and the sharp twist of hunger in me, Ruth lay her cheek against mine. It was cold as a tendril of mist. Agnes looked at me, then away.

"She looked at me," Ruth hissed. "Did you see?"

Agnes's eyes had snagged on the place where Ruth stood, but it was for such a little time that I couldn't be sure whether it had really happened.

Mama sighed. "I suppose a mother must do what is best for her daughter, and a rich lady as yourself can offer my darling Roosje more than an old poor woman. I shall accept this money."

She has sold me, I thought, and though I had feared she would ever since I was a little child and then more fiercely still when Mr. Mesman began to visit, I couldn't believe she actually had. I had thought, stupidly, desperately, that she cared for me, in a way. And maybe she did.

Only she cared for money more.

I shouldn't have been disappointed. She had always made it clear that I was a burden to her, and I wanted to go with Agnes, didn't I? More than I had ever wanted something before. But I couldn't help the hardening of my heart toward Mama.

In that moment, I think Agnes must have lost whatever little bit of respect she'd had for Mama, too. She gave her a lean little smile. "I'm glad to hear it. Will a check work for you?" She wrote it quickly, in a curious slanting hand. When she was done, she stood and smoothed down her hair. "Well, then it's all settled. Roos shall live with me from now on as my companion." She looked at me. "Unless you'd rather stay?"

I shook my head.

She smiled. "That's what I thought. I'll give you some time to pack. If you need me, I shall be outside." When she had gone, the smell of her perfume lingered, herbal and deep.

Mama sat stroking the check. "I suppose," she said, not looking at me, "that you must feel very pleased with yourself."

I shook my head. I didn't feel anything yet, as if afraid that it would all fall apart if I gave in to my emotions. "I'll go upstairs to pack," I whispered.

Once we were in my room, Ruth took my face in her hands and made me look into her eyes. Today they were shriveled and shrunken like raisins, with a curious orange color to them. "We'll never be forced by Mama to lie for our daily bread, and for that I know you'll be glad," she said. "Yet we must be careful all the same, Roos. I've not forgotten that male spirit that accompanied Agnes to the séance, and neither, I hope, have you."

I rested my head against her clavicle. "I can't think right now. If I do, I'll think and feel too much."

"Then I shall think and feel for you, my yokemate, my companion, my sweet."

"She has sold me, Ruth, as if I'm a chair, or a bag of potatoes, or a painting she wasn't particularly fond of, and to the first person who offered…"

"And that first person who offered just paid a small fortune for you. I don't know what her intentions are yet, but I do know she wants you very badly."

"That means she'll take good care of me, doesn't it?"

Ruth thought about it for a moment, then took my hand and

kissed it. I felt the press of her teeth against my palm. "Of course she will. Now go pack," she said. She sat herself down on top of the wardrobe. She had to twist and fold herself to fit.

I didn't own a suitcase. There had never been the need for one since Mama and I hardly left the house. I didn't have to pack much: my clothes, Ruth's box of treasures, her bottle of ground-up glass, some toiletries, the things my father had given me on his rare visits between sailing the world. Those gifts and a beribboned medal awarded posthumously, after his ship was sunk by a submarine during the war, were all that was left of him.

Sometimes Mama made me take the medal out and show it to our guests along with a photograph of him in uniform; she wanted them to know she was the widow of a decorated war hero because that made us more tragic and less fraudulent.

I tucked my treasures between my clothes, then wrapped them in a piece of old tablecloth Mr. Mesman had ruined. I bound the package with brown string. The feel of it against the scar between my index finger and thumb conjured memories of the hole under the floorboards, with its smell of mildew and dark earth. Fear made my palms slick with sweat.

When Mama came to look in on me, I was wiping my hands on my dress convulsively; they seemed to stay wet no matter how I rubbed at them. "Well," she said as she sat herself on the bed, her bangles jangling, "this is it then, at least for a little while."

"What do you mean? You needn't ever see me again after today."

She looked at a spool of thread I hadn't packed yet, then

slipped it into her pocket when she thought I wasn't looking. "Don't get any ideas, sweetheart. You're nothing special. Agnes just needs someone to alleviate the loneliness now that her husband is gone and someone to help look after her sister-in-law. The woman has consumption, didn't you know? You'll do the trick for a while. She said as much to me before you came in. Personally, I think you'll be back with me before the year is out. Fancy ladies like Agnes are famous for growing bored quickly, and you're a one-trick pony, aren't you?"

"She won't grow tired of me," I said stiffly.

"Poor little darling, I think she will. And when she does, you'll come back to me."

"I'll never come back to you," I spat. I balled my slick hands into fists.

"You will. How else would you make a living? You've got no skills. Hell, with your constant chattering to your invisible companion, you're not even suited to unskilled labor. Nobody wants a girl who's mad. The only thing left to a girl like that is to make use of what lies between her legs, but I think if it comes down to that, you'll find you prefer it here. Who knows, I might even take you back, though not if you insist on looking so sullen."

The blood flowed hot and quick in me then. It seemed to crash against the inside of my skull, little lapping waves of it. It was as if I had accidentally swallowed Ruth, but that couldn't be: she was still folded on top of the wardrobe.

"Of course you will," I said. "You'll do anything for money, won't you? You would've sold me to Mr. Mesman, had he ever offered. I suppose you would've offered it yourself, had Ruth not taken care of him first. You're no better than a common bawd."

I picked up my packages with trembling hands.

Two patches of color burned in Mama's cheeks. "Now, look here, girl. I've kept you fed and clothed through all these years, so don't you…" she began. She tried to take hold of my arm. In one quick ripple, Ruth came down from the wardrobe, her teeth bared. They were broken and sharp today. If I let her in, she'd commit violence. I jerked away from Mama.

"Don't you dare touch me," I hissed. "If you do, I won't answer for the consequences. Ruth doesn't take kindly to people who hurt me, and now that you've sold me, there's no reason for me to protect you from her anymore."

The color drained from her cheeks. Uncertain, she took a step back.

I moved past her, down the stairs, through the hallway and out onto the street, where Agnes stood waiting for me. She'd put on a chinchilla-fur coat, which looked wonderfully warm. She smiled when she saw me but frowned at my package. "Is that all? And don't you have a thicker coat?"

I shook my head.

She stroked my threadbare summer coat with the back of her hand. Had she been wearing her wedding ring, it might have caught on a button. As it was, her hand was still curiously naked. "We'll have to buy you some proper clothes and a nice thick coat then, won't we?"

FOURTH CASE EPISODE

PATIENT R–, A CASE STORY: INHABITED BY ANOTHER

(D = DOCTOR, P = PATIENT R–)

FOURTH EPISODE, CONDUCTED ON 8 OCTOBER 1954:

Notes to self: Previous session made it clear that copulation is a particularly sensitive topic. Key to unlocking the mystery? Likely, but avoid for now. Too early yet. Patient must trust me first. No doubt she'll tell me everything once she does.

Earlier talks seem to suggest patient may be schizophrenic; delusions are very vivid and elaborate. Keep pressing for inconsistencies. Response will reveal whether she's truly sick or merely manipulative. The sooner I know, the better. Would be unethical to have her stand trial if she can't be held responsible for what happened.

> **D:** "Do you often feel violent toward people?"
>
> **P:** "What do you mean?"
>
> **D:** "You've said that, when you were packing your things, you felt like you could have hurt your mother, and that it took a great effort of will not to. Do you often feel that way?"
>
> **P:** "You don't understand. I said it was Ruth who wanted to hurt Mama, not me."
>
> **D:** "Yes, and you said that, if you had let her in, you would've hurt Mama."
>
> **P:** "No. Not me. Ruth. When I'm possessed, it's all Ruth."

D: "Let's circle back a little. Does Ruth often want to hurt people?"

P: "Only if they mean me harm."

D: "What do you mean by that? What sort of harm?"

P: "If they want to hurt me."

D: "Hurt you how?"

P: "Just hurt me."

D: "So if I were to slap you now, would Ruth wish to hurt me?"

P: [*rubs the scars on hands in agitation; eyes start to wander; cocks head to the side, as if listening to some-one speak*] "Do you want to slap me?" [*voice quivers*]

D: "No. I don't want to hurt you, R—, I want to help you. Forgive me, this was a bad example. I only want to know what happens exactly when Ruth becomes angry with someone. What does she want to do to them then?"

P: "She wants to cause them pain."

D: "What sort of pain?"

P: "Physical pain. But only because she wants to scare them off, Doctor. She doesn't want to inflict violence just for the sake of it."

D: "And how would Ruth go about causing anyone pain?"

P: "She'd have to possess me first, then work through me."

D: "And why is that? Can spirits not interact with the physical world?"

P: [*starts to fidget*] "Only a little."

D: "So Ruth couldn't slap me, for instance, if she so pleased?"

P: "No."

D: "Not even when she's in her substantial state, and you can touch her, and she feels as real as I do?"

P: "Not even then. She can't touch someone who can't perceive her. But to me, she's often as substantial as you are."

D: "Interesting. Now tell me, R—: did Ruth want to hurt Mrs. K—?"

P: [*silence*]

D: "R—? Did Ruth want to hurt Mrs. K—? Or Miss K—, for that matter?"

P: "You make it out as if Ruth is a sadist. She isn't. It's just...I've read a theory once that prehistoric man sacrificed the most precious things they owned to the bogs to appease its gods and spirits. That's why we find swords and jewelry and other lovely things there. Ruth was drowned in a bog. That means she was someone's precious thing once, so precious they cut and choked and stabbed her till she finally died. It's not so strange then, is it, that Ruth sometimes shows her love for me through violence? And now I don't want to talk about it anymore."

D: "I am rushing things, aren't I? I'm sorry. I do not mean to be impatient. I merely want to understand you. Why don't you tell me what happened after you left Mama?"

Chapter 7

AGNES'S CAR WAS PARKED IN a different street. I'd been in a car only once before, when Mr. Mesman had thrown a party. He picked us up so we didn't have to take the bus. The journey took only twenty minutes, but I felt nauseous for the rest of the evening, though that may have been the nerves. When Mr. Mesman brought us home, I stumbled out of the car and was sick on the pavement. Mama blamed it on the champagne. I blamed it on Mr. Mesman's hand on my knee. He'd had to let go whenever he switched gears, and then I'd thought he'd leave me be, only for that horrible hand to creep back.

I felt slightly sick again now as Agnes held the door open for me. I should've eaten something, should have ensured my stomach wasn't trying to digest only sugar and blood. Agnes threw my package in the trunk. From it she drew an old coat of hers, which she draped over my lap and knees as if I were sick. "It'll be too long on you, you're such a slight slip of a thing, but it'll do until we get you something better this afternoon. I thought of having a hot lunch first, pasta or seafood, and plenty of coffee afterward. You could have an ice, of course."

I wondered how old she thought I was. I pulled the coat from my lap and draped it around my shoulders instead. It was wool, wonderfully thick and warm. Ruth snaked her arms into the sleeves and purred like a kitten.

Agnes took me to an Italian restaurant with gingham table-cloths, smelling deliciously of garlic and warm dough. The maître d' seemed to know Agnes, addressing her by name and bowing to her, then taking us to a table in the corner near the window. She ordered pasta and wine for herself, lasagna and lemonade for me. We were given some bread as we waited for our dishes. She buttered a slice for me. The butter was slightly salty, very rich, the bread still hot from the oven. As soon as I tasted it, I was lost. I wolfed it down, hardly chewing.

"Steady on," Agnes said, "or you'll ruin your appetite and get a bellyache in the bargain." But she buttered another slice for me, cutting it into little pieces and handing them to me one by one like she might have done for a child.

"I'm twenty-one, you know," I said.

"Are you? You don't look it. You're too thin."

"Mama wants me to look younger."

"What on earth for?"

"To help create the right ambience for the séances."

She took a sip of wine, exposing that light-brown throat of hers. She didn't look so tall now that she was seated. "Ah, yes, the séances," she said. "It's not all true, now, is it?"

I flushed, the color spreading like a glass of spilled wine. "It's not untrue."

She put the glass down and dabbed at her mouth with a napkin, leaving small purple stains. "But you weren't really possessed by Thomas, were you?"

I licked my finger, then used the wet tip to gather the crumbs on my plate. I put them in my mouth one by one.

She tucked a strand of hair behind her ear. Her hair was very thick and black. "Come, Roos, you needn't be loyal to your mama anymore now."

"I don't know about that. You might change your mind and take me back."

"I would never. Now please tell me: Thomas wasn't really there, was he?" That look of mingled horror and yearning was back again, so potent that I couldn't look at her.

"Tell her what she wants to hear," Ruth whispered in my ear, but there lay the trouble: I didn't know what she wanted. I couldn't tell Ruth that because I didn't want to talk to her in public and make people think I was mad. Even Mama liked to jeer at me for talking to Ruth when I was at home, and she at least half believed Ruth was real.

I finished eating the crumbs. Then I wiped my fingers on a napkin. "No," I said slowly, "he wasn't really there."

She leaned back in her chair, the tautness gone from her limbs, her face momentarily tilted back. The light of the overhead lamp bathed it in an orange glow, but even then it didn't really look yellow. I wondered why people described a skin as hers like that. "I see," she said, her voice flat. "Why did you pretend?"

"Because I thought you wanted to talk to your husband, and I had to give you everything you wanted."

She touched her ring finger, then remembered she wasn't wearing her wedding ring and dropped her hand in her lap. "You must be careful with that, Roos. It's a dangerous thing, to try and give someone everything. One day, you might find you've given away things you should've kept. Some parts of us must remain inviolate if we are to survive as a person."

I opened my mouth to respond, but we were served our lunch then, and for a while, I could do nothing but eat piping-hot lasagna. When I was done, the moment to reply had gone. I had eaten too much, but in a cheerful, only slightly uncomfortable way. It left me drowsy and content.

Agnes finished her food, then ordered coffee. She lit a cigarette and smoked it slowly, her eyes half-closed with the pleasure of it. "I hope," she said, "you shan't miss your mama too much."

I rubbed the scar from where I used to bite my hand as a child, the flesh thick and twisted like a cord. The scars from where that client had beaten me were different: thin strokes that changed color depending on whether my hands were warm or cold. "She's not really my mama, you know. She just makes me call her that because she thinks it makes us sound genteel. We're not even related." And thank God for that, really. It had often been my sole consolation. Well, that, and Ruth.

"Then how did you come to live with her?"

"My real mother died when I was very young, and my father was a sailor. He didn't want me to end up in an orphanage, so he gave me to Mama instead. He paid her to keep me, only then he died." Mama had read the letter with a frown, then looked up to me and said, *From now on, you'll have to start earning your keep, girl*, as if I hadn't done so as soon as I could pull a string. I had thought at first that my father had written to tell Mama he no longer wanted to bear the burden of my care. Later, when I found out he had drowned, I felt dirty for having thought so.

Agnes tapped the cigarette against the ashtray. A column of gritty ash collapsed onto the porcelain. "You've no other family?"

"No."

She took a drag, then held the smoke in her lungs for a good long while before blowing it out in a steady stream. She crushed the cigarette against the side of the ashtray. "So you're all alone, except for Ruth."

"I've never really thought about it like that. When you have someone like Ruth, you're not really alone."

"I understand," she said. I remembered the wolfish face in the windowpane, and a flush crept up my throat.

"Mrs. Knoop, do you…" I began.

She laughed. "Oh, please, do call me 'Agnes.' 'Mrs. Knoop' feels so cold and formal." She picked up the pepper shaker, and with one fluid motion, she tucked it into her handbag.

"You can't just take that," I gasped. My heart beat so fast, it didn't feel like a steady drumming anymore but like the hum of an insect's wings.

"Of course I can."

"But it belongs to the restaurant."

"Not for long. You'll find I'm a petty thief of pepper. Nutmeg, sugar, tobacco, and clove, too, when I can get it."

"But why?"

"Ever heard of *tanam paksa*?"

I shook my head. My throat still felt raw.

"You'll probably know it under its Dutch name of *cultuurstelsel*, cultivation system."

I did. Under the cultivation system, a specific part of Indonesia's—then still considered the Dutch Indies—ground had to be used to grow goods that could be exported. That way, Indonesia had earned a lot of money that went into the coffers of the Dutch state.

Next Agnes held the saltshaker to the light, then thought better of it and placed it back on the table. "My mother told me the stories her grandparents had told her, about the famines and epidemics. All that fertile soil used to grow indigo and tobacco and rubber, and none left for rice. And for what? To repay the costs the Dutch had made during the Java War to keep Indonesia from gaining independence. Nothing so sick as making a people pay for their own enslavement."

I shifted uncomfortably in my chair and kept quiet.

The tense cold look on Agnes's face broke, and she fixed me with a mischievous look. "It seems only fair I take back the products that made my people suffer. No matter if they're actually produced in Indonesia now; it still gives me a wicked sense of pleasure. Now, have you finished with that?" She nodded at my glass of lemonade.

"Not yet."

"Well, drink up then. We still have plenty to do today."

"Oh, but she's inscrutable," Ruth murmured.

Chapter 8

AGNES DROVE US TO THE city. She took me into a salon and had my hair cut stylishly short. My heart beat painfully quick as the scissors snipped near my ears and lock after lock came tumbling down. Mama's regime of starvation had caused my hair to fall out in little clumps, and what remained had become brittle. Cutting it was a good thing, but I still felt a lump in my throat as I looked at the dull strands curled sadly around the foot of my chair.

By the time the hairdresser was done, the melancholy had gone. The face in the mirror looking back was still pinched and wan, but the expensive cut made it look older, more sophisticated. I no longer looked like a nymphet.

Agnes touched my shorn nape. The color crept up my neck and throat, turning the skin red in ugly patches. She stroked a light line, once, twice. "So soft. Feel." She guided my hand. I felt the cut hair under my fingertips but mainly her fingers on mine. Ruth watched us, her eyes two black pits. I shuddered once, violently.

Misunderstanding, Agnes closed her hand around my neck and rubbed at it with her thumb to get the blood flowing. "It's chilly, isn't it, having your neck exposed? It'll take some getting used to, but what do you think? Do you like it?"

"It's so soft, and my head feels so light! I swear a gust of wind might blow away my head like dandelion fluff."

"Then we must be careful, you and I," Agnes said. She unknotted the little silk scarf around her throat and wound it around mine. "There, that should keep you warm and your head attached to your neck." She drew me out of the chair and linked arms with me.

Our next stop was a department store. There we bought two dresses, a pair of slacks, a skirt, two blouses, a jumper, and a pair of shoes. They were all rather big on me.

"In a few weeks, when you've had time to fill out, everything will fit. Unlike your Mama, I intend to feed you properly," Agnes said.

Besides those clothes she also selected a woolen coat for me in a gorgeous blue shade and a matching scarf and hat to go with it. Lastly, she took me to the department with underclothes, where she bought me slips in various shades of blush and cream. For stockings, she chose Lockhart. She took my hand in hers, softly, and moved the back of my fingers against the silk. "Soft as sin, aren't they?" she murmured. "When I was younger, I boarded at a convent school for a number of years. The nuns made us wear these horrible black stockings, so scratchy and cheap. It was beastly, making the daughter of a stocking manufacturer wear such inferior rags. When I finished, the first thing I did was rip up those horrible stockings and put on a pair of Lockharts."

She glanced at my stockings, then rooted around her purse and gave me a pair of nail scissors. In the changing room, I carefully cut the prickly shapeless wool until nothing was left but ragged strips.

After we had eaten dinner at another restaurant, Agnes took me to her rooms in the hotel where she had been staying for the past few weeks.

She put the key in the lock of the door but did not turn it. Instead, she looked to me. "You know, you needn't stay with me," she said.

I blinked. "But you've taken me away," I said.

"You don't owe me anything."

"But I do. I owe you everything."

"No. I know I've given your mama some money, but really that was only so she wouldn't make trouble later, and the clothes I bought were just because I couldn't bear to see you go about in those rags. If you find you and Ruth don't like to be with me, then I want you to know you can leave at any time."

I felt chilled. "Mrs. Knoop," I said slowly, "if you feel like you've made a mistake with me..."

She interrupted me with a nervous little laugh. "Oh dear, not at all. I'm not expressing myself very well. I suppose what I'm trying to say is that I'd hate for you to feel...beholden to me."

Beholden. It was such a funny, archaic word. Ruth might have used it. She was a smart one, my Ruth. Sometimes I got to thinking about who she might have been when she was still alive. Probably someone with a hunger for power. Perhaps she had been a pagan priestess. I could imagine her traveling into the bog to sacrifice a lamb with a silver dagger, the blood spouting hot and quick, the same bog where she would one day be sacrificed.

I imagined them staking and breaking her, a piece of rope around her throat so they could strangle her by degrees, leaving her in that strange liminal space of not-yet-dead-but-not-truly-alive-anymore for hours.

Ruth placed her hand on my shoulder. The fingers were crooked, twig thin. "Careful now," she whispered, her breath cold and tinged with the scent of freshly turned earth. "She sought us out, paid dearly for us to be with her. She may have her reasons for not wanting to seem eager, but eager she is."

"We don't feel beholden, but I'll tell you if we do," I told Agnes.

She smiled, twisted the key, and pushed the door open with her shoulder. "Please remove your shoes," she said and slipped out of her heels. Her stockings had a reinforced bit at the heel, a triangle of utter blackness.

The room was lovely, with high ceilings trimmed like a wedding cake. The marble fireplace with pink veins running through it, the crystal chandelier, the red velvet chairs standing comfortably around a scratchless coffee table, all of it spoke of money. There were two beds, both with snow-white sheets. How long had Agnes known she wanted me to be her companion? The room had clearly been lived in, yet I didn't dare touch anything for fear I'd sully or break something expensive.

I halted awkwardly in the middle of the room, my shoes in

hand. Agnes brushed past me, tossed her shoes in a corner, then shrugged out of her coat and threw it over a chair. It slithered to the ground and lay in a beautiful heap. She cursed softly, picked it up, and threw it on the bed instead. She went to the mirror, wiped at a bit of spilled powder with the side of her hand, began to unscrew her earrings. When she caught sight of me in the glass, she smiled.

"Hotel rooms are such strange places, don't you think? Even when we stay in them for weeks, they retain a sense of distance. I should know; I've seen so many of them." Agnes sighed. "Whenever I couldn't spend the holidays at school, my father paid a poor spinster cousin of his to look after me. He'd book hotel rooms for us at the coast, never the same place twice, and then we'd be at each other's mercy for several weeks until term started again. God, I hated her. Eunice was her name, though she made me call her 'Miss Finch.'"

From the quick eager way in which she spoke, I realized she was just as nervous as I was. Somehow that made it easier for me to feel at ease.

A caustic laugh escaped her lips. "*Miss Finch* had a mortal fear of people thinking she and I were related. She was very godly, so she found my very existence offensive. She once called my mother a 'slit-eyed whore of Babylon.' I was so furious with her then that I couldn't sleep for three nights straight; all I could do was imagine all the ways she deserved to be punished. Oh, she was a glutton for punishment, Miss Finch was, though for doling it out, not receiving it. If I did something naughty, she made me kneel on uncooked rice for hours while she prayed the rosary. Whenever I hear the clicking of beads, I feel a phantom pain in my knees."

"Did she make you kneel on rice because you're Indonesian?"

"Indo. My father was white. And you know, I never thought about that. You might well be right. Miss Finch wouldn't be able to point out Indonesia on a map, but even she must've known that people eat rice there."

"Mama used to beat me with a birch rod," I confessed. "She'd slap the back of my legs and knees till they were all inflamed. Though with her, the piousness is all pretense. She said she stopped believing in God when He made her keep me."

"How very lovely. It seems we're rather similar, you and I."

Again, she smiled at me.

I smiled back.

She dropped her earrings in a little dish. "Make yourself at home. I'll take a bath, give you some time to unpack."

My packages had been left on the coffee table. I unpacked them slowly, using Agnes's nail scissors to snip the twine. When my old clothes lay next to my new ones, they looked even more horrible to me than before. A sudden surge of hatred rose in my throat like bile.

"Let me," Ruth whispered. "Oh, please, let me in."

I let her in. Once she had stretched till she could stretch no more, she made me slash at the faux-silk slips, the sack-like white dresses that Mama had made me sew so I would arouse our male guests. *Mr. Mesman*, I thought and did not feel chilled but enraged. I imagined his face and all the ways he deserved to be punished. The phantom taste of blood welled up in my mouth, metallic and salty.

Enough, I told Ruth. Our rage spent, we sank on the edge of the bed. Ruth unhooked herself from my spine and crawled up my throat. I coughed softly to help her, then breathed her out, tendril after tendril of her until she sat beside me, clawlike hands curled in her lap. She worked her broken jaw, producing a series of rapid clicks. The sound was soothing to me. I rested my heavy head against her shoulder.

Bits of fabric and thread from my ripped-up dresses littered the carpet, seemed to grow from it like mold. In autumn, the space under the floorboards had sprouted mushrooms. Pale, bulbous things, soft to the touch. I would close my eyes and tell myself I was in the woods, and the still, rank air was just the smell of leaves and fungi—I could get up and walk away whenever I wished.

"Incredible," Agnes said.

I looked up. I hadn't heard her leave the bathroom, but there she was, flushed from the heat. A wet tendril of hair lay plastered against her throat. She swallowed, and the tendril shivered. "Ruth is sitting next to you, isn't she?" she asked.

"Yes. Can't you see her?"

"I see something very vaguely. An outline, nothing more."

"Then I shall describe her to you so you may see her clearly."

And I did. I talked of Ruth's hair dyed red and her skin dyed brown by the bog, her eyes that were sometimes a gleaming black like a beetle's wing case, sometimes dried-up raisins, and sometimes not there at all because the bog that preserved the down on her upper lip and the whorls on her knuckles ate away organs and eyeballs. I described the ragged clothes she wore, the bit of rope around her throat like a necklace with a knot so tight, it could never be plucked apart, how she could scuttle quick as a spider when the fancy took her, her voice like the wind in the reeds interspersed by the clicks from her broken jaw.

The more I told her, the bigger Agnes's smile became. "I can see you now," she told Ruth once I stopped talking. She held out her hand. Ruth laid hers in it, and Agnes did not hesitate, did not shudder at the dead flesh. She clasped it, stroked Ruth's knuckles with her thumb. After a few seconds, Ruth pulled back.

"I knew you were no fraud," Agnes said, turning to me. She took my hands. Her skin had already lost the warmth of her bath and taken on Ruth's cold, but I could see her pulse jump at the base of her throat, a little flickering throb. "And you?" she whispered. "Do you not see him?" Her eyes gleamed, and she spoke in a rather husky, breathless manner.

A delicious shiver went up my spine. Ruth squeezed my arm. If she were still breathing, she'd be panting with excitement. "Where is he?" I asked.

"Over there, in the chair by the window."

I looked over my shoulder. There he sat, the man with the wolfish face.

She went to him and fondly put a hand on his shoulder. "This is Peter Quint," she said. "My spirit companion."

FIFTH CASE EPISODE

PATIENT R—, A CASE STORY: INHABITED BY ANOTHER

(D = DOCTOR, P = PATIENT R—)

FIFTH EPISODE, CONDUCTED ON 11 OCTOBER 1954:

Notes to self: Patient took discussion on the true nature of Ruth (Ruth as a creation of a split psyche, Ruth as the shadow-self) rather well. Doesn't seem to believe me at all, of course, but didn't reject my theory with violence or hysterics, as sometimes happens in cases like these. Could argue her case rather well and is consistent.

Interesting.

D: "Have you ever considered that you created Ruth?"

P: "Created her how?"

D: "People fear the unknown. When your mama put you into that space under the floorboards, you were scared of precisely that: the unknown. It was dark, and all kinds of things could be hiding there. The unknown is a large thing to fear, bigger than what the mind may hold, especially that of a child as young as yourself. Your fear was so debilitating, so all-consuming, that your mind decided to make it comprehensible. It was the only way you could survive."

P: "You mean to say that I made up Ruth so I needn't be so terrified anymore?"

D: "Yes."

P: [*rubs scarred hand*] "I don't think that's right, Doctor.
I learned to love and trust Ruth very quickly. I wasn't
afraid of her anymore. Shouldn't she have gone away
then?"

D: "Not necessarily. You see, I think Ruth was a survival
mechanism. She became the embodiment of your fear
when you needed something concrete to be afraid of.
You were also intensely lonely and starved of love and
affection by your mother. Freud tells us that we all crave
our mother's love. Mama couldn't give you what you
needed, so your mind created a mother who could: Ruth."

P: "But don't you think that it's too much of a coincidence
that A– [Mrs. K–] and I both had spirit companions
that were so alike? If Ruth is just a part of me that I
made up, I mean?"

D: "No. I think you and Mrs. K–were very much alike. Both
of you missed the love of a parental figure when you
were young: you lost your father and only had Mama to
look after you, who seems to have done a poor job. Girls
at an age as young as you were when you made up Ruth
crave the love and approval of their mother, so your
survival mechanism took the shape of a woman. Mrs.
K–lost her mother, and though her father seems to have
taken excellent care of her material needs, there's little
question that he neglected her emotionally. So, like you,
she made up a parental figure to help her survive."

P: "Peter Quint."

D: "Exactly. Peter Quint. I'd like to talk about him. Firstly, does his name not strike you as odd?"

P: "No. Should it?"

D: "Peter Quint is the name of a ghost in the famous ghost story *The Turn of the Screw* by Henry James."

P: "I've never read that."

D: "It's the story of a governess who believes her charges are menaced by two ghosts. In the end, a young boy is killed. It is left to the reader to make up his own mind as to what really happened: whether there truly were ghosts harassing the governess, or whether she became mad and suffocated the child."

P: "What a sick little story. I don't care for it." [*shudders and starts to wipe hands on dress*]

D: "I feared you wouldn't. But don't you think it strange that Mrs. K—'s spirit companion used the name of a famous literary ghost, even though you think he must have been dead for a long time and therefore couldn't have read *The Turn of the Screw*?"

P: "You don't understand. Spirits like Peter and Ruth are quite nameless until they find a human companion."

D: "Didn't they have a name when they were alive?"

P: "Yes, but then they forget. They're tucked into the ground and don't decay, but sleep for so long that they forget a lot about what it was like being alive. We wake and name them, and in that way, we bind them to us, and ourselves to them."

D: "Why did you name your spirit Ruth?"

P: "In our street, there was a very old lady living with her family. Her mind had reverted to being a baby, and she couldn't speak anymore. If the weather was nice, they'd put her outside in a chair, and we could hear her grunt and cry out if something pleased or upset her. Her name was Ruth. When I first met my Ruth, before I'd bound her to me, she couldn't speak, either, only moan, so the name seemed apt."

D: "And Mrs. K— named her spirit companion Peter Quint in much the same way as you named Ruth? Because the name seemed apt?"

P: "Yes. Now that I know what that means, it doesn't surprise me. She was well-read and had a sense of humor, and Peter came to her much later than Ruth did to me."

D: "Do you know when he came to her?"

P: "When she was boarding at some horrid French convent school."

D: "Do you know how old she was then?"

P: "About sixteen or seventeen."

D: "That explains why her spirit companion took the shape of a man. Girls at that age have learned to displace their love for their mother onto their father and crave his love and approval."

P: "I don't think that had anything to do with it. I think Peter came to her because she was lonely and they were cruel to her, not because she missed her father."

D: "Who is 'they'?"

P: "Her classmates, the nuns. Everyone, really."

D: "R—, what did Mrs. K— tell you about her time at school?"

P: "Please don't rush me. If you do, I'll forget to tell you things, important things, things that'll help you understand."

D: "Such as?"

P: "Such as my first meeting with Peter Quint."

Chapter 9

FROM THE MOMENT I HAD clapped eyes on Agnes that morning, I had gone through an array of emotions: excitement, fear, shame, happiness, and more besides. Yet all had also felt somewhat dulled to me, somewhat removed and unreal. Dreamlike.

Yet as I sat looking at Peter, everything lost its haziness and came into sharp focus. All this was happening, and it was happening to me.

If Ruth had been a heathen priestess dating from the first century after Christ or so—and this period, if perhaps not the occupation, I thought roughly right—then Peter might have been a Roman soldier come to conquer hundreds of years before she had first drawn breath. Perhaps he was even older than that because didn't the Romans burn their dead? A warrior then, interred in one of the dolmen erected thousands of years ago. Certainly, he was much older than Ruth, for he looked even more wrong than she did.

He had a crick in his neck, making his head twist to one side. I had once seen a collection of mummies, not of the Egyptian kind, but bodies dried out and preserved by some quirk of nature.

Their skin had looked strange, dry and yellow and papery; Peter's skin looked like that, only it was stained black in places, not at all like Ruth's even tea tint, and mottled at his throat, perhaps from a particular kind of mold. His lips were perpetually drawn back from his too-big mouth, revealing a row of sharp little teeth. No wonder I had thought his grin wolfish! He had forgotten all sense of proportion; that explained his long limbs, so thin that the joints bulged, and the hands large as oven mittens.

I thought him rather beautiful.

"Hello," I said and blushed. I felt as if I might cry; already the tears pricked in my eyes. Now that my dreamer's trance had been lifted, I felt as raw and vulnerable as a newborn.

Agnes touched a fingertip to that soft pouch of skin under my eyes and caught the tear before it fell. It ran down her thumb, to be pocketed by the little web of skin between her fingers.

"Forgive me, I've never seen a spirit companion apart from Ruth. I don't know what to say," I murmured.

"Didn't you know about Peter until just know?"

"I suspected, but I wasn't sure."

"I whispered it to you during the séance. Didn't you hear?"

I shook my head. Two tears rolled down my cheeks. I laughed. "I was so afraid you'd tell everyone I was a fraud that I didn't understand a word you said. I was so sure you'd denounce me…"

"Denounce you? When you are like me? When all these years, I thought I was alone, and I feared that I was cursed or else quite mad, and then my Thomas…" Here she stopped herself, swallowed. She smiled at me, and her eyes were wet with tears.

She must love him to the point of speechlessness, I thought, and my heart ached for her. Yet, underneath that genuine ache, that sense of fellow feeling, there was the soft, insidious little twist of want. I readily admit it: in a way, I had already come to love her, and that love could never be quite free from need. I wish it were not so, but you must understand that, as a child, I only had Ruth to teach me love, and hers, though deep and fierce, was also a possessive love. What I felt for Agnes was right and true, yes, but it was not selfless.

Perhaps love never is.

I brought her chilled hand to my mouth and breathed on it to warm it. "You've got me now, and Ruth," I said, "and we shall have you and Peter, and there shall be no more loneliness, no more fear. Isn't that right?"

Ruth took a strand of Agnes's hair between her fingers and tucked it behind her ear. "Quite so," she said.

Peter came to his feet. He walked with a stoop but even so remained quite tall. Perhaps that was why Agnes had taken a room with such a high ceiling. He shuffled over to me and squeezed my shoulder gently. His fingers were so long that the tips pressed against my shoulder blade. They were hard and cold as icicles.

"Come, let's sit down. There's so much I've got to tell you and so much you'll have to tell me. I'll order something nice and hot to sustain us," Agnes said.

We sat down at the coffee table. For a while, we could hardly speak, only look at each other and laugh with the sheer joy of having found someone alike. It was only after an employee from the hotel brought us steaming cups of coffee and some pastries that we found our voices again.

"How did you find me?" I asked between bites of a cream pastry.

"Coincidence. I saw an ad your mama placed in the newspaper, and I decided to come. I'd been to this sort of thing before, but those people didn't really have spirit companions. But you…!"

And we laughed again.

That night, we spoke of all manner of things: my father, Lockhart stockings, religion. Most of all we talked about our spirit companions. Agnes was full of questions. How old was I when I met Ruth? How had I met her? Was she always with me? I told her everything, and it felt warm and good and right. As I spoke, I looked at Ruth fondly. She lay sprawled on the carpet next to me and was playing with the buttons she had ripped from my old clothes, clicking them together in her palms and imitating the sound with her broken jaw.

When I had explained everything, I had been talking so much, my mouth was dry and my throat was rough. I poured some coffee into a cup to wet my parched throat, the searing porcelain a painful pleasure against my palms. "And you? How did you and Peter meet?" I asked.

"At the Notre-Dame de la Compassion, the finishing school in France my father sent me to when I was sixteen."

"Why did he send you there?"

"I'd finished my education at boarding school, but I was too young to be married off, and his wife wouldn't allow me in their home, so this seemed the most elegant solution. Make no mistake:

my father cared for me. The school cost a lot and had an impeccable reputation. I don't know why, really. The food was just as bad as at boarding school, and the building was falling apart. The air was bad besides. At night, you could hear the girls with weak lungs cough as the damp settled on their chests."

I tried to imagine the sound of a dozen girls breathing around me, some wet and labored, others dry and light, and found that I couldn't. All I could imagine was Mama's soft snoring. I had no such trouble with the poor food and cold rooms, though.

"And there were no towns near or anything, just thick woods that we were forbidden from entering because it was easy to get lost in there," Agnes went on. "Though maybe the seclusion was a recommendation for some parents—no local men for us to get involved with." She drained her cup of coffee but kept holding the cup lazily in one hand.

"The girls, were they at least nice to you?" I asked.

"No, but I was used to that. They hadn't been nice in England either. They didn't like that my father was nouveau riche and that I was his bastard daughter with a foreign mother. They care less for that sort of thing in France, though. There, I suppose, they just didn't like me for me." She laughed bitterly.

I took her cup from her, my fingertips brushing the back of her hand, and my heart thumped painfully, and my hand felt hot and heavy, as if the blood wished to pool there. I poured her some more coffee.

"Thank you. That's sweet of you. I don't even have to ask! Already you and I are well attuned." She laughed, and this time there was no bitterness, just a pure beautiful sound that made the heat previously congealed in the place where she had touched me run all the way up to my chest.

Agnes took a sip and went on. "Every year, the older girls came up with initiation rituals for the new ones, and it was different for all of us. Every ritual was some sort of challenge, some task that had to be completed." She looked at her cup, frowned. "Cold," she said and put it down.

I drew up my knees and rested my chin on top. "What happened if you failed?"

"You were a pariah. Everyone ignored you. Apparently, the year before a girl didn't finish hers in time, so everyone acted as if she didn't exist. After a few months, she went into the woods with a piece of rope."

"She hanged herself?!" I exclaimed.

"Oh, she wasn't successful. The rope was rotten and broke when she jumped. The nuns did send her away, though. Officially because she'd broken the rules and gone into the woods by herself but, in reality, for fear her inclination to mortal sin would taint us all."

Shockingly, Agnes began to laugh. She clamped a hand over her mouth. After half a minute or so, her laughter petered out. She lowered her hand. "Forgive me. I didn't mean to laugh. Sometimes I can't help it. I must laugh or else go mad."

"I understand. I often felt that way with Mama," I said and shivered with the wickedness of having said something I felt so deeply out loud.

Agnes went to the bed, took a sheet, and draped it around me. She knelt in front of me, so our faces were level. "It shan't be like that anymore now, I promise."

As she rose, she lightly took my face between her hands and kissed my forehead. The place pulsed and burned long after she had seated herself again, her legs folded neatly, a pillow in her lap to toy with. "Where were we?" she asked, and I wondered how she could touch me so easily and why such an easy thing to her shattered me every time.

"You were telling me about the initiation rituals," I managed to say.

"Ah, yes, those. The older girls didn't take us all to be initiated at the same time, as is usual. Instead, they'd take one or two new girls each night. Not consecutively. Sometimes they took girls three nights in a row and then no one for a whole week. It was terrible. You'd lie awake for most of the night, listening to every creak, thinking they'd finally come for you, and then wishing they would, so you'd have it over with.

"They came for me after four weeks. They took me outside, gave me a torch and a compass, and told me I had to walk to the Roman watchtower and bring back something from there. We could see it from the classroom windows, but it was deep in the woods."

Ruth rolled a button down the seam where two floorboards met. Before it could get out of reach, she slapped it down and dragged it back to her, the button grating over the wood. "Were you scared?" she asked, looking at Agnes through one slitted eye.

"Of course. But I didn't want to be treated as if I didn't exist, so I forced my fear down."

"That's horrible!" I cried out. I curled my hands into the blanket so she wouldn't see how they trembled.

Agnes gave me a searching look. "It wasn't so bad, Roos," she said softly.

"I don't care. They had no right to do that to you."

"No, they didn't," she said and blinked as if surprised, as if she hadn't quite realized that before. She cleared her throat, went on. "Well, I walked through the woods. Soon, I couldn't see the tower anymore because of all the trees. I had to look at the compass and hope I was going in the right direction. After a mile or so, the torch went dead, but I'd found a deer path by then, and the moon overhead was full and bright, so I could still read the compass."

I looked at Ruth, sweet, sly, strong Ruth, and marveled at how brave Agnes was to go out in the dark all alone. I would have gone half-mad with fear, probably still would even with Ruth by my side.

"I climbed up to the tower and found a piece of broken rock to take back with me. When I went down the stone staircase, one of the steps broke, and I fell. I hit my head, and I was unconscious for a bit."

Agnes touched the back of her head, and I wondered if she felt a phantom pain there just like she did in her knees, just like I did at times in my scarred hands. "When I came to again, I couldn't see. I thought maybe I'd gone blind, and I panicked, but it was only clouds that had swept in and extinguished the moonlight. They moved away for a bit, and I could see again. I put the stone I'd found in my pocket, and I tried to find my way back to the school, but I'd not gone far before the clouds hid the moon again, and everything was plunged into darkness."

I imagined Agnes in some dark forest. I could smell it, and it smelled much the same as the space under the floorboards, which made my skin crawl. I imagined her making little noises of anguish as she whipped her head around and tried to see something, anything, and I wished to take that girl's hand into my own and guide her from darkness into light.

"Are you afraid of the dark?" I asked.

"I was then," she confessed.

"Roosje is terrified of the dark," Ruth said, "aren't you, darling Roosje mine? Even once she had me and therefore no reason to fear the darkness. If she had her way, the light would stay on all night long, only Mama never allowed it."

I laughed awkwardly. "Really, Ruth, what tall tales you tell!" And before she could respond, I turned to Agnes and asked, "What did you do next?"

"I couldn't go on like that, so I felt for some place to sit. I found a hill to the side of the road, all covered in moss, and I leaned against that and waited. I think I fell asleep again because the next thing I remember is that the sky was turning gray, and I realized I'd spent all night sitting not against a hill but against a kind of burial mound. I managed to hurry back to school before any of the nuns found me missing, only I hadn't come back alone: Peter had found me that night. It was his grave I had slept on, and he followed me because I had woken him, and he had gotten a taste of my blood as I rested my wounded head against the mound."

He turned his leathery face away from the window and looked at her lovingly. She caught his gaze and smiled.

"I saw him for the first time with his face pressed against one of the schoolroom windows, looking in, looking for me. I'd never seen anyone like him. I knew right away that he was some sort of ghost. God, but I was scared of him at first. My mother was a superstitious woman. She'd cook special meals whenever we moved, and she took care of our family's *kris* every five weeks with rituals and by cleaning it because she said it had a soul. It was such a pretty dagger, too, with a hilt of carved ivory and a wooden sheath coated in silver."

She drew the ritual dagger for me on a piece of paper, a quick sketch to give me a rough idea of what it looked like: the wavy blade, the ivory hilt I imagined had slightly yellowed with age, the sheath made of dark shiny wood with a floral pattern carved into it. She told me that every *kris* housed a soul, a spirit of a kind. Those who took care of their family's *kris* would be rewarded; those who neglected it, punished. The sort of soul that inhabited the *kris* she drew for me must've been a noble one indeed, stern but loving. Later, when I lived with Agnes at the Rozentuin, I looked up pictures of *kris* in an encyclopedia and made up stories of their characters. This one, its blade made of meteorite, must've been powerful yet with a good sense of humor; that one, with its sheath of gold crusted with gemstones, was probably a tad vain but also fiercely loyal.

Yet none seemed as lovely to me as the one that had once protected Agnes.

"Where is it now?" I asked.

"Lost to me. When my mother died, I asked to have it because if you don't take good care of your family's *kris*, it will bring bad luck and harm, but I was told they didn't find anything like a sword in our rooms. When I saw Peter for the first time, I wondered if he was the *kris*'s ghost come to punish me for losing it. Then I realized Peter was something else entirely. I thought that, perhaps if I could somehow make the whole situation darkly funny, I would be able to handle it better, so I called him 'Peter Quint.'"

"And in that way, you bound him to you," I said.

"Is that how it works? I had no idea."

Peter went to her. She lay her hand in his. "You're a blessing and a curse both, aren't you? You certainly didn't make my time at school any easier." She rested her cheek against his hand, which was so big, he could have held her entire head in it.

Ruth crawled over to me and raised herself by placing her hands on my knees. Her eyes were the shiny black shields of beetles today. "Am I a curse to you?" she whispered.

I kissed her forehead, which today had the color and consistency of a damp brown mushroom. "Of course not. You're my friend and protector, my companion and confidante."

"Good," she said and sank to the floor once more.

After Agnes told me about Peter, we talked of other things: Mama's séances, the dinner we had eaten, how much Agnes detested the watery cold of Dutch winters. There was only one thing of which we did not speak, and that was Agnes's husband.

The closest she came to talking about Thomas was by speaking of the estate she had inherited as his wife: the Rozentuin.

"I've not really inherited it, you know, but it's mine until I die, unless I marry again. It would've been different if there were children, but that can't be helped now. Of course, I have to share it with Willemijn—she's allowed to live there as long as she doesn't marry either. She is…"

Here Agnes hesitated, then pressed on. "She's a bit peculiar. You shouldn't let her frighten you."

"Frighten me how?"

Again, she hesitated. "She's sick, you know, and often in a lot of pain. It makes her short-tempered at times."

I remembered her from that picture in a magazine, the pale hair and eyes, the beautiful mouth with its bitter twist, and I felt a chill I couldn't quite explain. "Does she know I am coming?"

Agnes's eyes acquired a peculiar harshness. "It wouldn't matter if she didn't. I can do as I please. I don't need her permission. The Rozentuin is mine." Her gaze softened as she began to talk of the estate. She talked of the woods surrounding it on one side, the marshland on the other, the ground there so soft and treacherous that dogs and the occasional sheep or cow were lost there yearly. "It's a strange place, secluded and quite run-down, really, since families like the Knoops never seem to have any money nowadays and whatever I brought with me as my dowry just seemed to evaporate, but it's really rather beautiful in its way, too. I hope you'll come to love it as much as I do," she said.

I did.

Chapter 10

NEVER SHALL I FORGET THE first time I saw the Rozentuin. We came upon it in winter when its beauty was at its starkest. I had studied pictures of it in black and white, had imagined myself walking down the cobbled drive and smoking cigarettes in the library, but even so I was ill prepared for what awaited me.

We had left the hotel early. It was still dark outside. Peter was not with us. When I asked where he had gone, Agnes said casually, "Oh, I sent him up ahead. He doesn't care for car rides." I could imagine; those spidery limbs would likely get cramped quickly in small spaces. Still, the fact he had gone so far away from Agnes surprised me, perhaps chilled and excited me. Ruth and I were never far apart and never for long.

By the time we arrived at the Rozentuin, the sun was steadily mounting the sky. The light was of that pale, watery quality so typical of Dutch winters, slightly blurring everything it touched. It had rained the night before, and the land, which had been a marsh not quite so long ago, lay soggy and wet, with great wreaths of steam rising. Pools reflected the sky, lying like silver shards. Trees grew crooked, their bark stained with thick moss.

"We're almost there," Agnes assured me. Then, after a little while, she said, "There! Do you see those sunken gates? They mark the border of our land."

Our land, I thought and wondered if I was included in that *our.*

Gates of rusting iron stood crooked in the wet earth, gaping open. Agnes carefully turned the car onto the cobbled lane, and down the drive we went. Tendrils of mist crept between the trees. There was a hush in the air, as if everything held its breath with me.

"Ripping a flower apart between your hands," Ruth murmured in my ear, so softly that Agnes couldn't hear over the rattling the car made as we went down that bumpy lane. "A thrush singing in the woods. A woman running to you with outstretched hands." And she smiled. I clasped her hand and held it very tightly.

When I turned to look out the windscreen again, we had arrived. The tall windows flashed yellow in the light of the rising sun, which gave the impression the house was harnessing fire. Ivy had encroached upon the walls and clambered all the way to the roof, its tendrils nesting in the gutter, the waxy leaves obstructing the rainwater until the gutter had rusted and now sagged. Mustard-colored lichen with shades of blue and green grew on the walls, patterning them like lopsided flowers. It looked like mold was blooming at the windowsills. The lawn did not fare much better. Come spring, it would be filled with wildflowers growing thick as an army: rapeseed and dandelions and daisies; cow parsley and clover.

Now the grass lay brown and dead, the lawn sunken in places where the ground had grown soggy. A low wall had been built around the lawn and in all probability stretched around the gardens, its only opening for the driveway we so softly came down. Its brick had been bleached into a peculiar shade between pink and red. The mortar had crumbled and caused the wall to partially collapse in places. The pond behind the house, so broad that it could be seen even as we stood at the front, was choked with rotting leaves.

Still, the ravages of time could not take away from the house's classical beauty, its fearful symmetry softened by nature's touch so that its harsh perfection had blurred into a tragic loveliness.

"There," Agnes said, turning to look at me.

It was as if I had conjured up Thomas's ghost then, for my throat tightened with longing and pride.

SIXTH CASE EPISODE

PATIENT R–, A CASE STORY: INHABITED BY ANOTHER

(D = DOCTOR, P = PATIENT R–)

SIXTH EPISODE, CONDUCTED ON 12 OCTOBER 1954:

Notes to self: Today, patient didn't take my contradicting her at all well. Curiously, this happened only when I picked holes in Mrs. K—'s (alleged) story, not the patient's.

Patient seems to have very strong feelings toward Mrs. K—. Patient might be an invert. This could relate to her almost violent response to the topic of copulation. Might be worth watching her for more signs of homosexuality; after all, it's a known disorder of the mind.

> **D:** "I want you to listen carefully to what I am about to say and not get upset. Can you do that?"
>
> **P:** "How can I tell you if I don't know what you'll tell me?"
>
> **D:** "Just try to keep your emotions in check, all right? Try not to become hysterical."
>
> **P:** "All right."
>
> **D:** "I've thought about what you told me about Mrs. K— and her spirit companion Peter Quint, and I decided to do some research. I've written to Notre-Dame de la Compassion and requested information from them about Mrs. K—'s time there. It took a while. The school has closed down some years ago. Still, I managed to get into contact with a nun who taught Mrs. K—. She

described her as a troubled student who never quite fit in. She said she 'failed to thrive'. When I asked her about the incident in the woods you described so vividly to me, she denied that any such thing had ever happened. She did say that Mrs. K— had a penchant for telling lies."

P: [*interrupts*] "She would, wouldn't she? God can only imagine the consequences if the parents of their students found out. They would've stopped their donations and pulled their daughters out of the school. One nun's denial means nothing."

D: "Please don't raise your voice at me, and please don't interrupt me. I wasn't quite finished yet. To be absolutely certain, I also asked about the student who supposedly attempted suicide. She said no such thing had ever happened."

P: "Of course she'd say that. Would you want to admit that one of the girls left in your care was apparently so unhappy she tried to end her life?"

D: "R—, don't you think that's a bit far-fetched?"

P: "No."

D: "Don't you think it's even remotely possible that Mrs. K— made it all up? Not because she was a liar, but because she was ill and confused? I've no doubt that, in her mind, it was all true, just as I've no doubt that, in your mind, Ruth and Peter and all the rest are true, too."

P: [*puts hands over face*] "You're being like the police now."

D: "You mean like those men who questioned you?"

P: [*nods*] "There was one who said I made everything up. Not just Ruth, but Peter as well, and A— [Mrs. K—]'s stories. He said I was cruel and sick and that's why I made up mean tales about A— [Mrs. K—] and T— [Mr. K—] and W— [Miss K—]."

D: "I believe you, R—. I don't think you made up Mrs. K—'s stories."

P: "But you do think I made up all the rest."

D: "Perhaps 'made up' is not the right term for it."

P: "Why are you telling me this? About A— [Mrs. K—] and the convent school, I mean? Why do you always interrupt me to say that things aren't as I told them? Why can't you just let me tell you my story?"

D: "Because that's my job. I've been sent to see whether you can be held accountable for what happened, and if not, to find out why. Don't you understand that your whole future hinges on this? My verdict might be the only thing that saves you from a lifetime in prison."

P: [*puts hands in front of face and moans softly*] "Do you think I don't know? Do you think I'm stupid as well as mad? It's the first thing I think of when I wake, and the last thing I remember before falling asleep. I know very well what I am accused of!"

D: "Then why won't you tell me who murdered Mrs. K—?"

P: "I'm trying! I'm trying to tell you everything, but you keep interrupting me. Let me finish my story We can pick it apart at the end, but please, let me tell it to you first."

Part II

"Of course I was under the spell, and the wonderful part is that, even at the time, I perfectly knew I was. But I gave myself up to it; it was an antidote to any pain, and I had more pains than one."

—Henry James, *The Turn of the Screw*

Chapter 11

AGNES TOOK ME INSIDE. EVERY house has its own scent. The Rozentuin smelled like dust and damp and mold overlaid with wax and something spicy that I would later come to recognize as the herbs the cook used. The hallway was large but very dark due to the lack of windows. We carried our luggage ourselves; the time of valets and butlers had gone. The Rozentuin's staff was a humble one: a gardener, a cook, and a little maid who came in three times a week to clean.

"Please leave your shoes in the hallway. We wear slippers inside," she said.

"To protect the floors?"

"No, because my mother taught me, and wearing shoes inside has felt wrong ever since."

The hallway felt as cold as the weather outside. Agnes shivered. "It's the pond behind the house," she said. "The cold creeps in, and the Rozentuin was a draughty house if ever I saw one. It's no wonder the Knoops are such martyrs to lung complaints, really. Speaking of which: we must be quiet when we're upstairs. Willemijn is probably resting."

She took me up the staircase of carven wood that, she told me, came all the way from Italy. It was in need of a good scrub and wax. The window at the end of the upstairs hallway needed cleaning, too.

"I've given you the carmine room. My room is right next to yours, and then down the corridor is Willemijn's room. You might hear me move around at night to tend to her. I hope you won't mind that. I thought about giving you a different room, but it seemed wrong to put you so far away from us," Agnes said, her voice low. Using her shoulder to open the door, she said, "Careful, it sticks. It's the damp. It makes the wood shrink and swell. I like to think of it as the house breathing. You mustn't be scared if you hear things at night. It's usually just the house settling or else an animal outside. I suspect it'll take a little time to get used to." And with that she led me inside.

The room was lovely if dilapidated. The red wallpaper had been bleached by sunlight in places. The floorboards creaked and were uneven. Part of the ceiling had been stained by water, but the dark furniture was very handsome. "Here's your bed," Agnes said, touching it, "and your desk and chair. I tried to have that monstrous wardrobe moved, but woodworm has gotten into it, and I think it would fall apart if we tried, so I'm afraid you'll have to learn to live with it, though we can hang a sheet over it so you needn't look at it."

She touched everything as she spoke, as if to assure herself of its existence. The wardrobe earned a look of distaste. She touched it briefly, then shuddered. It was enormous, made of dark wood in which figures had been carved. I put down my parcels and went to take a closer look.

"My God," I said and laughed nervously.

Scenes of damnation had been lovingly carved into the wood. Grinning demons roasted emaciated men over little fires so that it would take hours, perhaps days, until they were dead, while goat-footed devils impaled screaming women with pitchforks. The wood-carver had taken great pains to portray the contorted faces of the damned. Outside, a cloud moved in front of the sun, and as the light faltered over the woodwork, the sinners seemed to be writhing.

"It's monstrous, isn't it? Like Hieronymus Bosch, but with none of the charm. Very vivid, too. It looks as if those women over there are being punished for the sin of lust by... Well, you can see for yourself what those demons are doing to them," Agnes whispered.

"Who would ever want to own such a thing?"

"I believe Thomas's grandfather had it made especially for the Rozentuin, though you should ask Willemijn if you want to be sure. She'll know. All I know is that he was quite fanatical. A bit of a sick bastard really." She laughed at my shocked expression. "You must forgive me. Sometimes I've got the mouth of a sailor on me. I blame my mother for that. She was a ballet dancer before she met my father. She picked up some rather colorful expressions."

Agnes opened the doors and showed me the cavernous insides of the wardrobe. "There, now you needn't look at those horrible carvings anymore."

"That's almost worse, isn't it? I feel like I have to keep watching them, or else they might move around." Then, because I didn't want to seem ungrateful, I added hastily, "I'm just being silly and morbid. I don't mind about the wardrobe. Truly I don't. There's a lot of room, much more than in my old wardrobe. And the wallpaper is lovely, and the bed, too. It's very big. Ruth and I shall be very comfortable here, very happy."

Agnes smoothed down the sheets with her palm. "I'll give you and Ruth some time to unpack and get settled. I shall be in my room, doing the same." She pulled the door closed behind her with a soft snick.

Had I displeased her? The mere thought made a light sweat break out over my body, and my stomach hurt.

Ruth closed the wardrobe door and studied the woodwork. "Not very accurate," she said, tracing the outlines of a horned face with her nail.

"Leave it open, please. I'll put my clothes away."

"You mustn't appear to be too grateful, you know. It shall be hard to keep up that level of gratitude, and I don't think Agnes is the sort of woman who desires that sort of power. If anything, she might want someone to stand tall and strong beside her, someone she may lean on. Do you think you can be that person for her?"

I looked into the full-length mirror in its gilded frame that stood in the corner. I had a cowlick on the back of my head that wouldn't be smoothed down, and I looked tired, anxious, both bird-like and fragile in my thinness.

If anyone leaned on me now, I looked as if I'd break.

But things might change. Agnes had shown me that. And if she wanted me to be strong for her, then I would be. I wanted to make her happy more than I wanted anything else.

"I can be whatever she needs, given a little time," I told Ruth.

I turned away from the mirror and began to unpack. Ruth stood at the window and looked outside. With her finger she drew shapes in the mist that had settled on the windowpane.

"We're at the back of the house," she said, "overlooking the pond. That's why it's so cold and damp here."

"Houses like these are hard to heat. It shall be better in summer. We're facing south, so the sun shall be upon this room then," I countered. Then, because I felt Ruth's anxiety, I went to her and lay my head on her sloping chest. "You needn't worry so. I think we shall be all right here," I said.

She wound her arms around me. "I must always look out for you, Roos. I must guard and protect you. You know that, don't you? I can't change this. It's the very essence of me."

"I know. You are what you are. Even so, you must try not to be jealous. I don't think Agnes will hurt us."

"If she does, I shall kill her."

I felt sick and weak then. "Like you tried with Mr. Mesman?" I whispered, and it was wrong of me to say his name in this place of new beginnings. I should have known better. To speak of evil is to invite it in.

Ruth stroked my hair. "Yes. Exactly so," she said, and with those simple words, she made a promise and damned us both. I stood in her embrace, breathing in her scent of earth and decay, and it was a comfort and a pain both.

When I was done unpacking, I went to find Agnes. I knocked on her door, but when no reply came, I opened the door a crack and peered inside.

The furniture in her room was curiously mismatched, as if it had been taken from all over the house. A huge black piano stood in the middle of the room, surrounded by coffee tables of various heights and designs. One held an assortment of pepper shakers and bags of spices, but most carried stacks of sheet music. Some of the sheets of paper had turned yellow and brittle with sunlight. One sheaf of music, the sheets connected with bits of sticking plaster, the paper foxed and furred from handling, had fallen and lay crumpled at the base of the table like a tongue.

"What a peculiar place for a piano," Ruth said. "Do you think they lugged it up the stairs? No, it wouldn't fit through the door. Through the window, then?"

I shrugged; I didn't know.

The rest of the room was cluttered and untidy, too: a blouse lay curled around the leg of the bed; a dusty teacup stood on the windowsill. The vanity was covered in bottles and tubes. A compact had fallen and spilled powder on the carpet and lay there still.

Agnes hadn't bothered to unpack at all; her suitcase's contents had been flung on the bed, the suitcase itself wiped clean and then left lolling on the ground. The only chair, a huge thing clothed in green velvet, dimpled under the weight of a huge stack of books. Its color clashed rather horribly with the lovely sea green of the wallpaper. The room must have been recently papered, for the color was vivid and there was a faint smell of glue.

The only picture in the room stood on her nightstand. To my surprise, it wasn't a picture of her husband, but an old, faded photograph of a woman who could only be Agnes's mother. They had the same coloring, the same eyes, the same curve to their jaw. I wondered if Agnes had been bullied in school with those eyes. Children could be so very vicious.

Peter lay in a sunny spot on the carpet, curled up like a cat. His skin was as yellow as some of the sheet music. He opened one eye, saw me, then pointed to his right, to the room from which came the sound of voices, the words too muffled to make out.

"Thank you," I said and left him to his sunbathing.

I went down the corridor to Willemijn's room. When I knocked on her door, the voices inside ceased. Anxiety dried my mouth and wet my palms. I knocked again.

"Agnes?" I asked, and my voice was a mere squeak.

"Just a moment," Agnes called. I could hear something rustling, a piece of furniture being moved, and then the quick patter of Agnes's footsteps. She opened the door for me, smiled. She had removed her stockings, and I saw she had a bruise blooming just above the little knub of her ankle. In the sunlight, her black hair had a blue sheen to it, like ink.

"In you come," she said.

This room was completely different from hers: all the furniture matched, and all was clean. It was also utterly impersonal. No knickknacks graced the mantelpiece or the mahogany cabinets. The desk, too, was completely empty. The nightstand held glass bottles with tablets and syrups, but those could be found in any sickroom.

The only hint that a living, breathing person with their own thoughts and memories and history lived there was a silver-framed picture of Thomas that stood next to an empty vase on a coffee table near the window. The wallpaper was yellow and had some sort of horrible pattern, a kind of floral that on closer inspection seemed to dissolve into random curls and whorls. The curtains of purple velvet made the yellow very vivid. The four-poster bed with carved legs also had purple curtains. These were drawn back and knotted around the bed's legs with tasseled cords of gold, revealing its occupant.

Willemijn Knoop lay in her bed like a queen. She was not dressed in a bathrobe, as I had expected she might have been since she had been described to me as ill. Instead, she wore a dress of watered silk and strings of pearls looped around her pale throat. Agnes's chinchilla-fur coat lay draped around her shoulders. Tuberculosis had sucked the meat off her bones, but it also lent her a strange and horrible beauty, placing roses in her cheeks and a luster in her eyes, making her lose that washed-out watery quality she had held in the one photograph I'd seen of her.

"So you are the girl who gets possessed," she said. Her voice was hoarse, a little whispery, roughened from coughing.

I flushed. "Pleased to meet you, ma'am," I murmured, and the words came out as hoarse as hers.

"Come closer," she ordered. I did as she asked. As soon as I was in reach, her hand shot out and clenched around mine. Instinctively, I made to pull back, but she held fast, smiled even, at the jerk of my arm, so hard and convulsive, I could never have hidden it from her. Yet that smile made me wish I could have. There was something cruel and knowing in it, something almost triumphant and something cold.

Her hand was cold, too, as cold as Ruth's, though hers was very white. Despite the twig-thin appearance of her fingers, her handclasp was strong. Up close, I could see her pupils were mere pinpricks. Perhaps, then, she was under the influence of some drug.

"But, Agnes, you've brought me a mere child," she said. Her eyes, so pale that they could have been chips of ice, never left my face. Behind me, I could hear Ruth work her jaw in anger. I felt ugly patches of red creep up my throat and cheeks.

"She's twenty-one," Agnes said.

"Then why does she look so thin and small?"

"Her mama starved her. A few weeks of good food, and she'll look her age," Agnes assured Willemijn. I wished she'd go back to being the Agnes of last night, the one whose hands I had held and with whom I had laughed from the sheer joy of having found someone alike. This woman who spoke carefully and did not look at me was a stranger.

"There's nothing wrong with you?" Willemijn asked me. "You're not sick?"

I shook my head.

"That's all right then. I'm afraid the part of the sick person has already been taken." She licked her lips. "The doctors told me I'm going to die, you see. They say my lungs are completely riddled with tuberculosis. Not even the triple therapy might save me. The last thing this house needs is another sick inhabitant."

"I'm sorry, ma'am."

She waved away the words with a little flick of the wrist. "What's your name?"

"Roos Beckman."

I thought she'd shake my hand then, but instead she bent over it and pressed her cold mouth to it before letting go. She looked at me through her lashes, through the long locks of pale hair that had fallen before her face, and smiled that cold hungry smile again.

"I think we might be good friends, Roos," she said.

Finally, she let go of my hand.

"Really, Willemijn, you're acting like a perfect witch. Stop scaring her," Agnes snapped. Willemijn laughed. Soon, the laughter turned into hacking wet coughs. Sweat pearled on her forehead.

"Serves her right," Ruth said wickedly.

When the coughing subsided, Agnes bent over Willemijn and dabbed at her forehead with a wet cloth. "That's what you get when you overexert yourself," she said curtly. She made the other woman sip something from a spoon, after which Willemijn sank back on her pillows and lay breathing in quick rasping breaths, her eyes closed.

Agnes came to me and lay a hand softly on my shoulder. "Best to leave now," she murmured. "She needs to rest. And try not to mind what she says and does. She simply likes to shock people."

Once back in my own room, I shuddered. "I don't know what to think of Willemijn. If I'm honest, I don't think I'll like her much," I said to Ruth.

"You don't have to. From the look and sound of her, she won't see another winter. And if she hurts you, well, then I'll take care of her," Ruth said. She went to the desk and stroked her bottle of ground-up glass with her fingernail, humming softly to herself and smiling.

Chapter 12

AGNES HAD BEEN AWAY FOR months, so the first few days at the Rozentuin, she spent the mornings taking care of the estate. She managed accounts, wrote letters. Those mornings, then, were mine to spend as I pleased.

The weather, though cold, was fine those first few days, so I began by exploring the grounds. This roused me; those first few nights were wretched. I kept waking up from nightmares in which I was back with Mama because Agnes hadn't wanted me after all. At other times, I woke from the strange sounds the house made. Mama's house had been too old and tired to do much but give the occasional wheeze, but the Rozentuin was very talkative. She liked to rattle her pipes and give a hearty groan when she stretched. Sometimes I even fancied I could hear someone walk around upstairs, moving things around.

The cold morning wind blew those fears away like cobwebs. Dressed in the wool coat Agnes had bought for me and a pair of her Wellingtons, I walked down little lanes of black earth frozen solid. I found a rose garden, now nothing more than bare shrub, and a little garden of broken marble statues stained with soot and lichen. To please Ruth, I picked up a broken finger and slipped it into my coat's pocket.

Following the garden wall, my fingertips brushing the pocked brick, I came upon the family chapel. It stood hemmed in by willows, dark and strangely foreboding. No warm-colored brick here, but hard gray stone pitted with age. The gutters had been choked with twigs and leaves, and the gargoyles hung from the lip of the roof with dry mouths, their harsh lines rounded by time and weather. I stood in the shadow the chapel cast for a while, studying the gargoyles and the gothic arches, the windows of painted glass grimy with dust.

Ruth stood by my side, her face grim. "This place is wicked," she said.

I laughed and squeezed her hand, which was as cold as the marble finger resting in my pocket. "You just don't like places of worship, you heathen. You needn't come inside if you don't want to."

"What if Agnes doesn't want you to go inside?"

That gave me pause, but Agnes hadn't told me I wasn't allowed into certain places, so I shrugged and tried to find the way in. The chapel door was of oak studded with metal. I tried to open it, but either the door was so heavy that I could not move it by myself, or it was locked. I walked around, trying to peer inside. One of the windows at the back had broken, probably in some winter storm. I found a heap of rotting furniture and dragged some of it to the wall so I could reach the window and look in.

I stood on the rickety chairs and tables, holding on to a seam between the stones with my fingertips. "Careful," Ruth said, and she put her hands on my waist to steady me.

I looked through the broken glass.

My heart began to pound at the first glance, and I felt weak and sick and scared, very scared. I looked, and dozens of faces looked back at me. They were covered in dust and veiled in cobwebs, an army of people with strange eyes and faces an unclean gray locked inside.

They're statues, I realized, the hot flush of panic beating at me in waves. *Just statues, statues of saints, not spirits at all.* Statues of painted plaster, dirty with neglect, the ones closest to me faded and abused by rain and hail. I saw Saint George with his lance, and Saint Sebastian writhing with arrows sticking out of him. I recognized them from Ruth's deck of cards.

There was something menacing about their flat stares, something malicious. I was afraid to look away; they might well move if I did. I remembered then that Thomas Knoop's grandfather had been religiously fanatical, and I wondered if his sick devotion had seeped into these statues somehow, tainting them. Like the wardrobe in my room, they felt evil.

I ran away blindly from that horrible place, promising myself I need never go there again. There could be no worship on Sundays there, the aisles choked with those statues, the dust finger thick. When I was out of breath and my head felt light, I leaned against a tree for a long while. Ruth sat on a branch above me. She worked her jaw, making the bones grind together.

"Let's explore someplace else," I said.

Ruth dropped down next to me and slipped her twisted fingers into mine. Together we walked away from the chapel, which continued to stand evil and unclean. Soon we stumbled upon the family graveyard. It was a Catholic one, full of marble angels and ornate slabs of stone. Wind and weather had rubbed at the inscriptions of the oldest ones, lichen staining them orange and yellow. The angels hunching over these graves were in poor shape, sour rain having eaten away at them until their features had almost been blotted out, soot leaving dark streaks on their robes and wings. The farther we went, the more recent the graves, yet the one I expected with dread and anticipation was so plain, I almost passed it.

No weeping angels for Thomas Knoop, no marble slab threaded with pink veins—only a stone marker with his name and dates and, underneath, *Beloved Brother and Husband*.

"It's not very ornate," I said.

Ruth shrugged. She did not care for graveyards, though whether that was because they reminded her she was dead or because she didn't care for holy ground, I never knew. Near the northern exit, we found a plot of unhallowed ground almost completely surrounded by bushes of holly. Little stone markers told of unbaptized babies, the most recent one from only a few years ago. There were only two adult graves: one so old, the stone had broken in half and thus become unreadable, the other a large slab inscribed only with *Hugo Knoop, Father and Husband, 1866–1936*.

Ruth touched the graves for the children one by one reverently, then threaded her arm through mine. "Let's go," she said.

The northern exit brought us to a sloping lawn, the grass brown and dead. What I initially took for a little summer house had been placed on the edge overlooking the graveyard. It was painted white and had windows on all sides. It was only when I moved closer and inspected the house all around that I realized it was a little tuberculosis house, a small building mounted on wheels so it could be turned around to let the occupant sit in the sun all day. The wheels had sunken into the muddy lawn, and the little house would not be moved now.

"Enjoying yourself?" someone asked.

Startled, I drew back. Willemijn's face appeared at one of the windows. She grinned at me and motioned for me to come inside. I mounted the little steps but would not cross the threshold. Willemijn lay on a chaise longue propped up by pillows, a heap of blankets covering her legs, a book open on her lap. She was dressed in red velvet today, which made her look exceptionally pale. "Do come inside," she said politely.

"My shoes are muddy, ma'am," I said.

"I don't care about that. I do care about you standing there in the doorway and blocking my light. I love the warmth, even though I never tan, unlike some in this house." She said this as if tanning were somehow uncouth.

I crimsoned and stepped inside quickly, moving into the shadows. Willemijn closed her eyes in pleasure as the light fell on her face and hands. It hit a silver frame standing on the little table next to her, which threw the light back in a dazzling flash. Inside was the same photograph of Thomas that stood in her room, one of those formal portraits in which he looked handsome and severe.

"You have been exploring," Willemijn said.

"Only a little."

"I saw you come through the graveyard. I like to look at it from the outside, you know, since soon I'll be on the inside looking out." Her eye opened to a slit to see if she had shocked me.

I twisted the fabric of my scarf between my fingers and said nothing.

"I wonder, did you perhaps come by the chapel before you went into the graveyard?"

"Yes."

"Then tell me: How are the statues doing?"

"Not so very well."

She smiled. She picked up an apple from the tray on the table next to her and began to peel it with a small silver knife. "They were my father's. He loved them more than he ever loved Thomas and me. It's a sin, to love an idol, isn't it? Only Daddy never saw it so."

"Is that why he's buried in unhallowed ground?"

"No, that's because he slit his own throat. He did it at the dinner table, with one of those small knives used for shucking oysters. You can't believe the mess. There was even blood on the ceiling." She pared the apple neatly and held out a piece for me. I took it from her, then stood holding the damp fruit, the flesh warming between my fingers.

"I'm sorry," I said.

"I'm not. Daddy was a brute after Mummy died. She had consumption, just as I do. Should never have had children, but Daddy wanted an heir. Perhaps she would've lived, had they stopped at Thomas. She died in here, did you know? As will I."

She broke a piece of apple between her fingers, licked at a trickle of juice running down her wrist. "Consumption runs in families. In that way it is like madness, I suppose. That, too, runs in my family, but you know that; you've seen those statues. Now come, eat your bit of apple. We need to fatten you up."

Reluctantly, I took a small bite. The fruit was hard and unexpectedly bitter.

"There you go. Now run along, little girl."

Once I was out of sight of the tuberculosis house, I threw the rest of my bit of apple into the bushes.

SEVENTH CASE EPISODE

PATIENT R—, A CASE STORY: INHABITED BY ANOTHER

(D = DOCTOR, P = PATIENT R—)

SEVENTH EPISODE, CONDUCTED ON 15 OCTOBER 1954:

Notes to self: It's becoming harder and harder to believe that patient is feigning madness. She can answer all my questions about her delusions without hesitating. Remains adverse to any logical explanation. Strong response to any suggestion she is mad, yet that's the only explanation that makes sense.

Unless she's an excellent actress, of course. I'm not so sure. High level of intelligence, yes, but intelligent enough to fool so many learned, world-wise men?

Careful now, Cornelius! Arrogance is a greater threat to justice than evil and ineptitude. Remain always wary, ever vigilant.

D: "Would you describe yourself as religious?"

P: "No."

D: "Why is that?"

P: [*shrugs*] "Mama didn't have much use for a church or God in our lives."

D: "You don't believe in God?"

P: "He hasn't yet given me much reason to believe in him."

D: "The K— household must have been quite a change, then. From what you've told me, several K—s' devotion to God bordered on the obsessive, if not the fanatical. Didn't that scare you?"

P: "W— [Miss K—]'s father and grandfather were already dead by the time I went to [the K— residence], so I never had anything to do with them."

D: "Miss K— told you stories, though, and from what you've just described, you saw the remnants of the K— family's obsession all around the house: those plaster saints, the wardrobe in your room. Didn't those frighten you?"

P: "Yes. I found them unsettling."

D: "Did you ever think perhaps the spirits of the old Mr. K—s could be haunting the place?"

P: "No. Spirits are very rare."

D: "And the mad things they believed? Did you see any truth of them while you stayed with Mrs. K—?"

P: "Shut up."

D: "Excuse me?"

P: [*rubs scarred hand irritably*] "Not you. Ruth. She's very chatty today, even though she knows I don't want to talk to her."

D: "Why don't you want to talk to her?"

P: "She knows she shouldn't talk to me when I'm with other people. We learned that the hard way. We talked all the time when I was little, regardless of who was with us, and then everyone in our neighborhood thought I was mad. I think it may have been the same for Agnes, and that's why Peter was always so quiet. Though it might just have been in his nature. Some people are like that, aren't they? As if every word they speak costs them money."

D: "What did Ruth just tell you?"

P: [*shivers, closes eyes briefly*] "I'd rather not say."

D: [*pauses*] "All right. Let's return to the question I asked before Ruth interrupted us. Did you see anything strange while you stayed with Mrs. K—, anything that tied into the delusions of the other K—s?"

P: "I heard footsteps sometimes, or smelled a male scent."

D: "What do you mean with a male scent?"

P: "Eau de cologne, very heavy, with cloves. I think I was especially sensitive to it because I'd only ever lived with Mama, and in a house of women, scents are very different."

D: "Anything else? Anything more..." [*gives a little chuckle*] "forgive me for using this word, but, well, anything more *spectacular*?"

P: "Only near the end, and then only briefly."

D: "Describe it to me."

P: "It had to do with the wardrobe in my room. I..." [*squeezes eyes shut again; shakes head quickly, as if trying to get rid of an unpleasant sensation; hisses*] "Be quiet!" [*opens eyes*] "You want to know whether there was a religious component to what happened, don't you?"

D: [*laughs uncomfortably*] "You've seen right through me.

Yes, I suppose that's what I've been getting at. Was there?"

P: "No. A— [Mrs. K—] didn't die because of religion."

D: "Then why did she die?"

P: "Because of love."

Chapter 13

DURING LUNCH—AGNES MADE A point of always taking her meals with me—I brought up the chapel with its army of rotting saints at the edge of the woods.

"Willemijn said they belonged to her father," I said before taking a sip of *sup bawang*, the onion soup Agnes's cook had made for us for lunch. She was a small lady from Indonesia who went by the name of Mrs. van Leeuwen, on account of her having married a Dutchman. I never found out whether she only knew how to make Indonesian dishes or whether she simply didn't care to make anything else, but during the time I lived at the Rozentuin, I was never served anything that wasn't Indonesian. It took my taste buds and digestive system a bit of time to get used to so much flavor—Mama preferred her food bland, else it would upset her stomach—but once they did, I wanted nothing else.

Agnes frowned. She dipped a bread crust into a little bowl with sambal. Mrs. van Leeuwen knew how to make at least a dozen different kinds. She used peppers, vinegar, shrimp, fried onions, peanuts, ginger, even fruit juice. Once the sauces were done, she kept them in glass jars. During my first night, she had served us *kroepoek* and toasted bread to dip into three small porcelain bowls of sambal.

"Don't try that one, miss," she'd told me and pointed at the red bowl. "It's sambal *gledek*, very spicy. You won't like it. The other ones are all very mild. I make them so for the one upstairs; she doesn't like anything very strong."

Agnes liberally spread the sambal *gledek* on a piece of toast and ate it slowly.

"Let me try a bite," I pleaded.

"It's far too hot for you."

"I'm a big girl. I'm sure I can handle it," I said.

"All right, but don't say we didn't warn you." Agnes laughed and held out the bread for me, her free hand cupped under the slice to catch potential crumbs.

To prove them wrong, I took a big bite. The sambal seared my tongue and the inside of my cheeks, burned my lips. I swallowed with great difficulty and felt the bite singe its way down my esophagus and into my stomach. Tears sprang in my eyes, and sweat pearled up at my hairline. "How white you are," Agnes teased me. Her comment gave me a strange jolt; I had never before thought of it so explicitly.

"This is just incredibly strong," I tried to defend myself while gulping down two cups of tea.

Agnes laughed. "Of course. No, don't drink so much. That won't help. Have some *kroepoek*." And she held the bowl out for me. I had then crammed two handfuls of the shrimp crisps into my mouth, chewing ferociously, tears streaming down my face, panting against that searing heat.

Now Agnes chewed her sambal-slathered crust of bread slowly, swallowed. "I haven't thought about those statues in forever. I'd almost forgotten about them." She lit a cigarette, took a puff, looked at me, and said, "You know, I can be so selfish. Thomas used to chide me for that. How many cigarettes have I smoked in your presence? At least a dozen, I'd wager, and yet I've never asked you if you want one."

"Oh, that's all right. I don't smoke. Mama wouldn't have it."

"Because she didn't find the smell attractive?"

"She said it might put our guests in mind of Hell."

"What a character your mama is. Well, she isn't here now. You can have a drag. I won't tell." She placed the cigarette between my fingers. The feel of her cool hand against mine made my insides clench with want. Because I did not want to disappoint her, I brought the cigarette to my mouth. Agnes's dark lipstick had stained the filter. Never before had I realized what an intimate thing it was to share a cigarette.

In a way, it was like kissing. I took into my mouth something still damp from Agnes's lips. I sucked at it, filled my lungs with smoke. Immediately, a sharp pain seized my chest and made my throat constrict. I began to cough, my eyes streaming.

Agnes did not laugh at me. She rubbed circles between my shoulder blades, took the cigarette before it could burn me, crushed it into the ashtray.

"I'm sorry," I gasped.

"It takes all of us like that the first time. Smoking is an acquired taste," she said, and lit another one.

"Like the Rozentuin," I said as soon as I stopped coughing.

"I suppose."

She began to talk of something else, but I placed my hand on hers and said, "Please, won't you tell me about those plaster saints?"

For a while she didn't say anything. Then, when she began to speak, the words came quickly, monotonously. "I don't know too much about it either. Thomas didn't want to speak of it. He could be so quiet, so brooding. If the past ever came up, it was as if a cloud passed over his fine face and plunged it into darkness. I learned not to ask. But there were bits he told me, little snippets here and there, and Willemijn could talk of it, so I know most of what happened from her."

She briefly closed her eyes, shivered. "After Thomas and Willemijn's mother died, their father, Hugo, went quite mad. He turned to religion to comfort him and bought all those statues. He had them blessed by a priest and then placed them around the house and treated them as if they were real people, had them dressed in real clothes, had meals prepared for them, that sort of thing. Willemijn broke one, Saint Cecilia, I believe, and Hugo had it wrapped in a shroud and buried in the cemetery as they said funeral rites over it. Not Willemijn—she'd been locked in her room because she was a murderess. Hugo died soon after. Thomas put all the statues into the chapel then and left them to rot."

A chill crawled up my spine, yet I couldn't stop myself. The matter was too strange, too exciting for a girl who had led such an isolated life as I had, so I went on. "Willemijn said Hugo butchered himself at the dinner table with an oyster knife."

"Did he? I had no idea. Thomas never spoke of him."

"He's buried in unhallowed ground."

"That I did know, yes." She blew out a plume of smoke from between her lips.

"Why didn't they throw the statues away?"

"They've been blessed and are quite holy. They can't be treated as trash."

"Maybe they should've been buried then. That seems more dignified than letting the elements eat them up."

"I think Thomas and Willemijn had quite enough of burials at that point. You know, when you think about it, it's hardly to be wondered at that they turned out the way they did," she said quietly.

I felt wicked and sordid then, having forced her to talk of her dead husband when it was clear that it was too fresh, too painful a topic. She had loved him deeply, after all, and his death, though the cause of it unknown to me, had been rather sudden and unexpected.

Yet if I had overstepped, Agnes did not show it. She crushed her cigarette and stood. She stretched, yawned. The tip of her tongue curled, catlike. "Come, let's make ourselves useful," she said, and with that the time of asking questions was over.

Chapter 14

AFTER LUNCH, AGNES AND I would clean a particular part of the house. That is, if she didn't have any pressing appointments that would take her far away from me. There were times when she left me alone for days, spending her nights in hotels. She'd call me up before bed, and I'd listen to her voice as she told me about her day—little, inconsequential things, like the food she'd had or a particular detail in her room that pleased her; never anything about the business of the estate that demanded her absence from me—and I'd do my best to be comforted. She told me she liked to listen to me talk, too, but I hadn't much to tell her. I whiled away my days by walking around the gardens and reading dusty tomes from the library or cuddling with Ruth. I felt quite useless and rather lonely. I was used to this, but I resented how easy it was to feel this way again now, when I had expected I need never be alone again.

It didn't help that the Rozentuin was such a strange house. At night, I was often woken by the sound of footsteps outside, heavy and sure, a man's tread. I tried to tell myself it was nothing, just the floorboards getting comfortable for the night, but it sounded very real. At first I thought it was Peter roaming—he was such a dreamy, restless creature, not at all like my Ruth, whose focus and stillness were really quite fearful sometimes—but he barely made any noise when he walked, perhaps because of the mosslike mold that had sprouted on his soles and underneath his toes and cushioned every step.

Yet there were no other men in the house, so it could be nothing more sinister than the damp warping the floorboards. Why there should be a faint smell of aftershave to accompany those sounds was a mystery to me, too, but I supposed that every house was entitled to its secrets. All the same, it made me uneasy. It was easier to ignore the sounds and strange smells when Agnes was in the room next to me. Perhaps it was a childish thing, to feel soothed by her presence, as if no harm could come to me then, but this was what I felt. When she was gone, I lay awake with my heart pounding, listening to that man pacing up and down, up and down the hallway or in the room overhead, and not even Ruth's cold body pressed against mine could make me feel at ease.

Yet I can't solely blame my fear of sleep on the house chattering around me. Part of it was because I was deathly afraid Willemijn would need me in the night and I wouldn't wake up when she called for me. Her medicine was locked away in a cupboard in Agnes's room, to prevent Willemijn from self-administering. Whenever she called for me, which didn't always happen, though sometimes it did multiple times a night, I'd get up and count out a number of pills for her or bring her a bottle of syrup. I'd sit with her until she dismissed me.

I asked Willemijn once what exactly it was that took Agnes

away from us. She was rubbing some grease on her lips, which were chapped and bloody. "Too many things here remind her of Thomas," she said.

"Oh. I thought she had to do things for the estate," I said. I handed her a handkerchief to wipe her fingers on.

Willemijn laughed. A scab on her lip cracked, which made her wince. She dabbed at it with the handkerchief, then carefully wiped her fingers one by one. "How much work do you think an estate as derelict as the Rozentuin could possibly be? We've no tenants, not like in the olden days."

"Wouldn't it be a lot of work precisely because it's so derelict? Maybe she's trying to raise money to restore the house."

Willemijn huffed with derision. "She couldn't raise two guilders if she tried, not with her reputation."

Something twisted in my stomach. "What do you mean?"

"In *our* circles," she said, and gave me a pitying little smile, which made me hate her, then hate myself because I felt a stab of shame, as no doubt she intended, "everyone knows Agnes is a little... How do I put this? *Touched*." She tapped her temple.

My hands began to shake. I snatched the handkerchief from Willemijn and folded it into little squares, careful not to touch the spots of blood and grease. "Just because she can see spirits doesn't mean she's insane."

"Perhaps, but it isn't very respectable, is it? Smacks of backroom séances, and those, in turn, smack of underage sluts. A few decades ago, it may have been all the rage for wealthy men to have a medium mistress, but it was always common."

Mr. Mesman, I thought, and bile burned its way up my throat. I wished Ruth were there to comfort me, but spirits feel a deep revulsion for the dying, so Ruth was in my room, curled up in my bed. I focused on the handkerchief in my hands, the feel of the cotton against my fingers. A loose thread snagged on the scar on my palm. "So you mean to say that people don't want to invest in whatever Agnes dreams up because they think she's insane?"

"Indeed. It doesn't help that she's a foreigner either. That's not to say she spends her days sitting in seedy little hotel rooms doing nothing. I suspect she might be looking to sell off some acres of land. God knows we could get a fair price for them. Farmers are looking to expand, and the soil here is fertile. The bog should be drained first, of course, and that's quite the investment, which may be why she hasn't struck a deal yet. Thomas once had an offer from an investor who wanted to build holiday bungalows here. He almost hounded that man off our property. Holiday bungalows. Can you imagine? How utterly vulgar."

I could fold the handkerchief no further. I shook it out and began again. "And the piano?" I asked.

"What about it?"

"Does she play it when she's gone? For other people?" I had harbored romantic notions of Agnes going out to play for people at select gatherings in the evenings after work, the kind of parties where the guests drank liquor from crystal glasses and the women had strands of pearls clasped around their throats and diamonds in their hair. Though maybe if those people thought her mad, it was better she didn't attend their parties.

"You think her some kind of famous pianist, do you?"

"Mama told me she was to become one, only nothing ever came of it."

Willemijn dipped her fingertips in the pot of grease and rubbed some on a dry spot on the back of her hand and the webbing between her fingers. "She had some sort of breakdown. I don't know all the details. Agnes keeps her cards close to her chest, as you've no doubt realized by now. All I know is that she spent some time in a private clinic before she met Thomas. She's a sly one, Agnes. If she had been upfront about it, Thomas might not have married her. We've enough madness in the family as is. And after she was married, well, it wouldn't be respectable for her to go on the stage, now, would it?"

"I don't suppose it would have been, not in your circles."

She shot me a curious look, then smiled. "Quite. Now, are you done interrogating me? Only I'd like to sleep."

I left her and crawled back into bed with Ruth. She cuddled against me, rubbing her leathery cheek against my hair.

I didn't feel like I'd truly learned anything new about where Agnes went when she wasn't with me. But what I did know was that, on the days she stayed at the Rozentuin, we invariably cleaned after lunch. Most rooms were no longer in use, the shutters closed, the furniture swathed in great yellowing sheets, the doors locked. The rooms that were still in use were filthy despite the efforts of the little maid. They smelled stale, musty, unlived-in. We took down the curtains and had them sent away to be washed; we dusted furniture, scrubbed floors, waxed wood.

It pained me, to see Agnes bind up her hair in rags and kneel on the stone flags till her knees were red and raw. "If I had my way," I told her, "you'd never have to clean."

"And you'd dress me in silk and velvet and have me recline on a couch for most of the day." She laughed. I flushed so quickly, the tears sprang into my eyes. I began to utter a stream of apologies.

Agnes hushed me by briefly placing her hand on mine and said gently, "I'm not mad at you, Roos. There's no need to say sorry."

"I just don't want you to be displeased with me. I want you to be happy." What else could I do? What else had she brought me to the Rozentuin for, if not this? If I could not make her happy, then I was useless and thus without worth. Mama had made that abundantly clear.

Agnes looked away. "Happy. Such a funny little word, don't you think? Perhaps not so hard a state to achieve, but nearly impossible to maintain, and different for everyone. I'm sure there are people out there who would be perfectly happy to never have to clean, but not me. Doing little has never agreed with me. It gives me too much time to dwell on things."

After dinner, Agnes and I would have tea in the drawing room. Of all the rooms the Rozentuin had, the drawing room had to be one of my least favorites. The chairs were uncomfortable, some strangely slippery, others too soft. They either rejected you or seemed to want to gobble you up. The wallpaper, I found ugly, too, though that might be because it was floral and, in that way, reminded me of Mama. I suppose it didn't help matters much that it was such a dark room, even with all the lamps lit. Unlike the dining room, which had windows so tall, we needed a stick with a hook at its end to draw the curtains, this room had just two little windows placed very close to each other. The glass had yellowed with age and struggled to let in any light, which meant we had to switch on lamps even when the sun shone if we wished to read anything. How often did I sit there and see something move in the shadows from the corner of my eye? For there were always pockets of darkness in that room no matter how many lamps and candles we lit.

Willemijn never came with us but went to bed early since she was required to rest. This, at least, was a small mercy; she scared me more than I dared to admit. Mrs. van Leeuwen did always join us for tea. She and Agnes spoke Javanese together.

"My mother came from Java," Agnes told me. "When it was just me and her, we spoke Javanese. I've forgotten a lot of it now because it wasn't allowed at the schools I attended, and there was no one to speak it with anyway, so Auntie van Leeuwen is helping me remember and teaching me what I never knew."

"Auntie van Leeuwen?"

"You may just call her 'Mrs. van Leeuwen,'" Agnes said. For an embarrassingly long period, this made me think Mrs. van Leeuwen was Agnes's aunt. It was only later that I found out it was a customary way of address among Indo people for respected nonfamily members.

And so, after dinner, I'd sit drowsing in my chair in the drawing room, stuffed to bursting with food, and I'd listen to this language I didn't understand and wonder what it was they spoke of.

Occasionally, Mrs. van Leeuwen would say a word in Dutch and repeat its Javanese counterpart, and then Agnes would jot it down in a notebook she kept for this purpose. Sometimes they laughed, and it felt strange and a little sad to me because I was excluded.

After three days or so, I asked Agnes why she wanted to relearn Indonesian.

"Javanese, Roos. And what do you mean, why?" She looked at me with a little frown.

"Why do you want to speak it when you live here, in the Netherlands? You speak so many languages already, Dutch and English and French. Is it because you want to go to Indonesia one day?"

"I'd like to go there, yes, even though I'm not sure I'd be welcome, but no, that's not why I want to speak my mother's language. If you grew up speaking Dutch, and then it was forbidden, would you not wish to speak it when you could? Especially if it was the language you shared with someone you loved, and that person is gone now?"

I felt ashamed then, ignorant. I lowered my eyes. "I suppose so, yes."

"People used to shame me for who I am." She spoke slowly, with a little tremor in her voice. "It's funny. I used to think my mother was the most beautiful woman on earth, and I was proud to look like her, only at school they told me that my very likeness to her was what made me ugly and inferior. I tried to eradicate so much of my identity during those years. But I am Indo, and that's not a source of shame but a source of pride."

She sought my eye; I managed to meet hers. How proud her gaze! How powerful, how harsh! Never had she looked more beautiful. Never had she felt so far removed from me.

"I understand," I said.

She softened and touched my cheek with her fingertips. They pulsed with heat. "No, you don't. There are things a girl with a face and skin like yours can never understand about a girl with a face and skin like mine. Know, yes, but not understand."

"What is the difference?"

She thought for a minute, and all the while, her long, lean fingers rested against my cheek until it felt burning hot. "Knowing is cold, I suppose," she said. "Cold and distant. You know things with your mind. Understanding is different. It's warm. You understand things with your mind, yes, but also with your heart."

"Why shan't I ever understand?"

"Some things must be experienced to be understood."

"Like having a spirit companion?"

She hesitated, then nodded. "Yes. It's not quite like it, but I suppose that's as near as you can get. Now come, let's have some tea. I believe Mrs. van Leeuwen has made us *spekkoek*."

"Might I take some upstairs with me, for Ruth? She loves cake."

"Of course. Just make sure you finish it tonight. I've started hearing mice in the walls at night, and I'm sure they would love some cake, too."

I heard them, too, though it was hard to believe they were mice and not small children trapped in the walls, scratching to be let out. It was as Agnes had said: it took some time to get used to the sounds of the Rozentuin. I often lay awake and listened to Agnes as she pottered around or went to Willemijn to put wet, cold handkerchiefs on her fevered brow and feed her sticky medicine with silver spoons, and then I'd fantasize about what it would be like to be tended to by Agnes if I were ill. More often I imagined myself tending to her, bringing her bowls of soup and plumping up pillows so she could rest her aching head on them.

Once, I heard sobbing, these desperate hoarse little sobs. "Thomas," she moaned—and then again, so loudly that I heard it very clearly. But when I knocked softly on the wall and called Agnes's name, the sobbing stopped, and all went quiet.

EIGHTH CASE EPISODE

PATIENT R—, A CASE STORY: INHABITED BY ANOTHER

(D = DOCTOR, P = PATIENT R—)

EIGHTH EPISODE, CONDUCTED ON 16 OCTOBER 1954:

D: "Based on what you've told me so far, I think now is the right time to talk to you about jealousy. Would you say you were jealous of Miss K— and Mrs. van L— [the cook]?"

P: "No."

D: "Really? Because it seems to me that you are a little jealous. It wouldn't be strange if you were, R—. Mrs. K— promised you a job as her companion, but from what you've told me so far, it seems that she spent most of her time away from you. That mustn't have been easy, seeing as you had... How shall I put this? Strong feelings for her."

P: [*stiffly*] "A— [Mrs. K—] had things that needed attending. I understood that. And you forget that A— [Mrs. K—] and I did spend time together; we had our meals together, and sometimes after Mrs. van L— went to bed, we'd stay up talking for a bit."

D: "Yet when you talk about Miss K— and Mrs. van L—..."

P: [*interrupts*] "W— [Miss K—] was very ill and needed to be looked after."

D: "You can understand why someone needs to spend time with someone else and still feel jealous."

P: "Well, I didn't. I rather pitied W— [Miss K—], and I never begrudged A— [Mrs. K—] her time with Mrs. van L—. I just felt excluded. If anything, that's not jealousy, but envy. But it wasn't that, either. It just hurt, is all."

D: "All right. You weren't jealous or envious, just hurt. What about Ruth? Would you say she's the jealous type?"

P: "Sometimes."

D: "Did she mind your interactions with Mrs. K—?"

P: "Not really. Ruth wants what's best for me."

D: "Wanting what is best for someone requires selfless-ness. I'd argue that this is the opposite of jealousy, which is inherently selfish."

P: "You want to hear that Ruth was madly jealous of A— [Mrs. K—] and me, don't you?"

D: "I merely want to find out what happened, and why."

P: "I know what you're doing. You're going through motives for murder, trying to see what fits. I told you that A— [Mrs. K—] died because of love, so now you're trying to understand how, exactly. You've already asked whether I desired A— [Mrs. K—], and whether Ruth and I have a tendency toward the violent; now you want to know if we're jealous. Next, you'll ask if I was ever afraid of Ruth, or afraid of A— [Mrs. K—]. That question answered, you'll want to know if I was pos-sessive, if Ruth was, even whether A— [Mrs. K—] was."

D: "And were you? Possessive, I mean?"

P: "Not in the way people usually are."

D: "Please elaborate."

P: "I wanted to know everything there was to know about her. I thought of her all the time. In a sense, I suppose you can say *she* had taken possession of *me*."

D: "So you were possessive of Mrs. K— in the same way a collector of shells or butterflies is?"

P: "No. Those are objects. I never saw A— [Mrs. K—] as such. I was just... I wanted to eat her up and drink her in. I was hungry for her touch and her words and her love. That's very different from collecting shells or butterflies."

D: "'Eat her up and drink her in.' Forgive me, but that sounds cannibalistic."

P: [*tiredly*] "You'd think that, wouldn't you?"

D: "In light of the state we found Mrs. K—'s remains in, you must concede it's a rather obvious question."

P: [*snaps*] "Look, do you want me to tell you this story, or not?"

D: "By all means."

Chapter 15

ONE NIGHT, AFTER MRS. VAN Leeuwen and Willemijn had both retired, Agnes tried to teach me how to dance. She had chosen one of the rooms that was usually locked on account of it being very large.

"We used to have our parties in here," she told me as she switched on the lamps one by one. The glass had gathered dust, leaving the light dull and low. I had been afraid of this room at first; much like the drawing room, it had patches of darkness that would not be dispelled. All the furniture had been moved to the sides and covered in great white sheets. *Anything could hide under there, and we would not know, we would not see,* I had thought. Not ghosts—those I didn't fear—but other things that might mean us harm, men like Mr. Mesman, for instance. My mind had fixed upon that idea, and my heart raced, and fear lashed my insides.

When Agnes pulled down one of the sheets, I flinched with fright. Underneath was only a table with a record player, and I tittered at my silliness but hated myself a little, too. I did not like how easy it was for me to become a frightened, foolish little girl again.

Agnes selected a record with different waltzes. As the music filled the room, she took me in her arms and explained the steps to me. Mr. Mesman had tried to teach me once, at one of Mama's New Year's Eve parties, but I had been so frightened of him, I had stood hard and stiff like a mannequin and could not concentrate on what he said.

It was different with Agnes. We went at it for over an hour and at some point laughed ourselves silly because we both kept going in different directions.

Now, tired and flushed from laughing, we stood gently swaying, her hand burning on my hip, my head resting against her chest. The heat came off her in gentle waves, mingled with the scent of her skin and hair. Peter lay underneath a sofa covered by a sheet, looking for dead bugs, and Ruth clung to the ceiling like a spider and watched over us with her empty sockets, and I felt safe and loved and useful. I wished it could be this way forever.

Agnes followed my gaze, smiled at Ruth. "What are you thinking about?" she asked me. I had my arms around her neck. A little lock of hair kept brushing the back of my hand.

"About how, in prehistoric times, people used to keep their dead relatives in the rafters of their house, like some sort of guardian angels." They'd fold the bodies, then smoke them till they were hard and dry. That way they would keep for decades.

Agnes shivered. "Oh, I don't like that idea at all."

"Why not?"

"I can just imagine all these terrible scenarios. Imagine you marry a widower, and his first wife is up in the rafters watching you, judging your cooking and how you rear her children." I felt her voice vibrate as she spoke, this delicious tickling against my ear and cheek.

"Maybe the children find it comforting. It's just a haunting of a different kind."

"Maybe, but not everyone gets along with everyone. There's a reason the word 'haunting' is rarely used in a positive way. To never be free of someone, well, that's not always a comfort."

I suddenly had a vision of Mama clinging to the ceiling, her eyes forever trained on me, silently judging me and finding me wanting. No, I'd never put her in the rafters of my home. If anything, I'd tuck her under the floorboards, see how she liked it.

"And wouldn't it get terribly crowded after a while?" Agnes went on. "There are only so many dead relatives you can stuff into your ceiling. Dead bodies are not exactly small now are they?"

"They'd be folded up, and the drying shrinks them."

"All the same, it's not like having a collection of butterflies that you can just tuck away in a drawer. The dead need to be stored properly—you can't just have them dangling from the ceiling like cured hams. That would be both disrespectful and inconvenient. What do you do when you run out of space? Who gets to stay and who gets to go? You're bound to hurt someone's feelings, aren't you, even if you don't want anyone to leave?"

As if this talk put her in mind of losing me, she pulled me a little tighter against her, interlacing her fingers in the small of my back. Though my cheek pressed hard against the bone between her breasts and my arms had to bend uncomfortably to stay around her neck, I felt so sweet and safe, I wished we could cleave together like that forever.

"It wouldn't have been like that," I murmured.

"No?" she asked, her breath stirring the little baby hairs at my right temple.

"No. Maybe," I said slowly, "they need only stay up there as long as their spirits haven't woken yet. Maybe that's why people preserved them. Maybe the dead weren't meant to watch over the living but the living over the dead. I think the old world must have been teeming with spirits. Death must have been a different thing to those people than it is to us. Not this unbearable ending, but a transformation. No need to grieve when someone died because they wouldn't be gone. Can you imagine if we still lived like that? Thomas could still be here, watching you, and…"

She shuddered and stepped out of my embrace. "Please don't. I know you mean well, but please, don't. I can't talk about him yet."

"But why? Is it too painful? Did you love him that much?"

"That's a rather personal question, don't you think? But if you must know, then yes. I was his creature utterly and completely. Sometimes I think I still am." She bit her lips with such force, spots of blood welled from the cuts.

"Oh, Agnes, I didn't mean…"

She raised a hand and hushed me. "It's late. I should get some sleep. Will you turn off the record player when you're done?" she said and would not look at me, would not touch me as she fled upstairs.

Self-hatred made me want to flay the web of skin between

my thumb and index finger. Ruth scuttled down the wall and took hold of my hand as I brought it to my mouth. Her hand was ice-cold, whereas Agnes's had been fever hot, but the body is easily tricked, so the sensation felt the same. "Come, you shouldn't have mentioned Thomas, but that's no reason to harm yourself. What good does it do?"

"It feels good."

"Only for a little while. This you know."

She was right on all accounts, of course. Hurting myself did more harm than good, and I shouldn't have talked of Thomas. But bringing him up had become like a sickness or, more accurately, a compulsion against which I was helpless. Every time I spoke of him, I hated myself. I promised I wouldn't do it again, but I had to know, didn't I?

I had to know how much she loved him because once I reburied his remains, there could be no going back.

Chapter 16

THIS UNTHINKABLE THING WOULD NEVER have come to me if it hadn't been for my fear of hunger. This fear was so crippling, so all-consuming, that I could not think beyond it. I simply needed to assuage it by collecting as much food as I could and ensuring I had access to it always, just in case. During my time at the Rozentuin, I began a nice little collection of pickled, fermented, and dried things.

Of course, during the final days, Agnes and Willemijn and I ate all the things I had collected, but we haven't reached that part yet.

My favorite day for scavenging was Sunday because I was left by myself at the Rozentuin as Agnes and Mrs. van Leeuwen went to church. Willemijn remained at home, but that didn't impede my exploring: she spent the afternoon dozing and dreaming, doped up on various medicines to ease the liquid fire in her chest. Peter was rarely there. Whereas Ruth stayed always close to me, Peter often roamed far and wide, returning to Agnes when called or when otherwise compelled. This made me think he must have belonged to a wandering people when he had lived. The land called to him still, and he walked it, finding things of value he brought home in cupped palms for Agnes to take pleasure in, mushrooms and seeds and pieces of flint.

And so, during those hours I was left alone with her, I explored the rooms closed up and left to molder in the hope I might find something edible that would keep. We took our time, Ruth and I. We didn't want to miss any food. And there was a certain pleasure in getting to know each floorboard, each spot of damp, each dirty windowpane. Besides, it wasn't as if I had anything else to do when Agnes was away.

I began at the top of the house and worked my way down. The attic contained the servants' quarters, small plain rooms with hard beds and a desk and chair each. No need for finery here. It smelled differently here, too, almost clean, just dusty and a bit muggy. These rooms had been unlived in for years. The damp had quite spoiled the wallpaper; it came down in strips. Ruth and I found some dead spiders, their legs curled up at beautiful angles, a dented thimble some maid had forgotten, some faded ribbons, but no food. We did find a dusty whiskey glass, which I put in my pocket so Ruth could have some fun later grinding it up with a file.

The rooms underneath the attic had been intended for use by the Knoops. I found little flakes of colored plaster in the hallway, a colored scratch on one of the walls. Hugo had moved his statues through there then. Sometimes, at night, when I was in that strange land between dream and wakefulness, I thought I could hear him drag them around, only that couldn't be because they were all safely locked away in the family chapel. A good thing, that—had I come upon one unawares in the dark of the shuttered rooms, I would've had a nasty shock.

In a room with ochre wallpaper, we met the companion to the haunted wardrobe in my room: a wooden screen with scenes of sin, placed so close to the door, I nearly stumbled against it as I stepped inside. Women with bulbous breasts copulated with goat-faced men in the deep dark woods while proud men dressed in finery played cards and stuffed themselves with meat shiny and dripping with fat. The edges of the screen were wreathed in carved fruit, all of it somehow distasteful. It seemed to me that I could press a finger to one of the apples or pears and feel the wood dimple underneath the pressure, as if it were flesh, and overripe at that.

It reminded me of the apple Willemijn had peeled and pared so neatly and then tried to share with me. The air in the room was even damper than in the rest of the house, and for one nasty moment, I imagined it was because the wooden figures breathed.

I shuddered.

"Hugo Knoop, patron of the arts," Ruth sneered before going behind the screen to inspect the rest of the room.

The hollow eyes of the figures seemed to look at me. Dust had settled in their empty sockets. I reached for the carved fruit to see if the skin really would split under my touch, then thought better of it and tucked my hands into my pockets.

"Oh, darling Roosje mine, you're simply going to love this," Ruth said from the other side of the room.

"What? What is it?"

I had to press myself against the wallpaper so I needn't touch that revolting screen. It stained my hands a fantastic yellow. "Oh," I said once I came out from behind it and saw the little desks with matching chairs, the blackboard upon the wall, the shelf of atlases and dictionaries and encyclopedias. This had to be the schoolroom where Thomas and Willemijn had received their lessons from an endless parade of governesses, none of whom had stayed long.

Ruth pinched a piece of chalk between her fingers, then made a face of disgust. "Moist," she said. She drifted over to one of the walls and studied the map upon it.

"This is beastly," I said. "Who would put a screen like that in a schoolroom?"

"Perhaps the governesses used it to help the children learn their catechism. There's a Bible on that shelf."

I shuddered with disgust and anger. Mushrooms could thrive here, in the damp and the dark, but surely not children. No wonder consumption had ravaged half the family and madness the other.

"Let's go. I've got a feeling those people on the screen are watching me, and I don't care for it," I said.

Next we inspected the storage room next to the schoolroom. Among dried-up inkwells, yellowed notebooks, and bent pen nips, we found a jar of pickles. "A strange place to find food, don't you think?" I said as I wiped away the dust from the glass with my handkerchief.

Ruth shook her head. "I think the children were given their meals in the schoolroom. The governesses must have prepared them here. Why else have that stone sink? And there are some plates and cups on that shelf over there."

I imagined eating under the watchful hollow eyes of the figures on the screen and felt like retching a little.

The final room we investigated that day was the nursery on the other side of the schoolroom. It was not nearly as dilapidated as I had thought it would be. The wallpaper was old and faded, yes, the ceiling stained black from an old leak, but someone had tried to bring the room to order not so very long ago by painting bright animals on the southern wall and hanging yellow curtains patterned with daisies. The crib near the window had matching sheets and a little pillow all plumped up. I touched the crib and set it swinging softly. It did not make a sound as it swayed.

My heart felt small and crumpled. "There was to be a baby," I whispered.

Ruth wound her arms around me, the skin brown and wrinkled like a wizened apple. "Poor Agnes," she said. "Though if the baby withered in her womb, who could blame it? You've said it yourself: this is no place to raise a child."

"But it didn't wither, Ruth. Don't you remember the graveyard? The plot of unhallowed ground with markers for unbaptized children? There was one grave that was only a few years old."

"No wonder Agnes lets the place go to rot and ruin."

I frowned. "But that isn't true. There's simply no money."

"Then how did she pay Mama? How could she afford the restaurants, your clothes, the fancy hotel?"

"Maybe she took out a loan. She cleans the Rozentuin every day. She scrubs her hands raw to do it. You can't possibly say she doesn't do her best to keep it neat and clean."

"Not every day. Only when she's here."

"When she isn't here, she's trying to raise money for the Rozentuin."

"Is she?"

"What else would she be doing? Please, Ruth, let's drop this."

"Don't you think it's all rather strange, though? Why not hire staff to clean? Why not hire a nurse to look after Willemijn?"

"Because there's no money."

"But there is."

I rubbed the scars on my hand. "We're talking in circles. Let's leave. This room makes me sad." I untangled myself from her arms. She kissed my forehead. I picked up the jar of pickles, stepped into the hallway, then froze.

Willemijn stood on the final step of the staircase. I had caught her unawares, and in that little sliver of a moment before she recognized me, in that heartbeat when I was someone else to her, I saw a desperate hatred and furious longing in her eyes, so potent that it made the breath catch in my throat. Then she saw me for who I was, and the emotion drained away, leaving only a dull sort of anger. "What, pray tell," she said, "are you doing snooping around my house?"

Chapter 17

THE SHOCK OF COMING UPON Willemijn unawares and of that ghoulish look on her face had made me dumb. I gaped at her as she ascended the final steps. The light faltering through the dirty window illuminated her face, showing me the sharp jut of her cheekbones, the veins thin as hairs around her eyes. Her skin was yellow as tallow, sickly, unhealthy. It was more akin to a dead woman's face than a living one's.

She glanced at the jar of pickles I was clutching so desperately, at the bulge in my trousers' pocket from where I had slipped in the whiskey glass, then peered into my face and smiled. "Scavenging, are we?" she said.

I looked at the jar sweating in my hands so I didn't have to look at her. "I didn't... I thought..." I stammered.

She lay her hand lightly on mine. It was searing hot with fever. "If you want something, you need only ask. Or does it bring you pleasure to pilfer like a common thief?"

She might have slapped me, so painful were her words to me.

"No. It's not like that at all, I..." But how could I tell her that

I was terrified of hunger, and even if I hadn't been, that I had to create some sort of purpose for myself for those times when I wasn't with Agnes because Mama had taught me that to be useless was the worst kind of sin?

Not that it would've mattered. Willemijn didn't let me finish anyway. "Come, I shall show you the rooms, and if there's something that takes your fancy, you need only say so, and I might give it to you." Her hand closed around mine, and she tugged me along. So strong was her grip that I was forced to stumble after her.

"Let's see. The nursery, you've already seen. Beautiful, isn't it? Thomas wanted an heir very badly. That's why he married Agnes, you know, only she didn't quite deliver." She laughed, or perhaps it was a sob. "I propose we leave the nursery for what it is. Have you discovered the schoolroom yet? I think you must have. You've got a yellow smudge on your sleeve. The wallpaper stains, you know. Agnes could tell you a pretty story about that! Now, the pickles you must've taken from the storage room, so that leaves Thomas's rooms and my old ones. Before he died, he had me moved a story lower so I needn't go up an extra flight of stairs with my bad lungs." She was so close, I could smell the decay on her breath, could hear the soft wet sounds her ruined lungs made with every breath.

"I don't want to see," I said.

"But you do," she insisted. She had dragged me to the end of the hallway now. From a pocket she drew a key with which she unlocked the door. All the while her other hand was still locked around mine.

"Yank your hand away," Ruth whispered. She had turned into

a glittering haze now, as brilliant as the glass she ground up and kept in a glass bottle with a lid one had to screw on. "Yank and run."

But Willemijn threw open the door and drew me inside, and I knew my chance to escape had gone. Her handclasp was too strong, or perhaps I had grown weak under her touch. There was something of the vampire about Willemijn Knoop. Yet I'd be lying if I said I didn't want to see those rooms, and many things I may be, but not a liar.

"Behold," she said, and in the mouth of another, that word would have been melodramatic, perhaps even ridiculous, but in hers it turned sinister, threatening. "Thomas's room."

There was nothing particularly special about his room. Dark furniture and upholstery, green wallpaper that matched the velvet of a chair whose mate I had seen before in Agnes's room. Yet I was uneasy, and not only because I felt I had no right to be there. I had thought Thomas's possessions would have been stored away, the furniture swathed to keep from turning dusty. But no, all was where it must have been when he was still alive: the cuff links in their saucer could be picked up by his long fingers and threaded through his cuffs; the pillow still bore the impression of his head; a book lay on the nightstand, a slip of paper marking the page where he had left off.

Only the smell betrayed that this room had been in disuse for months: it smelled stale, musty, slightly moldy.

"You didn't expect his rooms to be kept like this, did you? You thought everything would have been stored away. Agnes could bear it all better that way. She'd like to forget he ever existed, but not I. I

want him as close to me as I can. I loved him so. He was my dearest
friend in the world. Now go on," Willemijn said softly. Her mouth
was revoltingly close to my ear; it made the hairs on my nape rise.

"Go and look at his things. That's what you want, isn't it?" She
let go of my wrist and gave me a little shove. The liquid inside the
pickle jar sloshed against the glass. I felt as if I might be sick. Saliva
filled my mouth. I swallowed it.

Again, Willemijn shoved me, thrusting her palm between my
shoulder blades. Rather than be hounded by her, I went to the
dresser that held Thomas's brushes, his pomade and aftershave,
bottles topped with silver that Ruth would love to get her hands
on. On a little saucer lay a pair of cuff links and a watch.

"Go on, take something," Willemijn said, her voice soft and
sweet. It would have been better if she had sneered at me or called
me names, anything but this sudden kindness.

I closed my eyes and wildly thrust out my hand. It closed
around the watch, the metal so cold, it made a shiver ripple through
me. I opened my eyes and ran my fingers over it. The leather strap
was slightly oily. The face was cracked, the hands forever stopped at
the time when it happened. On the backside something had been
engraved. I had to bring it close to my face to read.

For Tom from A.

"Beautiful, isn't it?" Willemijn said. She took it from me and
held it reverently. I had to do my best not to shudder at her touch.
"Agnes gave it to him for his fortieth birthday. He wore it every
day, even though he owned more expensive watches. He even wore
it the day he died. Agnes said we couldn't bury him with it, not

when it was cracked, but I think she didn't want people to see and ask questions."

"Willemijn, how did Thomas die?"

"Like a dog." Her mouth turned down at the corners. "My poor, poor brother," she murmured. She rubbed the watch against her cheek like a cat might, then sniffed the strap for his scent, and I had to look away.

I could still see the inscription vividly in my mind's eye: *For Tom from A.*

She had called him *Tom* then, perhaps even *Tommy* when they were alone. It was easy, intimate. A chain of sensations ran through my mind. The soft, silky feel of a flower in my hand as I ripped it apart with my fingers to perfume the air; the steady tick of the watch around my wrist, a message of love flush against my skin; a woman running to me, her dark hair dancing around her face. I had the ridiculous urge to cry. But crying had never been of use to me when I had lived with Mama, and I did not think it'd be of use to me now.

I dashed the tears from my eyes with my fingertips, swallowed hard. Ruth brushed against my sore throat, cool as a tendril of mist.

"She loved him terribly, didn't she?" I asked slowly.

"Loved him? She worshipped him. He was a god. She submitted to his will utterly. You might not think anything of that, seeing as it's the nature of her kind to serve, but oh, she was his creature in every fiber of her being. She would give anything to have him back, as would I. Anything, anything…" Willemijn sobbed. Suddenly, she slumped against the dresser. As she fell, her arms swept its contents to the ground. The bottle of aftershave broke. The scent of clove and alcohol filled the room instantly, so potent that it made my eyes water. The saucer broke into three pieces; the watch landed with a twang.

One of the cuff links we never found again. I think it fell through a crack in the floor, and for all I know, it rests there still.

I managed to grab Willemijn just before she fell to the floor. I heaved her to the side to prevent her knees from grinding into the shards, then dropped her rather ungraciously on the carpet, the muscles in my arms screaming. She didn't weigh much, but after Mama's regime of starvation so I could look young and dainty, I had barely any strength in my arms. I mopped up the aftershave with a handkerchief the best I could, my mouth against the inside of my elbow so I wouldn't choke. With a shock, I recognized the scent: I had caught whiffs of it at times, usually at night, when it sounded like a man paced up and down the hallway beyond my bedroom door.

Was Thomas…?

I rejected that thought so violently, it couldn't even form properly. Had he been a spirit, I would've seen him. More likely that Willemijn sprayed his scent everywhere. Perhaps it was her I heard, dragging herself this way and that, and my fertile mind twisted it until I thought a man paced up and down. Men frightened me.

Having mopped up the aftershave, I opened a window. I threw the handkerchief out and wiped my reeking hands on the curtains. I took one of the pillows from Thomas's bed and placed it underneath Willemijn's head. Her face was wet with perspiration. Her chest rose and fell rapidly.

By the time I had collected the shards and thrown them in the bin—it still held twists of scrap paper from when Thomas was alive, and butts of cigarettes—Willemijn had come to. With her fever-bright eyes, she tracked my every movement.

I tried to smile at her. "Don't be frightened," I said. "You fainted. I hope you didn't hurt yourself."

"I'm not frightened," she hissed. She tried to sit up. I put my arm around her to support her. She was so thin, I could feel her spine through her clothes. She began to cough, so long and hard that I feared this would be the end of her.

"It's the aftershave," Ruth said. "It's settling on her lungs."

I placed my hands under her armpits and dragged her out of the room before shutting the door behind me with a firm kick. In the hallway, she lay gasping and choking, her face red. A vein pulsed on her forehead. She twisted on her side, retched, coughed up a little puddle of slime streaked with blood. I sat with her until the fit passed, holding her hair out of her face, rubbing her back, making soft shushing noises. She was soon so exhausted, she could barely speak.

With my sleeve I wiped the tears from her face. "You need to be in bed. You're burning up with fever," I said. "Do you think you can stand?"

Somehow, I managed to get her into her room. There I made her drink water and gave her some medication. I helped undress her. Tuberculosis had made the flesh melt from her body. Her ribs showed, as did the butterfly curve of her hips. Low on her belly, she had a jagged scar.

She saw me look and rubbed at it harshly with her fingertips, turning the corded flesh an angry purple. "No babies for me," she said.

"Is that why you never married?"

But she had closed her eyes and didn't answer. I tucked her into bed, placed a damp cloth on her forehead to ease the burning. "You must sleep now. This place…it isn't good for you. It's too close to the bogs. The air is damp and unwholesome."

Her eyelids flickered from exhaustion. "Why are you here?" she rasped. "What do you want?"

"I'm just trying to make sure you're comfortable."

She shook her head. "In general," she gasped.

I plucked at a loose thread on her sheets, wound it around my finger. When I had still lived with Mama, my dreams had been small: make it through this séance without demeaning myself too much; get a somewhat proper meal this evening; receive warm weather so I won't be damnably cold. I had hardly dared to dream of a life without her. Now that Agnes had given it to me, these pragmatic dreams were a thing of the past. Therefore, I could only want one thing.

"I want to make Agnes happy," I said.

She choked out a wheezing laugh. "You can't. Only he can, and he's gone."

"He might come back as a spirit."

Willemijn grimaced. "I don't believe that's possible."

"Just because you can't see them doesn't mean spirits don't exist. Or do you mean you think Thomas can't become a spirit? I think he might. It just takes time, and the right kind of burial place."

"What's the right kind?"

"A place where human remains don't really decay, like a marsh," I said. "That way, there's something tethering him to the earth. If the body decomposes, a spirit has nothing to keep them together, and they fall apart."

She grasped my hand again. Her grip was weak, her fingers stone-cold. Her eyes gleamed with a manic energy. "Then Thomas won't ever come back, not as long as he lies in the graveyard," she croaked.

The blood buzzed in my ears, and black spots danced in front of my eyes. "What are you saying?" I asked, but I knew already.

She took a shuddering breath and said, smiling all the while, "If you want to bring him back and make Agnes happy again, you shall need to dig up my brother's body and bury him in the bog. Do what must be done."

NINTH CASE EPISODE

PATIENT R—, A CASE STORY: INHABITED BY ANOTHER

(D = DOCTOR, P = PATIENT R—)

NINTH EPISODE, CONDUCTED ON 19 OCTOBER 1954:

Notes to self: Found myself growing frustrated with patient today, which isn't like me. Wish she'd simply tell me what happened. The sooner I know the truth, the better. Heard rumors that the prosecution hired Mr. van Vliet. He has a reputation for tearing defendants to shreds. If I can spare her that, I will. Find myself growing protective of patient.

Must confess I remain torn between the possibility she's mad and she's deceiving us all, though I never caught her in an outright lie before (N.B. she does deflect often). Doesn't help that we are given such little time each day to talk, but mustn't press too much. Must be satisfied she talks to me so readily. God knows they're not all like that. Mustn't forget we are making progress. She trusts me, knows I only want to help.

> **D:** "I'd like you to stop here for a moment, R—."
> **P:** "All right."
> **D:** "I want you to stop because I feel like you are not being honest with me."
> **P:** "I'm sorry."
> **D:** "You're sorry for being dishonest with me?"
> **P:** "No, I'm sorry that you think I am. I'm not. Why do you think that?"

D: "You said it was you who came up with the plan of reburying Mr. K—'s body, but now you're claiming it was Miss K—."

P: "I never said it was me who first thought of it."

D: "But claiming it was Miss K—? I find it impossible to believe that it was she who came up with the outrageous plan of digging up her brother's remains so that they could be thrown into a bog on the off chance he would come back as a spirit. She wouldn't even be able to perceive him. You could have chosen almost anyone else to suggest this plan: yourself, Ruth, Peter, even Mrs. K—, but Miss K—?"

P: "You're wrong, Doctor. W— [Miss K—] was actually the only one who could ever have come up with this plan."

D: "Why is that?"

P: "Because she loved T— [Mr. K—] so much it bordered on the fanatical. There was nothing she wouldn't have done, no lengths she wouldn't have gone to, to restore him to life. He wasn't just a brother to her."

D: "I remain unconvinced."

P: "Is it harder to believe than anything else I've told you so far?"

D: "Yes, because that I can easily explain as the fancies of a mind wounded in childhood, thus disturbing the normal Freudian processes we all go through. But digging up a corpse? I find it hard to believe that even a girl as damaged as you would do something so horrible, and even harder to believe that it was Miss

K— who made you do it. It's madness."

P: "That's what I thought at first, too."

Chapter 18

MY FIRST THOUGHT WAS, SHE'S *mad*.

My second thought was, *She's right.*

But the idea was so abhorrent to me that I balked from it instinctively. "You don't know what you're saying. It's the fever talking. You must rest now."

She clutched at my hand, but I drew it from her grasp easily. "Roos, please. My brother..." she began, but I did not wait for her to choke out the rest of her sentence. I ran to the hallway, and I shut the door behind me with such force, fragments of the wall came down.

My ears rang. I felt the blood drain from my face, and with it the color went from my sight. I sank shuddering against the wall and slumped there for I don't know how long.

When I came back to myself again, Ruth was cupping my face. "My sweet, my little love," she murmured. "You must wake up. It won't be so very long until Agnes and the others return, and then what shall they find?"

In a sudden panic, I ran back to Thomas's room. The scent of the spilled aftershave was cloying; the open window had helped somewhat but also turned the room icy. I placed the contents of the dresser back the way I remembered, then fetched a bucket, hot water, and soap and set to scrubbing the floorboards where the aftershave had begun to impregnate the wood. My nose was so full of the scent that I couldn't tell if I was doing any good.

When I had done the best I could, I fetched Willemijn's clothes and took them to one of the unused bathrooms. There I dumped her clothes along with mine into the tub to soak. With a sponge and a nailbrush, I scrubbed at myself until my skin felt flayed. I didn't want to smell of Thomas. Lastly, I took the jar of pickles and the whiskey glass from where I'd left them and hid them in my room, but not before I had eaten a few pickles, cramming them in my mouth feverishly.

That night I dreamed I was digging up Thomas from his grave.

Yet when the wood of the coffin broke and I shone my torch on it, it was Mr. Mesman who lay inside. He opened his eyes, smiled at me.

"Roos," he said, and his voice was no more than a hoarse whisper because Ruth had ruined his throat, "won't you let me worship you?" Appalled, I stumbled away, but he sat up and threw his arms around me, tried to draw me down into the grave with him.

I fought him. I kicked and screamed. Never again would I be helpless and frozen with fear, never again would my muteness be taken for submission.

A hand clapped over my mouth.

I bit at it like a dog would. I tasted blood, and the taste was so visceral, I had to retch, and the sharp pain in my tongue and stomach grounded me enough to realize that Mr. Mesman was screaming, and he sounded like a woman.

"Fuck!" he said, only he spoke with Agnes's voice.

"Agnes?" I whispered.

The lamp on my nightstand flickered to life and illuminated her face. She was sucking at her hand. "You bit me!" she said, and I saw her lips and teeth were stained with blood so dark, it looked almost black.

Shame twisted my insides. I thought I might well weep with it. Color crept up my throat and face, left patches on my chest. "I thought you were Mr. Mesman."

"Who the fuck is Mr. Mesman?"

But some things can't be talked about. "I'm sorry I bit you. Is it bad?"

"It's not terrible," she said and held out her hand for me to see. My teeth had dented the skin in a neat curved little row, breaking the skin in three places. Blood pearled up. I felt so terribly ashamed, I began to cry.

"I didn't mean to hurt you! I'm so sorry," I gasped. My throat felt small and tight, making the words come out all strangled.

Agnes sat next to me and put an arm around me. "Come now, it's not so bad as all that, now, is it?" she said softly. "Look, the blood is already clotting. By the end of the week, you won't see a thing."

"I bit you like an animal."

"I shouldn't have touched you the way I did. You were having some sort of night terror and lashed out. I should've understood. I have nightmares at times, too."

She stroked soft little lines on the nape of my neck. For a moment, my consciousness seemed to leave my body. Then it settled in that patch of skin she caressed with such tenderness. With every flick of her fingers, she drew out the fear and shame and tension, as if tugging at a thread. She made to move away.

I clasped her hand in both of mine. "Please," I asked, "will you hold me? Just until I feel a little calmer?"

"How do you want to be held?"

"I don't know. I've only ever had Ruth hold me, but she's stone-cold," I confessed.

"Then I'll show you," Agnes said.

She climbed into bed with me. She lay on her back. I nestled against her side, my head on her shoulder. She put her arm around me and traced little figures on my back. I didn't know what to do with my hand, but she took it in hers and placed it on the flat hard bit of her chest. My fingertips touched the bit of skin above her nightgown, all warm and soft. She was hard in some places—the jut of her hip bone against my thigh, the ridge of bone in the middle of her chest—but sweet and soft in others; on either side of my hand, I could feel the swell of her breasts, and it was a marvel to me how alike we were and yet so different. Already it was hard to imagine the terror that had gripped me moments before.

"Will you tell me something?" I murmured.

"What should I tell?"

"Anything. I like to hear you talk."

"I don't have anything interesting to tell you."

"Everything you say is interesting to me."

It took her so long to begin talking that I thought she had fallen asleep. But no, her breathing hadn't turned deep and slow; if anything, it was rather quick and shallow, as if something had excited or frightened her. She took my hand lying on her chest and moved the fingertips a little under the lacy edge of her nightgown. The skin was no longer soft and smooth there but hard and uneven. The scar ran the length of my finger.

"It's a stem with leaves, do you feel?" she whispered.

"I think so."

"You can't see now, but in a certain light, it looks almost silver."

"What can make such a scar?"

"A silver candlestick."

I imagined someone pressing a candlestick against Agnes's breast in much the same way one imprints hot wax with a seal. I imagined her gasp—the pain would not arrive straightaway, but when it did, it would be so fierce, it robbed her of breath to scream—imagined the hiss of her skin against the silver, the smell of smoke and burning flesh.

"Who dared do that to you?" I asked. *Who must I hate? Who must I destroy?*

She uncurled my fingers. Without realizing, I had balled my hands into fists. "I did," she said softly. "After my first week at boarding school."

I propped myself up so I could look into her face. The nightlight bathed one half of it in an orange glow, plunged the other into darkness. "Why did you do that?"

Agnes swallowed. The movement caused shadows to flicker over her throat like spidery fingers. "I wanted to blot out my feelings, but they were so strong that only something grand and terrible would do."

"You took a silver candlestick from the altar and burned yourself?"

"Exactly."

"Did it work?"

"Only for a little while. When the worst pain was gone, I felt sad again, and sick and ashamed and angry. Normal girls didn't burn themselves. No wonder I wasn't wanted. Self-mutilation didn't help, so I didn't try it again. A relief to the nuns, I'm sure."

"Mama always said Catholics like pain."

She laughed at that. I felt it vibrate through her chest. "And Protestants don't, with their constant anguish about whether God has handpicked them to be saved before they were born?"

I shrugged. "I don't know. Mama never took me to church. It wouldn't surprise me if I wasn't even baptized."

"And yet if we asked people to find the heathen, they'd be more likely to pick me than you. Funny how that works." She stroked the scarred skin between my thumb and index finger. "How did this happen, hm?"

"It's silly, not worth talking about," I murmured and made to pull away.

She clutched my hand, not enough to hurt but enough to make me stop. "Please, Roos, just tell me," she said softly.

I looked at Ruth swaying from the ceiling so I didn't have to look at Agnes. "I used to bite myself when I was frightened."

She placed my hand back on the scar on her chest. "Self-inflicted then, like mine."

"Aren't we alike?"

"Both rather damaged," she said softly.

"Only a little."

I felt the hard ridges of her skin, the sudden soft patches of flesh that lay unscarred between the twisted fronds. My finger found a vein, and I felt the blood stutter through it. Lying next to Agnes was very different from lying next to Ruth; she was much warmer, far less bony.

More pleasant, I thought, then felt a stab of guilt for thinking that. I felt safe with Ruth, didn't I? But then, I felt safe with Agnes, too.

"It wasn't all bad at boarding school, you know," she said. "Yes, the girls ignored me even though I'd completed their challenge, but I learned a lot there. Sister Bernadette taught me how to play the piano, and when she saw how it enraptured me, she made sure I could play it every day. There was Peter, too, of course, and when the whole boarding school affair was done, the Rozentuin. I don't want you to think all I ever lived through was misery."

"I don't think that."

"Funny. I don't think I've ever told anyone that story before."

I did not ask about Thomas, but there was no need. Her words had conjured him, and he lay hard and cold in the bed with us. We were quiet then, this soured quietness in which I desperately tried to think of a way to make things like they had been before. I still hadn't figured it out when we heard the deep hacking coughs of Willemijn through the wall separating the rooms. Agnes stood. "There, all better now. Sleep well, Roosje," she said. She went to the door, hesitated, then came back to give my neck a little squeeze.

Long after she had gone, I still felt her fingers upon my nape.

Chapter 19

THE MONTHS TURNED.

By the end of January, the effect of a few weeks of good food became apparent. Sometimes I undressed and stood myself in front of the full-length mirror in my room, and then I'd study the changes in me. My belly sloped; my breasts and buttocks had swollen and could now easily fill a hand. The thick down that had covered my skin had gone away, and though there was something to be said about having the texture of a peach, I found I preferred to be without so much fuzz.

I loved that I no longer looked like a child, but most of all I loved that my body didn't hurt so much anymore. My hip bones no longer stuck out like blades and made it painful to wear tight waistbands. My spine was no longer a ridge that grew sore if I rested it against the back of a chair for more than a few minutes. I was no longer cold all the time either.

My morning walks and afternoon cleaning meant I had finally built up some muscle, too. I could lift buckets full of soapy water now without my arms screaming, could walk briskly without growing faint. When I'd still lived with Mama, I had often been so tired, I could do very little. Now I had so much energy, it would have been frightening if it had not been so delightful.

These changes meant I had to let out my clothes at the seams, which had begun to strain and chafe. Each night as Agnes conversed with Mrs. van Leeuwen, I sat sewing by the light of a strong lamp. Sometimes Agnes would rest a hand on my shoulder as she bent over me to look at my work. "Fairy stitches," she'd marvel and give my neck another friendly squeeze, which drew the heat into my cheeks with such force, it felt as if I were being burned.

Agnes was free with her affection. She brought me little things to eat throughout the day; she took my hand and toyed with it during meals; she came to kiss me good night when I went to bed. I truly think I wasn't aware that I had a body before I met Agnes. I had felt things before, of course: hunger and cold and pain, all the small degradations of the body. Those were things to be ignored, and if they were too sharp to be ignored, they were to be borne.

With Agnes, my body no longer was an inconvenience to be brutalised into submission. It was as if she had woken me from a deep slumber with that lover's kiss at the séance. Is it any wonder that I loved her, that I wanted her to be happy? And to make her happy, I would have to dig up Thomas and tuck his body into the bog so he could be restored to her as a spirit. The more I thought about it, the more sense it began to make. A dreadful sense, yes, but sense nonetheless.

Still, I don't think I would have actually done it, had Agnes not revealed to me why she had brought me home with her.

———————

That day I was woken by Agnes playing the piano, and I knew something wasn't right. Normally, she played with the soft pedal pushed down to keep the volume at a minimum, but now the music rang through the house, shrill and strange.

When I went to her room to see what was wrong, Peter stood waiting in front of her door. Although he was so tall, his head brushed the ceiling when he stood upright, that morning he put me in mind of a little boy. He stood with hunched shoulders and a hanging head, like a dog who had been kicked by its master and waited to be forgiven. Spirits do not cry, but today his eyes were two wet caverns.

"Peter, are you all right?" I asked.

"Agnes is not well today," he said, and his voice was the low hum of a hundred insects.

I took one of his fingers in my hand and gave it a little squeeze. "I shall check on her then, shan't I?" I said and knocked on Agnes's door. She went to open it with such quick angry steps that I thought she might hit me.

"What?" she snapped, and her scowl did not soften when she saw it was me.

I swallowed. "Are you all right? Peter…"

She looked at him over my shoulder with a look of such hatred that I felt my mouth go dry. "Get out of my sight. You're the last thing on earth I want to see today," she spat.

He closed his eyes and shuddered.

She looked at me. "As for you: I want to be left alone today."

She slammed the door. After a minute or so, the music began again, wild and angry and discordant.

I worried my bottom lip between my teeth until I tasted blood. Ruth slipped her hand into mine. "Whatever it is that has her acting so, let her stew in it," she said.

But I couldn't let it go so easily. In my mind's eye, I kept seeing her face contorted by hatred, kept hearing her snap at me, and the more I thought about that, the bigger these things seemed to grow.

I didn't know what I'd done wrong, but clearly Agnes was upset with me. Otherwise she wouldn't have told me to leave her alone. If she was mad with me, she might come to dislike my presence. Worse, she might regret that she'd ever brought me here.

After all, what use was I to her?

She had said she'd like a companion, but I wasn't smart or educated. I couldn't speak Javanese or English, and though I could learn if I put my mind to it, there was no need: she had Mrs. van Leeuwen and Willemijn. I tried my best to clean the Rozentuin, but a little maid might have done that just as well and at half the cost, what with all the food I ate and the clothes Agnes had to buy for me, not to mention the money she had paid Mama to take me away in the first place. I was a lousy nurse besides, not in the least because Willemijn scared me.

In short, it was more than likely that Agnes had come to regret bringing me here. It was as Mama had said: she'd tire of me, and then she'd want to get rid of me. Maybe she'd even go so far as to bring me back to Mama and ask for her money back since I'd proven such a bad investment.

As I ate lunch and ate it alone—when I had asked Mrs. van Leeuwen where Agnes was, she'd told me she had asked for a tray in her room—I imagined what it would be like to be back with Mama. Much the same as before, I supposed. Starvation and cold and degradation, all much harder to bear because I had it so good with Agnes.

Already I could see Mama's gloating face. "Look, if it isn't Miss High-and-Mighty, come crawling back. I told you this is how it would be, didn't I?" And she'd squeeze my shoulder before telling me to change, that she had kept one of my old dresses and I might be able to squeeze into it. "I always knew you'd run to fat if I'd let you. But not to worry. You'll still fit in the space under the floorboards."

Darkness.

My limbs cramping from being folded in so small a space.

The smell of mold and damp.

And she might not let me out for a long time, just to show me who's in charge. She'd keep me in there for so long, I'd think she had forgotten about me, and maybe she had, or maybe she did remember, but this was my punishment for leaving her, and *I will die in there, I will hunger and thirst until my tongue swells up to thrice its size and I bite it in half in a moment of madness, or the walls might collapse, and I'll choke to death on black earth, and I will die, I will die, I will die…*

I burst into Agnes's room, interrupting the mournful tune she was playing. Startled, she looked up at me. "What is it? Has something happened?" she asked and came to her feet.

"Please," I begged. "Please don't be mad at me anymore. Please don't make me go back to Mama. I'll do anything, but don't send me back."

I fell at her feet and clasped her ankles, rested my forehead against her knees. I was shaking so hard, I felt as if I might break a bone. The satin of her skirt was soft against my cheek, and from its folds rose the scent of her body.

"Please don't ever make me go away," I whispered.

She made me look up at her. Her eyes were of the deepest black, the lashes thick and short. Her hands were soft and warm against the sides of my face, and though the kneeling hurt my knees, it was bliss to sit as I did, enveloped in her warmth and scent.

"Never, never," she promised. She drew me up and kissed me to seal her promise, and so deep was that kiss, so sweet, that first I shuddered, then she did.

"Oh," I breathed. She brushed her thumb over my bottom lip, kissed me again. The soft touch of her lips against mine made my blood quicken. Heat crawled up my spine, flooded my brain, and it was like being possessed.

Suddenly, Agnes drew away from me. "We mustn't, oh, Roos, we really mustn't," she said. She came to her feet, went to the window, clasped the sill with such force, the blood drained from her knuckles. Her shuddering breaths clouded the glass.

I still felt the ghost of her mouth on mine, of her hand so easily placed against my nape, the fingers against my scalp. Those places burned, but the rest of me grew icy now that I was bereft of her touch and warmth.

"What did I do wrong?" I asked.

Agnes said nothing. A gust of rain against the pane made her flinch.

A pain crept up my throat. Instinctively, I laid my hand against it. "Agnes?" I asked, and I sounded weak and small and pitiful.

She whipped around. "God, must I explain everything to you? I can't, not after Thomas!" She stooped to pick up a pair of shoes, crammed them on her feet.

"Where are you going?" I asked.

"Out!" She grabbed her coat from a chair and slammed the door behind her. I heard her run down the stairs and slam the front door, then all was quiet.

I began to cry, softly at first, then with gulping sobs I tried to stifle behind my hands. I had tried to make things right, but all I had done was anger Agnes further. Ruth threw her arms around me and guided my face to her shoulder. I pressed my mouth against the hard line of her collarbone. Occasionally, she wiped the tears from my face and sucked them from her fingers; spirits have a love for salt, be it blood or be it tears.

After a while, she made me look at her. "I shall hurt her for this," she said.

"No, no!"

"I shall. She has made my beloved weep, and for that she must pay."

"Please, Ruth, no!"

"I must protect you. I must, I must…" She trembled so hard, her ruined jaw clicked rapidly, as if she were composing a message in Morse code. I held her tight. She was scarecrow thin today, her shoulder blades poking out like wings, her ribs jutting out. I stroked her long red hair, kissed the damp flesh of her cavernous cheeks.

"You're not going to hurt anyone." I soothed her.

"But you want me to. Sometimes you want me to. Don't deny it."

"Not today, Ruth. Today I want you to be with me and not think dark thoughts. I've got too many of my own already. Mama, the space underneath the floorboards... I need you to keep them at bay for me."

I rocked her to the rhythm of the rain splashing on the house until the trembling stopped. The odd thing was that caring for Ruth soothed my fears and self-hatred. I wasn't utterly locked in my own head anymore.

I blew my nose and wiped the dried salt from the corners of my eyes. Once in my room, I stepped into my boots, laced them up.

"What are you doing?" Ruth asked. Her reedy voice was hoarse with emotion. Nervously, she plucked at the piece of rope she wore knotted tightly around her throat, the same piece someone had used many years ago to strangle her by degrees.

"Going after Agnes."

"Perhaps she wants to be alone."

"Perhaps, but with this weather, it'll be better if she's inside. And I must do whatever I can to look after her. I must be useful to her, somehow."

As soon as I stepped outside, the rain drummed on my umbrella, drowning out the squelching of my boots. My breath streamed in plumes from my mouth and nose. A drop of water ran down my wrist and into my sleeve, which made my hairs rise.

It didn't take long to find Agnes, but then I'd had a good idea where she might be. I found her kneeling at Thomas's grave, dirtying her stockings and ruining her shoes. She was ripping apart a crocus between her fingers, releasing the sharp green smell of its sap. I stood next to her, held the umbrella over her to shelter her from the rain.

"You could've spared yourself the trouble," she said, glancing up at the umbrella. "I'm already sopping wet."

"I'm sorry," I said.

"I didn't mean to shout at you just now. I've not been myself today. It's been exactly a year since Thomas died."

Of course, I thought and felt stupid for not having realized it before. "I'm sorry," I said.

"You don't have to apologize."

"I'm sorry."

She dropped the pieces of crocus, ripped another one from the soil. "You know, you're like a dog sometimes, Roos. You get kicked, and then you trail after the person who kicked you with your tail between your legs, trying to apologize and be forgiven, as if it were somehow right for them to kick you, when really you're only a little dog."

The pain rose again in my throat. "I don't mean to be like that," I said.

"I know. I understand. I could be like that too with my husband. He wasn't a good man, you know. He could be domineering, jealous, vindictive, narrow-minded, at times even cruel. Possessive, too. Often, I think it is a good thing he's gone, even though I loved him, though I did so in an ugly manner, violently and entirely. But then I remember that, in his own fucked-up little way, he loved me, really loved me, and for a girl like me, with no one in the world to call my own, that's not a small thing."

But you do have someone to call your own! You have me now, me! my heart cried. I swallowed those words, buried them deep within me.

"Do you want him back?" I asked, and I couldn't help that my voice quavered.

She didn't answer but instead doubled over as if in pain, pressed her hands into the wet earth. Mud squelched between her fingers.

"I can't, I can't!" She sobbed.

I understood everything then: why she had been overjoyed to find someone who could see spirits, why she had bought me from Mama and taken me into her home. She wanted Thomas to be restored to her, and she needed me to do it for her because she didn't know how. Even if she had known, I was sure she couldn't do it herself. It would be too horrible for her.

But not for me.

This, then, was my purpose.

I dropped the umbrella and drew her into my embrace. I had expected she might resist, but instead she melted into me, her dirty hands clawing at the back of my coat, leaving gray slimy streaks. "I'm going to make it all right," I promised her.

TENTH CASE EPISODE

PATIENT R—, A CASE STORY: INHABITED BY ANOTHER

(D = DOCTOR, P = PATIENT R—)

TENTH EPISODE, CONDUCTED ON 21 OCTOBER 1954:

D: "Remind me again why you thought this plan would work."

P: "Because the spirit falls apart like the body does. Spirits take time to wake. If the body has been annihilated before that time, the spirit disintegrates. But if the spirit wakes and the body has been preserved in some way, then the spirit survives. It's like those spiritualists said: spirits are shackled to the earth, though not only by the nature of their deaths, but by the survival of their bodies. That's why there are so very few of them."

D: "There is something I don't quite understand yet. Why, exactly, was it so important to you that Mr. K— become a spirit?"

P: "I've told you already. A— [Mrs. K—] wanted him back."

D: "Then why didn't she just do it herself?"

P: "She couldn't. That's why she had taken me in: so I could help her with this."

D: "Yet a little while ago you told me Mrs. K— was selfless and took care of you out of the goodness of her heart. Why did you change your mind about that?"

P: [*silence*]

D: "R—?"

P: "I didn't believe she could love me without wanting anything in return, but then I also believed she and her husband had the perfect marriage. That just goes to show how wrong I was, doesn't it?" [*begins to cry softly*]

Chapter 20

THAT NIGHT I DREAMED ONE of my Ruth dreams and woke with the smell of peat in my nose. I took this as a sign that I had made the right decision.

"That's all very well," Ruth said, rubbing away the little crust of salt that had gummed my lashes together in sleep, "but how on earth are you ever going to get it done? You're not strong enough to dig up a body and move it by yourself. Digging up a coffin is the work of a few strong men, not one scrawny girl. And how are you going to get it done without being caught? Grave robbing is a punishable offense."

I took hold of her hand and kissed the shriveled mound at the base of her thumb. "I'm growing stronger every week, and there's still time to figure out all the rest. Besides, I'm not going to do it all by myself, now, am I? I've got you."

"You flatter me," she said and gave my hand a hard squeeze.

Still, Ruth had some good points. I needed to prepare everything and prepare it well. There could be no second chances. I walked from the graveyard to the bog several times to see how far it was and to find the best place to rebury Thomas. To get to the bog, I had to leave the estate and cross the main road, which was used by farmers living nearby to get to town.

It was therefore important to get Thomas to the bog in one piece or at least not lose any bits near that main road and risk them being found and the whole thing discovered. The police would get involved then, and they'd inevitably pay the Rozentuin a visit and force Agnes to talk about her husband. This I had to prevent at any cost. Thomas was still too painful a topic for Agnes.

But Willemijn was a different story. The whole thing had been her idea, and though she frightened me, Agnes's happiness was more important than my personal feelings. One morning, as Agnes was going over the Rozentuin's accounts, I slipped into Willemijn's room and told her I was going to rebury her brother to maximize his chances of coming back as a spirit.

She looked at me with her skull's face, then smiled. "I see. And how exactly are you going to do it?"

I rubbed the scar on my hand. "I hoped you might help me with that. I've gone to the bog several times now, so I think I should be able to find my way even when it's dark, but I'm not sure how I'm going to manage to dig up Thomas's coffin all by myself, let alone carry him those few miles."

"You haven't asked Agnes for help, have you? Because that would be most unwise."

I shook my head. "No. I don't think she could bear to see his body. I don't want her to think about it either. It would be too painful. I won't tell her a single thing."

Her smile broadened. "That's good of you, Roos. Very smart, very thoughtful. These things are distasteful, aren't they? And so much better to have it all be a surprise to her. That way, you won't raise her hopes only to dash them when it doesn't work after all. Now, I've been reading about all this. You needn't lift out the whole coffin. You need only unearth the top of the coffin and throw the earth down on the opposite end. The weight of the earth will crack the wood, and then you can drag the body out with a hook."

She mimed pulling something up with a jerky motion, then looked at me and smiled. "It's what the resurrection men used to do. And you forget my brother has been dead for a year now. He won't weigh so very much anymore. All you need to do is wrap him in a sheet. That way, you won't lose anything on the way to the bogs. You could place his remains in a wheelbarrow so you don't have to carry him all the way."

I looked at her in astonishment. "You've thought it all through, haven't you?"

"When you're as ill as I am, there's little else you can do but think. Now, you'll need the key to the front door if you want to slip out at night." She handed me her copy of the key. It lay heavy in my hand, slightly tarnished.

"Thank you," I said.

"You'll need to collect some tools, too," she went on. "Do you need me to make a list?"

I shook my head. "Thank you. I think I'll manage."

Ruth regarded me with big black eyes. "When, I wonder," she

whispered with her reedy voice, "did it become inevitable you dig up Thomas?"

"Hush, you," I said and set out to find the tools Willemijn had described to me. I found a shovel, a crowbar, a ladder, some wooden planks, and a wheelbarrow in the garden shed as well as a pair of waders. From the icehouse, a little square building once used to store meat, I took a meat hook so I could drag Thomas out of his coffin. I took two pairs of mice-nibbled sheets from the linen cupboard in the servants' quarters and an old uniform that I could get dirty with impunity. Willemijn gave me a little lamp to light my way. All that done, I only needed to wait for the right sort of night. It couldn't have rained, or the earth would turn to mud and show my tracks and make it impossible to push the wheelbarrow. It couldn't have been freezing, or I'd never manage to dig Thomas up.

In the end, I only had to wait two weeks.

Chapter 21

I KNEW IT WOULD BE the right night the moment I got up. Though the wind still carried the bite of frost, the air itself felt mellow. I spent the morning walking the stretch between the graveyard and the bog several times, just so it would all be fresh in my mind. After lunch, I checked the tools I had gathered and racked my brains for anything I might have forgotten.

Still, there was only so much I could prepare.

The rest of the day, I simply had to wait. Time crawled. From nerves, I rubbed at the scars on my hand till they bled.

"Roos, what is it?" Agnes asked me during dinner.

I dropped my fork, flushed. "Nothing."

"Then why are you so nervy? Did something happen?"

"I'm just feeling a bit under the weather," I lied.

"Then you must have an early night, you poor thing," she said, so I had no other option but to go to bed while she and Willemijn were still up. At one point, Agnes came to check on me. I pretended to be asleep. She brushed the hair from my forehead, whispered my name. A delicious thrill ran through me. I opened my eyes, smiled at her.

"You feel a bit hot," Agnes told me. "Here, I've brought you something. If you're feeling ill, you must make sure you eat and drink enough. Your body needs it." She had brought me a bit of soft cake and a hot drink of water and sugar. Under her watchful gaze, I ate and drank. When I was finished, she smiled at me and briefly gave my neck a squeeze again. "Your hair is getting long. We must cut it soon. Now sleep well."

I lay in bed after that, staring at the ceiling, my stomach making little happy flips. I listened to Agnes play the piano for a little while, listened to her tend to Willemijn when she called. After she got into bed, it was just the house creaking around me and the wardrobe groaning as the damp made the wood expand. I waited for at least an hour before I got up and dressed in the darkness, putting on a maid's old uniform. I had to be very quiet; Willemijn's illness had made a light sleeper out of Agnes.

With every moan from the floorboards, every whisper from the drafts roaming through the house, I tensed, the blood buzzing in my ears, certain she would switch on the lamp on her nightstand and get up to see what was going on. But either she was more tired than I had thought, or I was quieter than I gave myself credit for, because I made it out of the house undetected.

I collected the tools from the garden shed and made my way to the graveyard.

How different it looked by night! The moonlight made the tombstones pale as chalk. I made a brief detour to the little plot where the stillborn babies were buried and left some narcissi on their graves; I thought the buttery yellow might bring them joy. I kissed the stone marking the resting place of Agnes's baby, then walked to Thomas's grave.

Once there, I spread out one of the two sheets and began to dig. The earth was soft and sticky. I threw each clod on the outspread sheet so I could dump all of it back easily once I was done. Soon, the muscles in my arms and back and shoulders felt tight and sore.

Blisters sprang up on my palms, making me wince every time I pushed the shovel back into the earth. The night was cold, but I felt burning hot. My mouth turned dry as paste. I hadn't thought to bring any water, and for that I cursed myself now.

Yet despite the pain and discomfort, I fell into a rhythm. I pushed the shovel down with my foot. I tilted it, lifted it out. I threw the earth on the sheet, where it landed with a slithering thud. I aimed the shovel at the next spot. I pushed the shovel down with my foot. I tilted it, lifted it out.

After a while, I had to stand in the pit I'd dug to continue digging. I had to lift the shovel high whenever the blade was loaded with earth, making my shoulders and upper arms scream. "Oh, Ruth, I'm going to be wicked sore tomorrow," I whispered.

She wiped the sweat from my brow. "Let me help. Let me bear it for a little while."

I let her in. It had been a long time since she'd possessed me, but it was something that, once learned, you never forgot how to do, like riding a bike. She picked up the shovel, began to dig. On and on she dug, and we fell into the rhythm again of the soft silky sounds of the shovel and earth.

Soon, we were surrounded by walls of earth. It was a good thing

Ruth had taken possession of me then. Standing in a grave was eerily similar to hiding in the space underneath the floorboards, but these walls were not supported and might cave in and bury us. It was dark besides. Had her grip on me not been so firm, I might have panicked.

When she hit the coffin, the impact juddered up my arms. I coughed Ruth up. She took my face between her spidery hands. "Keep your wits about you," she said.

I nodded, lay my hand on hers for a moment.

With the shovel I exposed the contours of the coffin. I had feared it might be a lacquered affair, the wood inches thick, but it was really rather plain, the wood stained from a year underground. I ran my hand over it, hissed as a splinter bit into my palm and made one of my blisters weep.

Ruth gripped my hand, plucked out the splinter, and sucked at the blister.

"The wood has started to rot," I told her as I stroked her cheek with my thumb.

"Then you won't need to pile on too much earth to get it to crack."

"Thank God for small blessings."

"Not God: nature and its tendency to decay."

Using the wooden planks I had brought, I sectioned off the bottom of the coffin. I climbed out of the grave. Next I grabbed the edges of the sheet, lifted it until the mound of earth shifted and clods began to rain down. Then, because I was afraid the whole mound would slide down and undo all my hard work, I used the shovel and threw down little measured heaps.

It didn't take long for the wood to splinter. I stopped heaping earth on the bottom of the coffin, wiped the sweat from my brow and held the lamp high. Through one of the cracks, I could glimpse the collar of a shirt, all yellow.

I paused. I felt thoroughly chilled. A drop of sweat ran into my eye. I rubbed at it, but that just made it sting more.

"What is it, my little love?" Ruth whispered.

"I'm afraid of what he'll look like," I confessed. Despite conversing with the dead for as long as I could remember, I had never seen a corpse before. I didn't have the faintest idea what Thomas would look like. He could be a collection of bones and dust. He could look very much the same as the day he'd died. He could be anything in between. After all, this graveyard was close to the bogs, so who knew what properties the soil here held?

"Then let me do it. I'm not afraid," Ruth said.

I shook my head. "Some things I must do myself."

With the crowbar I carefully pulled away bits of wood. I winced at every creak, every groan. From the coffin came a strange musty smell. I pressed my mouth to the inside of my arm and coughed.

"Look!" Ruth whispered.

My hands tightened around the crowbar until I felt my heartbeat in every fluid-filled blister. I turned to him and looked. Relief made me want to laugh. He wasn't as frightening as I had feared. In fact, he wasn't frightening at all. With his sunken cheeks, taut yellow skin and dried-up eyes, he looked like Peter and Ruth. I had never found them frightening, and they could do far more harm than Thomas could, so why should I be scared of him now?

"Good evening, Mr. Knoop. My name is Roos Beckman," I said because it seemed only polite to introduce myself. I took hold of his hand, the skin dry and slightly brittle. My fingers brushed the cold face of his watch. Not his favorite, not the one engraved *For Tom from A*, which rested on its saucer upstairs, kept there by Agnes, who could not bear to have him buried with it.

"I'm sorry to have disturbed you, but I need to dig you up and put you in the bog so you can come back as a spirit. Agnes really wants you to, and I'd do anything to make Agnes happy."

I draped my handkerchief over his face to keep it somewhat safe as I continued to remove more wood. When I felt I had created an opening large enough to pull him out, I grabbed the meat hook. I had blunted the tip so I wouldn't accidentally impale him with it. I pushed it into a hole in his suit and tried to drag him out that way, but the cloth tore, exposing a shoulder blooming with green mold. I tried again, hooking it under his shoulder, but he groaned so much that I was afraid I'd pull him apart. I had no choice but to shovel out all the earth I had dumped back in and pry the lid off.

"So much for Willemijn and her ideas," Ruth remarked.

"I guess some things can only be learned through experience," I said through gritted teeth as I threw handfuls of earth out of the grave. When I had finally managed to expose his entire body, I had to sit down on the edge of the coffin and rest for a while. My stolen uniform stuck to my body. I drew the collar from my neck, and it let go with a soft sucking sound. I scraped my teeth over my furred tongue, spat. I was so thirsty that it dulled the pain in my muscles and hands.

Ruth blew on the burst skin of my palms to cool them. "When you're done, you must disinfect these blisters. All kind of filth has gotten into them."

"I should've brought gloves. I'll remember that next time," I said and laughed, though more from nerves than anything else. Afraid I might go into hysterics after all, I came to my feet and set about finishing what I had started. I placed my hands under Thomas's armpits and heaved. He was not as heavy as I had expected, but my arms still strained to lift him. His size made him unwieldy. I was glad Willemijn had suggested I bring a wheelbarrow; I could never have carried him to the bog. I couldn't even carry him up the ladder.

Instead, I bound ropes around him, clambered up and lifted him out that way. I placed him on the other spread-out sheet. He was smeared with mud and earth now. I tried to wipe it from his rotting clothes and face, but all that did was make his ear fall off, taking a good chunk of skin with it.

"I am so sorry," I murmured, appalled. I bound my handkerchief around his head to keep the ear in place. The back of his skull had already been wrapped with bandages, so at least I didn't have to worry that whatever was left of his brains would fall out.

I wrapped the sheet around him like a shroud and lifted him into the wheelbarrow. His body had become rather rigid during the past year, so he wouldn't fold into it nicely, but with a bit of rope, he'd stay in place as I pushed the wheelbarrow toward the bog. I tore off a bit of the sheet and bandaged my hands as well as I could before removing my tools and the planks from the grave.

That done, I dumped the earth back in and patted it all down the best I could.

In a fit of inspiration, I placed the shovel under Thomas, the blade supporting his head. The terrible image of his head jolting loose from his neck as we made our way to the bog had suddenly popped into my mind.

The journey to the bog proved far harder than I had imagined. The wheelbarrow had a faulty wheel, or perhaps it had become unbalanced with Thomas bound to it, but it had the tendency to run to the left. I had to use all my strength to keep it going in a straight line, causing the muscles in my side and arms to become sore within moments.

Near the main road, I hit a rock in the dark, causing the wheelbarrow to tip sideways. Thomas's arm scraped over the ground as I struggled to right the thing. When I took his hand in mine to apologize, I found the skin was horribly scraped and some of his nails had gone. I searched for them with the lamp. When I found them, I tucked them into the pocket of his trousers to keep them safe.

Yet despite all this, Ruth and I managed to reach the bog. It smelled of water and rotting plants and wet earth. The wind tugged at tufts of grass, made the dead husks of reed rustle.

"You have to be careful. The ground here is treacherous. One misstep, and you'll sink into the mud up to your crown," Ruth warned me.

I used the shaft of the shovel to test the ground and found a path to the edge of the water. Somewhere a bird called out. It sounded as if it were being strangled.

All the hairs on my body rose.

I untied Thomas from the wheelbarrow. By now my arms had lost their strength to such an extent, I almost dropped him as I lifted him out. The only way I managed to get him to the water was by grabbing him under his armpits and dragging him, which was rather undignified but couldn't be helped. With every tug, a fusty smell rose from his clothes, and his bones and tendons creaked alarmingly. After what seemed like forever, I reached the water. I gently placed him on the ground, then pushed him in, creating beautiful ripples.

He didn't sink.

Instead, he floated.

I pushed him in farther, thinking that perhaps the water was so shallow, he only appeared to be floating but was really resting on the bottom, only when I pushed my hand underneath him, I felt nothing but freezing water lapping at me. I tried pushing Thomas under, but grotesquely, he bobbed back to the surface again after I had let him go.

"He won't sink, Ruth!" I cried.

"Don't panic! Drag him back to shore so he doesn't drift out of reach. Then go and find something to weigh him down."

I did as she suggested. My eyes darted over the squelchy ground to try and find something to wrap into Thomas's shroud to make him sink. I found a big branch, but when I lifted it, the wood turned to pulp in my hands; the branch was as soft as a rotten tooth. I needed a stone, but everywhere I looked, I only saw mud and brown grass and bits of yellow reed, none of it heavy. My heart was hammering so hard, it hurt.

To have come so far, only to risk it all going wrong because Thomas floated…

In a sudden flash of inspiration, I remembered the wheelbarrow. The heavy metal would surely sink. All I needed to do was lift Thomas into it, then roll the thing into the water. Only I was so tired, I could hardly stand, let alone lift Thomas again. I tried, but I kept banging him against the lip of the wheelbarrow, causing two of his fingers to snap off and, I feared, some of his ribs to crack. In the end, I had to throw the wheelbarrow on its side, roll Thomas into it, bind him, then try to lift the whole thing till it stood upright again.

It was so heavy with Thomas's added weight that I couldn't do it. My arms trembled so much with the effort, I feared they might shiver out of their sockets.

"Let me help," Ruth said.

She wrapped her arms around me and pulled. Together we fell back, using our weight to our advantage. The wheelbarrow tottered, then landed neatly on its wheels, spraying foul-smelling mud everywhere. Panting, I wiped my muddy hands on some grass. They felt like raw pieces of steak. I began to push the contraption to the water, but the greedy ground sucked at the wheels like a toothless mouth and made them get stuck. I threw myself against the wheelbarrow to jolt it loose. All I accomplished was bruising my shoulder.

I began to cry then, from frustration and exhaustion both.

Ruth wiped the tears from my face. "My sweet, my love, let me help you."

"What's the use? You can possess me, but this body won't change. I'm not strong enough. I was stupid to think I could do this. I'm just a pathetic, stupid little girl."

"Let me bear the pain and the weariness for you then, if only for a little while." She placed kisses all over my face, little icy nips. I hugged her, rested my face into the curve of her collarbone. My eyes burned. If only I could rest them for a bit, I might feel better.

"You mustn't go to sleep," Ruth murmured.

"But I'm so tired…"

"I know, but you can't go to sleep. Come, get to your feet. I've got an idea that might just work. If you dig a little furrow into the mud for the wheels, you might be able to push the wheelbarrow into the bog after all."

Wearily I hoisted myself up and stood swaying like a drunkard. Ruth steadied me. Afraid I might not be able to get up again if I sat down now, I used my fingers to draw lines in the mud toward the water. With my feet I scraped some of the worst mud away from the wheels, then tried to push the thing forward again. The ground was so soft, my feet slipped. I scrabbled for purchase, gritted my teeth, shoved against the wheelbarrow.

"Come on, Thomas, you bastard!" I screamed.

Suddenly, the wheelbarrow shot forward. I fell to my knees, mud splattering against my face. I grabbed the handles to help myself up, pushed forward. Slowly but surely, the wheelbarrow with Thomas tied on top began to roll toward the water. Occasionally, I had to deepen the rut I had made, but at least the thing was moving. It was easiest once I reached the water's edge because the ground there sloped. Softly, the water lapped at the front wheel, then the metal tray. It reached Thomas's feet and washed the caked-on mud from his heels.

I was up to my ankles in it now, and though my galoshes had managed to keep out water and mud, they didn't keep out the cold; my toes were numb with it. None of that mattered as long as I managed to rebury Thomas. Only a little farther now...

The wheelbarrow, Thomas, and I went in so quickly, I didn't even have time to catch my breath. One moment I was slowly pushing him to his watery grave, and the next, I was submerged in water so cold and dirty, it burned my eyes and nose. I began to kick and flail. My hand hit something hard, probably the wheelbarrow. Pain shot up my arm. I screamed, swallowed water. I fought my way to the surface. I came up gasping and spluttering.

"Take my hand!" Ruth screamed. She lay on her belly and reached out a hand the exact shade of the bog swallowing me. I tried to take hold of it, but as soon as she touched me, the pain was so intense, I pulled back instinctively. Again, I went under, cold water filling my mouth and nose. I thrashed wildly, then somehow managed to kick my way up.

This time, Ruth grabbed the collar of my stolen uniform and, with a tremendous heave, managed to drag half of me onto firmer ground.

I coughed, retched. Muddy water sprayed from my mouth. I had nothing to wipe my tongue and lips on; I was covered in mud and reeking bits of rotting plant from sole to crown. I inched forward bit by bit until my legs and feet were no longer submerged in water. Then I flopped onto my back and lay panting, staring at the sky.

Clouds had come in from the sea, extinguishing the light of the stars and moon.

Ruth curled up against me, shivering with fright. She tried to clasp my hand, but the burning pain made me cry out. Tears leaked from my eyes.

"I think you've broken your hand," she said.

"I think so, too. A small price to pay, though. I almost became a little Ruth before my time, and all for a man I've never met." I wheezed.

"If Agnes isn't grateful for all you've done for her tonight, I won't answer for my actions," she said, and then we both had to laugh at the absurdity of the situation.

When I finally managed to get up so I could begin to make my way back to the Rozentuin, there was no trace of Thomas. The water had swallowed him whole and lay still as a silver salver.

ELEVENTH CASE EPISODE

PATIENT R—, A CASE STORY: INHABITED BY ANOTHER

(D = DOCTOR, P = PATIENT R—)

ELEVENTH EPISODE, CONDUCTED ON 22 OCTOBER 1954:

D: "Before we continue, I'd like to ask you a few questions about Miss K—. Firstly, what did you think of her?"

P: "I pitied her. She was very ill."

D: "Did that make her ill-tempered?"

P: "Sometimes, when the pain was bad. When it wasn't, I think her illness mainly bored her."

D: "You've said before that you were scared of her."

P: "Yes."

D: "Why was that?"

P: "I sensed she might mean me harm. 'Making mischief,' Ruth called it, though she meant it in the old sense, when mischief still meant something malevolent."

D: "And what sort of mischief might Miss K— make, according to Ruth?"

P: "She didn't know. Neither did I. It was just a feeling."

D: "Yet you still carried out Miss K—'s plan to rebury Mr. K—."

P: "Because I thought it was what A— [Mrs. K—] wanted."

D: "Did it never occur to you that Miss K—'s plan to relocate her brother's remains might be a form of 'making mischief', to use Ruth's words?"

P: [*presses the palms of hands against eyes*] "No. I know

now that I shouldn't have trusted her. I'll have to carry the weight of that knowledge with me for the rest of my life, won't I?"

D: "Is that why you killed her, too?"

P: [*looks at me through fingers, eyes filled with hate*] "If you're going to say things like that, I won't talk to you anymore. In fact, I think I'm done for today."

Part III

"I caught him, yes, I held him—it may be imagined with what a passion; but at the end of a minute I began to feel what it truly was that I held. We were alone with the quiet day, and his little heart, dispossessed, had stopped."

—Henry James, *The Turn of the Screw*

Chapter 22

OF THE WAY BACK, I remember only flashes.

I remember Ruth sucking at my broken hand. I must have cut the skin on the lip of the wheelbarrow's tray as I thrashed about in the water, a mean gash ran from knuckle to knuckle. Because I was so cold, the blood swiftly slowed to a trickle. I held my hand pressed to my chest, using the other one to carry the shovel back to the graveyard; I had to go there to collect the other tools and drag them back to the garden shed.

At some point, it began to rain. I tilted back my head and caught the drops in my mouth, and that made the thirst somewhat more bearable.

Somehow, I arrived at the garden shed. I must have wrapped the tools into the sheet and dragged them behind me, but I've no memory of that. I stripped, having to tear the uniform because I couldn't undo the buttons with one freezing hand. With the dirty sheet, I tried to wipe the worst of the wet and mud from my body. I was shaking so hard from cold that my teeth clicked together, producing much the same sound as Ruth's broken jaw.

Tears blurred my vision, but I was too tired to cry for long. I wrapped the uniform into the sheet and dumped the whole package into the bushes. I'd come back for it later and dispose of it properly.

The next thing I remember is being in the bathroom, doubled up with pain. It felt as if someone were stabbing my insides with a hot knife. I reached the toilet just in time before hot water sprayed out of me. I cleaned that up as well as I could, then clambered into the tub and washed myself with the tap still running. I was so cold that even Ruth felt warm, but gradually the water warmed me. Everything burned then as the blood began to quicken.

The gash that ran the width of my hand started to bleed again, adding a pink tinge to the water. Once out of the tub, I clumsily wrapped bandages around my hand. When I tightened them, the pain was such that I nearly fainted.

After that, everything became rather strange.

I lay in the hole under the floorboards, and no matter how much I pushed against the hatch, it wouldn't open. *They've nailed it shut*, I realized, and began to scream and scream and scream, but though I heard people talking overhead, heard the scrape of their chairs as they settled, no one came to rescue me. I grew cold and weak, but still I screamed. Only when my vocal cords ruptured did I cease. Above me, I heard Mama laugh.

Mr. Mesman and I stood in front of a mirror.

"Witness me transform you into a god," he whispered, his voice rough and damaged. He put his hands around my throat and began to squeeze. The pain was so intense, it drew tears to my eyes, yet I still saw his reflection smirk at me as my face turned first red, then black.

I was in the tuberculosis house, and outside were Hugo Knoop's plaster saints. Whenever I didn't look at them, they crept closer. I spun around till I was dizzy, trying to look at all of them, but the little house had windows all around, and there were so many plaster statues that I couldn't keep them from creeping.

Closer and closer they crept and crawled, until they were pressed against the glass, their lurid faces full of quiet menace. And I saw that one of them wasn't a plaster saint but Thomas's corpse, clambered out of the bog. Behind me, I heard the glass crack. The hairs on my body rose. I whipped around to see, but then the glass broke, and in they came.

And all these things happened to me alone because Ruth was gone, and her absence mutilated me more than anything Mama or Mr. Mesman or any strange evil could ever do to me. I felt I could bear anything, as long as she was there to bear it with me. I felt so alone, I thought I might well die of it.

———

I woke from the pain in my hand. It throbbed, each heartbeat echoing in the swollen flesh. I groaned. My mouth was dry, my tongue coated in plaque. It felt as if a rat had crawled inside and died in there.

"My love, my little sweet, my darling thing, you're awake," Ruth purred. She lay beside me, and the coldness of her body was a delight to me. I flung myself into her arms, relishing the peaty scent rising from the pleats of her dress.

"You were gone." I sobbed. "You had left me."

"I never left your side. It was you who had gone far away from me, in there," she said and touched my forehead. "Now come, you must drink a little, and then rest. You've been very sick."

I drank water from a pitcher on the nightstand, spilling it down my front because I was weak from fever and I could only use one hand, the other one being tightly bandaged. My thirst sated, I sank back against the pillows and twined fingers with Ruth. "You must never leave me again," I murmured, exhaustion slurring my words.

"Never, never," she promised.

The next time I woke, Agnes was there.

She was sitting at my little desk. Before her lay my nail file, the damaged whiskey glass Ruth had begun to grind up, and the bottle of powdered glass. Ruth lay on the carpet, playing with the contents of Agnes's jewelry box.

"You're awake," Agnes said and rushed to me to help me sit up. She filled a glass with water for me and helped me drink, cupping the back of my skull as if I were an infant. "I've put some painkillers in there, which is why it tastes so bitter. I can never swallow pills whole myself—I always have to crush them up. I didn't know if it was the same with you," she said.

Groggily, I rubbed at my sleep-gummed eyes. She dipped her handkerchief in the water and wiped at my eyes until I could open them.

"I stink," I said and felt ashamed.

"Don't worry about any of that. I'll help wash you in a bit. Now, are you hungry?"

I nodded. I was starving.

Agnes fetched me a cup of broth and some bread. I dipped the bread in the broth and wolfed it down. That done, I leaned back against the pillows, winded. I looked at my hand all wrapped up. My knuckles itched. I tried to worm a finger between the bandages to scratch, but they were wrapped too tight, and besides, when I rubbed my knuckles, the pain was such that I let off straight away.

"You mustn't touch it," Agnes said. She was sitting at my desk again, her hands folded in her lap. She looked tired, and her clothes were creased, as if she'd slept in them.

"What happened to me?" I asked.

"You don't remember?"

I remembered I had dug up Thomas and laid him to rest in the bog, but that I couldn't say out loud. Instead, I shrugged. "I went to the bathroom. I felt sick. I think I may have fainted. Then all these strange things happened."

"I think you cut your hand when you fainted, and the wound got infected. The doctor had to come. I've been giving you antibiotics against the infection. You didn't want to take them, and you didn't want to go to sleep either because you were afraid your mama would come to fetch you back when you were asleep, and I'd let her."

She fiddled with the switch of the lamp on my desk. I hadn't seen it before. It was on, the light very faint now that it was day. *She has let it burn throughout the night because she remembered I'm afraid of the dark,* I thought, and felt so full of love for her, I could've choked on it. I felt this intense desire to touch her, like an itch under my skin.

"That sounds like something I'd be afraid of," I said.

"You also talked about plaster saints and bogs, but you mumbled so much, I couldn't make out half the words you said. You don't remember any of that?"

"I don't remember talking to you about it."

"Oh, you were very talkative. It was the fever, of course. You were burning up with it. Ruth held you, and then Peter, but even their cool bodies couldn't force it to break. You were delirious with it."

"Indeed. She accused me of leaving her," Ruth said. She was toying with a little gold necklace, letting the chain slither through her fingers and down into the palm of her other hand. Her eyes were sly slits today, gleaming as golden as the necklace.

"Did I break my hand?" I asked.

"No, you've just badly cut and bruised it."

"I'm sorry. I must've made a lot of work for you. You must've run yourself ragged, tending to me and Willemijn."

"You mustn't think of it like that. You can't blame yourself for getting sick." Agnes touched the damaged whiskey glass, moving her finger along the rim. "Now, you also talked a bit about this. You wanted me to take it out of the drawer, though I'm not sure what you wanted me to do with it. Why do you have this?" she asked, though from the look of pity and compassion on her face, I knew she had already guessed at their significance.

"That's mine," Ruth said. "I like to rub glass to powder. I'm like a magpie. I like shiny things, like Peter likes things dead and shriveled."

Agnes didn't look at her but at me when she asked, "Why do you keep the dust?"

I looked at the knotted scar on my hand, the flesh thick and twisted. Perhaps my other hand would be scarred now, too. "Because they say that if you mix ground-up glass through someone's food, it'll surely kill them without leaving a trace. But I wasn't going to use it. I'm not wicked, and neither is Ruth. It's just that having that bottle at hand and knowing I could use it, well…it made living with Mama more bearable."

"And now? Does it still make life more bearable?"

"I don't need it anymore."

"Then shall I get rid of it for you?"

"I'd rather keep it. Don't worry, I won't use it." I reached my hand out to her beautiful face. It was delicious to touch her, but the itch under my skin did not still. If anything, it intensified. I suppose I was, and continue to be, a hungry thing. "I'll keep it to remind me of what my life used to be like, so I can be grateful that it isn't like that anymore."

"And I still like to rub glass to powder," Ruth said sulkily. "I like to hold the powder to the light and see it sparkle, like ice, like diamonds."

"If you like shiny things so much, feel free to keep that necklace you're playing with, and those pearl earrings, too. I'd rather you toy with those than with glass," Agnes said, and she put the file and the glass and the bottle away, a frown ruffling her brow.

Chapter 23

I HAD TO KEEP TO my bed for the next few days until I had regained my strength. It's strange perhaps, but despite the pain in my hand and the feeling of weakness like a tremble in my bones, those days were very happy. I ate and drank and slept, and when I was doing none of that, I was so restless, I couldn't keep still.

When, I wondered, would Thomas's spirit rise from the bog?

I had an intense feeling of happy anticipation, very much the same as when I was a child and my birthday or Saint Nicholas's day was approaching. Mama had never gotten me much, but our guests had brought me little presents: bars of chocolate, thick woolen socks, a wooden spinning top with bright stripes.

"You need to manage your expectations," Ruth told me. "Don't you know it took me centuries to wake? If Thomas ever becomes a spirit, you and Agnes may well be long dead."

"You're being very pessimistic."

"Not at all. I'm being realistic." She placed the little golden necklace Agnes had given her around my throat.

"I don't know about that, Ruth. And you forget I gave Thomas a good taste of my blood when I cracked my knuckles on the lip of the wheelbarrow. That might wake him if nothing else will. You know like no other how your kind thirsts for blood," I said.

"You've already bound me to you."

"Is there a limit on how many spirits a person can have?"

"I don't know, but I find it distasteful."

Peter often came to sit with me and bring me little gifts. The first time, he held out his cupped hands to me, but when I reached out to take his offering, he pulled back and grinned shyly at Ruth.

"Go on," Ruth said.

Carefully, he placed the skull of some small woodland animal onto my palm. The bone had been bleached a beautiful white.

"Thank you," I said and put it on my nightstand.

His other gifts included a dead butterfly, a piece of quartz, a crow's feather of inky black, several vertebrae small as pebbles, and a piece of glass with its edges worn smooth by wind and rain.

"Peter, how long did it take you to become a spirit?" I asked him after he had given me some coins blooming with verdigris. Ruth had put them in a small empty bottle with a cork stopper and rolled the bottle around on the floor, delighting in the soft chime of the coins against the glass.

"I don't remember," he said. He was sitting on the windowsill, soaking up the brittle sunlight, the mold growing on his throat and shoulders the same color as the blight on the coins. A bee had gotten in and droned around his head for a while, then landed on the soft dimple where his spine and skull met and was still.

"Well, were you awake before Agnes fell asleep on your grave?"

He carefully stroked a fingertip over the bee's fuzzy body as he thought, smoothing down its hairs. I wondered why the bee let him. Perhaps it was attracted to Peter because he was so sweet. "Sometimes I woke, and then I slumbered again," he said finally.

Triumphant, I turned to Ruth. "See?"

She twirled the nail file between her spidery fingers. "That means nothing. He's much older than I am. Maybe spirits are bound to wake at one time or another, and the naming and the blood merely binds us, but it's not what disrupts our slumber. Though you cried loud enough to wake the dead when you cut your hand, little yokemate."

"Agnes cried, too, and then I couldn't sleep anymore," Peter said softly.

"Perhaps we should all scream over Thomas's body then. That's bound to wake him up. Though if Agnes's weeping over his grave didn't do the trick, I wonder if anything will."

"Don't," Peter said sharply.

I looked at him with astonishment. I had never heard him angry before. "She doesn't mean it, Peter," I said.

He left without saying anything.

"Do you think we offended him somehow?" I asked.

She shrugged. "Who knows? I don't pretend to understand him. I don't understand anyone without a sense of humor." She began to file away at the whiskey glass, having spread a piece of paper underneath to catch the grains so she could pour them into her bottle easily.

Every evening, when Willemijn was resting, Agnes changed the bandages around my hand. The flesh around the cut was still puffy and inflamed, but she assured me it looked far better than before. The stitches were an ugly black, pulling the skin taut.

"That cut will turn into a scar, but no permanent damage was done," Agnes assured me. "Speaking of cuts: we must cut your hair. It's getting rather long. If we hurry, we can do it before the light dies away."

Before we could cut my hair, I had to wash first. She helped me with that, pouring water over my head with a pitcher, using her other hand to shield my eyes. A sudden memory came to me then. I was five years old and sat in the tub, Mama behind me. She scooped up water with her hands and let it dribble down my neck and shoulders.

We had folded a boat out of newspaper, and as I blew on it to move it around the tub, the ink had bled purple into the water.

"Did your mother wash you like this?" I asked Agnes.

"No. The apartment we lived in didn't have a tub, just a lavatory we had to share with five other families. We used a bowl of hot water and washcloths instead. In winter, the water took forever to heat up, and it was always tepid by the time we had undressed."

"I'm sorry. Were you very poor?"

"My mother preferred to spend money on other things. Besides, at the time I didn't know any better. It was only after my mother died and I slept in my father's house for a few nights until he could send me to boarding school that I realized not everyone lived like we did. But then that's probably true for a lot of children, don't you think?"

"I always thought other little girls also had to perform séances."

She carefully brushed a bit of soap from my forehead with her thumb. "Did you think they had spirit companions, too?"

"No, somehow I knew I was alone in that."

"Not quite as alone as you thought," she said and drew a quick teasing little line down my neck with her soapy finger.

After I had dried myself and dressed—"Don't put on your shirt just yet, the hair will get in and stick to the fabric and make your neck and back itch,"—Agnes sat me down on a chair, newspaper spread under and around so it would be easy to clean up the cut hair afterward, a towel draped around my shoulders. She combed out my hair, divided it into sections.

"You know, I think your hair has gotten a lot thicker." She took a handful and gave a playful tug.

"It's because you're so good to me," I said.

"How kind you are! You mustn't talk when I start to cut, or I'll cut it unevenly. I always have trouble cutting in a straight line somehow."

For a while we didn't speak. There was only the snipping of the scissors and the little thuds of pieces of hair hitting the spread-out newspaper. When she had cut it all, she wiped the scissors on the towel around my shoulders. "I'll have to shave your neck," she said, and went to fetch a razor.

Some water from my hair dripped down my throat and made me shiver.

"Now, this will only take a minute," Agnes said. She lathered my neck with soap. With decisive strokes, she shaved away the hair that grew on the sides of my neck, and I wondered, had she done this with Thomas? Did she wash his hair for him, then sit him down in a chair near the window so she could cut his hair for him and shave his throat?

I closed my eyes, and after I quickly ran the chain of sensations I had knotted together for Thomas through my mind, I could imagine it vividly.

I am sitting on this hard-backed chair, wearing only my pajama trousers because I don't want any hairs to get into my shirt and drive me crazy with their itching later. Agnes takes locks of my hair between her fingers and cuts them. She's dressed in her underwear, also to prevent my hairs from getting into her clothes.

"I don't think that's quite straight," I tease her. She frowns at me, keeps cutting. With those beautiful warm hands of hers, she brushes bits of wet hair from my shoulders, and it inflames me. As she moves in front of me to cut the hair at my brow, I place my hand on her thigh, on that lovely strip of skin between stocking and knickers, hot as a fevered brow, cold as cutlery in its box.

"Stop it! I can't focus like that," she says and slaps my hand away, but she does it softly. I move my hand back. She gives a little tug at a lock of hair, which makes me wince and her smile. "Men are such babies," she says. "You barely touch their hair, and already they squirm."

"I know how to make a woman squirm," I say, and I pull her down onto my lap and place kisses all over her face, making her laugh.

"What are you thinking about?" Agnes asked.

I opened my eyes. The confidence I felt when I imagined myself as Thomas still lingered, and I said, "That it's easy to love you."

She stilled. "I don't think many people would agree with you on that."

"Then many people are fools," I said.

"I think you're still a little silly from having been so ill," she said, but she gave my neck a playful squeeze as usual, then put her arms around me from behind and rested her chin on the top of my head. "You smell nice," she murmured and kissed my crown.

I pressed her hands against my breastbone and nursed the soft little pain of loving her, this tender ache that left me breathless and quiet.

TWELFTH CASE EPISODE

PATIENT R—, A CASE STORY: INHABITED BY ANOTHER

(D = DOCTOR, P = PATIENT R—)

TWELFTH EPISODE, CONDUCTED ON 25 OCTOBER 1954:

D: "I'd like to focus a bit more on the ground-up glass, if you don't mind."

P: "Why would I mind?"

D: "Right. Who told you that powdered glass can kill a man?"

P: "No one did. I read it in a library book."

D: "Do you remember what book?"

P: "A mystery novel, I believe. I don't remember the title or much of the plot, but the idea of powdered glass as a murder weapon stuck with me. Ruth began to grind up glass soon after. It gave her something to do and it gave me peace of mind."

D: "Did you ever come close to using it when you still lived with Mama?"

P: "I thought about it often, but I never dared. I couldn't really imagine a life without her."

D: "The devil you know rather than the devil you don't?"

P: "I guess."

D: "So why was Mrs. K— any different?"

P: "What do you mean?"

D: "I mean, why did you lace her food with powdered glass? Why did you try to kill her?"

P: [*suddenly stands and sweeps notebook, pencil, and her cup of water off the table; shouts*] "You don't understand! After all I've told you, you still don't understand!" [*screams wordlessly*]

D: [*tries to talk over screaming*] "Don't shout at me and don't touch my things. You know this isn't allowed. If you don't hush soon, they'll remove you from this room, and then I can't tell you what I've found out about the powdered glass."

[*keeps screaming, begins to scratch and bite herself; here the interview had to be suspended for my safety and that of the patient*]

Chapter 24

THE DOCTOR REMOVED MY STITCHES a week after I'd regained consciousness. After that, my flesh was left to its own devices. It knitted itself together the best it could, leaving a scar. Whenever I balled my hand into a fist, the skin around the scar felt taut, but apart from that, I could do everything quite as well as before the accident.

There was no longer any need for bandages, nor for me to keep to my bed, yet still Agnes came to sit with me every evening after everyone else had gone to sleep. She'd take my hand in hers and drip a little oil on the knuckles, then massage it into my skin.

Afterward, she'd toy with my fingers, moving them this way and that. "To make sure everything is as it should be," she'd say, but then she'd sit holding my hand in hers until she, too, went to bed, and it felt like that first night in the hotel, only the wild excitement we had felt then had turned into something slower and deeper.

During one of these evenings, she took a letter out of her pocket and placed it on my lap. "I almost forgot. A letter has come for you."

"For me? But I don't know anyone."

"But someone must know you, otherwise they wouldn't have written." She laughed and nodded at the envelope. It was dirty and torn in one corner. It had my name on it. I didn't recognize the handwriting, which was rather hard to read. Whoever had written to me was not a very skilled writer; the letters were uneven in shape and size, the strokes tremulous like that of a child or a sick person who had lost the strength in their fingers.

I turned the envelope over to see who had written to me, but they had left no return address.

"Come on, open it," Agnes said.

I stuck my thumb into the tear and ripped open the envelope. The paper inside was cheap, onion thin. It seemed rather yellowed, but then that could easily be a trick of the dying summer light, so warm and golden. The writing slanted peculiarly. It took some time to read. When I finished, I felt cold and sick. I threw the letter on the table and rested my face in my hands, trying to steady my breathing.

I could not see the letter, but I was hyperaware of its presence; my mind was fixed upon it, and so clearly did I see that feeble imperfect handwriting in my mind's eye that I might have been looking at it still.

"Roosje, what is it? Who wrote to you?" Agnes asked.

I lowered my hands. "A nurse who has been employed by my mama. She says I must come quick. She says Mama is dying."

I could not leave that very night. Though the warm weather did Willemijn good, she was always poorest during the night and needed Agnes's care. If Agnes couldn't drive me to Mama, I needed to use the bus and train, but the latest one had already left by the time I had packed my things.

"I shall take you to the station first thing in the morning," Agnes promised me, and she did. Because the trip by train took several hours and there was no telling what would happen once I'd reached Mama, Agnes booked a room in a hotel for me.

"You needn't stay with your mama unless you want to. And remember, Roosje: your home is at the Rozentuin now, with me," she said.

I wondered if she was afraid I wouldn't come back. I wished to say something to soothe her, but by then the train had already started moving, and all I could do was wave at her through the window until she disappeared from view.

All through the journey, I fretted. Ruth had turned into a silvery haze and flitted around my face and wrists to cool them; the air was hot, oppressive. The stifling heat promised thunder.

Walking into the street I had lived on for almost twenty-one years gave me a queer feeling in the pit of my belly. All was as I had left it. This terrifying thought entered my mind then, made my steps falter: What if I had never gotten away? What if my time with Agnes was merely the fancy of a desperate mind? What if I opened the door to my old home and found Mama and her guests waiting for me, the spluttering candles lit, the curtains drawn?

But no, I had Agnes's necklace around my throat to prove she was real, that it had all really happened. I touched it for comfort.

"Remember," Ruth whispered, "you are not alone."

When I had still lived in this house, I'd always use the kitchen door. It had never been locked. I no longer lived here, though, and guests always used the front door. I went to ring the doorbell, then wondered if that would upset Mama. I knocked on the door instead, softly so as not to disturb her. After a while, just when I was about to knock again, I heard soft footfalls. A nurse opened the door. Her uniform was pristine, her face rather equine, long and thin with wide-spaced, pale eyes.

"Nurse Caris?" I asked.

"Yes?"

"I'm Roos. I believe you wrote me a letter." I took it out of my purse and held it out for her to see. She bent close to read it. The light fell on her hands, which were rough and red, the nails short and unpainted. Her hair, so blond that it was almost white, she wore in a ponytail. She had slickened it with gel or hairspray; it looked both shiny and hard, almost like plastic.

"You must be very quiet. Your mama is asleep. You'll have to wait till she's awake again to speak to her," she said. She spoke in a brusque way, rather harsh, brooking no argument, as if she expected me to make trouble. Did she speak to Mama that way? I'd find it rather unappealing if I were sick, but then Mama and I were nothing alike in many ways.

I stepped inside. The familiar smell of incense mixed with cheap perfume and starch made a sadness unfurl inside me. Nurse Caris

MY DARLING DREADFUL THING   225

took me through the hallway into the parlour at the front of the house, which was where Mama had always received her guests before taking them to the little room in which we conducted the séances. I remembered it well, and though not a stick of furniture had been replaced, all of it was changed, so much so that it made me stagger.

Had those curtains always been so threadbare, the table and chairs so old and worn? It was as if someone had put a spell on the house, leaving everything where I remembered it yet making it appear shabby and cheap.

A pain rose in my throat. I swallowed against it, but it lingered. "Could you get me a glass of water?" I asked the nurse. She sighed deeply, raised her eyes to heaven, but went to fetch it for me all the same. She came back almost at once with a dripping glass, the water lukewarm because she had not let it run before thrusting the glass under the spout. She had brought a basketful of laundry and began to fold it as I sipped from the glass. "Does Mama still perform séances?" I asked.

She snorted. "I wouldn't be here if she did. Filthy business."

"In your letter, you didn't tell me what's ailing her."

"It's not for me to divulge sensitive patient information."

"No. No, of course not." I paused, took another sip of water. There was a chalky taste to it, bitter, unpleasant. I forced myself to swallow. "Does she treat you well?"

She looked me up and down, her hands never stilling but plucking handkerchiefs and towels and undershirts from the basket and folding them with speed and precision. "What a strange question. Wouldn't you do better to ask me how I treat her?"

"She can be difficult."

"Really? That's not the impression I got."

I flushed, drank more from the unappealing water to give myself something to do, then put the glass down on a yellowed lace doily. I opened my purse and made a great show of rooting through it. "Oh, dear," I said, and my voice sounded fake in its brightness. "I seem to have run out of cigarettes. Would you mind getting me some?"

Again she snorted. "I'm a nurse, not a maid."

"What a piece of work she is," Ruth murmured in my ear.

I forced myself to smile. "I wouldn't dream of treating you like a maid. I merely thought you might like to have a little break? The shop also sells caramels and other sweets. I thought you might buy some of those, too, as a little treat."

She locked gazes with me. There was nothing horselike about her eyes; they were extraordinarily pale and cold, the lashes mere stubs. "Feel bad that you came here with empty hands, do you?"

The blood pooled in my cheeks with such a vengeance, it pricked my eyes to the point of tears. I forced myself to smile. "I bought her flowers, but they wilted in the heat." Such an obvious lie, but I hadn't thought to bring Mama anything, though no doubt a beribboned basket with apples and oranges and grapes with the bloom of the sun still on them would have pleased her.

Nurse Caris sighed again, then held out her hand. "I'll go fetch you your cigarettes and something nice for the patient. In my experience, the promise of a little treat helps a great deal. I'll also buy myself something, mind."

I gave her some money. She didn't go, not until I had given her some more. As soon as she had pulled the kitchen door shut behind her, I went into the little room at the front of the house. This, too, was as I remembered and yet not the same: there stood the cabinet in which Mama stored her tarot cards, chipped and dusty now; there, the piano on whose keys I had made an empty tin crash countless times, but the keys had yellowed, and some lay curiously sunken.

A pair of curtains had not been drawn properly, letting in a strip of daylight. Had Mama been well, she'd never have allowed a sliver to show. I took hold of the curtain to close it; it felt unpleasant, slightly oily. I drew it over the rod, which produced a strange sound, almost like the soft, shrill little sobs of a frightened child.

My skin broke out in gooseflesh. Chilled, I turned to look at the table with its tablecloth of black velvet. The ghost of that child's sobbing went on, faint now but shriller still.

In a sudden panic, I shoved at the table. It moved easily since it was made from cheap light wood painted to look expensive and therefore heavy. Mama once had experimented with making the table float during our séances. I pushed the table until it crashed against the wall and stood juddering.

My shoving had bunched up the faux Persian carpet, its colors bright in patches where the daylight hadn't touched it in years. I took hold of a corner and tugged at it until the carpet folded into two, exposing the floorboards. I went to my knees and rubbed my hands over the boards until I found what I was looking for: a hole disguised as just another black knot in the grain of the wood. I hooked my finger in and pulled, lifting out a square part of floor.

The gasping little sobs stopped.

The space underneath the floorboards was much smaller than I remembered. I doubted I could fit in it now. It still smelled of mildew and earth. Bits of string were tied around their hooks. I took hold of one; it had not been taken care of properly and had frayed.

Were those spots flecks of my blood, or did I just imagine that? The whole experience was so visceral, I began to tremble and then, softly, to weep.

"She had no right," I whispered. "She had no right at all to put me in here. I begged her so often not to. I was so afraid. At times I thought my heart would give out…"

Ruth slid an arm around me. "But it's not all bad, darling Roosje mine. This is where we met," she whispered. "This is where I became your yokemate, and you became mine. Here we played together, worked together, suffered together."

Her jaw clicked when she kissed my sodden cheek. I looked at the cheap table covered with velvet cloth.

"Mr. Mesman," I said and shuddered so violently, I bit my tongue and tasted blood.

"Nurse Caris? Nurse Caris, I need something against the pain." Mama groaned from upstairs.

"Come, Ruth. Let's pay Mama a visit," I said. I kicked the trapdoor shut and went up the stairs, my heart hammering against my ribs. My eyes felt dry and tight from weeping, as if I had cut the inside of my lids. I resisted the urge to rub at them.

"Nurse Caris!" Mama gasped, her voice laced with panic and pain. I confess it gave me a wicked thrill to hear her call thus.

I stood on the threshold of her room and looked in. Mama's room had been transformed into a sickroom. Glass bottles with sticky stoppers and peeling labels stood cheek by jowl with jars of cold cream and brown bottles of pills. Crumpled handkerchiefs littered the floor. Vases of flowers and baskets of overripe fruit stood on the windowsill, the flowers drooping, the water cloudy. There was a smell in that room, one of sickness and of rot.

In the bed with its creased sheets lay Mama. She seemed to have shrunken. In my mind, she had been much taller than I was, but I saw now she and I had always been of a height. She had never been a big woman, but now what little flesh she had possessed had fallen away from her. Her skin was gouged with lines now and, like her lips, tinged slightly blue.

For a moment she stared at me, bewildered and frightened. Then recognition dawned. She looked me over, taking in my patent-leather shoes, the silver buckle on my belt, the expensive cut of my silk blouse, the delicate gold necklace, the little pearls in my ears.

"Well, well, well," she said, "look who has come back at last. Now won't you give your dear old mama a kiss?"

I bent over her, brushed my lips against her cold dry cheek. She smelled of face cream, cough syrup, cheap perfume, and under that, very faintly, of stale urine. Pearls of sweat beaded on her forehead, settled in the lines there.

"Little Roosje, won't you be a good girl and hand me that green bottle over there?"

She pointed to an assortment of bottles on the vanity, out of her reach. I went and picked up the green bottle. It was heavy and slightly sticky. In the mirror, I could see Mama nervously plucking at her sheets. As soon as I was in reach, she snatched the bottle from me and began to suck on it like a teat, her eyes closed. After a little while, she sank back against the pillows.

The strain went from her face, and she moaned. The sound was distasteful to me, strangely sensual. "Where's Nurse Caris?" Mama asked.

"I sent her on an errand."

"And she let you?"

"I gave her some money."

"Cold, greedy little bitch."

"I wanted some time alone with you. I heard you were sick. That's why I've come to see you," I said. I suddenly felt very young, very foolish. I pinched the scar on my hand to ground myself. "What's ailing you?"

"My heart. It's swollen and won't beat regularly anymore, but in fits and starts. In time, it'll give out."

"I always suspected you didn't have a heart."

Perhaps I was cruel. She was, after all, only an old sick woman. But my eyes still stung from weeping, and the dust from the séance room clung to my trousers, and I did not care if I hurt her. She looked at me with astonishment, then with cold hatred.

"If you've come only to reproach me, I'd rather you leave. God knows I did the best I could with you," she snapped.

I felt suddenly drained. I wondered why I had come. "At least Agnes paid you handsomely for your troubles," I said slowly.

She snorted in derision. "She didn't pay me half of what you're worth."

"It pains me that it was necessary for me to leave for you to realize that."

Mama laughed bitterly. The loose flesh of her throat jiggled. "Don't lie to me, Roos. You abandoned me the first chance you had. You never cared a jot for me. You always were an ungrateful child." She took another swig from her bottle. The tip of her tongue entered the bottle's neck. The green glass discolored it horribly, made it look like a wriggling maggot.

"I'm sorry you think of me like that. I've always done my best to please you," I said slowly.

"Another lie. And after all I've done for you. Your very own mother."

"Stop it. That tale has long since gotten stale."

"Do you know I still haven't found someone to replace you? Mad girls are easy enough to come by, but none have your particular brand of madness, and I was too old to have another child. Though I doubt another daughter of mine would be as mad as you. To imagine a constant spirit companion, my God." And she laughed.

A flush hit my face like scalding water. "I'm not mad," I said through gritted teeth.

Mama didn't even deign to reply. She just continued laughing, her whole frame shaking with it. Illness had sucked the fat out of her and so left the skin sagging. Each breath of laughter made her skin ripple horribly.

"I'm *not* mad," I repeated. I realized I had balled my hands into fists and relaxed my fingers. My nails had dug little half-moon dents into my palms. They flushed crimson.

"Of course not. Everyone has a Ruth," she gasped, tears streaming from her eyes.

"Stop that. You'll just soil yourself," I said, but she took no notice. Still she laughed, choking on it now. This hacking, wheezing laughter was so horrible, so degrading, that it caused wrath to take hold of me, like a fever of the brain. It dried my mouth and made me tremble.

"Let me show her," Ruth whispered in my ear. "Let me show her just how real I am. Let me deal with her as I did with Mr. Mesman." She brushed against my lips, eager to slip inside.

Oh, but it was tempting to let her in and unleash violence on Mama.

Did she not deserve it? I imagined pushing the heel of my hand against her throat until the cartilage buckled and her eyes grew cloudy.

I might have done it; I confess it readily. I could easily have murdered Mama. I didn't need to mix ground-up glass into her food either; I could simply press my arm against her throat and choke the life out of her.

The only thing that kept me from it was the thought of Agnes and what her life would be without me, living between the Rozentuin's rotting walls under the petty tyranny of Willemijn. Mama wasn't worth the hassle. So, no, I didn't stave in her head with one of the glass bottles she nipped from with such pleasure, nor did I strangle her with the soiled sheets.

But I did not refrain from harming her altogether.

I licked my dry lips and bent close to her. "You might laugh now, but you'll be dead soon. I'll laugh then, all the way to the churchyard and beyond. You know what happens once you're dead?" I hissed. "They'll put your body in a coffin, and that coffin they shall put into the ground. It'll be dark there and cold. I hope your spirit shall be trapped inside that coffin forever so that you may know what it was like for me to be put in that small hole under the floorboards every single day when I was a child."

She worked her mouth, wrung the bottle between her hands. For one awful moment, I thought she might cry. Instead, she began to speak.

"I tried to get rid of you. As soon as I knew the seed had caught, I tried everything I could think of. I even drank turpentine. But already when you were as small as my little nail, you were determined to bring me grief, and you wouldn't go. I wish now I'd tried harder. You're goddamned cruel. I think I'll write you out of my will, child of mine or no."

I went cold all over, as if plunged in freezing water.

"You're lying," I said. "You're not my mother. My real mother died shortly after I was born, and my father gave me to you to keep me safe."

She couldn't even bring herself to laugh. "That man probably isn't even your father. In those days, there were a few fellas, just to tide me over, just until my paintings started selling. Only then you came. I told that man you were his because he seemed like he might help and keep me from being ruined, and he did."

"You're lying. You're lying to hurt me."

At this she smiled, revealing little gray teeth. "Perhaps I am, Roosje, but how can you be sure? You've never been very good at separating fiction from reality. And no matter who your real parents are, I am the one who raised you. Everything you are, you are because of me. You're more me than anyone else."

Had she knifed me, it would have hurt less. So horrible was the idea that Mama and I were alike, so revolting, that I felt everything inside me contract. I bent double with the pain, so fierce and sharp that it drained the whole room of color and sound, leaving only grays and blacks and this horrible humming in my ears.

Just when I thought I might faint, something snapped. There was no time to get up and make a run for the toilet, not even enough time to draw Mama's bedpan out from under the bed. Instead, I vomited all over the bed, drenching her legs and lap.

One surge of vomit, two, three.

My stomach was empty, and still I retched, as if I could physically expel her words and all she had done to me over the years.

"You horrible, filthy child! You did that on purpose!" Mama shrieked.

"I'm sorry," I murmured, "I'm so sorry." I tried to strip the bed of its soiled sheets, but Mama had picked up a heavy book from her nightstand and whacked it against my face with such force, I stumbled and fell. An explosion of pain radiated out from my right temple.

With my hand pressed against my face, I stumbled down the stairs, heedless of Mama's screams.

"I'll kill her for this!" Ruth wailed as she flew down the stairs beside me, "Oh, but I'll see her dead before we leave here, darling Roosje mine!"

"Hush!" I snapped. "Don't you see it'll leave a bruise at worst, no more? We've had a lot worse."

But she frightened me all the same, and I dashed down the hall, pushed my way past Nurse Caris, her arms laden with brown paper bags. She shouted something after me, but then I was already out in the street, running still.

THIRTEENTH CASE EPISODE

PATIENT R—, A CASE STORY: INHABITED BY ANOTHER

(D = DOCTOR, P = PATIENT R—)

THIRTEENTH EPISODE, CONDUCTED ON 2 NOVEMBER 1954:

Notes to self: Wasn't allowed to visit for a whole week. Patient very distraught after our last exchange; had to be sedated. Don't want to upset her but feel it's vital to press on now. Wish I could've talked to her sooner. Don't quite think she's feigning madness and deceiving us all anymore, but now the ill-willed could claim she had a whole week to get her story straight and think of new lies.

Therefore decided to go all in and ask her about Mr. M—. Heard rumors the prosecution might ask him to act as a witness to prove patient has a history of violent behavior.

Feared that patient might not talk to me again. She was very agitated, but I managed to force a breakthrough!

D: "In light of what happened between you and Mrs. K—, I want to talk about Mr. M—."

P: [*silence*]

D: "Do you remember who he is?"

P: "I don't want to talk about him."

D: "Why not?"

P: "He's not important."

D: "I don't think that's true. In fact, I think it's vital we talk about him. You have mentioned him several times now. Once, you even said Ruth promised to do to Mrs.

K— what she did to him, should she ever hurt you. It says in your file you nearly ripped out Mr. M—'s throat with your teeth, and now Mrs. K— is dead, her body mutilated by bite marks. I've read her autopsy report. I've seen the pictures. Her left hand was almost torn from her wrist, and that must have taken a lot of time and determination. Do you understand the significance of this? The prosecution will try to establish a pattern, and I fear many a judge will be convinced. So yes, I do think it's time we talk about Mr. M—."

P: [*silence*]

D: "R—, you can trust me. I've come to know you. You wouldn't just bite a man's throat. Won't you tell me why you did it?"

P: [*silence*]

D: "Are you still angry with me because of last week?"

P: [*glares*] "Do you need to ask that?"

D: "I didn't mean to upset you."

P: "Well, you did. You did, and then they forced pills down my throat, huge, bitter pills that made me feel like I was dead. I didn't feel anything anymore. And Ruth..." [*sobs*]

D: "What about her?"

P: [*wipes away tears angrily*] "She was gone. I couldn't see her anymore because of the pills. Not that I want to, not after what happened, but it should be my choice, not anyone else's."

D: "You couldn't see Ruth anymore after they gave you pills?"

P: "Don't."

D: "Don't do what?"

P: "Don't use this fact as a weapon against me. You'll tell me that me not being able to perceive Ruth when I was under the influence of those pills is clear proof that she's not real, when in reality, it doesn't prove anything at all."

D: "Doesn't it?"

P: [*shouts*] "No it doesn't! It just means my brain is different from yours! If there was a pill that would make you unable to see colors, would you then think colors are just an illusion? Of course you wouldn't! And I bet there are pills out there that could make you see spirits in the same way I can. So no, this doesn't prove anything!"

D: "I see. You've argued that well, R—, and I'm sorry this happened to you. If you want, I can talk to the people here, make sure they never give you those exact pills again. But we must talk about Mr. M— first."

P: [*refuses to look up from clenched fists; presses lips tightly together*]

D: "All right. If you won't tell me, I'll tell you what I think happened. I think he was one of your mother's guests. Someone with a lot of money. I think your mother..."

P: [*interrupts*] "Mama wasn't my mother. She just said that to hurt me."

D: "Do you know that, for people traumatized when they were children, admitting that they were abused by someone who ought to have protected and loved them, someone such as a parent, is often the hardest?"

P: "That may well be, but she wasn't my mother."

D: "All right. What do you want me to call her then?"

P: "Call her what you like, just don't suggest she was my real mother."

D: "I shall stick with 'Mama' then, since that's what you and I have been calling her so far. Is that all right?"

P: [*nods*]

D: "As I said, I think Mr. M— was wealthy. I think Mama wanted him to become a patron to you. To accomplish that, you had to please him. Only then he hurt you, and so you hurt him back."

P: "Not me. Ruth."

Chapter 25

I SUPPOSE I MIGHT AS well explain what happened with Mr. Mesman. I've brought him up several times now, after all, and to understand everything that happened, it might help to know what he did to me and what Ruth and I did to him in return. Simply put, Mr. Mesman thought I was a piece of fruit he could pluck, but when he tasted me, he found me rather more bitter than he had expected.

He was one of our guests. He attended his first séance when I was almost eighteen, after his only child had died in a horrific accident for which he blamed himself. His wife blamed him, too, and as a result, their marriage had collapsed, although they were not officially divorced by the time I met him.

He was unlike our other guests in the sense that he came from money. For this reason, Mama desperately wanted to please him.

"Think, child," she told me in the days before he was to come visit, "what might happen if he is satisfied with us! He'll come again, and his pockets run deep. Perhaps he might even become our patron." And she rubbed her hands in gleeful anticipation.

The séances made me feel sordid and cheap, as you know, yet the idea of having a patron appealed to me, as the idea of being free of want must always appeal to those living on the brink of poverty. Besides, if he became our benefactor, we needn't hold séances so often.

I put on my best dress and brushed my hair the day we were to meet. Mama even applied some lipstick to my lips and pinched my cheeks till they were pink and sore.

When we were introduced, I lowered my eyes demurely, then studied him through my lashes. He was beautiful in a cold, stilted way, with a sharp bone structure and severely parted hair that made me think him a fascist. I thought of him as a statue but had to correct myself almost immediately because marble at least gives the impression of warmth; he seemed bloodless and strange.

"But he's not dead," Ruth whispered. "Do you not see the pulse jump in the vein at his temple?"

"Miss Beckman," he said, then took my hand and kissed the back of it. He was like that, gallant in a deeply chauvinistic way. His fingertips brushed against the scars from the incident with the birch rod, accidentally at first, then with intent. I flushed but didn't dare to pull back my hand for fear of offending him. I see now he was possessive from the first.

If only Ruth and I had performed poorly that day, things might have gone very differently. We should have made Mr. Mesman believe we were frauds. Instead, we convinced him we were possessed by the spirit of his child, convinced him so absolutely that his white face flushed an ugly crimson as he fought off tears. He attended our séances every week for the next two years.

Although he had shown that fearful streak of entitlement to my body the moment we met, it took months before he stopped being anything but cold to me outside the séances. I suppose he knew he had to keep his distance or else fall prey to his dark desires. Yet when he could keep his distance no longer, he was not immediately and utterly lost. His unravelling was a slow process and, for that, all the more dangerous. Ruth and I had never felt at ease with him, yet his immense self-control lulled us both.

The first sign of his slipping were the gifts: chocolate in silver wrappers, bars of scented soap, flowers. The things you might give to a lover as well as to a friend or relative, and since he invariably handed them to Mama, there could be no sense of impropriety. Only on my birthday did he bring me a gift that was for me and me alone: a sleek little kitten of the purest white, which I named Trudy and loved like I had loved my doll.

She slept at the foot of my bed and brought me little gifts of dead leaves and, once, a mummified moth. Mama had her drowned after two weeks because she clawed at her furniture and lace curtains. They weren't genuine lace, but Mama didn't want them ripped all the same.

Mr. Mesman was the only guest we ever entertained who had no trouble obeying Mama's rules. Never did he reach for me; never did he touch me. The only exception was when he drove us to his party, but I blamed that on him being slightly drunk. Perhaps that's why, when it all went to hell, it went so spectacularly.

Mama only left the house once a month, to settle her accounts with the shopkeepers. I usually spent those free hours in my little room with Ruth. We'd lie together under the covers, Ruth holding me as if I were her child, stroking little figures on my arms and hands. The day it all went wrong, she had caressed me almost to sleep. I lay drowsy and content, nestled against her, when a voice rang out, startling us both.

"Hello?"

"I'd better go and see who it is," Ruth said, but I pulled her back.

"Don't. I'll go."

I hastily put on a dress. My fingers fumbled with the buttons.

"Hello?" the voice called again.

"Just a minute!" I called back. Ruth plaited my hair for me as I clipped my stockings into place. I ran downstairs.

Mr. Mesman stood in the kitchen. He held his hat in one hand, his leather gloves in the other. When he saw me, he smiled. "Miss Beckman," he said and inclined his head. Never in those two years had he called me by my Christian name.

"What are you doing here?" I asked.

"My, you're all red and panting. Did you run so quickly for me?" He laughed.

"I didn't know it was you."

He cleared his throat. "Forgive me for dropping by like this. I rang the bell, but there was no answer. Is your mama not here?"

"She's settling her accounts with the shopkeepers."

"I see. And Ruth?"

"Upstairs."

"Well, I came to give you this." He drew a package from his

coat pocket, which he tossed on the kitchen table rather carelessly. I stared at it, my heart thumping. My hands went cold with fear. I didn't dare look him in the eye, but all the same I didn't dare to let him out of my sight.

"I shall give it to Mama," I said.

"It would be utterly wasted on her. It's for you."

"You needn't have."

"Perhaps." He squeezed his gloves, making them creak. "Won't you open it?"

Reluctantly, I picked up the gift. It was small enough to fit in the palm of my hand. I fumbled with the knotted ribbon until Mr. Mesman, in his impatience, took the gift from me and slashed at the ribbon with his pocketknife.

"Hold out your hand," he said and dropped a velvet-covered box into it. I opened it. The hinges snapped open with hardly a sound. Inside were the loveliest earrings I'd ever seen, tear shaped and glittering like stars. I was afraid to touch them. When I did, I found them cold and brilliant and hard.

"Do you like them? They're diamond earrings. You've a lovely throat. If you put up your hair, the earrings would fall past your face and draw attention to that. It's a family heirloom. My mother used to wear them."

My hands were clammy. A pain rose in my throat, which made it hard to talk. "They're very pretty," I whispered. "But I can't accept."

I held out the box to him, but he didn't take it.

"What nonsense," he said. He threw down his gloves and hat

and grabbed my arm. The shock of his touch made me sick to my stomach. He dragged me to the mirror on the wall, then plucked an earring from its bed of satin and held it next to my face.

His hands were yellow with cold. "Don't you see how pretty they'd look on you?"

"Please, Mr. Mesman, you shouldn't give me gifts like this. It's too much, and I…I'm not worthy…" I stammered. I took the earring from him and tucked it back in its box, then put the box into his coat's pocket. The leather felt revolting, cold in great patches but warm in the places it had rested against his body.

Mr. Mesman clasped my hand. "How can you possibly say that?" he said, and his voice was soft, horribly intimate. He put an arm around me. "Glorious Roos, do you know how many mediums I have visited after my son died? And all of them frauds, trying to trick with wires and hidden pockets and poor lighting. But not you. With you, it's real. None can compare to you. You stand alone. Had you been born in another age, people would have venerated you. Won't you let me worship you as you deserve to be worshipped?"

I was so utterly terrified of him that I must have blacked out, but only for a moment. The next thing I remember is lying on the table, the wrapping paper crinkling underneath me with every move. Mr. Mesman was on top of me, his hand clamped over my mouth and nose to keep me from screaming, almost choking me.

But Ruth didn't need me to scream to know something horrible was being done to me. She had rushed down the stairs and now stood beside me, splendid and terrible in her wrath. The very air crackled with it. She was so large, she had to bend her head; her crown brushed the rafters.

"Let me in," she commanded, and her voice boomed and rolled over me like waves breaking on the shore.

I twisted my face away from Mr. Mesman's hot hand and opened my mouth. She went down my throat so fast, it felt as if I'd swallowed a razor. She took hold of my spine and flooded me. I shivered with the force of her rippling through me, which made Mr. Mesman groan.

Ruth put her arms about him to draw him closer. He smelled of leather and expensive eau de cologne and, underneath that, sweat. His Adam's apple bobbed in his throat as he swallowed; he salivated a lot when excited. Ruth drew him closer still until his throat was against my nose and lips.

I didn't know what Ruth was going to do. If I had, I would have stopped her. Mr. Mesman deserved what he got, but all the same, I wouldn't have let her.

This you must believe.

He was gaining speed when Ruth opened my mouth and bit his throat. She didn't do it quite right at first, and the skin brushed my teeth and chin like sandpaper. She pulled back a little, then tried again, aiming for that juddering Adam's apple. This time, she managed to get it between my teeth, and she clenched my jaw shut.

Mr. Mesman screamed and tried to pull away, but she wouldn't let go. His cartilage crunched. He smacked his fist against my face, and still Ruth wouldn't open my mouth.

Again, he punched. She bit harder. Blood spouted into my mouth, hot and rich and thick.

It tasted like money.

Ruth unclenched my jaw. Mr. Mesman staggered away, his hand pressed against his throat. Blood gushed through his fingers, sleek and shiny as ribbons of raw silk. In that queer half-light of the room, it seemed black.

Ruth wiped my mouth with the back of my hand. "Lay a finger on Roos again, and I'll rip out your throat properly, you fucking bastard," she said.

He tried to say something, but no words came. His eyes still showed madness, yes, but now tinged with fear. He made for the door and stumbled out, leaving a bloody handprint on the wood. With all that blood gushing out of him, I thought he might well bleed out and die, but then so might I; blood was still trickling out of me.

Ruth took a towel and pressed it against the bruised flesh to stem the flow. "It shall be all right, sweet one. He shall never come here again," she said.

"Of course he shan't. We've killed him." I sobbed, though more from fright than anything else.

I've said before that I'm not a violent person. Maybe that wasn't right. Maybe I am. All I know is that, in that moment, I wished Mr. Mesman would bleed out slowly.

Chapter 26

AFTER MY VISIT WITH MAMA, I was in such a state that I could do nothing but wander the streets for a few hours. I must've looked quite crazy, grimacing and mumbling as I talked to Ruth, but I couldn't stop.

When my feet hurt and my throat was parched from the heat, I walked to the hotel. There I found Nurse Caris had left a message for me from Mama. In the neat handwriting of one of the receptionists, I learned that she had decided to write me out of her will.

I squeezed my hand into a fist, turning the paper into a hard wrinkled ball. The skin on my scarred knuckles turned white and tight.

I took a bath to wash the sweat and dust from me. The room was stiflingly hot. "I wish it would rain," I said to Ruth. She clambered into the tub with me, cooling the water as effectively as a slab of ice would have done, pressing her twiggy fingers against the little bruise forming at my temple where the book's corner had caught.

After a simple dinner, I lay down in bed. I had intended to just rest my eyes a bit before calling Agnes to let her know what had happened, but my visit to Mama had drained me and I slept like the dead, waking in the afternoon the next day. I drank three glasses of water and had another cold bath in an attempt to stop feeling groggy.

"Thank God we are going home," I said out loud.

I tried calling the Rozentuin to let Agnes know I'd be at the station in the evening, but though the phone rang and rang, no one picked up. "Perhaps there's something wrong with Willemijn," I said. Ruth took my hand and squeezed it. With a gnawing pain in my belly, I began the journey back.

Once I had arrived at the station, I used a payphone to call the Rozentuin.

"Mrs. Knoop speaking," Agnes said after I'd let it ring for a long time, prompting the operator to ask me twice whether it wouldn't be better to disconnect the call since it seemed like no one was going to answer it.

"Agnes, it's me. I'm at the station. Could you come fetch me? If not, I'll just walk. That's not a problem either. I tried to call before to let you know when I'd be back, but—"

She cut me off. "I'll be there in twenty minutes."

"Thank you. I…" But the line had already gone dead.

I sat in the shade with my suitcase, watching the heat ripple the air as if it were water. The sky had lost its vibrant blue color and had turned a milky white instead. It would storm soon. This wind-quiet moment where all seemed hushed and queer was just the world holding its breath.

When Agnes pulled up, I ran to her. "Thank you for coming to pick me up," I said and meant to kiss her cheek. She moved away, took the suitcase from me. Her face was tight, and she wouldn't look at me.

"Was the train ride all right?" she asked, and her voice was tight, too.

That little pain in the pit of my stomach hardened. "Yes. Yes, it was quite all right. Just very hot, but I had Ruth to help me keep cool."

We settled into the car, yet still she wouldn't look at me. I began to flex my hand so I could feel the tug of the flesh around my scarred knuckles. I had done something wrong, something that upset her terribly. If only I knew what it was, I could try and make it right.

To break that strained silence, I talked of my trip to Mama. I stumbled over the words, made poor jokes, accidentally skipped bits so I had to backtrack and retell whole parts. The car trip didn't take long. By the time we arrived at the Rozentuin, I had not finished my story, but Agnes interrupted me.

"I must go check on Willemijn. She's had a poor night. She says my cooking is inedible, and it gave her heartburn." Mrs. van Leeuwen had left yesterday to visit a cousin and wouldn't be back until the end of the week.

"How uncharitable."

She shrugged tiredly.

"Can I do something to help?"

She shook her head.

"Then I'll just go upstairs and put my things away, all right?"

When I was in my room, I felt paralyzed with dread. I had done something wrong, and if the worst happened, I didn't even have Mama to fall back upon.

Around and around my thoughts went, ever deeper, ever darker, until I couldn't stand it anymore. What use was it, this chewing over all the ways things could go wrong? Being caught in my own head was exhausting. Worse, it was useless, and I despised being useless. I couldn't make anything right and avoid all the horrors I could so vividly imagine if I didn't know what it was I had done wrong. As soon as I heard Agnes go into her room, I followed her there. She stood at the window, looking at the bruising sky. I closed the door behind me, pressed my palms flat against the wood to steady myself. "Tell me," I said, "what I've done to displease you, and give me a chance to make it right."

She did not answer right away. Instead, she pressed her fingers against her temples. "This heat has given me a headache. It's so oppressive. If only it would rain…"

I waited for her to speak, but she remained standing with her hands at her face, so I brought her a glass of water and some aspirin instead. She dropped the tablets into the water. We both watched them fizz. I hadn't filled the glass all the way, and some sediment drifted to the bottom and lay there like white clay. She took a few sips, grimaced at the taste.

"Won't you tell me?" I begged.

She brought the sweating glass to her face and rested it against her forehead, her eyes closed. "The police came," she said.

My heart began to thump painfully.

"Someone had found Thomas's watch near the main road and brought it to the station. The police were quite sure it was his because it had its name engraved on the back; he had a thing about marking his possessions in case any of the servants ever got it in their heads to steal something from him. What they didn't understand was how it ended up lying in the dirt. Had we perhaps been burgled? I told them no, we hadn't. And then I lied to them, Roos."

She opened her eyes. A drop of water ran from the glass down her face like a tear. "I lied to them," she repeated. "I said I had asked Josephine to take it to the watchmaker in the city because the strap had broken, and I wanted it fixed. I said she had lost it along the way, and we had looked for it but hadn't found it. Hardly surprising, since the way from the Rozentuin to the city is long, and she might have lost it anywhere. I was beyond happy it had been found; it meant so much to me, since it belonged to my dead husband."

Then all is well, I thought longingly, desperately. Yet if that were true, then why was she so upset with me?

Agnes put the glass down, began to turn it around and around so that the water inside sloshed against the sides, almost reaching the rim but never spilling over. "I thought that might be the end of it, but no, they were a suspicious lot. They asked me why I had entrusted it to a mere maid if it meant so much to me. I told them I didn't have the time to go all the way to the city, not with Willemijn being so ill. I had meant to report the watch as missing, but I hadn't had the time yet for that either. I offered them tea and *spekkoek*, but they declined and left me, which was just as well because I had a lot to think about, mainly how the watch my husband was buried with ended up lying near a road. And I couldn't explain that, but I think you might."

I twisted the stuff of my skirt between my fingers.

"I'm sorry, Agnes. I'm so sorry. It must've fallen off when I moved him. At some point, the wheelbarrow overturned, and I think that's when the strap broke, and I lost it. I didn't realize. If I had, I would've looked for it."

She stared at me, a thumbprint of a frown between her brows. "When you moved him?" she asked slowly.

I suddenly had the insane urge to giggle. "Yes, when I moved him."

"What do you mean, you moved him?"

I got the horrible sense I had failed her or, worse, had hurt her without meaning to. I rubbed the fabric of my skirt over the scars on my palm, turning the flesh an angry purple. "You know, when I moved him. When I dug him up and reburied him in the bog."

She swallowed, and the muscles of her throat rippled beautifully. "You dug up Thomas's body and reburied it in the bog?"

I thought I might cry. "Yes. I wanted to bring him back. I thought that's what you wanted."

She looked at me as if I were a stranger. "What are you talking about?"

My breath hitched in my throat, and the words came out in desperate little sobs. "I tried to turn him into a spirit so you and he could be together. I thought it would please you. Please don't look at me that way…"

"What way?" she snapped.

"As if you don't know me, as if you're mad with me. I didn't want to do it. I didn't like it. I only did it because I wanted to make you happy, because I want to give you anything you want…"

"You've dug up his body and moved it. My God. I think I shall be sick," she murmured. She sank down on a chair, her hands clapped over her mouth. She was trembling, and her face had taken on a peculiar grayish hue.

I refilled her glass of water, stirred it to get the aspirin dust to dissolve, and fetched a wet cloth. With the cloth I dabbed her temples and throat. She took the glass from me, but she was trembling so much, the water sloshed over the rim and ran down her wrists. I steadied her hands, helped her drink. For a while, the only sounds were her teeth clicking against the rim, her gulping breaths, the little wet sounds of her swallowing.

When she was done, she sank back, her eyes closed. Her hands were stone-cold. I chafed at them until the backs looked bruised, trying to warm them. I forced myself not to babble, as I might have done, but choose my words carefully. "Please don't be angry with me. I thought bringing Thomas back would make you happy, and to make him come back, I had to bury him in the right sort of ground. That's why I did it. I only wanted to please you."

"Why," she said, and she sounded drained and a little ill, "did you think bringing Thomas back would make me happy?"

"Because you loved him. You love him still. You told me so yourself. You love him so much, you can't even talk of him. You had the perfect marriage."

She laughed in disbelief. "The perfect marriage? You thought we had the perfect marriage? Who the fuck told you that?"

"Everyone! Mama, Willemijn, the newspapers and magazines..."

"My God," she said, and again she laughed or perhaps sobbed. She pulled her hands from mine. "A perfect marriage, don't make me laugh."

"Agnes, what do you mean?"

She sprang to her feet. "I mean that my marriage was nothing like what you seem to think it was. If you can call a union marred by jealousy and rage a perfect marriage, then I suppose Thomas and I did have a perfect marriage, yes. Personally, I wouldn't call it that. I'd call it poisonous, rotten. The things he did to me..."

She pressed a hand to her belly, her fingers curling hard.

"Of course, it didn't start out that way. Oh no. Thomas was very charismatic. He could fool anyone, if only he put his mind to it. And God, did I want to be fooled. I admit that readily. I had such a hunger for love, for companionship, for acceptance. And it isn't as if he didn't love me. It wasn't merely animal magnetism, though there was plenty of that, too. No, from the beginning, we had this connection, as if we had known each other for a long time. He seemed to read my mind."

"Like you and I did," I said.

She paused, then shook her head quickly. "No. Yes, but no. Not like you and I. Never like that. How could it be? You're not vicious and rotten and twisted."

A ripple that might be pain, that might be love ran from my throat down between my breasts. I thumped the palm of my hand against my chest to make it stop.

"But I didn't know what he was, not yet. Within a month after we first met, we were married. It's not good, to make such a big commitment so swiftly, but I wanted a home of my own, and he wanted a wife and children. I should not have been so rash, or perhaps I should have told him about Peter before we got married. But Peter isn't someone you can bring up easily, and the right moment never seemed to arrive." She talked very rapidly, paced around as she did so, making quick little movements with her hands.

"So we got married. Not at the Rozentuin, as you might expect. It was a seaside wedding, rather sober. I wore a cotton frock and wildflowers in my hair. In a way, it was an elopement, and that made it feel dangerous and exciting." She laughed, and it was not this bitter resentful thing, but something sweet and pure, something that, once heard, I would wish to draw from her again and again and again.

"No one we knew attended—we had to ask two passersby to be our witnesses. At the hotel we ate steaks weeping blood and drank wine sour as vinegar before he took me to his bed, and the sea pounded on the beach all night." She shuddered and, for a moment, couldn't go on. I sat very still, afraid that anything I'd say or do would make her stop talking and lock all this back into herself.

"After three days, I finally told him about Peter. I had thought he'd be kind to me about it because he had so many family members deemed mad. I should've known then that he wouldn't take the news well precisely because madness ran in his family, but I was young and naive and so terribly in love. Though looking back on it now, perhaps a part of me already sensed he'd be displeased, and that's why I didn't tell him sooner."

She picked up her sweating glass, brought it to her mouth, took a messy sip. She almost dropped it back onto the table because her hands were unsteady. This time, the water sloshed over the rim again, pooling onto the table and reflecting the ceiling. Carelessly, she mopped it up using her sleeve, leaving a wet smear, and all the while, she kept talking, very quickly, very nervously, the sentences broken up at odd moments by choked laughter, by choked sobs.

"God, I'll never forget the way he looked at me, so full of loathing, as if I were something dirty stuck to his shoes. If he had become angry with me, I think I could have borne that. If he had screamed at me or even hit me, I would have understood. To draw blood is just another kind of passion, isn't it? But Thomas rarely used violence of that kind because it opened a door with a long corridor, and at the end of that corridor lay sex and, eventually, reconciliation. Instead he ignored me. He didn't talk to me, didn't touch me. For the rest of our honeymoon, he treated me as if I didn't exist, and it was like I was back at school again. I couldn't handle it. I cried and begged and goaded, anything to get a response from him."

"Oh, Agnes," I whispered. I wanted to rush to her, take her in my arms, take away all this pain and horror, but it was as if I were enchanted: as long as her tale remained unfinished, I was rooted to my spot, only allowed to listen. Maybe that was a good thing. Wasn't she tearing out all this rot herself by telling me about it, and did I not help her most by listening, at least for now?

Agnes rolled up her sodden sleeve, squeezed the fabric until drops ran down her wrist and dangled from her fingertips. "It was only when we were on our way to the Rozentuin that he parked the car by the side of the road and finally turned to me. He offered me a deal. If I agreed to see a doctor and take pills that would make Peter go away, he would forgive me for tricking him into marrying a madwoman. And I did. God forgive me, but I did. I forsook Peter for a man I'd barely known two months so I could finally have a home."

She pressed her hands to her face and groaned.

I thought of sending Ruth away, and a sharp little pain started at my breastbone, so fierce and sudden, it made me gasp. "But that must have mutilated you," I said.

"It did. I remember waking and finding him gone, as if he had been blotted out, and I panicked. I searched for him everywhere, screaming his name. Thomas had to call in the doctor to sedate me. He gave me more pills, pills that dulled everything until I felt nothing. It's easy, pretending to be a perfect wife when you feel only a little more than, say, a tomato."

Despite myself, I laughed. Startled, Agnes looked at me; then she began to laugh, too.

"I'm sorry," I gasped. "I didn't mean to laugh. It's not funny at all, feeling as much as a vegetable, but…"

"But you must laugh or else go mad," Agnes said, and we laughed till we were aching with it, this desperate, hysterical laughter. When it petered out, then died away, my belly was sore and my cheeks were wet.

"What happened? How did you come to see Peter again?" I asked.

Agnes drank some water, offered me the rest of her weeping glass to soothe my throat flagellated by our shared laughing fit. I drank quickly, gratefully.

"The war happened," she said, "and with it came a shortage of medicine. I ran out of pills. This is how Peter was restored to me, and with him all my feelings came back. When he woke me, stroking my hair, I could do nothing but embrace him and weep. I held him so tightly, I bruised us both. I never wanted to let him go. Dear Peter. He wasn't even mad with me, just wildly concerned. I hadn't perceived him during those years, but he had never gone far from me, and he had seen and heard a lot more than I had. He told me Thomas wasn't worth my affections, that he betrayed me." She took the glass from me, then drank the final bit of water with her head thrown back as if it were liquor.

"He wouldn't tell me how, not at first, at any rate, but I kept pressing him until he finally broke down and said Thomas made a mockery of my marriage with Willemijn."

She brought the glass to her mouth again, remembered she had drained it, lowered it. "I guessed what he meant straightaway, but I didn't want to believe it. It was such a horrible, filthy thing... But I couldn't stop thinking about it. I began to pay attention, to follow them around. And then I caught them together, in the schoolroom."

Shockingly, she laughed. "Finally, those yellow smudges on their clothes were explained!"

I felt cold and sick. The water I had just drunk chilled my stomach. "You mean they...?"

"Yes."

That familiar chain of sensations ran through my mind: the soft, silky feel of a flower in my hand as I ripped it apart with my fingers to perfume the air; the steady tick of the watch around my wrist, a message of love flush against my skin; a woman running to me, her dark hair dancing around her face. Only this time, the chain broke apart, and the true Thomas stepped out of the shadows and was revealed to me in a flash of sights and smells and sounds.

Thomas, standing straight and tall and superior, Agnes weeping at his feet as she begged for him to speak to her, to touch her, to acknowledge that she existed. Thomas, unscrewing the cap from a bottle of pills and putting them in Agnes's mouth one by one, smiling in triumph as he watched her crush them between her teeth and swallow. Thomas, his nose buried in his sister's hair, his mouth sucking a bruise on her throat as his fingers rubbed at her and she panted in his ear…

I felt empty then but not bereft. It was a good kind of emptiness, as if I had purged myself from something harmful. I almost laughed. All this time, I had strained and striven after a phantom. I was free of him now.

Meanwhile, Agnes went on talking. "I had done everything for him. I'd denied myself, torn myself apart, and given parts of me away I should have kept, and for what? For love? If that was love, it came at much too steep a price. I couldn't pay it anymore. Something had to give."

"Why didn't you leave?"

"I had paid so much and so dearly for living in this house that

I couldn't well give it up. From the very start, I was also determined to make everyone think my marriage was a roaring success. You don't know, you can't know, how Thomas's friends and acquaintances responded to me when they found out he had married me. They'd look at me, and I could almost hear them wonder, where did he find this ill-bred little bitch with her lack of pedigree? Besides, I couldn't have left. I had very little money and no family."

"But what about your father?"

"When he heard of my marriage, he wrote me a check and a letter telling me it would be the last time he paid for me, seeing as I now had a husband to support me. A few years later, he died. So, you see, even if I had wanted to go, I couldn't have." She fumbled for a cigarette in her pocket, lit one, and smoked it, still talking and pacing.

"The strange thing is that it wasn't all bad, even after the war ended and I had to pretend I was numb and sane and taking my pills again. Like I said, Thomas could charm the devil himself, and I believe that, in his way, he genuinely loved me. We had these periods in which things were almost good. The sex always was. But then Willemijn became pregnant."

She took a drag from her cigarette, making the tip glow.

"Thomas told me and told me, too, that we would pretend the baby was his and mine, because that would save Willemijn from disgrace and provide the Rozentuin with an heir. It had become clear by then that I couldn't conceive. I sat very still as he broke the news to me, and I thought: Shall I tell him? Shall I tell him I know the child is his? Shall I tell him I know, and I won't go along with all this because there's only so much disgrace and shame a person can suffer? But I lost my nerve."

Agnes dropped her cigarette into the empty glass of water, where it sizzled and died. She lit another one, the smoke curling around her fine face.

I thought of the nursery all done up, of the plain little marker in the graveyard for a stillborn baby, and it all began to make a horrible sort of sense.

"But the baby died, didn't it?" I asked.

"Something was wrong with it. Maybe it was because Willemijn had kept to her bed for months, trying in vain to keep her lungs from getting buggered by the strain of pregnancy, or maybe it was simply because her brother was the child's father. I don't know. But it was very sick when it was born, and it only lived for a few hours." She laughed brokenly, and for the first time, tears dripped down her cheeks.

"Willemijn wasn't well—there was all this blood coming out of her, black and thick like rope—so I looked after the baby. It was very small. I put it flush against my chest, skin to skin, because I thought a baby that tiny couldn't keep itself warm. I held it and listened to its little rattling breaths, and though I knew it couldn't possibly live, I kept hoping that it would. Only it died."

Agnes hugged herself, shuddering as her wet sleeve touched the naked skin of her neck and throat.

"Thomas came to look at it, and I told him the child was dead, but it was all right, he and Willemijn could try again some other time. And then I began to laugh. I didn't mean to do it. There was

no mirth in it. I only laughed because I thought I'd go mad otherwise. I shouldn't have laughed, and I shouldn't have let him know
that I knew what he and his sister did. With a man like Thomas,
you must keep your cards close to your chest, because everything he
knows about you, he will use to destroy you if it suits him."

She stopped talking, took a shaky breath.

"Agnes, why did you never tell me any of this? I could've helped
you. You needn't have carried all this alone."

"Because I was ashamed. I let these things happen to me. And
you forget: I've never had anyone I could trust enough to talk to
before, only Peter. And some things one just doesn't talk about, not
with anyone. Some things are so shameful, so painful, that we lock
them away deep inside us and pretend they don't exist. You have
things like that, too, things your mama did to you; I know you do.
And I..."

She gave a little cry and dropped her cigarette; she had been
talking so feverishly, she had forgotten to smoke, and the thing had
burned her. I picked up the glass she had been using as an ashtray
and flicked the butt in with my fingertip before it could mark the
carpet, hissing at its searing heat. Agnes leaned against the windowsill, trembling and sucking at her fingers. She didn't even curse.

I kept silent, thinking she would pick up the thread of her story,
but she just stood there, her black hair falling into her face, looking
at something back in time that I could not share with her unless
she put it into words.

I scraped my throat and said softly, "Agnes, tell me honestly.
How did Thomas die?"

FOURTEENTH CASE EPISODE

PATIENT R—, A CASE STORY: INHABITED BY ANOTHER

(D = DOCTOR, P = PATIENT R—)

FOURTEENTH EPISODE, CONDUCTED ON 3 NOVEMBER 1954:

D: "R—, do you know what 'defamation' is?"

P: "No."

D: "Defamation is a criminal act that consists of any sort of statement made about a person that could seriously harm their reputation. Furthermore, the statement must be untrue, and the person making it must know it's untrue when making it."

P: "All right."

D: "Do you know why I am telling you this?"

P: "No."

D: "Because I fear that the prosecution might charge you with defamation if you recount any of what you've just told me about Mr. K— in court."

P: "But what I'm telling you is true. A— [Mrs. K—] told me so herself. Therefore, it isn't defamation."

D: "It's true that the prosecution might have a hard time proving defamation. It's never easy to prove that a person knowingly spread information both untrue and harmful. Nevertheless, I'm afraid they might try it. It is likely in their interest to make you look untrustworthy."

P: [*tiredly rubs her eyes*] "Why?"

D: "If you plead innocent..."

P: "Who says I'll plead innocent?"

D: "Ultimately, that's something to discuss with your lawyer, but assuming you do, the prosecution will likely strive to prove that you are actually guilty because they want you convicted. The fastest way to do that is by making you out to be a liar."

P: "You make them sound like predators, and the pursuit of justice nothing more than blood sport."

D: "Because a young widow lies dead and mutilated, and then we haven't even talked about the fact that you let another body rot on the lawn until it stank to high heaven. Don't you see that someone will be made to pay? I fear you're setting yourself up to be an easy scapegoat."

P: "You want to protect me?"

D: "Against yourself, yes. That is my task as your doctor."

P: "Not against the wolves from the prosecution?"

D: "I urge you to carefully go over what you mean to testify with your lawyer. The accusation of murder is very serious, but defamation and perjury aren't exactly laughing matters, either."

P: "If the prosecution already won't like me telling the court what sort of man T— [Mr. K—] really was, then they're not going to like a lot of things I have to say."

D: "Such as?"

P: "Such as how T— [Mr. K—] really died."

Chapter 27

AT FIRST, IT SEEMED AS if Agnes hadn't heard me. She still stood sucking her burnt finger. Yet, just when I was about to repeat my question, she removed her glistening finger from her mouth and said, "I killed him."

For a moment, I felt nothing. Then so many feelings flooded me at once that it felt like a hemorrhage of the brain. Color bled into my cheeks. *She killed her husband*, I thought and could make no sense of all I felt.

Meanwhile, Agnes kept talking. "He wasn't right after the baby died. In his mind, I mean. At first, I didn't pay any heed. Willemijn was very sick, and she needed my care. She had some sort of infection—puerperal fever, I think they call it. The doctor had to cut out her womb."

The scar on Willemijn's belly, I thought and felt stupid for not having wondered sooner why it was there.

"For months I had to tend to her, and when I wasn't looking after her, I slept. That's why I didn't really notice the changes in Thomas, and I didn't sense any danger when he asked to speak to me in his room one night. He sat at the open window, looking so still and beautiful, as if he'd been hewn from a piece of marble. He was such a handsome man…"

She rubbed her eyes roughly, with multiple fingertips at once. "He lit a cigarette for me, asked me how I was. For a while, we talked pleasantly. Then he suddenly told me he wanted to divorce me. The baby dying and Willemijn becoming so sick had brought it home to him how short and fragile life was. He needed an heir, and it was clear I wouldn't give him one, so he wanted to find himself another wife and try again."

Anger surged from my belly, traveled up my throat, and settled in ugly red patches on my neck and cheeks. *How dare he!* I thought.

"Men like Thomas dare a lot of things," Agnes said, and I realized that in my seething anger for his treatment of her, I had spoken those words out loud.

I fought down my hatred for him and asked, "How on earth did you bear it? His telling you that, I mean?"

"Badly. While he told me, all my feelings drained away, and I became as numb again as if I'd swallowed a handful of pills. I remember sitting there, listening to him, and thinking, 'Soon, the feeling will return to me,' and waiting for it to happen. Meanwhile, I noticed all these silly things: how a corner of the carpet had been kicked up, how the air coming in through the open window smelled of rain…"

She went to the window, squeezed some drops from her wet sleeve on the sill, and began to draw figures with her blistered finger, grimacing all the while. "By the time Thomas had finished talking, I was still utterly without feeling. He asked me what I was thinking. I said I didn't want to leave. For better or worse, the Rozentuin was my home as well as his. I didn't tell him I had no place to go if he turned me out and almost no money, and he had none to give me because he was as poor as a church mouse. It was useless to state those things because he knew them, and one can only appeal to another person's sense of pity if they have one."

"What did he say when you told him you wanted to stay?"

"He was ruthless. He told me I had no claim to the Rozentuin outside my marriage, and a wife only belongs when she breeds. I told him that was all very well, but he couldn't divorce me without my consent, and consent I didn't. I had given and given and given while I was with him. I was empty. I couldn't give him any more."

Again, she rubbed her eyes, turning the whites pink. "Well, since I didn't immediately bend to his wishes, he thought he'd bring me to heel. He told me in that clear cold way of his that if I wouldn't consent to a divorce, he would have me committed to an asylum. I had a long history of mental disturbance, didn't I, and there were the endless prescriptions for pills and the doctor's case notes to prove that. If that wasn't enough, he could ask any of his friends to testify that I was mad. While I had been looking after Willemijn, Thomas had been telling his friends and acquaintances I had lost the baby and had taken it very hard. He feared for my sanity. Over the course of months, he had slowly convinced everyone we knew that I had become unhinged."

That bastard. He deserved what he got. I would've killed him for that, too, would kill him again for her if I had the chance, I thought and felt such burning hatred for him that, for a moment, I thought I'd burst into tears. "You must have felt so frustrated, so powerless," I said.

"I did, and never more so than when he smiled at me and said, 'See, darling? I can have you put away anytime I like.' I knew he was right. Once people believe you're mad, anything you do will convince them more. But I couldn't be put away in an asylum; that would kill me. They would force pills down my throat, and Peter would disappear once more. I could bear almost anything, but not that. To be alone again…it would destroy me. To prevent that from happening, I killed him."

She put her hands to her face and looked at me from between the fingers like a child might have done. "It was a moment of passion, perhaps of madness. I just got up, went to him, and shoved him. I'll never forget the look of surprise on his face as he fell, as if he couldn't believe I would actually harm him despite everything he'd done to me. And then he was gone from sight. It took an eternity before I heard the thud of his body and the crack of his skull. When I finally dared to look down, I saw his brain splattered on the terrace, and that I'll never forget either…"

She ground the heels of her hands against her eyes and moaned softly. It was a strange thing, seeing her so discomposed. Stranger still was how calm it made me feel. I thought of what Ruth had said when we had arrived at the Rozentuin, how Agnes might want a person to lean on. I could be that person for her now.

I went to her and drew her hands away. The palms were wet

with her tears. "I understand," I said. "I'd kill for Ruth, too. Now tell me: Does anyone know what you did?"

"The police ruled it an accident. I think they thought it might've been suicide, but they had too much respect for Thomas and too much compassion for Willemijn and me to suggest that out loud."

"And Willemijn?"

"She suspects. She's never said anything, but I know she does. Was it her idea to rebury Thomas?"

I nodded.

"That doesn't surprise me. No doubt she wanted me to find out and be horrified and scared. If we're not careful, she'll call the police and tell them what you've done, just to make things hard on me. She would've just loved it if I had to send you away. I'd be completely at her mercy then. Hell, she might even try and tell the police it was all my idea and have me declared insane, just as her brother tried before her. There's no telling with her. Tell me honestly, Roos. Will anyone find Thomas?"

"I don't think it very likely. I buried him well."

She sank down in her chair again, looking grave and spent. "There's no chance of you tucking him back in his first grave now, is there?" she asked, and it was only half a joke.

"I'd rather not. It was hard enough to get him from his grave into the bog. I don't think the other way around is much easier."

She massaged her temples. "God, what a mess."

"I'm sorry. Had I known, I'd never have done it."

"Don't apologize. If anyone's to blame, it is me. I shouldn't have left you alone so much. Thomas always said that women with too much time on their hands turn to mischief or madness. I suppose there's some truth in that."

I twisted the little necklace she had given me around my throat, doing it hard and fast, relishing the bite of the gold. "Then why did you? Leave me alone so much, I mean. Could you not stand to be here because everything here reminds you of Thomas and all the things he did to you?"

She dropped her hands in her lap and shook her head. "No. I've always loved this place, no matter how much Thomas has tried to taint it for me. Whenever I was gone from here, it was to talk to banks, to try and scrape together the enormous amount of money needed to keep this place from falling apart even more. I've a set income every year, courtesy of being a widow, but it's not enough, and what I am allowed to do to the estate is very limited. I may live here, but I cannot sell so much as a foot of land without permission from half a dozen parties. It's a damned shame. I've been talking to lawyers for years but without any results."

"How did you pay Mama if you had no money?"

"I had sold my wedding ring before our first séance. The family jewels had gone a long time before, and even if they hadn't, I didn't have the right to do anything but wear them, or I'd have sold those, too, but that ring was solid gold and worth something. As for the stores where I bought your clothes: having an illustrious name is worth something. They let you buy things on credit. Not for long, of course, not once they realize you can't pay the bills, but until then, you can get the things you need to try and keep up appearances."

"Was that what you did when you were gone? Try to keep up appearances?"

A soft sad smile. "Not all of it. I've also been talking to a detective. I've been trying to track down my family's *kris* for over a decade now so I can give it the love and care it deserves. I've also been trying to find out if I've any family left on my mother's side. Sadly, both of those endeavors have also been without any results so far." She laughed again. The sound was almost a groan. "If Thomas only knew, he'd be laughing himself silly. He always did say that everything I touched blackened and withered. He's dead, and I have long ceased to love him, but I'm still not free of him. I still hear his voice, still strive for his approval…"

She pinched the base of her ring finger, which still bore the white mark of her wedding ring, now sold. "Sometimes, I think that all I am is what he made me," she murmured.

I knelt at her feet and took her hands in mine. I kissed the knuckles one by one, then the fleshy pads at the base of her thumbs. "But you're not. You're kind and funny and smart, and so much more besides. He couldn't take that away from you. He might've tried, but he couldn't because you're stronger than him and stronger than what he did to you."

She stroked the back of my hand with her thumb. "I love you, Roos."

"I love you, Agnes."

She drew me up to her to kiss me.

I placed my hand on her knee, then moved it up, slowly, softly, feeling first the silk of her stocking under my fingertips, then the lace border, and finally, deliciously, her skin, hot and silky as sun-baked sand.

Agnes slithered down from the chair and pushed me down onto the carpet, and the weight and heat of her were sweet as sin. Together we undressed me, tugging at buttons and hooks with impatient fingers. The room was oppressively hot, but as she touched me, gooseflesh rippled down my limbs and pimpled my chest and throat. She stroked my belly, which was no longer concave but curved outward after months of good food.

Her fingers were scalding. She squeezed my buttocks, mapped the stretch marks on my thighs, cupped the swell of my breasts. "My little darling thing, how you've grown since I first saw you," she murmured. She took my crimsoned earlobe into her mouth and tugged at it until I gasped. I took her hand in mine and brought it between my thighs so she might feel how much I desired her.

With those lovely long fingers of hers, she began to stroke me, inflaming me. I put my hand over hers and pressed it harder against me. She rubbed, and then she chafed at me with the heel of her hand, her fingers curled against my slick flesh so deliciously, I bit the sleeve of my shirt in delight. In this way she pleasured me once, twice, thrice; in this, like most things, Agnes was generous.

After the third time, I pulled her hand away. I felt sensitive, raw, deliciously weak. She kissed my mouth, made me suck her fingers. They tasted like brine, and I wondered why it was that spirits who desire salt so much always strain to obtain it through tears and blood but never through lovemaking.

When the strength returned to my limbs, I planted a row of

kisses from Agnes's mouth down her throat, between her breasts. She was right; the scar on her right breast did look silver in a certain light. I kissed that raised ridge of puckered skin until she placed a hand on my head.

"That flesh is all dead. I don't feel it anymore," she said.

I went lower then, down her belly and lower still, rubbing my cheek against her black hair, so different from mine, not at all rough and bushy but almost soft. When I parted her with my fingers and kissed her wet, soft flesh, she moaned and arched her back. Her fingers curled into my hair. I kissed and licked and sucked. Soon, she began to flow. A light sheen of sweat sprung up on her body.

"You're a pearl," I whispered against her downy thigh. That place between my legs contracted and began to ache again, as if she had not stroked it to satiation moments before. I wondered if perhaps, from this moment on, it would always be sore with want for her.

Her thighs trembled around my head, then tightened. As she came, she began to howl so loudly that it scared me. I crawled up over her body and clamped my hand over her mouth, and still she screamed.

"Hush, or Willemijn might think you're being murdered," I whispered. The howl petered out into a sobbing groan, and then she was quiet. She might have been sleeping if it weren't for the quick rise and fall of her chest. From between her closed lids, a tear slipped slowly down her temple. I caught it on the tip of my tongue before it ran into her hair.

She smiled. She looked like a fairy princess waiting to be kissed awake, so beautiful, her cheeks and mouth all flushed. I moved my mouth from her temple to her lips.

It began to rain.

Chapter 28

TOGETHER WE LISTENED TO THE drops drumming on the roof. The rain had been expected and was most welcome. We had opened all the windows to let in the cool fresh air.

"We should close some of the windows, make sure the rain doesn't come in," Agnes said, but neither of us got up. Why would we, when it was utter bliss to lie on that threadbare carpet, imparadised in each other's arms?

After a while, Peter came inside. He was bejewelled with raindrops. They had caught most beautifully in the mold at his throat. He regarded us for a little while, then came over and squatted next to us, his joints popping like green wood in a fire. He took Agnes's hand and kissed the back of it. Me, he patted gently on the head. That done, he went to sit at the window, waiting for the sun to come out and dry him.

I nuzzled Agnes's shoulder. "I'm glad we're in your room and not in mine. I don't think I could make love to you with the devils and sinners carved in the wardrobe watching."

She choked back a laugh. "Sweet funny thing," she said and hugged me tighter.

Together we dozed, then woke and made love again. When we were done, I fetched some food from the kitchen—*spekkoek* and *kroepoek* and a jar of pickles, humble but filling and lovely in its different textures. We ate between the sheets, using a cracked plate to catch the crumbs and juice. We drank water from a cup on her nightstand. The summer heat had made it lukewarm. It had a strange aftertaste, slightly metallic.

The bell in the corner of Agnes's room began to ring. It was connected to Willemijn's room; if she pulled the cord, it rang. The ringing carried much farther than her voice these days.

Agnes groaned and made to get up.

Gently, I pulled her back. "I'll do it," I said. "You stay here and rest." I kissed her brow before I got dressed. She had made me weak in the legs; they felt like reeds, all hollow inside, and I struggled to get into my skirt because I kept stumbling. Ruth appeared next to me and gripped my arm to steady me.

At the door, I turned around and ran to Agnes so I could kiss her again.

"Go!" She laughed and pushed me away. Just before my hand slid out of hers, she clutched it tight and pulled me back into her embrace. "Go, but come back to me as quickly as you can. I don't want to be alone," she murmured.

In the hallway, I leaned against the wall and laughed for no reason other than that I was happy. Agnes had killed her husband, and I had desecrated his grave in the mistaken belief that would please her, and I was so happy, it felt like my heart was too big for my chest.

"Who knew," Ruth whispered, "that Agnes Knoop wanted a bedfellow as well as a companion?"

"Hush, you," I said.

Willemijn rang the bell again. I combed my fingers through my hair and stepped into her room. It smelled muggy. She wasn't in bed as I had expected but was seated near the window, a big shawl draped around her shoulders. In the dying light of day, she looked especially wan and sickly. Yet that listlessness disappeared when she saw me.

"Have you come to say goodbye to me?" she asked with the eagerness of a child.

I felt calm and clean and cool. "Why would I say goodbye to you? I'm not going away."

That cruel childish delight in her face faltered. "But I thought… the police came…"

"Oh, I know all about that. Agnes told me."

Her brow furrowed furiously. "But then…why?"

I smiled coldly. "She's not angry with me. Why would she be? She knows I reburied Thomas because I had the best of intentions. Though, from what you've just said, it's clear to me that you hadn't."

"I…" she began, but I wouldn't let her continue.

"You wanted me to rebury your brother and you wanted Agnes to find out because you thought it would shock and upset her, and then she'd send me away. What I don't understand is why. What have I ever done to you? You can't accuse me of having taken your brother's place, and I've been nothing but kind to you, so why did you want to get rid of me?"

She began to twist the fringe of her shawl between her long white fingers. Her mouth was set in a hard line. "You've got some nerve, pretending it was all my idea. Don't forget it was you who told me about the connection between burial practices and spirits. My suggestion to rebury my brother was merely the inevitable conclusion to your madness, you silly little girl."

The calm that had possessed me only moments ago turned to hot anger. "How dare you talk to me that way!"

She fixed me with a cool, superior stare. "Stop making everything about you, will you? None of this is about you. It never was. I hardly ever think about you. I just needed you because I couldn't do what needed to be done myself. You were a tool, no more," she said and looked at her weakened hands in disgust.

"I see. You wanted to hurt Agnes, and I was collateral damage. God, how horrible! After all Agnes has done for you. Hasn't she suffered enough?" I said.

Her eyes flashed with tears and anger both. "And what about me? Haven't I suffered, and far more than she has? She seduced Thomas, didn't she? Before she came, I was everything to him. What use did he have for a wife? Together, we'd keep the family line pure. But then came Agnes. Amazing, exotic little Agnes. She stole him from me with her filthy foreign ways. When I heard the news, I thought Thomas was playing a sick joke on me. Did he really mean to breed with this yellow slit-eyed bitch and leave the Rozentuin to her and her little bastards, this estate that has been in our family for centuries? Only it wasn't a joke. When he came back from his honeymoon, I told him in no uncertain terms he had made the worst mistake of his life, but by then, he already knew. He had married her in a moment of madness, he told me, and now he was punished for it. If anyone suffered, it was he, and through him, I suffered, too!"

"Don't you call her that!" I said hotly.

"Slit-eyed, slit-eyed, slit-eyed!" She laughed, taunting me. I thought of hitting her, of dashing her head against the wall, and burning rage suffused my head and limbs. Meanwhile, she kept talking.

"Of course, I don't expect you to understand," she spat. "How could you, when you never met my brother? He was perfect. When our parents were roaming Europe for a cure for our mother's consumption and that endless string of governesses abused and abandoned us, he cared for me. When our mother died and our father filled the rooms with plaster saints, Thomas shielded me from his madness. And when he could shield me no longer, he took a knife to our father's throat and liberated us both. His love is all I've ever known. I know his love made monsters out of us both, but he is a god to me, and I can deny him nothing. But you're wrong, you know. Reburying him wasn't about hurting Agnes, though I knew it would, and if nothing else comes of it, I'll be content. After all, she deserves to burn in hell for what she did to him, and so her suffering pleases me." Winded, she pressed a hand against her chest. I could hear her breath whistle through her throat.

"If it wasn't about hurting Agnes, then what was it about?" I asked.

She turned her head to the window. Tears dripped down her

hollowed cheeks. "Making sure he can find his way back to me. My entire being cries out for him. I have to take every chance I can get to restore him to me, no matter how small, no matter how insane," she whispered.

I wanted to laugh. I wanted to cry. "But what use would it be to you if he came back? You can't even see spirits."

"I might learn. If two people as different as you and Agnes can share the same brand of madness, then why not I? My father thought saints spoke to him. My grandfather saw angels and demons crawling up against the wall and hiding in the rafters. Lunacy lies in my very marrow, so why shouldn't I be able to see spirits if I want it hard enough?"

She hugged herself and began to rock to and fro. With her brittle hair and ravaged face, she looked like a scarecrow buffeted by the wind. Whatever watery beauty she had once possessed, whatever beauty the first stages of consumption had given her, all of it was gone now. She just looked very poorly, very sick. I felt a stab of pity, strangely cool amid the heat of my anger. I could not quite bring myself to touch her, but I knelt in front of her.

"Willemijn, look at me," I said.

She kept looking out the window, sobbing softly to herself, her mouth a black wet hole. Glistening streaks ran down her cheeks like the tracks of a snail. So close to her, I smelled the wet rot on her breath.

"You say you've suffered horribly. I believe you. You say all this pain was inflicted on you and you had no choice but to bear it. I know what that's like. But that's no reason to inflict it on others.

What you did to Agnes…it's wicked, and it's cruel, and it isn't right."

"If you're looking for remorse and apologies, look elsewhere. You'll have none of mine."

"Why do you insist on inflicting pain? It won't bring your brother back. Nothing will!" I exclaimed in frustration.

"Madness might, and so madness is what I choose," she whispered.

Suddenly, she stopped her sobbing. Fear flickered on her face, but only for a moment. When it was gone, she began to laugh, softly at first, then with great wheezing hacks, making a pulse in her forehead jump. She curled forward, spat into a handkerchief, turned her face back to the window, and continued that horrible choking laughter. Something deep in her chest rattled, like a loose penny in an empty tin.

The sound repulsed and frightened me. "Stop it!" I cried. "Do you mean to laugh yourself to death? There's nothing to laugh about."

She fixed her burning eyes on me and smiled. It looked more like a snarl, her upper lip curling back and revealing her large teeth, which seemed even larger because consumption had turned her face gaunt. Blood colored the lines between the teeth pink and brown.

"Do you not see him?"

My heart began to thump painfully fast inside my chest, yet my hands and feet turned to ice. Sweat prickled underneath my armpits. A shiver tore through me, raising all the little hairs on my body. "What are you talking about?" I asked.

"Go look out the window, and then tell me I've got nothing to laugh about."

Mechanically, I did as she ordered, though dread made my limbs heavy. The window had fogged over slightly; I wiped at it with the side of my hand, smearing it until it dripped. The raindrops on the outside shivered, then began to run; the glass lay rather loose in its frame and juddered at my touch. The clouds were moving away, revealing a sky drenched in shades of orange and red and purple. A red twilight meant more rain, didn't it? Or was that a red dawn? I suddenly couldn't remember.

"Do you not see him? Look, look!" Willemijn jeered.

"There's no one there," I said. Relief washed through me. My knees, still weak from Agnes's attentions, threatened to buckle, and I leaned heavily against the sill. A splinter bit into my palm. I plucked it out, watched a bead of blood well up, growing bigger and bigger. Before it could run, I brought my hand to my mouth and sucked it away.

"You're not looking at the right spot then. He's at the edge of the pond."

I scanned the lawn, looked at the filthy water of the pond, completely green with duckweed now. "I don't see anyone." Of course I didn't. What were the chances of Thomas coming back as a spirit? Ruth and Peter had taken centuries, and their bodies had been in the right conditions from the moment they'd died. There had been someone to wake them besides, but who was there to wake Thomas with their crying? No one but the odd fox or bird.

"You're a liar! He's right there!" Willemijn screamed.

I laughed, shortly, bitterly. "I'm sorry, but there's no one there, Willemijn."

"Don't you dare laugh at me, you fucking blind bitch!" She stabbed me in the chest with her finger. I beat her hand away.

"I've had just about enough of you! If you think your brother is there, then you might truly be mad." I made to turn, but Willemijn gripped the back of my neck and slammed my face against the window. She wasn't very strong, not anymore, but she had surprised me. Hot pain throbbed through my orbital bone. Her long nails dug into the skin of my nape. Her hand was cold and clammy, her touch deeply unpleasant.

"Follow my finger and try and tell me again that you can't see him," she hissed. She placed her finger along my cheek, then stabbed the glass with the tip, leaving a little smudge.

This time, I did see.

Thomas stood outside on the lawn.

FIFTEENTH CASE EPISODE

PATIENT R—, A CASE STORY: INHABITED BY ANOTHER

(D = DOCTOR, P = PATIENT R—)

FIFTEENTH EPISODE, CONDUCTED ON 4 NOVEMBER 1954:

D: "Do you know what schizophrenia is?"

P: "A sickness of the mind."

D: "Indeed. A patient suffering from schizophrenia has trouble telling fantasy from reality. The illness is characterized by psychotic episodes. When a person has one of those, they may behave in bizarre ways. They can become delusional and experience hallucinations, and they may appear confused and are unable to talk coherently. Did you know that Mrs. K— had been diagnosed with paranoid schizophrenia?"

P: [*silence*]

D: "She spent some time in a mental institution after she had her breakdown. There, she was treated for auditory and visual hallucinations. Did you never wonder what she did in the years between finishing school and meeting her husband?"

P: [*whispers*] "She never told me."

D: "Why do you think that is?"

P: "It's as she said. Some things are too horrible to talk about. I never told her about Mr. Mesman, either. I allowed her to have secrets, as she allowed me."

D: "I'll be frank with you, R—. The police think you may have triggered a psychotic episode in Mrs. K—, or at the very least that you encouraged her in her paranoid delusions."

P: "But it wasn't me who began it! It was W— [Miss K—]. She was the first one to see T— [Mr. K—]. How do you explain that?"

D: "The K— family has a long history of illnesses of the mind. From what you've told me, I wouldn't be surprised if Miss K—'s father and grandfather suffered from a kind of psychotic disorder. It may well be that Miss K— was susceptible, too. And she was so ill by that point she was given morphine daily, wasn't she? Morphine can play strange tricks upon the mind. Regardless of what Miss K—'s mental state was at the time, the police think you are responsible for what happened. Some of them think you may have wanted Mrs. K— to come to harm. Do you understand?"

P: [*visibly agitated*] "But that's not true! I loved A— [Mrs. K—]!" [*pauses; inhales deeply*] "I loved A—. I loved her so much I feel sore and sick with it. It makes a pain rise, from here to here," [*touches breastbone and moves it over throat*] "so that I can scarce swallow for love. I'd never harm her, never..." [*begins to weep into hands*]

D: "I believe you, R—. I don't think you meant to hurt her. I think there's a different explanation. Have you heard of *folie à trois*?"

P: [*shakes head*]

D: "It is a psychiatric syndrome in which three people come to share the same delusion. Usually one person is the instigator, although it can also happen that the delusion occurs simultaneously in all three people. Because Mrs. K— suffered from schizophrenia, she was particularly susceptible to delusions. Miss K—, too, was vulnerable to suggestions because of her long family history of mental instability and use of morphine, and you..."

P: [*interrupts*] "You think I'm having delusions, too. You think I can't tell reality from fantasy. Why can't you just believe me?" [*bites the skin between the index finger and thumb of left hand*]

D: "I believe it is real to you."

P: "Why can't it simply be real, and not just to me? Just because you can't explain how it could be real doesn't mean it's not real."

D: "All right. Please don't bite your hand. I don't want you to hurt yourself. Why don't you tell me how Mrs. K— ended up dead?"

Chapter 29

DEATH HAD BEEN FAR KINDER to Thomas than to Ruth and Peter, or perhaps Thomas just remembered better what human beings were supposed to look like because he hadn't been dead long. There was some mold spotting his gray skin, and the flesh had sloughed off his frame, leaving his long lean face cadaverous, but the proportions were as they should be.

Yet somehow everything he had gotten right only served to make him look more wrong. Peter and Ruth, I found beautiful; Thomas made my flesh crawl.

He looked up and fixed his eyes upon me. They weren't black holes or dried-up raisins but looked very much as I supposed they did when he was alive: pale and cold. Such malevolence lay in them, such hatred, that I felt my mind buckle. Ruth and Peter remembered nothing from when they were alive. From the way Thomas looked at me, I was sure he remembered more than was good for Agnes and me.

Once my brain thawed a little, the first thing I thought was that I could not let Agnes see. The second thought was that I must lock all the windows and doors to deny him entrance to the house.

I turned to Willemijn. She had pressed her hands and face to the glass, fogging it with her breath and warmth. That ghoulish look, that mixture of hatred and yearning I had seen when she had met me on the stairs once had taken possession of her face once more. Slowly, her hand crept over the glass toward the window's fastenings.

"No!" I yelled. I lunged at her and tried to drag her away from the window, but she began to scream and buck. I had to slap her with an open hand, once, twice, thrice, to get her to stop. I clutched the fabric of her blouse and brought my face so close to hers, I felt the scrabble of her lashes against mine.

"I am sorry I hit you, but you can't let him in! If you do, he'll harm us. Don't think you are exempt. You weren't when he was still alive, so I don't see why you would be now that he's dead."

"Never me! I was the only one he ever loved!" she spat.

"That's why he made you have the baby that triggered the tuberculosis that has been killing you slowly ever since. Now stay here while I go and close all the windows and doors."

She opened her mouth and coughed in my face, spraying it with droplets of blood and phlegm. I reared back with a cry and rubbed my face against the inside of my elbow. Willemijn fell to the ground and lay there laughing and coughing. For a moment I thought about tying her down so she could not reach the window, but she seemed so weak, I doubted she could get up unless someone helped her, so I left her lying there, giggling and gagging.

I had gone downstairs not a moment too soon: as I jumped down the final steps, the handle to the front door began to turn. I launched myself at the door and clutched the doorknob with one hand; with the other, I fumbled for the key Agnes had left in the lock.

Thomas battered the door then with such might, the key shuddered out of the lock and clattered to the floor.

I cried out, pushing back as hard as I could. I held the knob so hard, the little joints in my fingers began to burn and throb, yet it started to turn anyway. Through the fear and horror, one thought came to me with terrifying clarity: I was no match against Thomas. I could not hold this door closed. My only chance was to lock it, but for that I needed to retrieve the key, and to do that I needed to let go of the handle.

As if he could sense my despair, Thomas redoubled his efforts to get inside. The knob twisted inside my hand, slowly, almost gleefully. I clutched at it with both hands, but with my sweat-slick palms, I couldn't get a good grip on the metal. It rotated against my flesh. I held it so tight, the turning felt searing hot. With a horrifying click, it reached the point where it could turn no more.

All was silent then, and all was still.

Please, I begged, or thought, or prayed, *please, leave us in peace. Please don't...*

Thomas launched himself against the door again. It shot open at least a few handspans, the wood colliding with my shoulder. I felt as if I had been hit with a sledgehammer. Pain enflamed the joint and shot down my arm. I turned and fell with my back against the door in an effort to keep it shut. My stockinged feet began to slip on the tiles. I rucked up my skirt and felt for the straps of my garter belt, tore at them so my stockings would slither down my legs.

Something cold stroked a little line on the inside of my arm.

I could not bring myself to look down straightaway. Instead, I pressed myself even harder against the door, and though the places where the bones of my hips and spine were flush against the wood must have turned sore, and though my shoulder and arm and hand were on fire, my entire consciousness seemed to concentrate on that little patch of skin where something drew figures I couldn't comprehend so softly, it might almost be called tenderness.

I let my head fall forward; there was no other way I could have made myself look down. The fear was too potent.

Thomas had wormed his arm through the crack between the door and the frame and was now hungrily tracing my veins with a corpse-cold finger.

"Ruth!" I screamed.

She was next to me then, her teeth bared and a snarl in her throat. She threw her weight against the door. There was a snap of bone, then a moment of silence before Thomas started howling. Ruth stood back a little, allowing Thomas to drag his arm back. Just before he could pull out his hand, she bashed her shoulder against the door again. The little wet crunch of his hand being crushed made me flinch.

When he had finally extracted himself from the doorway, she pressed her shoulder against the door to keep it shut and placed a cold hand over mine while she felt for the fallen key with the other. Once she found it, she locked the door and placed the key between my fingers.

Someone groaned.

"Hush, my little love," Ruth said, touching her forehead against mine, and I realized it was me.

"Thank you," I said. I stood back from the door and massaged my shoulder. The flesh was bruised and tender, but I could still move my arm.

Thomas pressed his face to the small glass pane next to the front door. In the pictures I had seen of him, he had been handsome. The lines and proportions that had lent beauty to his face were still present, but all of it was marred by the sheer hatred that radiated off him. His eyes traveled over my face, then fixed themselves on a point behind me. His mouth split into a grin.

I turned to look. Agnes stood on the staircase, her face a mask of fear, her fingers clawlike as she clutched the banister.

"Oh, Agnes!" I said. I ran to her, nearly stumbling over my stockings as they slithered down my legs with a silky hiss. I stripped them off, cast them aside. When I reached Agnes, I put my arm around her waist in case she should stumble. She trembled, yet her body was rigid, too, like a bowstring that had been plucked.

Thomas laughed. He waved at Agnes, then stuck his hands in the pockets of his trousers and walked away, whistling a tune. When he turned, I got a queasy feeling in my stomach. The back of his head gaped open and empty, like a cracked eggshell that had been hollowed out. Looking at it was like looking at a spoon from a wrong angle: I couldn't be quite sure which way it curved.

"He'll try to find his way in through another door. We must lock all doors, and the windows, too," Agnes said, and she did not hesitate, she did not falter. "I shall do the ground floor if you make sure everything upstairs is secure."

My love for her did not banish the terror I felt, but it made it easier to handle somehow. "No. Ruth and I will take the ground floor. You and Peter head upstairs. I've left Willemijn on the floor, but I'm not quite sure she won't crawl to the window and call to her brother to creep in that way."

Agnes briefly closed her eyes, and a look of pain and exhaustion passed over it like a dark cloud. Yet when she opened them again, they glittered fiercely.

"Let's hurry then, Roos. Hurry, hurry!"

She dashed up the stairs, her bare feet drumming on the steps. I ran down, took Ruth's outstretched hand. She pulled me along, out of the hallway and into the library. From one of its mullioned windows, we could see Thomas standing on the lawn, rocking back and forth on his heels, his hands still tucked in his pockets, his head tilted back as he inspected the house. When he saw us, he ceased rocking and sauntered to one of the windows, grinning like the devil.

"No you don't!" Ruth spat through clenched teeth. She yanked me to the window with her so hard, my joints popped. With fingers cold and wet with fear, I managed to lock it just before he pressed his hand against the glass. It was the one Ruth had crushed between the door, all dented and wrong, with gristle showing through ragged strips of skin.

When the window wouldn't budge, he shrugged and moved to the next window.

I've had nightmares of this ever since, dread-laden dreams in which I see Thomas approaching an open window and I run to close it, but my legs won't obey or the distance between me and the window lengthens rather than shortens with each step, and I know it'll be too late, but I must try because of the horrors that shall happen if he enters the house.

But I wasn't too late. Every time Thomas approached a window or door, I managed to lock it just before he could place his ruined hand against it and try and push it open. When I had locked the final door, I ran up the stairs. I found Agnes in her room, standing at the window next to Peter and looking out. Willemijn sat sullenly in the green velvet chair, combing her fingers through the fringe of her scarf.

"I've locked all the doors and windows downstairs," I said.

"Then he shan't be able to come in," Agnes said, but this thought did not seem to comfort her. Little lines of worry had appeared around her mouth and between her eyebrows.

"What is it? What's wrong?" I asked.

"I feel as if we have made a mistake somewhere. If Thomas wanted to get inside, surely he could have done so."

I remembered the way he went from window to window, his hands tucked in his pockets, as if he were simply taking a stroll. "Perhaps he could have tried a little harder," I admitted.

"I don't like it. I feel as if he's playing with us like a cat with a frog," she said. She folded her lips around her cigarette with a soft papery sound. The lines on her brow deepened.

"But why?"

She blew out a cloud of smoke. "It's his nature to be cruel."

"No, I mean, why does he choose to stay outside? What use is that to him? If he wants to torment us, isn't it better for him to be in the house with us?"

Willemijn began to giggle again, a cough rumbling in her chest. Agnes froze, the cigarette halfway to her mouth. Realization hit me a second later, chilling me to the bone.

"As long as we are in here, and he's out there," I said slowly, "there's no way for us to leave, now is there?"

Willemijn spread her scarf on her lap and began to braid some of the tassels together. "None," she said with glee. "None at all."

Chapter 30

FOR A WHILE THERE WAS only the silky, slippery sound of Willemijn's scarf slithering around on her lap as she tugged on the tassels and the sizzling of Agnes's cigarette. She squashed it carefully in the tray, then rubbed her fingers together to get rid of the ash and a little fleck of tobacco that stuck to her skin.

"Right," she said, "I suppose that means we are in deep fucking trouble."

"Don't say that!" I took her hand in mine. She had a blister on her finger from where her cigarette had burned her some hours before. It looked pearly, the skin painful and taut. Peter rested his cheek against her shoulder to comfort her.

She gave me a sad, sour smile. "You don't know him like I do."

"There must be something we can do."

"Oh, I don't mean to say we should just roll over and die. I don't intend to go down without a fight. I'd rather not go down at all if I can help it."

"But go down you will," Willemijn said. She did not say it with any malice or glee; she was merely stating a fact.

"Bitch," Ruth hissed.

I ignored Willemijn. "Look, why don't we send Ruth to him to tell him he is not welcome here?" I suggested.

"He knows he's not welcome. We've made that abundantly clear," Agnes said.

"Well, maybe she can see if there's a way to exorcise him, or perhaps we can reach an agreement. We don't even know how much he remembers from when he was alive. Maybe all he has is this feeling of hatred toward you, but how long can you keep on hating someone if you can't remember the reason?"

"I don't think it'll make much of a difference, but trying it can do no harm," Agnes said, and so Ruth went outside. She spoke to Thomas for no more than five minutes. When she came back, her tea-colored face had worry lines carved between the brows and around the mouth. She looked at me, her eyes like sharp pieces of flint. "He won't go. He says you have summoned him, and he is bound to you because you named him and bled for him."

I balled my hands into fists and felt the tug of the scarred flesh on my knuckles where I had cut them on the lip of the wheelbarrow.

"Did you tell him the position of spirit companion has been taken and there's no vacancy?" Agnes asked. She lit a cigarette and smoked it quickly.

Ruth shrugged. "It won't make any difference. He has been bound; he can't be banished. He must leave of his own accord or not at all."

"Like I said," Agnes murmured, "we are in deep fucking trouble."

We spent thirty-three days holed up inside the house.

I think we went a little mad.

So much of what happened then has blurred together, the way raindrops do when they've lain against a windowpane for a while and gravity drags them down.

But some things stand out vividly, the images, the sounds and smells and textures, all of it so sharp and crisp that, at times, it seems to bleed over into the now. I can feel Agnes's soft breaths against my throat and upon my cheeks then, I can taste the bitterness of pills blooming on my tongue, I can smell putrefaction.

I shall tell you what I remember.

Despite everything Agnes had told me of Thomas and despite my own experiences with people like Mama and Mr. Mesman, I didn't think things would turn out as badly as they did—a stubborn streak of optimism, or perhaps a lack of imagination, though I don't think anyone could have guessed how spectacularly everything would go to hell during those thirty-three days.

The first few days, I did not yet fully grasp the gravity of the situation, but then there was so much to do that I had little time to think. We prepared as if for a siege. We gathered all the food, ate the perishables, then decided on daily rations.

"Finally a good use for your acts of petty thievery," I quipped as I looked through Agnes's assortment of pepper shakers, boxes of sugar, and little bags of nutmeg and cardamon. We could still laugh then.

Agnes and I barricaded the doors downstairs and shuttered the windows in case Thomas should change his mind and come inside after all. We weren't quite sure what he would do if he managed it, but we weren't particularly keen to find out. We also moved Willemijn's things into Agnes's room so the three of us could stay there. It had become necessary to watch Willemijn at all times, not only because she was rapidly deteriorating but also because she tried to call her doctor and tell him Agnes and I had lost our minds and were holding her hostage.

Agnes wrested the phone from her, then apologized to the doctor with a cool crisp voice. "It's the morphine, I think. It makes her hallucinate. She also thinks her brother's spirit is outside." She gave a soulless chuckle at this. "Yes, quite distressing for all of us. The way she describes him, you could almost see him. But not to worry, Doctor; we will manage. No, there's no need to drop by. Yes, I shall call if there are any changes. Thank you. Goodbye." When she had severed the connection, she rubbed her eyes and sighed. "Thank God for the well-known hallucinogenic properties of morphine."

Willemijn glowered at her. "You unnatural yellow bitch," she snarled.

I made to strike her, but Agnes clasped my wrist. "Do not seek to correct what you don't understand," she said.

"But she called you…"

"I know what she called me. Don't waste any more breath on it."

She proceeded to call the staff to tell them they were not needed for a while since we were taking Willemijn to a private clinic, not in the hope that she could be saved, but to ease her suffering. This done, she cut the telephone wires.

We were now completely severed from the outside world.

The seventh night, it was my turn to sit up and watch over Willemijn. Because we gave her morphine in the evenings, she usually slept quite well for a few consecutive hours, but even then we never left her unattended.

She watched me hungrily as I took the tablets out of their bottle one by one, her face tight with pain. Agnes kept the bottle locked in a drawer to prevent Willemijn from self-administering and accidentally taking too much.

I dropped some on her open palm. She counted them. "Do give me one more." Her illness had reduced her voice to a hoarse whisper.

"You know I can't."

She scowled but did not argue. Instead, she popped the tablets into her mouth one by one. Unlike Agnes, she had no trouble with pills and could even swallow them dry. Her nightly dosage taken, she fell back against the pillows and waited for the morphine to numb the pain.

Just when I thought she had gone to sleep, she opened her eyes a crack and said, "You have got me all wrong, you know."

"Have I?" I said.

"Yes. You think Thomas harmed me. You think he forced me to have his baby. That's not true." She coughed softly, her face twisting with pain.

"You don't have to speak," I said.

She shook her head. "I want to. I want you to know. Thomas didn't want me to get pregnant. He knew what might happen if I did. He was always very careful. Only it caught anyway. I shouldn't have kept it, but I wanted it. I wanted an heir for the Rozentuin. I couldn't bear the thought of all this falling into the hands of some other family and him and me being responsible for the end of our line. This was the only thing in which I ever opposed him. Now I wish I hadn't."

"I don't know what to say," I admitted.

"You don't have to say anything. I just wanted to tell you this." She swallowed. The skin at her throat twitched like a horse's flank when it tried to dislodge a fly. "Now please let me sleep."

"Of course."

She screwed up her eyes in the way a child might have done. As the drug took effect and tamed the liquid fire in her chest, her face lost that tight, masklike quality. Soon, she slept, a beatific smile upon her lips.

The next day, we woke up to a little surprise from Thomas.

The plaster saints from the chapel were spread out on the lawn.

Their paint was scratched, their plaster chipped. One of them was hung about with winding sheets. The fabric had torn and decomposed in places, the white all stained, making it look like an Egyptian mummy. They should've looked utterly ridiculous in the searing summer light, but they didn't.

They looked like an army ready to lay siege to the house.

"But that isn't right," Willemijn said when she saw them. She worked her mouth like an old lady might and wrung her tasselled scarf between her hands. "He knows I hate them. He would never..."

Agnes knelt beside her and clasped her hands with her own. "That dreadful thing outside isn't your brother anymore. He doesn't care that this hurts you. In fact, I'm sure he'll hurt you if he thinks it'll get him closer to me. You don't matter to him anymore. Only I do."

Willemijn tore her hands from Agnes's grasp. "You're wrong! You have never been more important to him than I am. This is all about me, don't you see? He's punishing me. He must think I've sided with you, and that hurts him more than those statues could ever hurt me," she said.

"Believe that if it makes any of this easier."

"You're cruel. My poor, poor brother," she whined and began to cry with her mouth open.

Over the next few days, Thomas moved the statues a little closer to the house when we weren't watching.

Or maybe they moved of their own accord. Neither Ruth nor Peter could move such heavy objects by themselves. If Thomas could, he was far more powerful than I had initially thought, and that made him infinitely more dangerous.

The day after, the statues had come a little closer still.

I kept a very close watch on Willemijn for the next few days, afraid that she would do something desperate, like hurt herself or try to let her brother in. But it wasn't her I should have worried about.

It was Agnes.

During the night cleaving the twelfth and thirteenth day, I woke to find Agnes at the window trying to undo the locks. Thomas was outside, his horrible face so close to the glass, it had partly misted over. Ghosts do not generally breathe, but they do draw air inside their lungs and expel it when they talk, and his lips were moving.

"Agnes, no!" I yelled and threw myself at her. We had a sort of fight then, a kind of tussle where she pulled away and I tried to hold her fast.

"Let me go!" she screamed.

"You can't let him in!"

She dashed her elbow into my stomach. I grunted with pain, but I did not let her go. She let out a wordless howl of frustration and strained against me, but I had locked my limbs together, and she could barely move. It did not seem to last very long, yet by the time she slackened and sank to the floor, my arms hurt almost as much as the night I had dug up Thomas. I felt as if weights were knotted around each finger, pulling on my arms, straining the muscles and bone.

Agnes rested her forehead against the wall. "He'll win. You know that as well as I do. At some point, I will let him in. Look how close I came tonight..."

"What did he say to you?"

She looked up at me, and her face was a mask, drawn and tight and pale. "That he'd spare you if I let him in. That he wouldn't harm you in any way, but only if I opened the window for him. And if I didn't let him in, well, he'd find a way, only then we'd wish we'd chosen differently because…" She stopped talking and gasped as if in pain.

"Because?"

"I can't say it."

"You can and you must, Agnes. I have to know what we're up against."

She squeezed her eyes shut and began to talk rapidly, monotonously. "He said he'd possess you and use you to have me declared insane. He'd make you go to the police and tell them of all this madness: how I had kept you and Willemijn hostage, had beaten and starved you because I thought there was something terrible outside that shouldn't be let in. Or he'd use you to murder me bit by bit, that I may know what it was like to be killed by someone I had loved and trusted. He'd dispose of you then. Once he had possessed you, he'd know your deepest fears and use them against you. Or he'd possess me and use me to destroy you, force me to kill you by degrees. He hadn't quite made up his mind. The possibilities for fun, he said, were near endless."

I thought of Thomas forcing his way inside me, ripping my throat to shreds. It would be like Mr. Mesman all over again, only worse, because Mr. Mesman had only been inside me a little way. Thomas would flood my whole body with his poisonous presence, anchor himself to my spine, and then use me to hurt Agnes. The worst part would be that I would be fully present but powerless to stop him as he did so. And then he'd know all about me, all my shameful little secrets and fears: Mr. Mesman, my terror of hunger, my childlike fear of the dark, my plans for the powdered glass and Mama...

"So you see now why I wanted to let him in," Agnes whispered. "I couldn't bear to let him hurt you. And then I thought..." She bit her lip, shook her head quickly, let out a dark chuckle. "I might as well tell you. I thought, 'Why not get it over with now? Why draw out this suffering? He's so much stronger than I am.' I'm starting to think I'm his creature still." She hung her head in shame.

I pushed away the images that had risen in my mind. I had to be strong now. "You're not. You're more than what he did to you, Agnes, just as I'm more than what Mama did to me. They may have done their best to twist us with their hatred and bitterness, and we might never forget the horrors they inflicted on us, but we won't let them succeed. We've both been maimed, but maybe if we're together, we can learn how to be a whole person."

"Oh, Roos, how easy you are to love and admire when you talk like that. But you're wrong, you know. At some point, I will let Thomas in, and you will let me. There'll come a time when anything is better than this endless waiting, when pain and degradation become preferable to this not knowing what it is exactly that he shall do to us."

I lifted my burning arms with a gasp and placed my hands on her shoulders, which made her look up at me. "I won't give that bastard the satisfaction. I'd rather die than let him do anything to you," I said.

"We will if we don't find a way to get rid of him. He is dead already; there's no thirst or hunger to plague him. All he needs to do is wait, and he has all the time in the world."

I looked out the window. His hateful face was there still, the eyes strangely luminous. It reminded me of a drawing I had seen once in a library book, of a corpse laid out with two coins on his eyes so he could pay the ferryman to shepherd his soul to the after-life. I drew the curtains to shut him out and said boldly, "Well, maybe there'll come a time for him when anything is better than this endless waiting, too. I'll make it so."

She contemplated this for a moment, then smiled, placed a cool hand on the back of my neck, and gave it a little squeeze.

SIXTEENTH CASE EPISODE

PATIENT R–, A CASE STORY: INHABITED BY ANOTHER

(D = DOCTOR, P = PATIENT R–)

SIXTEENTH EPISODE, CONDUCTED ON 5 NOVEMBER 1954:

D: "Thirty-three days is a long time to spend holed up inside. What did you do to make the time pass?"

P: "We tended to W— [Miss K—], cooked, kept the rooms clean. When we had free time, A— [Mrs. K—] played the piano for us or read out stories. We'd also play cards, using cents or cigarettes or sweets for bets. They taught me how to play poker, but W— [Miss K] was a bad loser and accused A— [Mrs. K—] of cheating, so we stopped playing after a while because it only led to fights."

D: "She didn't accuse you of cheating?"

P: "I don't think she thought I was smart enough to cheat."

D: "It mustn't have been easy, being cooped up with Miss K—, especially after she had used you."

P: "I didn't hate her as much as you might think. I had bigger things on my mind."

D: "Such as?"

P: "Keeping the peace between W— [Miss K] and A— [Mrs. K—]. Making sure A— [Mrs. K—] could bear the mental strain of knowing her husband's vengeful spirit was trying to kill her, and me too, as collateral damage. I also had to come up with a plan to defeat or escape him before we ran out of food."

D: "We've established before that you have a particular fear of going hungry. Seeing the food dwindle as the siege lasted must have been agony for you."

P: "I suppose."

D: "Hunger truly is a terrible thing, R—, and it can make people do terrible things. We know of people who have eaten their beloved pets, people who dug up the dead. Hell, if the hunger is bad enough, people might even kill each other."

P: [*tiredly*] "I didn't try and eat A— [Mrs. K—], if that's what you're suggesting."

D: "But you did bite her corpse, didn't you? You almost severed her left hand at the wrist. Why, if not to eat her?"

P: "Who says it was me who bit her hand?"

Chapter 31

THE STRANGE THING IS THAT the more depressed and defeatist Agnes grew, the more determined I became. I'd look outside and see Thomas standing on the lawn with this cruel smile twisting what would otherwise have been a handsome face, and this wild hot feeling would flood my brain like blood.

Let him try and match his will to mine, I'd think, *and we'll see who shall bend and bow in the end.*

On day fifteen, Agnes ran out of cigarettes. She had been rationing them, but now she had smoked them all up, even the butts she had rescued from the ashtray in the library. All day she was twitchy and irritable, and she refused to play cards with me. I tried to play with Willemijn instead, but a sudden flare-up of pain in her chest made her squeeze her hands into fists, folding the ace of spades, the diamond ten and three, the knave of hearts. I played solitaire instead and pretended I didn't know what the cards with the creases were.

I woke that night to find Agnes sitting on the windowsill and brushing her hair. The bristles moving through her hair produced this lovely sound, almost painful, like silk snagging. When she was done, Peter lay a finger on her head and stroked her with the same delicate movements he had used to caress that bee all those days ago, when I had asked him how long he had been alone after he'd woken as a spirit.

She took his hand and shook her head at him.

The seventeenth day, a poacher wandered onto the lawn at twilight, a dead pheasant and two dead rabbits slung over one shoulder. He stopped dead when he saw the plaster saints. Their slow procession toward the house had left dark ruts in the lawn. The poacher laughed uneasily, then began to whistle a tune to try and calm his nerves. Thomas joined him, and although the man could not see him—he nearly walked right into him—perhaps he could hear him, for he cocked his head and listened, then visibly shuddered and walked away briskly, breaking into a run when close to the trees.

I had a nightmare on the twenty-first night. Agnes woke me and held me tight. I don't know what it is I dreamed, but the terror and helplessness that usually lingered for hours after I woke quickly shifted to desire as she began to kiss me. I drew her on top of me. We locked together with a gasp, damp flesh against damp flesh. Together we strove and strained, lost ourselves, were found by the other.

The twenty-second day, Agnes burst into tears during lunch.

"What is it?" I asked.

She pressed her fingers against her eyes and murmured, "I think I might be to blame for everything that's happening right now. If I still had my family's *kris*, it would've protected us from Thomas. Maybe this is revenge from its spirit. I've had nothing but bad luck since I've lost that damned dagger, haven't I? I should've tried harder to find it. That detective I hired was shit."

I wished I knew what to say to comfort her, but sometimes, nothing we can say has the power to console.

"Or maybe it's because I didn't honor Thomas in death," she went on, gulping against the sobs. "I should've held a *selamatan* for him on the fortieth day after his death, and I should have left a plate with his favorite food out for him on his birthday, kept his chair empty for him. He wouldn't have woken if I had carried out the rituals, like Auntie van Leeuwen said I should."

I drew her hands from her eyes and kissed the wet knuckles one by one. "You're not to blame, Agnes. If anyone is, it's me."

"I'd like to take some credit, too," Willemijn whispered cheerfully from her bed.

I gave her a cold look. "Don't worry. I've not forgotten your part in all this."

She closed her eyes and smiled a smile of pure pleasure.

By day twenty-three we had been reduced to eating the pickled things I had squirreled away. One of the jars had gone bad; the stench that wafted from the jar turned the room noxious. "Maybe I'm already dead," Willemijn said, every word followed by a little gasping breath. "Maybe this is Hell." She pressed her scarf against her face.

"Wait till she runs out of morphine tablets," Ruth said.

But we did not have to wait for that: Willemijn died just before the twenty-ninth day broke.

She didn't go quietly.

She had been waging war against her body as soon as it had begun to fail her, and those final days and nights she raged with all the strength that was left. With burning eyes, she lay gasping for breath, her hands clawing into the blankets.

Agnes had tried to give her some sleeping pills and painkillers to ease the pain and let her drift off into sleep, then death, but Willemijn had spat them out and stared at her sister-in-law with a mixture of fear and cool indignation. It's not a pretty sight, to see someone's willpower being chipped away slowly by fatigue and pain.

During her last night, she kept drifting in and out of consciousness. Her eyes would flutter shut, and we'd think that, this time, there would be no more waking, only for her to surge up out of slumber, her face contorted. Her eyes would wander around wildly before fixing on something we couldn't see. At that point, she was beyond speaking, though her cracked lips kept forming one name over and over.

"Agnes," I said softly, "don't you think we should let her go to him?"

She dipped a small bit of sponge into a saucer of water, then dabbed Willemijn's lips with it. A drop coursed down her chin. Agnes wiped it away with her thumb.

"It might temper his wrath," I said.

"Nothing can."

"It might make him leave us alone. Spirits don't like the dying."

Ruth and Peter had left the room around the twenty-sixth day and had kept away ever since; I had known then that Willemijn wouldn't live long.

Agnes briefly closed her eyes and touched her fingertips to her forehead. "I don't know," she said. "I don't know what Thomas will do when he sees his sister like this. It might provoke him further. But I also know that it'll be cruel to keep her away from him when it's so very clear that she longs to be with him. I am not cruel." She sighed. "We'll grant her this final wish, and we'll accept the consequences, whatever they may be."

We dressed her, brushed her hair, then let Peter carry her outside. It was no easy thing to convince him to do this for us; as I have said, the dead do not care for the dying. But Peter was a sweet one, and Agnes's distress upset him more than Willemijn's dying did.

Once he had gone, Agnes and I did not stand at the window to see how Thomas would respond. We crawled into bed together and clung to each other like two frightened children.

In the hour before dawn, Thomas began to howl. That's how we knew she had died.

"What shall we do if he takes her body to the bog and turns her into a spirit, too?" I asked.

"I don't know," Agnes said. Her teeth were chattering, even though it wasn't cold. "Maybe it won't come to that."

She was right, though I soon wished she hadn't been. Thomas left his sister's body lying on the lawn, among the plaster saints, as if she were one of them and had fallen in battle. The summer heat soon turned it ripe with rot. No fox from the woods would go near it, nor any bird either, but insects were not deterred. Soon, a rippling sheet of flies covered her. They glistened like jewels in the sunlight, emerald and sapphire. It seemed I could hear their constant buzzing everywhere I went, harping at my nerves till I felt sure I'd go mad if it didn't stop soon. Sometimes, I stopped hearing it, but then my mind would fix on it again, and I could hear nothing but that incessant droning of hundreds of wings.

The worst was the smell, though. Even with the windows closed, it soon permeated everything. I could taste it with every breath: this putrid, almost-sweet scent of rot. Our stomachs, already shriveled and sensitive from lack of food, soon became sore with nausea.

Agnes ceased playing the piano. She no longer read out any stories; in fact, she didn't read at all. We didn't play cards anymore, either. All we did was lie together in the nest of pillows and blankets where we slept, waiting for something to give, growing weaker and more desperate with every passing hour.

On the thirty-second day of our confinement, Thomas hurled something through our bedroom window. The glass spat apart with a noise as sharp as a keening fox. Shards thudded against the furniture, drummed down onto the floorboards, dashed against the walls. The object he had thrown bounced several times until it collided with the bedside table. It did not stop moving straight away but lay swaying softly for a little while, producing a grating sound not unlike the rocking of a chair.

We had been asleep but now sat upright, clutching each other like frightened children, our hearts racing and our bellies and throats constricted.

A second window exploded in a rain of splinters. I cried out and threw myself on top of Agnes to shield her as fragments of glass hailed down upon us. By the time the third window went, Agnes had had the presence of mind to crawl under the bed and pull me with her. From there, we flinched every time another window broke, our hands pressed hard against our mouths to keep us from crying out.

When all the windows had been smashed and it became clear Thomas wouldn't throw in anything else, we dragged ourselves out from under the bed, careful to avoid any glass. I stooped next to the bedside table and picked up the object he had used to break the first window. It was heavy and coated my fingers in a fine layer of dust. When I turned it over in my hands, I saw that it was the face of one of the plaster saints. She had lost her nose on the way in, and her forehead and chin were chipped. Her eyes were coated with grit, giving them the appearance of being clouded with cataracts.

Thomas had also thrown in one of her hands, a sandaled foot, and an unidentifiable chunk that could have belonged to any part of her robed body.

"I guess she didn't like it outside very much. Who can blame her? Quite a dead crowd out there," I quipped tiredly. The corners of my mouth had turned into little wounds; every time I spoke, the scabs that formed there split.

In any other situation, Agnes would have been the one to make that joke. Now she didn't even laugh. Instead, she sank onto the edge of the bed, clutching another piece of the saint in her hands.

I carefully placed the head back on the floor and went to her. "Did you get hurt?" I asked.

She shook her head.

"What have you got there?"

She hesitated, then opened her hands. On her palms rested the head of a lamb. Most of the saints had looked malevolent, or at the very least sly, but the lamb looked terrified. Part of the other hand of the saint was attached to the lamb's head; clawlike, the fingers dug into the white fleece. "I know who she is," she said and nodded at the plaster head.

"Do you?" I plucked a glass splinter from her knuckle, brought my mouth to the nick in her skin and sucked at it. The taste of her blood made me salivate. My stomach cramped with hunger.

"It's Saint Agnes. She's always portrayed with a little lamb."

I didn't know what to say to that. I took the blankets from the bed and shook them. Fragments of glass clattered to the floor. Before I could sweep them up, Agnes pulled me down next to her and began to check me for cuts. She pulled a bit of glass out of my cheek with a pair of tweezers before placing it on a saucer. It lay there, wet with my blood, glistening like a tear.

"It's a good thing it's summer. We won't get cold at night, even without windows," I said.

I tried to soothe her with more silly chatter, but she sat up suddenly and said, "I can't stand this anymore." She rubbed her eyes viciously with her knuckles. The skin underneath was purplish and lined, as if someone had beaten her.

"Let's eat something. That'll make you feel better. We still have some of those pickled beets you like so much, or…"

"What good will that do? We'll still be stuck in here. We'll still be living this living death, slowly starving, slowly dying."

"We're not dying. We're surviving," I said. I took her hand in mine, stroked the knuckles, taking care not to touch the one ripped open by the glass.

She tore her hand from mine. "If that's true, then why have Ruth and Peter kept their distance from us these past few days?"

I didn't know what to say. Tears pricked my eyes. I bowed my head so she wouldn't see.

She got to her feet and began to pace. "I'm not going to die in here. I refuse. I didn't get this far for it to end like this. I didn't survive my fucking husband and find you, only for us to die in here like dogs."

She stirred something in me then. I looked up at her. "Tell me what I must do, and I shall do it."

"There's only one thing we can do, one horrible, dreadful thing," she said. She rummaged in her nightstand and plucked out a brown glass bottle filled with pills.

Chapter 32

IMMEDIATELY, I FELT MY DETERMINATION shrivel. "No," I said and held out my hands as if to fend off a blow.

"What other choice do we have? If we can't see Thomas, he can't torment us. You know this is true. It is the only way."

"Ruth is a part of me. I can deny her no more than I can deny these hands, this face, this beating heart. If I take those pills and she is torn from me, it shall be as if I have lost a limb."

Her hand tightened around the bottle, bleaching her knuckles. "People lose limbs every day and continue living."

"You are willfully misunderstanding me. I'm trying to say that losing Ruth shall mutilate me. I shall forever be incomplete."

She was shaking. The pills rattled softly against one another and the glass. "When I told you I'd surrender to Thomas, you said we are more than what is done to us. You said that, together, we might learn how to be whole. Other people don't need spirits. They can't even see them. Perhaps that's what being whole means."

I shook my head wildly. "I can't! I can't give up Ruth. And you can't give up Peter either. Don't you remember that's how we got into this mess in the first place?"

She began to cry. "Do you think this comes easy to me? I don't want to lose Peter. But I don't want to lose you either. And if I have to choose, I choose you. I love you, Roos."

How I had longed for those words! But not like this, never like this. "Oh, Agnes, you are breaking my heart," I murmured. I sat down and pressed the heels of my hands against my eyes until fantastic colors bled all over my vision. My throat was so tight, I felt as if she had wrapped her hand around it and was slowly but surely strangling me.

Agnes sniffed. "I'm sorry. If there were another way, I wouldn't ask this of you. But I've turned the matter over and over in my mind, and I can't see what else we might do."

I sobbed; my throat felt cut. "Ruth would rather I die."

She gave a little cry and took me in her arms. "Don't talk like that! Ruth loves you. She wants you to be safe and happy. And we don't have to take these pills forever, just for a while, just until Thomas grows tired of us and leaves us. Then we can stop and restore Ruth and Peter to us."

"You know better than I that he'll never grow tired until he has seen you destroyed, and perhaps me as well because you love me. Once we swallow these pills, we shall have to keep on taking them. We shan't see Ruth or Peter ever again."

She pressed her sodden cheek against my shoulder. "I know, I know! But what's the alternative? Die and rot like Willemijn out there? Or wait till he destroys us in the most terrifying way?

Because it's one or the other, Roos. Either we die, or we let him torture us to death. You've seen what he can do. The only reason he's still outside is because he wants to be. He wants to break me, wants me to submit to him utterly, and the only way to do that is to terrify and terrorize me until I let him in. If I do that, he has brought me to heel one final time."

"He shan't, he shan't!" I cried out.

She went on, heedless of me. "But he's growing restless. If he waits too long, if I turn out to be too willful for him, you and I will die before he can have his fun with us. Should it come to that, he'll simply force his way inside. That's why he smashed all these windows: it's both a warning and a promise. He can come in, should he want to, and that I cannot allow. Not because I'm proud; God knows I've little dignity left. No, I cannot wait for him to make his final move because of what he would do to you."

I tried to shush her, but she shook her head wildly.

"No! You must listen to me, Roos, because you need to understand! Thomas delights in cruelty, and he desires to punish me. There's no limit to what he will do to see me cast low, and that includes hurting you. You think you've suffered already? This is nothing compared to what he'd do to you, should we ever give him the chance! But you know as well as I do that he can't hurt us if we can't perceive him, just as Peter couldn't hurt him when he was still living, and Ruth couldn't hurt your mama. Think about it: taking these pills is the only way you and I can make it out of here alive!"

I disentangled myself from her embrace. "I need to be alone. I can't think right now," I said. I went to one of the maid's rooms.

It was frightfully hot, the air close and choked with dust. A drop of sweat coursed down my back, then another. I licked my cracked lips, but that didn't make them feel any less dry.

"Ruth!" I called out. "Please come to me. There's something I have to say to you."

I knew she was behind me when a sudden chill cooled my fevered skin. I turned around. As if to match me, she had become thin and gaunt, her lips peeling.

"What is it, my little love?" she asked.

I swallowed. My saliva had turned thick with thirst and would not go down very easily. "Agnes has found a way out for us. She wants us to take pills so we will stop seeing spirits."

For a moment, she swayed as if I had struck her. Then she threw herself at my feet. I tried to raise her, but she clutched my hands and drew me down with her and cupped my face so I could do nothing but look at her, at that strange haunted face I had feared before I had learned to love it. "We are wedded to each other, you and I. You're my helpmeet and yokemate, and I am yours. My love for you is as strong as death. You can't send me away. Do you hear me? I won't let you!"

I took hold of her hands and softly pulled them away. She clutched my hand and dropped kisses on the knuckles, cold and quick and sharp as insect bites.

"But, Ruth, what else am I supposed to do?"

"Let Agnes send you away. Thomas is bound to you. Where you go, he must follow."

"He won't let me leave. He'll forcefully possess me and use me to destroy Agnes, and then he'll dispose of me."

"He shan't hurt you. I won't let him. I'd rip out his throat first, tear him limb from limb."

"He'd fight you."

"Let him try."

I shook my head wildly. "He's stronger than you are. I don't want you to get hurt!"

"I won't mind."

"But I would."

"And you think abandoning me is somehow better?"

I rubbed my eyes so hard, they hurt. "All right. Say that your plan works, and we can leave here without consequence. Say we bore Thomas, and he'll leave us in peace rather than torment me to death. What would we do then, Ruth? Go back to Mama? I don't think I'd survive the shame. Besides, she won't take us in because we are of no use to her anymore now that she's dying. How would we live?"

Her grip around my hand tightened. I felt the little bones in my hand grind together. Scalding tears sprang into my eyes. I gasped, but either she did not notice, or she did not care, because her handclasp only seemed to gain in strength.

"My little love, my sweet, my darling," she said, and she spoke eagerly, quickly, "you need not worry about any of that. I'll take care of you."

As the rest of my hand turned numb, I began to feel the blood beat in my fingertips, a rapid unpleasant thumping. I closed my eyes and groaned. "But you wouldn't manage it this time! That's what I'm trying to tell you. What place does a spirit have in the outside world?"

"The only place I need is beside my beloved."

I slammed my free hand on the ground in frustration. "Oh, Ruth! Don't you see, or don't you want to see? If you force me to choose you, you condemn me to a life of sordid backroom séances."

"There are other ways to make a living."

"You know as well as I that I'm fit for nothing else! My pact with you has made it so!"

She tightened the grip on my hand further, making a flaming pain tear through the flesh I had thought numbed. "You'd do well to remember that you were the one who let me in." She hissed, "I didn't ask to be woken from my slumber by your pitiful crying, did I? I didn't ask for you to name me and slake my thirst, to be bound to you forever. Yet I've never complained, not even once, because I would bear anything and everything for love of you. Now, does my love mean so little to you that you would not suffer for it as I have for yours?"

"Must love be about suffering?"

She looked at me with eyes so black, I wondered how she could even see. "How else does one show the strength and sincerity of one's love if not through suffering and sacrifice?"

My glorious, imperfect Ruth, who had been stabbed and hit and strangled and drowned. How could I have expected her to understand love in any other terms?

With a cry, I tore my hand from her grasp. She had held it so tight that the skin first had turned red, then black. "I can't, Ruth! Please understand! I can't anymore. Don't you see that choosing you would kill me?"

"Then die! Die, die, die, only do not abandon me!" she wailed. Tears of black coursed down her cheeks.

I began to cry then, too. I had a pain in my chest so sharp and fierce, I thought it might strangle me. "Forgive me, but I want to live. I'm sorry, Ruth, I'm so sorry." I turned from her and ran to Agnes.

She was sitting in the green velvet chair, turning the bottle of pills between her hands, making the pills inside swirl. When I burst into the room, she sat up and leaned toward me.

"I can learn how to be normal for you." I wept. "This third eye of mine, or whatever it is that allows me to see spirits, I will gouge it out for you. You have given me so much; I can give this to you."

"Roos…" she began, but I would not let her finish.

"Do you want me to renounce Ruth? I'll do that for you. I'll renounce her, though it breaks my heart…" I couldn't speak anymore then, only sob. An iron hand seemed locked around my heart, making every beat agony. And yet every gasp for breath, every thump of my heart told me, *I am alive, I am here.*

Agnes took me in her arms. She did not speak, and for that I was grateful; anything she could have said would only have sharpened my grief. Instead, she held me and rocked me. She blew softly on my swollen eyelids, and when my sadness clawed at my lungs to the point where I couldn't breathe without agony, she made me look into her eyes and match my breathing to hers until I no longer thought I'd die. When the first wave of grief had spent itself and I grew quiet, she held my head in her lap and stroked my hair.

After a while, she got up. She brought me a glass of water. I drank it thirstily. It tasted slightly of pennies. Still without speaking, she took the glass from me when I had finished and placed it on the dresser. There she began to grind some pills to dust with the bottom of the bottle, and I wondered why it was that she had taken pills for years but still wasn't able to swallow them whole and had to bash them to powder instead. Perhaps the sensation had become unbearable to her; Thomas had made her swallow so many of them, after all.

She tore a page from a notebook, folded it a few times, then brushed the ground-up remains of the pills into it. "I'll mix it into our food and drink," she said, yet before she could, Ruth came in and clasped her wrist so hard, her skin dimpled. She winced but did not pull away.

"Please," Ruth begged, "please give me one last night with Roos before you make her deaf and blind to me. This you owe me."

Agnes thought for a moment, then nodded. "All right. One last night." She hesitated, then reached out to stroke Ruth's cheek. Instantly, Ruth shied away from her, the little gray pips of her teeth bared in a snarl.

That night I spent in my old room, Ruth in bed beside me. I stared at her dear face, trying to drink it all in so I would forget nothing. I traced the little wisps of her eyebrows with my fingertips, felt the ridge of bone protruding from her jaw where she had broken the bone. I listened to the little grinding click it made when she swallowed and thought that such a sound would always be a comfort to me, because it would remind me of her.

"My little yokemate, you don't have to do this," she whispered. "We can still leave and build a life elsewhere."

I said nothing, just pressed my face against her throat and breathed in her particular peaty scent, wishing this moment had passed already, then wishing it could last forever.

Chapter 33

I WOKE LATE IN THE morning. It had rained in the night; the drops had dried in the morning sun, leaving the windows dirty. Ruth had crept out of bed without waking me. I washed, then dressed. When I stepped into the hallway, I almost upset a plate with some pickled carrots and a glass of water. The glass had white grit at the bottom.

Agnes has put the pills in there, I thought and felt sick. I left the plate and glass to sweat and went to look for her.

I found her in her room. I saw straightaway something was wrong with her. Her skin, usually such a beautiful light brown, had a strange gray hue to it. She lay limp, her mouth slightly open. I ran to her and found she had been sick; vomit coated her chin and soiled the sheets. It smelled so strong and sour, I gagged.

"Agnes!" I screamed and shook her. Her head rolled, her limbs flailed; she did nothing to resist me, only moaned a little. Through her flickering eyelids, I saw only the whites of her eyes. I couldn't feel her pulse in her wrist, yet when I lay my ear to her chest, I found her heart was still beating, albeit slowly. She had rolled around in the glass when she fell, and it had cut her in a myriad of places, gotten tangled in her hair, and clung to the strands as drops of water.

"Agnes, you must wake up!"

She groaned again, then convulsed. More vomit dribbled from between her lips, this time streaked with ribbons of blood. Afraid she'd suffocate, I stuck my finger in her mouth and scooped out the sick.

"There's nothing you can do for her," Ruth said. She stood with folded hands, looking like some goddess of old, strange and terrible.

"What do you mean?" I asked.

From the folds of her ragged dress, she drew a stoppered bottle. It was empty, save for some grit on the bottom that glittered like snow.

An ice-cold hand gripped my heart and throat and squeezed. "Ruth, what have you done?" I asked.

"What I needed to keep us together and to set us free from this house," she said calmly.

"You've mixed ground glass into her food. Oh, Ruth…"

Agnes groaned and rolled her head, then choked softly. I took her face between my hands and lifted her head into my lap. A trickle of blood ran down her chin; it was so vivid, I could scarcely bear to look at it. I tried to wipe it away with my thumb. It was hot and sticky.

"I must call a doctor," I said.

"He won't be able to help. Anyone who eats powdered glass will surely die. You know that as well as I. Besides, Agnes has cut the lines, remember?"

I clutched Agnes's hand so hard, my knuckles turned yellow with the strain. "You're a monster, Ruth."

"If I am, it's because you've made me one! You're the one who would abandon me, who would discard me like a piece of rent cloth, as if I am worthless! You replaced me, and you sacrificed me!" she screeched, and her voice was like a hundred nails raking down a piece of glass.

Agnes grimaced, moaned a little. I wondered if she was in pain. I wiped the vomit and blood from her chin with the hem of my shirt. "If you think I won't take pills after what you've done to Agnes, you're sorely mistaken," I said through gritted teeth.

"Oh, but you won't take pills."

"I'd do anything to be rid of you now."

"Even give up your only chance to ever see Agnes again?"

I looked at her, at her gleaming eyes, at the slash of her mouth and the sharp teeth inside, small as pearls. "What do you mean?" I whispered.

"Agnes is dying. This, you can't stop. But if you bind her to you now, she might come back to you as a spirit. Yet if you took pills to blot me out, you'd never know she'd returned to you, now, would you? You won't survive losing us both, and so you shall do as I suggest."

"You bitch!" I screamed. I got to my feet and struck her face. Her head stayed perfectly still, but her jaw snapped to the side. She cried out in dismay, and clutching her twice-broken jaw, she fled from me.

I sank next to Agnes. A line of excruciating pain ran down

my sternum. I felt as if the bone would split. I swallowed, and the
pain pulsed.

"Why did you eat all alone?" I whispered. "You made a point
of always taking our meals together. Why didn't you wait for me?
Were you that frightened, that desperate?" I stroked the hair from
her face. Her flesh felt cold and clammy, and I couldn't find a pulse
anymore. She was still breathing, though; when I held Ruth's bottle
with ground-up glass under her nose, the glass fogged up. There
was very little time left.

What else could I do but what Ruth had so slyly planned?

I brought my hand to my mouth and tore at the skin between
index finger and thumb. When blood beaded from the punctures,
I held my hand over Agnes's mouth and saw to it that the drops
fell between her lips.

"You are Agnes," I told her, "and you are beholden to me. I am
Roos, and I am beholden to you. We are bound fast together now.
This you shall remember: you must return to me."

I don't know how long I sat with her then, but it must have
been hours; the pools of sunlight traveled along the floor, then
up the walls, turning ever softer and more orange. At some point,
Peter stormed into the room. Maybe the scent of blood had drawn
him out of whatever place he had been hiding these past few days;
maybe a person and their spirit companion are connected, and he
had felt the string between Agnes's heart and his grow slack.

Seeing what had happened, he shoved me aside and gathered
Agnes in his arms. He bit at her face, her throat, her hands, and
her arms, like a dog who found its owner dead and nipped at him

in a desperate effort to revive him. Blood beaded from the nicks in her skin, thick and black. He dug his teeth into her wrist and drank deeply, keening all the while, stroking her face with his huge fingers.

I hugged him tight, and though his spine pressed bruises into my flesh, I did not mind. After a while, I sat up straight and laid my hand on his shoulder, and he turned to look at me. His face was contorted with grief.

"We must take Agnes to the bog and bury her there if we want her to come back as a spirit," I said.

He pressed his forehead briefly against mine, then came to his feet. He would have carried her straight to the bog, had I not stopped him. Spirits care little for the way things look, but I couldn't let Agnes be buried looking all dirty and torn. I undressed her, washed her body, bound her wounds. The blood came sluggishly now that her heart had ceased to beat, but it still came, trickling from the tears Peter had made. In a moment of desperation, perhaps even of grief-induced madness, I fastened my mouth over the wound at her wrist. The flesh was torn and wet. I began to drink in the same way Peter had. Her blood was thick and hot and rich, and it filled me and sustained me, and I understood why spirits craved it, why Ruth had so often sucked at my scrapes and cuts. It was an act of utter intimacy.

When I was done, I wiped my mouth with the back of my hand and wrapped the wound with strips ripped from my silk chemise. "We are doubly bound now, tighter than any human and their spirit ever before. This you shall remember: you must come to me."

I put her favorite dress on her, dabbed scent at her wrists and throat.

Peter picked her up when I was finished, rubbed his cheek against hers. He did not move, only stood there with Agnes in his arms as if she were his doll and he, a little child seeking comfort from the feel and heft and scent of her.

"Let's go, Peter," I said softly and gave a little tug on his arm. Together we walked down the stairs, leaving prints in the dust. It took me a while to remember where I had left the key to the front door; it had seemed so long ago since I had locked it.

"Do you dare to go outside?" Peter asked when I inserted the key into the lock.

I gave him a tremulous smile. "Yes. I don't think Thomas means me any harm, and even if he does, I don't much care what happens to me now."

I pushed the door open.

Someone tried to come in.

I screamed and backed away, my hands raised to ward off blows that never came. Peter growled, this threatening hum that I felt vibrating in my chest and bones. When I lowered my arms, blood running through my veins with such force, it thrummed, I saw it was a nun. She held a rosary in her folded hands and wore a crown of roses. The thorns had dug into her brow, piercing it; the blood ran into her eyes, turning them pink.

A plaster saint. Just another plaster saint meant to frighten and intimidate. Thomas had chosen one adorned with roses specifically to target me, my name being the Dutch word for *rose*, just as he had terrorized Agnes by throwing broken pieces of her namesake's statue through the windows. My nun wasn't the only saint cluttering up the steps. I could squeeze past the one meant to represent me, but I couldn't walk past the other ones without touching them; for that, there were too many standing too close together. In a sudden fit of anger, I shoved the one closest to me: a female saint I didn't recognize, with a leering expression and veined hands painted in great detail. She teetered, then seemed to right herself. I shoved her again, harder this time, causing her to topple down the stone steps. On the way down, she left behind her folded hands and her nose. She crashed onto the lawn, sank into the mud.

I hurled down the other saints with a cry of rage, then stood looking down at their broken faces, my eyes and lungs smarting from the plaster dust drifting from their supine forms.

"Let's go find Thomas," I told Peter.

We didn't have to look long. He stood on the lawn, next to the bug-eaten corpse of his sister. The stench was such that I had to press my nose and mouth against the inside of my elbow. It made my eyes water.

"Agnes has died," I called out to him and then could not go on. I swallowed thickly, balled my hands into fists. The tug of my scars grounded me a little. "My spirit companion killed her. You have been avenged. Now, please, be gone and trouble me no more. Your quarrel was never with me, and though I bound you to me, I did so unwittingly."

He came toward me and raised his mangled hand to my face. With the other, he pulled away my arm from my mouth. I shut my eyes in terror, but he only rested the tips of his fingers against my cheek. "Oh, but how you could amuse me. When I slithered into Agnes's bedroom last night and she saw me, she drank and drank and drank her pill-laced water so fast, she nearly choked on it. And when I didn't disappear straightaway but began to whisper to her of all the things I'd do to her, to you, she powdered her food with it, the same food your companion so thoughtfully sprinkled with glass, and stuffed bite after bite down her craw. There are no pills left for you. I've made sure of that. No escape, just endless suffering," he whispered, his bog-tainted breath ghosting over my face. It was the first time I heard him speak; his voice was like water running over stone, not at all unpleasant, but his words and touch seemed to chill my very marrow.

He climbed inside, I thought. *He crept up the wall and clambered inside our room, and Agnes was left to face him alone because I was with Ruth. I left her unguarded and thus condemned her.*

Sick with grief and hate, I opened my eyes. In his silvered eyes, I read the pleasure that the truly sadistic derive from the pain of others, and somehow that calmed me. To struggle against him would please him; instead, I had to feign utter indifference to whatever he might do to me.

"Do as you please to me. I won't resist," I said coolly.

A flicker of confusion flitted over his face.

You really are a small, simple soul, aren't you, Thomas Knoop? I thought. Suddenly, I felt nothing but contempt for him, contempt and boredom. Was this the man I had thought of so much, whom I had wanted to emulate?

When Agnes had told me what he had really been like, I had reeled back from that desire in horror and relief, but in a way, he had still fascinated me. Now I saw that he was truly not at all interesting. Emboldened by this realization, I pressed on.

"Do you think I care what happens to me, whether I live or die, now that my spirit companion murdered Agnes? I've lost everyone I care about. I've a good mind to drown myself in the bog. So, you see, I don't give a damn what you might do to me."

Instantly, he withdrew his hand from my face. In the luminescence of his eyes, I saw my own boredom reflected; if he could not torment me, I was of no interest.

"I release you," he said and then was gone.

Relief made me sway. I leaned heavily against Peter, buried my face against his spotted skin, and inhaled his good, honest scent of moss and earth.

"Will you truly drown yourself?" he asked.

"I don't know," I confessed. "Now come, let's go and bury Agnes."

He placed a finger against my shoulder, holding me back. "I'll go alone," he said.

"Please," I begged, but he shook his head. "Will you at least let me say goodbye?"

He bent his knees until I could reach Agnes. She didn't quite look like she was sleeping, but her face had lost the strain of the past few days, and that made her look strangely young. I could look back into time and see all the girls she had once been: the one who had married Thomas in a simple summer frock, her eyes shiny with excitement and hope; the one who had slept on a mound with a brick in hand to show her classmates the stuff she was made of; the one standing on her father's doorstep in a thin coat with a suicide note pinned to her lapel.

I kissed her cold brow and murmured, "I did not mean for you to suffer, and I did not mean for you to die. I am sorry. Please forgive me." A little blood had dried on her temple. I sucked on my fingers and rubbed at it. She had a gash near her hairline; it opened and closed like a little mouth as I rubbed. "Your poor body is all battered now, and for that I'm sorry, too. But Peter will tuck you into the bog, and there, your broken flesh will be of no account. You'll sleep in the water, and you'll dream of good things. I shall do my best to make sure no one will disturb your slumber." And then, because three times makes it real: "This you shall remember: when you wake, please come haunt me."

Peter straightened himself and pressed Agnes closer to his chest. He began to keen again, the sound like the wind whistling through rock. Long after he had disappeared between the trees, I still heard him cry.

———

I dug a hole for Willemijn in the graveyard and buried her there. Of this I only remember flashes: the wet gritty sound the soil made as I dug in the spade; the burning of vomit surging up my throat; the sight of worms breaking out of the ground because my patting down of the earth sounded like rain to them.

In the house, I went directly to my room to sleep. I was too tired to wash myself, but I couldn't bear to go to Agnes's room, not when she wasn't there but her scent and stray hairs still clung to the bedclothes.

The sheet I had hung in front of the wardrobe had partly fallen away, revealing the demons and sinners cut into the wood. Not even the hot rays of sunlight pooling into the room could make those cruel carven figures any less horrible to look at. I took hold of a corner of the sheet and tried to throw it on top of the wardrobe. The sheet billowed like a sail, then fluttered softly down, dislodging motes of dust that danced in the light like fairies.

I tried again and then a third time, but I wasn't tall enough, and those horrible wood carvings kept leering at me. The blood that buzzed in my ears from the exertion faintly sounded like the swelling and falling of laughter, or perhaps of sobbing, and then I realized that the sound came from the figures carved in the wood. Their mouths were moving, and they shook with mirth as they watched me.

"Be quiet," I said, but that just made them laugh all the more. The sound rose in volume, fell a little, only to rise again, this deranged sobbing, these high-pitched hysterical shrieks.

"Shut up!" I yelled and punched the face of a demon spooning out a sinner's eye, of a person being flayed, of a devil who had his arm up to the elbow in a human's mouth, and still the sound swelled around me till I thought my mind would crack. The house seemed to bend and ripple around me. In a sort of frenzy, I punched the wooden faces as quickly as I could, making the wardrobe's hinges creak. *But how can I make this stop when it's not coming from the wardrobe but from inside my head?* I thought and felt my mind warp under the strain.

That was how the police found me after a poacher had alerted them to the fact that Willemijn Knoop's body lay festering on the lawn: stinking of rot and smeared with earth, muttering unintelligibly and grimacing as I battered a wardrobe with bloodied hands.

SEVENTEENTH CASE EPISODE

PATIENT R—, A CASE STORY: INHABITED BY ANOTHER

(D = DOCTOR, P = PATIENT R—)

SEVENTEENTH EPISODE, CONDUCTED ON 6 NOVEMBER 1954:

Notes to self: Am as appalled as I am shaken. Patient describes things so viscerally. What horrors must she have experienced to make these delusions filled with spirits, corpses, and partial cannibalism preferable to reality? She is wedded to them as only one truly mad can be.

Poor thing.

D: "R—, there is something I have been meaning to ask you for a while now. Do you hold yourself responsible for Mrs. K—'s death?"

P: "Yes."

D: "Can you tell me why?"

P: "It's simple. If I hadn't brought T—'s [Mr. K—'s] spirit back, A— [Mrs. K—] wouldn't have asked me to renounce Ruth or else be sent away. If I hadn't renounced Ruth, she wouldn't have mixed the ground-up glass in A—'s food."

D: "You think Ruth killed Mrs. K—?"

P: "Of course. Mr T— [Mr. K—] killed her, too, but I'm to blame."

D: "R—, I meant to ask you this before, but then you became so angry I didn't have the chance. I will ask you now. Are you aware that mixing powdered glass into a person's food does not kill them?"

P: [*looks stricken; talks incoherently for a moment*] "But it does! Everyone knows it does."

D: "I have written to three different doctors, all experts on the digestive system. I asked them whether eating ground-up glass could kill a person. They told me that it can't. If the glass has been turned into a powder so fine it won't be detected when eaten—and it must be very fine indeed, because we can taste grit and sand just fine—then it won't harm the oesophagus, stomach or intestines. At worst, the victim might experience mild irritation and a little bleeding. Only swallowing large shards may tear the lining of those organs or even rupture them, but no one can eat shards without noticing, if only because they'd cut the mouth before you could swallow. Do you understand? You can't have killed Mrs. K— with powdered glass because it's impossible to kill anyone with powdered glass."

P: "You're wrong! A— [Mrs. K—] ate powdered glass and then she was dying. She kept vomiting, and blood dribbled from her mouth. What else could have caused that?"

D: "I've read Mrs. K—'s autopsy report. The doctor found some powdered glass in her stomach, but he also found a large number of ground-up pills. Such a large

amount, in fact, that she would have lost consciousness and started vomiting."

P: "I don't understand."

D: "Mrs. K— had taken an overdose, probably accidentally. The fact that she was unconscious and vomiting attests to that. She may have consumed powdered
glass, but that's not what made her so sick."

P: "But the blood..."

D: "She probably bit her tongue when you shook her."

P: [*silence*]

D: "R—, do you understand what I am trying to tell you?
Mrs. K— was sick, yes, but not because of you or Ruth.
She was confused and scared, probably because she
was in the throes of psychosis, and in that muddled
state, she must have taken the wrong amount of pills."

P: "Why are you telling me this?"

D: "Because this is what might save you."

P: "Forgive me, Doctor, but I don't see how. Now, I think I
am going to faint." [*faints*]

Chapter 34

I MIGHT HAVE DISAGREED WITH Doctor Montague on a lot of things, but he was right on two accounts. Firstly, the prosecution went after me like a pack of wolves.

Secondly, the key to my salvation lay in powdered glass.

Never shall I forget all the prosecutor said and did to get me convicted for murdering Agnes. His name was Mr. van Vliet, and he was a man with hair like copper wire and a strange sensual mouth that did not match up with the hard lines of his lean body and face. With lurid imagery, he tried to paint me as a volatile woman who delighted in planning and then executing elaborate acts of cruelty and violence.

"Imagine," he told the judges, "Miss Beckman grinding up pills with a pestle and mixing them into the food and drink of the unsuspecting Mrs. Knoop, a lady who, we must never forget, had taken Miss Beckman into her home out of the goodness of her heart. To ensure she shall die, she even mixes some ground glass into her food."

He mimed sprinkling powder over an imaginary dish.

"But I didn't!" I exclaimed.

One of the judges pounded his gavel against the sound block, making me jump. "I will have order in my courtroom, Miss Beckman, and if you can't keep it, I'll see you removed," he barked.

Helplessly, I turned to my lawyer. Mr. Lindelauf was a big man, with fingers like sausages and ears large and round as saucers. "And you will have order, Your Honor, never you fear," he said. He placed his hand on mine, dwarfing it, and said in a low voice that only I could hear, "Patience, my dear. Let Mr. van Vliet have his little bit of fun. I'll have his head on a silver platter for you soon enough."

Mr. van Vliet cleared his throat and went on. "Now imagine Miss Beckman creeping to Mrs. Knoop's limp body, licking her lips and rubbing her hands together. She attacks her benefactress like a rabid dog, ripping at her flesh with such force that she nearly separates the left hand from its wrist. She has done this before, when she almost ripped out Mr. Mesman's throat without provocation. Once she has sated her lust for blood and to cover up her crime, she drags the body to the nearby marshes and dumps it there as if it's no more than a sack of rotten spuds."

Doctor Montague did all he could to defend me.

"Miss Beckman is ill," he said. "From an early age, she has been horribly abused. To survive, her mind created a kind of companion for her, a creature she calls 'Ruth.' She thinks that Ruth is the ghost of a woman who died a long time ago."

He did not smile as he might have, as others had, and for this, if not much else, I was grateful to him. It's no small thing, to be allowed to keep one's dignity.

Doctor Montague cleared his throat and continued talking. "Miss Beckman further believes that certain rituals can make a person turn into a spirit once they have died. When she found Mrs. Knoop unconscious, she believed Mrs. Knoop was going to die, and so Miss Beckman carried out these rituals in a desperate attempt to ensure her beloved friend would not desert her. These rituals may seem extreme and violent, but we must not forget that, in Miss Beckman's mind, they were the best thing she could do for Mrs. Knoop."

"That's a far cry from the deliberately violent creature Mr. van Vliet has painted for us," one of the judges remarked.

"Indeed. I have had extensive talks with Miss Beckman, and I can assure you that she means well. Yes, her behavior is disturbing to sane men like you and me, but intentionally malevolent it is not."

"But this behavior has had dire consequences, Doctor Montague. In light of these consequences, I have to ask: Do you think Miss Beckman can be held responsible for her actions?" the same judge asked.

Doctor Montague's eyes met mine, and in them I saw not the almost-voyeuristic enthusiasm he had displayed during our talks, when his desire to probe a deviant mind had been met, but true compassion mingled with pity. I felt thoroughly chilled by it.

Don't, I mouthed.

He gave me a sad little smile and almost imperceptibly shook his head at me, then tore away his gaze so he could look at the judges. "In my expert opinion? No, she can't."

Heartfelt words, yes, and words that would undoubtedly have

had me committed to his hospital if it hadn't been for my lawyer. Mr. Lindelauf's voice was big, rich, and pleasant. When he began to speak, you couldn't help but listen.

"It doesn't matter whether Doctor Montague thinks Miss Beckman can be held responsible for what happened because I will prove that, despite what she and the prosecution might say, she didn't do any of the things she's currently on trial for. Let's begin with the prosecution's claim that Miss Beckman ground up dozens of pills and fed them to Mrs. Knoop without her knowledge. This is so unlikely as to be laughable," he said.

As he spoke, he stroked the golden links in the chain of his pocket watch; he was as vain as he was big, always dressed like a dapper gentleman.

"Any doctor worth their salt," he went on, "will tell you that these pills, when turned to powder, will make any kind of dish bitter to the point where it is hardly edible. Mrs. Knoop could therefore never have eaten a dish laced with pills without knowing what she was doing. It is instead far more likely that Mrs. Knoop ground up the pills herself and mixed them through her food. Perhaps she was confused and ill, as Doctor Montague has suggested. Perhaps she had become indifferent to life; after all, she had lost her husband and her sister-in-law, her only real family. Both scenarios could potentially explain why she ate powdered glass, though we shall never know for certain what motivated her to eat pills and glass. What we do know for certain, however, is that Miss Beckman can't have fed those to her without her knowing."

One of the judges leaned toward his neighbor and whispered

something. Mr. Lindelauf made sure to catch this man's eye when he laid down his next argument. "Furthermore, Miss Beckman can't have made the wounds on Mrs. Knoop's body. The teeth marks don't match up with Miss Beckman's teeth. In fact, those marks look more like something a wild animal might leave behind, perhaps a dog or fox. In all likelihood, they were inflicted after Mrs. Knoop's body had been taken to the bog."

Mr. Lindelauf stopped speaking. He took off his glasses and began to polish them with a handkerchief of virginal white. He held them to the light, tutted, polished them some more. They seemed comically small between his large hands, like something a child might adorn her doll with.

"Lastly," he said, replacing his glasses and shaking out his handkerchief with a flourish before folding it neatly and tucking it into his pocket, "it's impossible for Miss Beckman to have gotten rid of the body in the way the prosecution claims. The prosecution asserts she dragged Mrs. Knoop to the marshes, but the police found no signs of any dragging. They think the body must have been carried instead. How, I'd like to know, would Miss Beckman have done that? She's a small slip of a thing weighing barely forty-five kilos! And we know no one could have helped Miss Beckman. There was no one at the Rozentuin to assist her, and everything we've heard in here has told us she had no friends she could ask for help."

"Then who do you suppose brought Mrs. Knoop's body to the bog?" one of the judges asked.

Mr. Lindelauf shrugged. "I wouldn't know, Your Honor. It's not my place to speculate. I am only giving you the facts, and those are that Miss Beckman cannot logically be found guilty of the charges laid before her. There's no proof she gave the pills to Mrs. Knoop, no proof she mutilated her after she had died, and no proof she brought the body to the bog."

"What about the powdered glass?" Mr. van Vliet asked, his mouth puckered as if he was sucking on a lemon rind. His cheeks were still flecked with red.

"Multiple doctors we consulted have said that powdered glass won't kill a person. It won't even harm them."

"The accused didn't know that. She told the police that she thought Mrs. Knoop lay dying because of the powdered glass she had slipped into her food. That shows the accused's clear intent to do Mrs. Knoop harm."

Mr. Lindelauf dismissed Mr. van Vliet's accusations with one contemptuous flick of the wrist. "Miss Beckman is not on trial for her intentions."

"It wasn't mere intent. Your client confessed to attempted murder by giving her employer food with powdered glass," Mr. van Vliet persisted.

"She didn't. She said it was Ruth. Ruth, Miss Beckman's imaginary friend and avenging angel. She also told the police that another spirit with the ludicrous name of Peter Quint mutilated Mrs. Knoop's body, then carried it to the bogs. I think I've proven by now that what Miss Beckman says is not always what actually happened."

And because Mr. Lindelauf convinced the judges of this, and

because the prosecution couldn't prove beyond a doubt that I had done the things they accused me of, I was acquitted.

———————

"But I am guilty," I told Mr. Lindelauf. He had taken me and Doctor Montague to a restaurant to celebrate my acquittal and had ordered cake for all of us.

"Not according to the law," Mr. Lindelauf said. He sipped from his glass of scotch and closed his eyes in bliss.

"In every other way I am, though. Agnes wouldn't have taken those pills if it weren't for me. So, you see, I truly am guilty."

Mr. Lindelauf laughed, spraying crumbs from between the bristles of his mustache.

"My dear girl, are you upset I got you acquitted? I thought you enjoyed playing Salome to Mr. van Vliet's John the Baptist. If you didn't want that, you should've taken on a worse lawyer than me. You really are a funny one. A good thing I didn't let you speak. Some people really will hang themselves if you give them enough rope, won't they?"

He downed his drink, then counted out some money and laid it on the table. "Well, children, this has been pleasant, but I must run. This should cover the bill and give that pretty waitress a nice tip. Make sure she knows it's from me." He picked up his coat and hat, gave us a little bow, and left us to our cake and tea.

"I am not ungrateful to Mr. Lindelauf per se," I told Doctor Montague as I gathered the crumbs of cake from my plate with a fingertip. "It's just that I don't like how he made me out to be a liar or a madwoman, possibly both."

"He did get you acquitted."

"That he did."

Doctor Montague moved his finger over the rim of his teacup. "If you think you are guilty of Agnes's death, then why won't you commit yourself to my care?"

I suddenly felt so drained, I could scarcely believe I could still sit upright. "What will become of me if I do?" I asked him wearily.

"You'll be committed to a hospital, where you'll be my responsibility," he said gently. He hesitated, then put his hand over mine. His knuckles were dusted with hair. "I'll look after you. There'll be no Mr. Mesmans, no spaces under floorboards, just your own room, clean and bright, and regular meals and people who want only to help you."

"And pills," I said. "So many pills that I wouldn't be able to see a spirit if it stood right in front of me."

He leaned back in his chair and rubbed his eyes under his glasses. "Where will you go if you won't come with me?"

I looked at my hands folded on the table. Funny. I had stiffened at Doctor Montague's touch, but now that his hand no longer rested on mine, I felt oddly cold. I suppose that, during my time with Agnes, I'd learned not to automatically associate the touch of someone living with pain and degradation. "I don't know," I confessed.

Mama had died while I was in custody. I had not been invited to the funeral. I don't think the police would have allowed me to go anyway, and I'm not sure if I would've gone if they had, but all the same, it would have been nice to have been asked. After all, I did live with Mama for twenty-one years. True to her word, she had written me out of her will, leaving me with nothing. Agnes might have made provisions for me, if there had been time, if she had known, but as it stood, I had very few possessions: some clothes, two pairs of shoes, a suitcase, half a dozen books.

"If you won't let me treat you, will you at least allow me to help you?" Doctor Montague asked.

"I don't much like to be beholden to anyone anymore. It hasn't worked out so well for me before."

He smiled. "I understand, but you wouldn't be beholden to me. If anything, I'd be beholden to you." The word sounded funny when he said it, not at all solemn, but almost kind.

"I don't see how."

"I feel responsible for you. I want you to be safe and happy. The pleasure you'd give me in helping you would be enormous."

Ruth might have whispered in my ear that it was a trap, that he was manipulating me into accepting his help, that his true reasons for doing so were hidden from us and might be nefarious, only she wasn't there to fuel my wariness. I had to think for myself, make my own decisions, almost as if I were a normal girl.

"I don't think I deserve to be safe and happy, not after what I did to Agnes," I confessed.

He leaned closer to me, his chin resting on his steepled hands. "I don't pretend to know what Mrs. Knoop thought or felt, but from what you told me, she seemed kind and selfless. Do you think she'd rest easier, knowing that you are tormenting and punishing yourself for what happened to her?"

"But spirits aren't drawn to those who are happy," I said helplessly.

He thought for a while, then said, "From what you told me, I don't think she has to be drawn anymore. You bound her to you already, didn't you? You named her, fed her your blood, cried over her. You have done all you could. Now you can only wait. In the meantime, you should try to make a life for yourself. If she ever wakes and comes to you, I bet she'd be well pleased to find you healthy, and if not happy, at least not sad. Content, perhaps, if you think you can manage it."

I didn't think Doctor Montague believed in spirits. I suppose some things must be seen and felt to be believed. But that he was willing to go along with what was true to me, not indulging me as one might a child but with the reverence one might show another's religion, well, that made me feel a stab of profound fondness for him.

"May I tell you no whenever something you offer or want me to do displeases or upsets me?" I asked.

"Naturally."

"And you ask nothing in return for what you give me? No work, no…no touch?"

"I wouldn't dream of it."

I didn't quite trust him, but that didn't matter. If I rejected his offer, what was there for me but an uncertain future probably filled with hunger and exploitation? Besides, I could always flee from him if he proved dishonest.

"All right," I said slowly, "I'll allow you to help me."

Chapter 35

THE FIRST THING DOCTOR MONTAGUE did after we had finished our celebratory cake was make some calls. That done, he took me to a department store. It wasn't the same one Agnes had taken me to the day she had come to rescue me from Mama, but it made my throat constrict all the same.

When we entered the store, I was both wary and nervy. The doctor didn't look like Mr. Mesman at all, but this expedition put me in mind of all the gifts that horrible man had bought for me and what he'd wanted in return. Thanks to him, I would always find a man buying clothes and jewelry for me sinister and frightening.

Only Doctor Montague didn't want to dress me in clothes he found appealing, didn't want to bind me to him with gold and velvet. He had taken me to the store merely to get some small items he knew I must lack but would need now that the police would no longer house me: soap, a toothbrush, a comb.

"I'm sorry. I should've found a woman to do this with you. I know you're not very comfortable around men," he apologized.

"I don't mind," I lied.

When we were done at the department store, we took a bus to the university. I was still cagey, my hands slippery with sweat, my face grimacing. I saw people look at me and felt scalded with shame, but I couldn't help it. It didn't help that I wasn't used to being on a bus. The swaying and the starts and stops made me feel sick. When we finally climbed out, I had to bend over and vomited the cake and tea I'd had earlier.

Doctor Montague seemed out of his depth now that I showed signs of physical rather than mental illness, but he rallied to the challenge admirably. He patted my back and gave me his handkerchief to wipe my mouth with. When he was sure I could stand, he took me not to his lodgings as I had feared but to an apartment building where he knew the landlady. She was the one he had called earlier. While I had been licking his plate and that of Mr. Lindelauf clean, he had inquired about a room for me.

"It's small and a little shabby, and the windows make it cold and draughty, but I thought you wouldn't mind that because they let in a lot of light. I know you don't like small dark spaces. I know men sometimes frighten you, too, but you don't have to worry about that: the landlady only rents to women, and she doesn't allow them to bring men back to their rooms," he told me as we waited for the landlady to let us in.

"You've given it a lot of thought," I said.

"Of course I have," Doctor Montague said, his smile a bit incredulous, as if he couldn't believe I'd ever doubt him. "I want you to succeed in life, Roos. Since I can't force you to let me treat you, the very least I can do is create circumstances that will maximize your chances of thriving." He glanced at his watch. "Do you mind if I go to the shops while the landlady shows you the room? They'll close soon, and I'd like to get you some food so you don't have to worry about that either. We both had a very intense, tiring day, didn't we?"

"Of course," I said. I pretended to tie my shoelaces to keep him from seeing the relief spreading over my face. There was much still to fear and much still to worry over, but I didn't think I'd have to worry about Doctor Montague's intentions anymore.

The room was small and old and draughty as the doctor had said, but it was clean and full of light. More importantly, it was a place all my own. Because I had no money, the doctor arranged everything; I only had to sign a few papers. He also arranged for me to take typing lessons. I was terrified of going out those first few weeks, certain that people would recognize me from all the lurid articles in the papers, that they would hound and hurt me, but I knew I had to earn my keep. Since séances were no longer a possibility, I'd have to learn some other skill that would prove useful. I suppose I could have vetoed the idea, but I didn't want the doctor to be disappointed in me, and he had already bought me a typewriter and reams of paper. In a way, I was beholden to him, no matter what he said.

I may have been lonely, but I was never alone. During the first few days after the trial, the medication I had been given during custody and the trial began to wear off, and Ruth came back to me. She did not really show herself to me, but I began to see her from the corner of my eye like a smudge, and at night I heard the familiar click of her jaw.

I didn't acknowledge her. What she had done to Agnes was too horrible, too recent. But what is a year, or even three, to a spirit as old as Ruth? She could afford to be patient.

One night, I sat on my bed and said, "I have many things a girl needs to be happy."

From the tail of my eye, I saw her watching me, her long hair sheeting down her chest, her crooked hands folded uncertainly against her belly.

"I've got a roof over my head. I've got useful employment I enjoy. I've got plenty of food I like, and books to read, and records to listen to. Beautiful things surround me, such as that little marble statue on the sill and the striped paper I've put on the wall. By all rights, I should be happy."

I smoothed a fold out of the sheets. They were cotton, freshly washed. "But I'm not happy. I've thought long and hard why that may be, and I've come to the conclusion that there's something missing from my life, something dreadful, something darling. You see, I don't think I can ever be truly happy without the company of my Ruth."

She sobbed and crept to me like a beaten dog. She smelled achingly familiar, of peat and sweet rot.

I bent over her and kissed her cold crown.

"Please don't ever make me go away again," she whispered, the words slurred almost to the point of incomprehensibility by her twice-broken jaw.

"Never, never," I promised. With one decisive push, I slotted her jaw back into its socket, and we were at peace.

EXCERPTS FROM A. M. MONTAGUE, *A WAR IN MY MIND:
THE EFFECTS OF CHILDHOOD TRAUMA ON THE ADULT
PSYCHE* **(AMSTERDAM: ELSEVIER, 1958)**

"Trauma sustained in childhood can linger long after the child
has grown, and may show itself in a variety of ways, ranging from
the annoying but manageable to completely debilitating. Take,
for example, the case of Patient M—, a man beaten to the point
of blindness by his uncle. Not considering his blindness, Patient
M— has recovered remarkably well from his ordeal. Although the
sound of a man removing his belt—his uncle strapped him with a
leather belt, the heavy silver buckle of which ultimately caused
Patient M—'s blindness—[1]still causes him no small amount of
anguish, it is this sound alone that triggers such a response.

Compare this to the case of Patient T—, a woman who caused
the drowning of her little brother in the family's very own bathtub
when she was seven years old. She developed a mortal fear of
water, and that prevented her from carrying out such a simple act
as washing the dishes or cleaning the windows, let alone washing
herself.[2]

Also highly interesting is the case of Patient R—. Her trauma
manifested itself not in a fear of a particular sound or sensation
but in a complete inability to separate reality from fantasy. She

---

1   It is perhaps no small wonder then that Patient M— refused to wear a belt
     and forbade his sons from doing so.
2   It needs no explaining that her inability to maintain even the most basic
     principles of personal hygiene made her a pariah unable to secure a job or
     start, let alone maintain, any kind of relationship.

was under my care while she was detained by the police for her involvement in the death and subsequent mutilation and unlawful burial of her caretaker's body."

(...)

"The transcriptions of the case notes referred to in these pages can be found in Appendix C: Case Stories. I would like to draw special attention to the case notes of Patient M—, Patient R—, Patient T—, Patient Jo—, and Patient Ja—, since these are the cases I shall be referring to the most throughout the main text."

—Introduction, pages ix–x and xviii

"The first time I went to visit Patient R— was to determine whether she was mentally fit to stand trial. She stood accused of the murder of her employer/caretaker, as well as the mutilation of her corpse and its unlawful burial in order to hide her crime. I expected to find a middle-aged, masculine woman, sullen and unintelligent. Instead, I found a pinched, thin young girl who trembled a little when she spoke and tilted her head to the side whenever she listened, a symptom I have often observed in lunatics. Her twitchiness did not abate as we got to know each other better. She spoke in a peculiar way, her choice of words often somewhat old-fashioned. Her eyes were large and expressive, though a little mad."

(...)

"Patient R— developed an intricate alternate reality populated by ghosts in order to survive what had been done to her during her childhood. Similar to the fancies of the schizophrenic, Patient R— claimed she could see ghosts and talked to them frequently. Also similar to the schizophrenic was her belief that these ghosts occasionally infiltrated her body, at which times she was not herself and could subsequently not be held accountable for anything she said, did, or failed to do. It is interesting that her spirit companion—the ghost she claimed was with her constantly—was female, although this may not be too surprising if we take into account Patient R—'s homosexual tendencies, which later transferred from her spirit companion to her unfortunate employer."

—Possessed by Another: The Case of Patient R—, pages 37 and 45

"It remains a sad fact that my colleagues and I are as of yet unable to cure all the unfortunates brought to us. At times, the damage runs too deep to heal. Although we may find ways to make its effects more manageable, they will not go away entirely.

This does not mean our work is not worth doing. Certainly, it is most rewarding when a patient learns to cope with their fears; I laughed with joy when Patient M— proudly showed me his son's new belt made of beautiful black leather with a thick silver buckle and treated myself and Patient T— to a celebratory glass of champagne when she managed to wash her hands under the running tap in my presence. She will never go swimming, but at least she can now maintain a decent level of personal hygiene.

Unfortunately, such compromises are not always possible, not

360 JOHANNA VAN VEEN

in the least because some patients do not want to or simply cannot understand that they are sick and in need of help. Such sentiments are somewhat common when treatment begins, especially when the patient has not sought out my help themselves but has instead been brought to me by a concerned family member or GP, but it is rare that a patient will continue to refuse my aid after multiple sessions.

Rare, yes, but not unheard of. Despite my numerous conversations with Patient R—, she clings to her delusions to this day. In such cases, all I can do is continue to offer my help and hope that, one day, I shall be taken up on my offer. Nothing would please me more than to find Patient R— banishing her ghosts to the realm of fantasy for good."

—Conclusion, page 394

Epilogue

ALL THIS HAPPENED SOME YEARS ago. I live a simple life now: I type things for Doctor Montague; I clean my house to keep it neat and attractive; I cook wholesome meals for myself.

Most of all I wait for Agnes.

I've been waiting for a long time now. Sometimes I don't believe she'll come. In my darkest moments, I am sure she has forsaken me and I shall wither away for want of her.

But all this love, all this yearning, it has to mean something.

If I should die before she has found her way back to me, then I shall simply have to find her. I shan't be mere bone and tendon rotting in a coffin. I'll slumber, and when I wake, I'll rise—up, up, up, out of the earth and into the sky.

I might have forgotten everything by then—Mama, Ruth, even my name—but Agnes I won't forget. She'll be there because she's a strong one, my Agnes: if anyone can become a spirit, it is she. She'll be waiting for me, and no matter how changed she'll be, everything of me shall leap to everything of her in joyful recognition.

I don't think it needs to come to that, though.

Lately, I've begun to feel a presence.

I seem to feel the ghost of her hand on the nape of my neck. I catch whiffs of her scent. I catch myself straining my ears, listening for a voice so faint, I can barely make out the words.

She is stirring.

Not long now until she wakes and I can close her in my arms again.

Until then, I'll let the memory of her possess me.

READING GROUP GUIDE

1. Ruth is an unusual character. Describe her physical appearance and her behavior. What sets her apart from what we think of as "typical" ghosts?

2. While Roos and Mama's séances are fake, do you think they still helped people? Why or why not?

3. What qualities are necessary for someone to become a spirit?

4. Describe the different forms of oppression Agnes faces. In what ways does she overcome it?

5. Roos is an unreliable narrator. As you read, did you trust her perspective? When did she surprise you?

6. Consider Doctor Montague's treatment of Roos. How do you think he sees her? And why do you think Doctor Montague ultimately helps Roos?

7. How would you characterize the relationship between Roos
    and Ruth? Is it possible to define the kind of love they share?

8. In this story, worship, love, and sacrifice all tangle together.
    How do you see that reflected in the characters' relationships
    with one another?

9. Do you think Agnes and Roos will be together again?

A CONVERSATION
WITH THE AUTHOR

Bog bodies aren't particularly common in Gothic fiction. What inspired you to make them so integral to the story?

I've always found bog bodies absolutely fascinating. I've been aware of their existence from an early age because I live in the Netherlands, where a number of bog bodies have been found, including the famous Yde girl. These bodies offer us a wealth of historical information, usually about a time and people we don't know that much about because they left no written records. By examining bog bodies, we can discover what these people looked like, what they ate, how they made their clothes. Yet there is one question that we can never answer: *Why* did these people end up in the bog?

When researching bog bodies, I came upon several theories that aim to answer this question. Some bog bodies probably belong to people who accidentally wandered into the bog and drowned, but a number of others have clearly been murdered, often in a very violent manner that smacks of overkill (stabbing, strangling, bludgeoning). One theory poses that these people

must have been sacrificed and that these victims were chosen
specifically for two reasons: 1) they were young and therefore
valuable to the tribe, thus making their death a true sacrifice,
and 2) they were marked in some way by the gods, often through
disability. Indeed, a large number of bog bodies were what we
would now consider physically disabled: the Yde girl, for example, suffered from severe scoliosis and the Kayhausen boy had
an infected hip socket that meant he could not walk without
assistance. The bog bodies that were not physically disabled,
the theory poses, may have been mentally disabled or mentally
ill, which means they may have been considered touched by the
gods and gifted with the powers of divination and of seeing
things others couldn't.

During my research, I also stumbled upon the following idea:
that, on bright, sunny days, the bog water might have been clear
enough for people to see the bodies thrown in, some of which were
staked down to keep them in one place, and that people may have
regularly visited these bodies because they were considered holy or
otherwise imbued with power.

All of this is utterly fascinating and, in my view, utterly Gothic:
violence inflicted upon the young and the disabled and mentally
ill, secrets we will never unravel, the possibility that these bodies
would flicker in and out of view and thus come back again and
again in the same way that a spirit might… Wonderfully fitting
ingredients for a Gothic novel exploring obsession, desire, and
madness!

Agnes and Roos fall deeply, passionately, and somewhat tempestuously in love. At the time, what was the overall public stance on queer relationships?

In the Netherlands, homosexuality was no longer punishable by law since 1811, although a law that was in effect from 1911 until 1971 did criminalize queer relationships between an adult and anyone under the age of twenty-one (for the straights, that age was sixteen). Of course, just because something is not punishable by law does not mean it is condoned. Queer relationships at the time this novel is set wouldn't have been accepted, though they would have been tolerated if not conducted too openly.

We mustn't forget that, unlike what certain people want us to believe, the nuclear family—consisting of only a father, mother, and children—isn't the only way to live. In fact, it wasn't all that common throughout history. People often lived together with other family members, with friends, with employees. It was also perfectly common for two women or two men to live together (e.g. two spinsters or two bachelors), offering the queer community plenty of ways to pursue queer relationships. In the situation of Agnes and Roos, people would probably not assume that they were having a romantic and sexual relationship; instead, they would consider Agnes taking Roos in as an act of Christian charity, thus allowing both of them to conduct their relationship in private.

How much research did you have to do to write this novel? What did that look like?

I had already done a lot of research into the Second World

War in the Netherlands and the 1950s for a different project, and I had researched Freud's theories and psychoanalysis for my BA thesis. Additionally, I had read a number of books on Victorian spiritualism out of personal interest before I began writing. There's no doubt that all this information helped form the setting and plot for *My Darling Dreadful Thing* before I even began working on it!

The two topics I did read up on whilst writing were bog bodies and hysteria. I wanted to make sure that Ruth's portrayal as a bog-body-esque spirit was realistic. Similarly, I didn't want Dr. Montague's notes on Roos's case to be anachronistic. On the one hand, I wanted to make it clear that he acts out of a genuine intent to help Roos; on the other hand, I wanted to show that he has his own blind spots because of the scientific theories of mental illness and trauma that he works with.

It's interesting that two of our key antagonists—Thomas and Mr. Mesman—loom large yet have very little time on-page. Was that a purposeful choice? What would you say characterizes the villains of this story?

Much like Daphne du Maurier said when writing *Rebecca*: it was an exercise in technique. Can I make an antagonist feel threatening even if they are barely there? At the same time, I also wanted to show how trauma can continue to affect a person even if the perpetrator of that trauma is no longer there. In a sense, the trauma that Roos and Agnes (and, to an extent, Ruth as well) have suffered is its own kind of haunting.

As for what characterizes the villains of this story: I think that almost all the characters in *My Darling Dreadful Thing* are driven by intense desire. What sets the villains apart is that they will selfishly pursue that desire to the exclusion of all else: if they must hurt someone to achieve what they crave, they will.

Mama and Willemijn are both intensely unlikable characters, in no small part because of their racism and prejudice. Were those views common for the time? Why did you choose to include them in the narrative?

There have always been racists. This, of course, is no excuse; just as there have always been racists, there have always been people battling against racism and prejudice. That being said, Mama's and Willemijn's views on race and mental illness, though definitely not shared by everyone, were a lot more common in the 1950s than they are now.

I have decided to include them, a choice I did not make lightly (the inclusion of such views may be painful and triggering), because I firmly believe it is important that we acknowledge the wrongs of the past, no matter how uncomfortable they may make us. Only through acknowledgment can we offer dignity and justice to the victims and learn to do better in the future. Such acknowledgment, of course, is not always appropriate; had this been a romance novel, I probably would not have included these comments, because the mentally ill and people of color also deserve to read fun and sexy stuff without being confronted with the very stigma they face every day. However, *My Darling Dreadful Thing* is a sapphic Gothic horror novel, and what better place to explore racism and prejudice than within a genre that aims to show just how horrifying those things are?

Can you talk a little bit about your writing process? How did you manage to balance Roos's perspective and Montague's transcripts?

At the time I wrote the first draft of *My Darling Dreadful Thing*, I was working at a bookstore five days a week. I had to be there at 9:15 AM, which meant I had to leave home around 8:50. Because my dog, Teuntje, was still a puppy, I was often up before 7:00, giving me plenty of time to write in the mornings. I used the time I traveled to and from work—like a lot of Dutch people, I biked—to think intensely about the book, which ensured that, as soon as I actually sat down to write (I often wrote a bit more in the evenings), the writing would go relatively smoothly. It also helped that I had a rough outline. (I can't go in blindly, because then I'll get stuck, but I can't have everything planned out too much, either, because then the project loses its spark.) I no longer work at the bookstore, but my process is still roughly the same: I will write a rough outline, then write in the mornings before work and again after dinner, using my commuting time to think about the book.

As for Roos's perspective and Montague's transcripts: the first draft actually had way fewer transcripts! I was afraid they would break up the flow of Roos's story. My agent, however, pointed out that the transcripts were a great narrative tool: by reminding the reader constantly of what was at stake, the novel became taut and suspenseful. They were also a great way of informing the reader about spirits. Thus, I used them to drive suspense and to incorporate some world-building in an organic way. To balance them out, I tried to stick to a formula: for every two or three chapters with Roos's perspective, I could have one chapter of Montague's transcripts.

Roos and Agnes face intense stigma—even abuse—due to their perceived "insanity." What drew you to this topic? How did you go about exploring it with care?

Not only is "insanity" a staple of the Gothic, people who are mentally ill still face a lot of stigma and abuse for something they cannot help, which really clashes with my sense of what is right.

As for how I went about exploring it with care: though I did not shy away from showing the dark side of being perceived as "insane," I tried my hardest to treat these characters with compassion and respect, even when they behave in ways we might find unappealing or even disturbing. One such way is by showing Roos's rich inner life and highlighting certain character traits such as her loyalty and determination. In this way, I tried to show that, even if she is mentally ill (which, if you have read the book, you know is questionable), she is so many other things besides.

What are you hoping readers take away from this book?

That you can find hope, love, and compassion even in the darkest of places.

And last: Would you consider *My Darling Dreadful Thing* a love story?

Absolutely!

ACKNOWLEDGMENTS

They say it takes a village to raise a child. In that sense, it's not very different from writing a book. There are many people without whom I could not have written *My Darling Dreadful Thing*. I'd like to thank my agent, Kristina Pérez, for immediately believing in this story and being a wonderful agent. You're always on top of things and great at promoting my interests, but you're also a warm, smart person with a great sense of humor. I couldn't wish for a better agent!

I am also very grateful to my editor, Jenna Jankowski, for her sharp insights, her thorough commentary, and our lovely conversations. I genuinely believe *My Darling Dreadful Thing* wouldn't have been half as good without your help. I hope we will work on many more projects together, all of which will no doubt improve under your loving care.

I must also thank my copy editor and my sensitivity reader for their thoughtful commentary. I like to think my English is pretty good, but it's clear there's always room for improvement!

On a similar note, I'd like to express my gratitude to the team at Sourcebooks and Katie Klimowicz in particular for their support and for making this book look good both on the inside and the outside.

I would also like to thank my sisters, Lieke and Hilke, for reading an early version of this story and supporting me along the way (and a long time before I started writing this, too). Lieke, I know this story scared you so much you couldn't finish it the first time around—always good news for a horror writer—but I hope you'll be able to finish the final product. I'll hold your hand throughout the scary bits, I promise. Hilke, you did manage to finish it even though you really don't like horror, so look at you go! You're much braver than you think. I know I won't make a horror convert out of you, but I hope this is one horror book you'll love forever.

There are also some people I must thank, not for their direct contribution to this novel but for their general love and support. Mama and Papa, I know I always crack jokes about how you didn't believe I'd ever become a published writer—not because I'm not good enough but because it's a tough business—but I've always felt supported by you. You've been there for me through all the disappointments and rejections. Now, we can finally celebrate the successes together!

This list wouldn't be complete without my bookish friends, namely Nita and my Paagman buddies. Nita, thanks for your words of affirmation and for fangirling about our books. My Paagman friends—Adrienne, Anita, Anne, Benjamin, Emma, Guus, Jozet, Sasha, and Sandy—thank you for all your enthusiasm and love. I couldn't wish for better friends.

Last but never least, my darling Corinna. You've been my staunchest and most loving supporter, even though you had to suffer through all my complaining and the occasional bout of despair. I know you didn't dare to read *My Darling Dreadful Thing* until it would actually be out—you silly superstitious sweetie—but the curse is broken now. I can't wait for you to read it and tell me all your thoughts. Most of all though, I can't wait for us to live the rest of our lives together. I love you to bits, my darling girl.

ABOUT THE AUTHOR

© Wijnand Geuze

Johanna grew up in the Netherlands together with her two sisters. The three of them are triplets, though her sisters are identical to each other and she's different, a fact she didn't discover until she was five years old; at least, unlike most people, she can pinpoint the exact moment she became self-aware.

She has received an MA in English literature with a specialization in early modern literature, as well as an MA in book and digital media with a specialization in early modern book history, both of them at Leiden University. She currently works as an editor for a big company that sends a lot of reports and letters out every day, all of them requiring a lot of love and attention to make sure that every comma is where it should be (which doesn't mean she's any good at placing them correctly when it's her own work though). This job gives her enough time to write (mostly queer Gothic) novels. When she isn't doing any of those things, she enjoys spending time with her girlfriend, her sisters, and her dog, though not necessarily all at the same time.